JOURNEY TO PLUBORIA

Books By LG Rice

SECRETS OF SAGE MANOR BOOK SERIES
Through The Crystal Gate, Book One
Shadows Over Tanzlora, Book Two
Battle For Pisgah, Book Three

What If ETs Are Real?

GALEN VALLEY CHRONICLES BOOK SERIES
When The Past Comes Home, Book One
What Happened on Wren Hollow Trail, Book Two

Journey To Pluboria

LG Rice

DEDICATION
For anyone who has ever felt broken or far from
whole—
This story is a reminder that healing is possible.
Like Bronte, you may walk through darkness before you
find the light.
But even if your body isn't restored, your heart and
spirit can be.
Through love, faith, and the support of those who truly
care,
wholeness can return.
You are not alone.
You are not beyond healing.
You are worthy of joy.

1

The sterile light of the examining room reflected off the polished metal instruments arranged neatly on a tray. Dr. Madre Walsh stood near the door, her arms crossed tightly against her chest, watching as Dr. Wilson Reedly worked on Bronte Sutton, who sat scowling on the edge of the exam table.

Bronte's grizzled face twisted into a grimace as Dr. Reedly pricked the sole of his foot with a pin.

"Of course, I can feel you pricking me with a pin," Bronte barked, his tone sharp enough to cut steel. "I've felt every single thing anyone's done to me since I hit my head on that damn rock! What I can't do is move my blasted legs. I can feel 'em—just can't use 'em. So unless you've got some miracle up your sleeve, maybe stick to something that helps instead of poking me like I'm a frog in science class."

Dr. Reedly, a middle-aged man with prematurely gray hair and a calm demeanor, simply nodded as if Bronte's outburst was par for the course. "That's helpful information, Mr. Sutton," he replied evenly, jotting something down on his clipboard. "The fact that you can feel sensation but not initiate movement gives us a better understanding of your condition."

Bronte snorted. "You know what would give me a better understanding? Being able to walk out of here instead of being prodded like a pincushion."

Dr. Madre Walsh stepped forward, placing a hand lightly on Bronte's arm. Her voice, soft but firm, cut through his tirade. "Bronte," she said, her tone carrying the weight of time spent corralling his cantankerous ways. "Let's give Dr. Reedly a chance to explain what he's doing before you scare off another specialist."

This was their third neurologist visit in six months because Bronte had managed to completely exasperate the first two specialists to the point that they declined to see or treat him. Bronte grumbled something under his breath but clamped his mouth shut.

Dr. Marshall Stern, Madre's husband, standing at the head of the table, adjusted his glasses and offered a sympathetic smile to Dr. Reedly. "You'll have to excuse Bronte," he said. "He has a unique way of expressing himself. It's part of his charm."

Dr. Reedly raised an eyebrow but said nothing as he moved to examine Bronte's knee reflexes with a small hammer. He tapped lightly, watching for a response that never came.

Madre took the opportunity to redirect the conversation, hoping to stave off any further outbursts. "Dr. Reedly," she began, her tone professional, "since Bronte can feel sensation but has no motor control, what does that suggest? Is it a spinal issue? Something in the brain?"

Dr. Reedly straightened and folded his arms, resting his clipboard against his chest. "The symptoms suggest a disconnect between the sensory and motor pathways," he explained. "It's not uncommon in head injuries, but it's unusual for sensation to remain intact without motor function."

"Unusual," Bronte muttered darkly. "That's one way to put it. I'd call it a cosmic joke."

Madre shot him a warning glance before turning back to Dr. Reedly. "What kind of tests or treatments would you recommend next?"

"We'll need to run a full set of imaging scans—an MRI, possibly a functional MRI to see how the brain is communicating with the rest of the body," Dr. Reedly replied. "It's possible there's inflammation or a lesion disrupting the motor pathways."

Bronte perked up slightly, his interest piqued. "And if you find it? What then? You gonna zap it with one of those lasers or drill a hole in my skull?"

Dr. Reedly blinked, caught off guard by the question. "Not exactly. Treatment would depend on the findings. It could involve physical therapy, medication, or, in some cases, surgery. But let's not get ahead of ourselves."

"That's easy for you to say," Bronte shot back. "You're not the one stuck in this useless body."

Madre sighed, her patience beginning to fray. "Bronte, please. Let the man do his job."

Dr. Marshall Stern stepped in again, his calm voice cutting through the tension. "Bronte, we're all here because we want to help. You've got Madre worried sick, and we've already exhausted conventional treatments. Let's at least hear what Dr. Reedly has to say before jumping to conclusions."

Bronte scowled but relented, leaning back slightly on the exam table. "Fine. But if this turns into another dead end, I'm calling it quits."

Madre's expression softened as she placed a hand on his shoulder. "It won't be a dead end," she said quietly, more for herself than for him.

Dr. Reedly adjusted his glasses and nodded. "We'll get to the bottom of this, Mr. Sutton. I promise."

As the tension in the room eased, Madre exchanged a glance with her husband. Both knew that finding answers for Bronte would be anything but simple—but they also knew that giving up was not an option.

The midday sun warmed the patio as Madre guided Bronte's wheelchair up the recently constructed ramp to Sage Manor's kitchen entrance. The wheels bumped slightly on the threshold, and Bronte let out an exaggerated groan.

"Really?" he muttered. "A ramp? A chair lift? What's next? Bubble wrap on all the furniture so I don't stub my toe?"

Marshall, walking alongside, chuckled. "You're right, Bronte. Next, we're going to get you a horn for that wheelchair so you can warn people to get out of your way."

Bronte snorted. "Hilarious, Stern. Just get me inside."

Madre held back a sigh as she pushed Bronte over the smooth tile floor of the kitchen. The room smelled of fresh bread and herbs, a comforting aroma that contrasted with Bronte's persistent grumbling. The wheelchair hummed as Madre maneuvered him into the parlor, where Gran Celia and Lorinda sat by the window. Sunlight streamed over their table, illuminating plates of scones and a delicate porcelain tea set.

"Well, well," Gran Celia said, setting down her teacup. Her sharp eyes swept over the trio. "Look who's back. I assume the visit to Dr. Reedly was... enlightening?"

Bronte wasted no time. "Enlightening? Sure, if you like being poked and prodded like a science experiment." He waved his hands theatrically. "'Oh, Mr. Sutton, can you feel this? Can you feel that?' Yes, I can feel it, but I can't do a dang thing about it! And what's their big solution? More tests. Always more tests. They don't have a clue."

Gran Celia raised an eyebrow but said nothing, sipping her tea as Bronte's tirade wound down. Lorinda, sitting beside her, frowned and opened her mouth to speak, but Madre quickly stepped in.

"Well, if you'll let me explain," Madre said, her voice firm but calm, "Dr. Reedly actually had some very useful insights. He confirmed that Bronte's sensory pathways are intact but that the issue lies in the motor pathways. He's ordered imaging tests to pinpoint the problem."

She turned to Gran Celia. "Dr. Reedly was professional and thorough, and he's determined to find answers. It's going to take time, but we're making progress."

"That's a much better version," Gran Celia said, smiling slightly. She turned her sharp gaze to Bronte. "You might take a page from Madre's book, Bronte. She makes things sound almost hopeful."

Bronte crossed his arms and muttered something under his breath, clearly unimpressed.

Lorinda leaned forward, her expression warm. "Bronte, I know this is frustrating, but at least it sounds like they're working toward a solution. And in the meantime, you've got us to help you through this."

"Lucky me," Bronte said dryly, though there was a faint flicker of gratitude in his eyes.

Gran Celia set her teacup down with a decisive clink. "Bronte, you're part of this family, whether you like it or not. And families stick together, especially when things get tough. So, grumble all you want, but you're not doing this alone."

Bronte's lips twitched as though he wanted to argue, but he finally sighed and slumped back in his wheelchair. "Fine. But if I hear the words 'be patient' one more time, I might lose my mind."

Madre chuckled softly and rested a hand on his shoulder. "Then we'll try not to say it out loud."

The room settled into a comfortable silence, the warmth of the tea and the scent of freshly baked scones softening the tension. Bronte may not have been the most cooperative patient, but here, surrounded by the people who cared about him, his gruff edges seemed a little less sharp.

"Speaking of people who care, where are the rest of the crew at?" Bronte asked, his voice rough but tinged with curiosity.

Gran Celia, who had been quietly observing him, answered, "They're down in the chamber under the gazebo, meeting with Keelee and Elara. The Tanzloran and Arcmyrin councils have sent their latest communications regarding the alliance with Earth's leaders."

Dr. Stern perked up at that and turned toward Bronte. "Would you like to go down there and join them? I'm sure they'd want to see you."

Bronte immediately waved off the suggestion. "Nah, I think I'll just head to my room and get some rest."

Madre, ever persistent, placed a gentle hand on his arm. "You sure? I know you don't want to sit through long discussions, but it might be good for you to hear what's going on firsthand."

"I'm sure," Bronte said.

"Well, ok then," Madre replied as she looked to her husband, "Marshall, dear, will you help Bronte to his room before you go to the chamber?"

Bronte turned to her with an arched brow. "Madre, I can get to my room on my own, especially since you all insisted on installing that fancy contraption that lifts me up the stairs like some kind of royal highness. So, no need for a send-off party."

Madre sighed and held up both hands in surrender. "I give up."

She shook her head as Bronte rolled himself toward the door.

"Bout time," Bronte muttered before pushing himself through the entryway and disappearing down the hall.

A moment of silence hung in the room as they all watched him leave.

Gran Celia finally broke it with a tired sigh, shaking her head. "Honestly, I don't understand him sometimes. Why be so negative all the time? I mean, I get it—I do. I'm not the one who's lost the ability to walk, and I can only imagine how frustrating that is for him. But the way he communicates, the way he shuts people out—sometimes it erases the sympathy I have for him."

Madre lowered herself onto the couch, a contemplative look in her eyes. "I agree," she admitted. "But it's just who Bronte is. He's always been stubborn and set in his ways. I think... we have to love people where they are, even if they're not in a good place. Even when they push us away."

Lorinda, who had been silently listening, nodded in agreement. "He's been through a lot. And this... well, this is just another battle for him."

Marshall, who had been quietly absorbing the conversation, finally stood from the wing chair beside Celia and stretched. "Well, while you all sit here psychoanalyzing Bronte, I'm going to head down to the chamber and see how the meeting is going."

Celia smirked at him as he adjusted his belt and turned toward the door. "Good luck with that. If Ridge and Lincoln are leading the charge, you might be down there all night."

Marshall chuckled, "Wouldn't be the first time."

With that, he made his way toward the gazebo, leaving the women to their conversation.

2

The air in the underground chamber beneath the gazebo hummed with energy as the Crystal Gate vibrated at a high frequency, its iridescent glow casting shifting patterns of light across the stone walls. The steady whirring sound, once a comforting sign of progress, now seemed like an ominous reminder of the strain on the Triad.

Marshall walked into the room and took a seat on the bench placed against the stone wall as Ridge Beaumont adjusted his position at the oval table. Ridge's face was tense as he glanced at the crystal panels that displayed the spirits Ambreela, Ignissa, Terraveta, and Mistara, each silently observing. Ridge, Lincoln, Waverly, and Lynx sat around the table, their expressions as heavy as the charged atmosphere in the room.

"This was supposed to get easier after the Umbralox was defeated," Waverly said, her voice low but sharp. "But instead, it feels like we're unraveling. Every time we think we've made progress, another issue crops up."

Lincoln ran a hand through his dark hair, his face lined with frustration. "Earth's leaders are still dragging their feet. They want assurances Tanzlora and Arcmyrin can provide resources, but they won't commit to sharing anything in return. Tanzlora and Arcmyrin see it as greed and mistrust, and frankly, I can't blame them."

"Ignissa says that fire burns brightest in conflict," Mistara's cool voice echoed from her panel, her watery image shimmering like a rippling lake. "But if left unchecked, fire consumes everything. This fracture must be resolved before it spreads."

"It's not just Earth," Lynx added, his voice calm but edged with worry. "Tanzlora's council is split. Some believe sharing their agricultural advancements with Earth will drain their resources, while others fear that Arcmyrin will gain more from the alliance and leave them vulnerable."

Ridge sighed, leaning forward on the table. "And Arcmyrin isn't blameless either. Elara told me some of their council members are skeptical about Earth's intentions. They're afraid Earth's history of war and environmental destruction will spill over into the alliance."

"They're not wrong," Waverly said bluntly, crossing her arms. "But we can't afford to let this fall apart. The Triad's alliance is our best hope for preventing another catastrophe like the Umbralox—or worse."

The communication orb pulsed brightly, and Keelee's holographic form shimmered into view. The Tanzloran envoy's silver hair and violet hued skin were glowing and striking as ever, but his face bore the same weariness that the Beaumonts felt.

"Apologies for the delay," Keelee began, his voice carrying a slight edge. "The Tanzloran council has been in session for hours, debating the latest proposal from Earth. They're skeptical, to say the least."

Moments later, Elara's image materialized beside Keelee's. The Arcmyrin envoy's calm demeanor was a sharp contrast to Keelee's frustration, but her tone betrayed a simmering tension. "And the Arcmyrin council is equally wary. They've requested additional assurances that Earth's leaders will adhere to the agreed-upon terms. They're concerned about a lack of accountability."

Ridge exchanged a glance with Lincoln. "We understand their concerns," he said, his tone measured. "But if this alliance is going to work, we need trust on all sides. Right now, everyone's treating this like a negotiation for leverage, instead of the collaboration it's supposed to be."

Ambreela, Spirit of Air, chimed in, her voice a gentle breeze. "Unity requires more than agreements on paper. It demands trust, vulnerability, and the willingness to compromise. The seeds of discord have been sown by fear and suspicion. How will you address them?"

Keelee folded his arms, his gaze fixed on Ridge. "It's not that simple. Tanzlora's people have been self-sufficient for centuries. Sharing resources is one thing, but relying on Earth, after everything we've seen and heard about its history? That's a leap of faith some aren't willing to take."

"And Arcmyrin doesn't want to risk becoming the intermediary," Elara added. "We already share knowledge with Tanzlora, and there's concern that adding Earth into the mix will dilute our autonomy."

Waverly leaned forward, her tone firm. "We've all fought side by side against the Umbralox. We've seen what we're capable of when we work together. Is that really worth throwing away over politics and old grudges?"

Mistara's watery voice echoed again, steady and soothing. "Remind them of what is at stake, not only for their planets but for the galaxy as a whole. The alliance is not merely about resources; it is about survival and evolution."

Ridge nodded, his jaw tightening with resolve. "We'll bring that message back to Earth's leaders, but Keelee, Elara—you need to do the same with your councils. We're stronger together, and we all know it. The alternative isn't just a fractured alliance; it's chaos."

The spirits observed silently, their shimmering forms radiating an unspoken sense of urgency.

Keelee sighed and glanced at Elara. "I'll try," he said. "But this is a deeply rooted apprehension, Ridge. It won't be easy."

"It never is," Lynx said, his voice steady. "But we've faced worse, and we've come through it. This is just another battle, and we'll fight it together."

As the Crystal Gate hummed louder, signaling yet another impending journey, the Beaumonts prepared themselves for the long road ahead. The promise of galactic peace and harmony felt further away than ever, but they weren't ready to give up. Not yet.

The soft glow of twilight blanketed Galen Valley, its rolling hills dotted with wildflowers that swayed gently in the cool evening breeze. Ridge guided Lorinda down a winding stone path toward a secluded terrace overlooking a serene lake. Lanterns hung from the branches of nearby trees, casting warm golden light on the intimate dining spot he had arranged.

Lorinda's eyes sparkled as she took in the scene. "Ridge, this is... breathtaking," she said, her voice tinged with awe.

"I thought you deserved something special," Ridge replied, pulling out her chair and gesturing for her to sit. "With everything going on, we don't get enough time to just... be."

As they sat down, the soft strains of a string quartet began to play in the distance. The table was adorned with delicate floral arrangements, a nod to Lorinda's love of natural beauty, and a meal prepared with ingredients sourced from both Earth and Tanzlora awaited them.

Throughout dinner, their conversation flowed easily, touching on their shared memories, the challenges of uniting the sister planets, and their hopes for the future. But as the last rays of sunlight dipped below the horizon, Ridge grew quiet, his usual confidence replaced by a flicker of nervousness.

Lorinda noticed and tilted her head, a soft smile playing on her lips. "What is it?"

Ridge took a deep breath and reached across the table to take her hand. "Lorinda," he began, his voice steady despite the pounding of his heart, "we've been through a lot together. From battling the Umbralox to navigating the chaos of this alliance... you've been my anchor through it all. And every step of the way, I've realized that no matter how uncertain the future is, one thing is clear: I don't want to face it without you."

He stood, pulling a small velvet box from his pocket, and knelt before her.

"Lorinda Rooney, will you marry me?"

Lorinda's hands flew to her mouth, tears welling in her eyes as she nodded furiously. "Yes! Of course, yes!"

Ridge grinned, sliding the intricate ring—a beautiful Earth grown diamond surrounded by iridescent Tanzloran crystal all set into gorgeous Arcmyrian metalwork—onto her finger. As they embraced, the distant quartet began playing a joyful melody, and for a moment, the weight of the Triad's troubles lifted, leaving only the joy of their shared commitment.

The kitchen at Sage Manor was a flurry of activity as Ridge and Lorinda returned home. Gran Celia, Lynx, Waverly, Lincoln, and Bethany were gathered around the table, sipping tea and sharing updates on the alliance efforts. When Ridge cleared his throat, all heads turned toward him.

"Well, we've got some news," Ridge announced, his arm around Lorinda.

Lorinda held up her hand, revealing the glimmering ring. "We're engaged!"

Gran Celia let out a delighted gasp, rising from her chair with a speed that belied her age. "Oh, my stars! This is wonderful! Absolutely wonderful!" She enveloped them both in a tight hug before stepping back to examine the ring. "And what a stunning piece of jewelry! It's perfect."

Waverly beamed. "Finally! I was starting to wonder when you'd make it official, Ridge."

Lynx grinned, clapping his uncle on the shoulder. "About time. Congratulations, both of you."

Bethany's eyes glistened with emotion as she embraced Lorinda. "You're going to be so happy, I just know it."

The room buzzed with excitement as the family began discussing the wedding. Gran Celia, ever the planner, was already listing ideas aloud.

"We'll have to make it a grand affair," she declared. "And what better place than Tanzlora? A crystal cathedral, of course! It'll symbolize the unity we're working so hard to achieve."

Ridge chuckled, exchanging a glance with Lorinda. "We were thinking the same thing."

Lynx, his eyes gleaming with curiosity, leaned forward. "Wait a second, Ridge—did you actually get down on one knee for the proposal?"

Lorinda grinned before Ridge could respond. "He did. Right in the middle of dinner. Caught me completely off guard."

Ridge shrugged, smirking. "Figured I'd do it the traditional way, make sure she knew I was serious."

Bethany clapped her hands together, her face glowing with excitement. "Lorinda, we already feel like sisters, but now it's official! I'm so happy about this." She beamed. "And I can't wait to see Monica's reaction. She's going to love this!"

Waverly nodded eagerly. "Yes! When do you plan to tell her?"

Lorinda shared a warm glance with Ridge before answering. "First thing in the morning. Ridge and I want her to start her day with good news."

Lynx grinned, leaning back with his arms crossed. "That will be one happy girl when she hears this great news!"

The thought of Monica's wide-eyed joy and bouncing excitement brought smiles all around. The warmth of the moment settled between them, reinforcing the love and unity that made their family so special.

Lincoln, who had been quietly enjoying the conversation, leaned forward with a curious expression. "So, Ridge, Lorinda... what's the timeline? When are we looking at for the big day?"

Ridge glanced at Lorinda, squeezing her hand before answering. "We touched on that a little bit in the car. We both agree that to give proper planning time, we should look at dates around six to nine months from now."

Gran Celia nodded approvingly. "That sounds reasonable, and we'll need plenty of time—especially if you're serious about getting married on Tanzlora."

Ridge nodded. "We are."

Celia sighed wistfully, her expression softening. "This will be a first... a wedding uniting all three sister planets. I just wish there was some way Galen and Victoria could be alive to witness this."

At the mention of Victoria, the room grew quiet for a beat, the weight of her absence settling over them.

Lorinda, her voice warm but tinged with longing, whispered, "I wish I had her here to plan it." She looked toward Celia with a small, sad smile. "I've seen pictures of the lavish events she hosted. If she were here, I'd put every bit of it in her capable hands."

Celia chuckled softly. "Oh, you wouldn't have had a choice. She would've taken over in a heartbeat."

Lincoln smirked. "And it would've been grand—like something straight out of a royal ball."

Lorinda laughed. "Exactly! Which is why I know she would've loved the idea of a Tanzloran wedding. She had an eye for the spectacular."

Bethany, ever the optimist, squeezed Lorinda's arm. "Maybe she's still watching over us, helping in ways we can't see."

Celia's eyes twinkled with emotion. "Maybe she is."

The warmth of that thought filled the room as everyone shared a moment of reflection before turning back to the exciting task ahead—planning a wedding unlike any the Triad had ever seen.

As the evening wore on, everyone toasted to the future, their laughter echoing through Sage Manor. For the first time in months, it felt like they weren't just fighting for the entire Triad—they were building something beautiful within it.

3

The phone in Sage Manor's office rang, breaking the tranquil morning silence. Gran Celia, seated at the desk going over some estate documentation, set the paperwork down and reached to answer. She picked up the receiver, her voice calm and steady.

"Hello, Beaumont residence," she said.

"Good morning, is this Mrs. Celia Beaumont?," came the voice on the other end. It was warm yet formal. "This is Vice President Charles P. Houston. I hope I'm not disturbing you."

Celia straightened, her tone polite but curious. "Not at all, Mr. Vice President. To what do I owe the honor of your call?"

"We need your insight and guidance," Houston said, his voice tinged with urgency. "The President and I have been discussing the situation with Tanzlora and Arcmyrin. We believe it's crucial to establish a formal interstellar agreement with the councils of both planets. Their trust in you and your family is evident, and we'd like you to join us in Washington to help navigate this process."

Celia's brow furrowed as she considered his words. "Mr. Vice President, Tanzlora and Arcmyrin have coexisted in peace and harmony for centuries without formal agreements. Introducing the idea of a treaty or contract could send the wrong message—one of mistrust. Earth's insistence on such a measure might be seen as a lack of faith in the alliance."

Houston was silent for a moment before responding. "You make a valid point, Mrs. Beaumont. But Earth's leaders are... pragmatic, let's say. They want something concrete, something binding, to reassure the skeptics here. Your perspective could help us find common ground."

Celia sighed softly. "Perhaps it's time for a face-to-face discussion, then. I'd be willing to come to Washington, but I'll need to bring someone with me. I'd prefer not to travel alone."

"Of course," Houston replied. "We'll take care of all the arrangements—transportation, accommodations, everything. Just let us know when you're ready to leave, and my office will handle the rest."

"Very well," Celia said, her voice firm. "I'll speak with my family and let you know. Good day, Mr. Vice President."

"Good day, Mrs. Beaumont. And thank you."

Celia hung up the phone and stood for a moment, gazing out the window. The morning sun cast golden light over the garden, but her thoughts were clouded with the complexities of interstellar diplomacy.

She found the family gathered in the library, their voices low but animated. Dr. Madre Walsh, Dr. Marshall Stern, Ridge, Lorinda, and Lincoln sat in a loose circle, the topic of their conversation immediately apparent as Celia entered.

"I'm telling you, it wasn't just a dream," Madre was saying, her tone insistent. "It was a vision. Bronte needs to go to Pluboria. I don't know how, but as a starseed of Pluboria, that planet is the key to his recovery."

Ridge frowned, leaning back in his chair. "Pluboria? Madre, we don't even know exactly where it is located. It may not even be in our galaxy, we know that we can't use the portal system we currently utilize for travel to Tanzlora and Arcmyrin. We have absolutely no information at all about this planet other than what you and Bronte know. Are you sure about this?"

Madre met his gaze, her expression unwavering. "I've never been more certain. Every conventional approach has failed. Pluboria can offer what Earth, Tanzlora, and Arcmyrin cannot. We just have to get there and I know that we will be given direction on that once Bronte agrees to go."

Lincoln nodded thoughtfully. "It's a long shot, but if Madre's right, it could be Bronte's best chance. Have you spoken with him about this yet?"

Celia stepped forward, drawing their attention. "I hate to interrupt," she said, "but I just received a call from Vice President Houston."

The room went quiet as the family turned toward her.

"What's going on?" Lincoln asked.

"The Vice President wants me to go to Washington," Celia explained. "He and the President are insistent on creating a formal interstellar agreement with Tanzlora and Arcmyrin. They believe it's necessary to reassure Earth's leadership, but I told him it might send the wrong message to our allies. He's invited me to discuss the matter in person."

"That's... a lot," Lorinda said, glancing at Ridge.

"It is," Celia agreed. "But I think it's important to go. The alliance is fragile enough as it is. If Earth's leaders are this concerned, it's better to address it now before it becomes another point of contention."

"Are you going alone?" Marshall asked, concern in his voice.

"No," Celia said firmly, taking a seat next to Lorinda. "I requested that someone accompany me, and Houston agreed to arrange it. I'll need to decide who will go with me."

The family exchanged glances, a mix of excitement and apprehension filling the room.

Celia leaned forward in her chair, hands clasped as she addressed the group. "If I'm going to Washington, I'll need someone to accompany me. Ridge or Lincoln, I'd like one of you to come along. Your experience with diplomacy and the alliance would be invaluable."

Ridge and Lincoln exchanged a glance, but before either could respond, Madre sat up straighter, her expression resolute.

"I don't think that's possible," she said, her voice calm but firm. "In the vision I had, I was clearly instructed that Ridge, Lincoln, and I are to take Bronte to Pluboria."

Celia raised an eyebrow clearly taken aback by Madre's statement. The atmosphere in the library grew quiet and tense with all eyes on Celia.

Gran Celia shifted in her chair as they all waited for her response. When she finally spoke, her tone was skeptical, "Instructed by whom, Madre? Who is giving you these visions, and why would they demand that Ridge and Lincoln go with you? Why not Marshall, your husband?"

Madre met her gaze steadily. "I don't know who they are, but the message was clear. This isn't about just healing Bronte—it's about something much bigger. The Beaumonts have a role to play in this."

Lincoln frowned, leaning forward. "That doesn't make any sense, Madre. Until you and Bronte brought up Pluboria, none of us had even heard of it. Why would any entity from Pluboria specifically request us?"

"I don't have all the answers," Madre admitted, her voice softening. "But I know what I saw and heard. The energy in the vision... it wasn't just a dream. It felt like something—someone—was reaching out, guiding me. It was overwhelming."

Ridge rubbed his chin thoughtfully. "I get that it felt real, Madre, but we're talking about uprooting everything to chase a hunch. What if there's a better option for Bronte right here?"

Madre's eyes flashed with a mix of determination and frustration. "You think I'd suggest this lightly? This isn't a hunch, Ridge. Every attempt we've made to help Bronte has failed. He's suffering, and I believe this is his best chance. If I'm wrong, I'll own that—but I don't think I am."

Celia tapped her fingers on the armrest of her chair, her brow furrowed. "It's still a leap. Why would Pluboria even care about the Beaumonts? What's our connection to that planet?"

Madre hesitated, then looked down, as if searching for the right words. "Maybe it's not about us specifically," she said at last. "Maybe it's about what we represent—something tied to the alliance, or the harmony we're trying to create. All I know is, I saw it. The three of us, taking Bronte to Pluboria. It was vivid, Celia, and it felt... urgent."

Ridge and Lincoln exchanged another glance, their skepticism evident.

"Even if we entertain this idea," Lincoln said slowly, "we still don't know why us. Marshall has been in the trenches with Bronte's case. He has medical expertise like you do. Wouldn't he make more sense?"

Madre shook her head. "I thought the same thing at first, but the vision was clear. It has to be the three of us. Maybe it's not just about healing Bronte physically. Maybe it's about something more."

Celia sighed deeply and leaned back in her chair, pinching the bridge of her nose. "I'm trying to keep an open mind, but this is asking a lot, Madre. We're juggling an alliance that's hanging by a thread, and now we're supposed to send Ridge and Lincoln on a trip to a planet none of us know anything about?"

Madre's gaze softened as she looked at Celia. "I know how it sounds. But this isn't just about Bronte, or even Pluboria. It's about the bigger picture. Everything we've been working toward—the alliance, the harmony—it's all connected. I feel it in my bones. I can imagine this is how Galen Beaumont felt all those years ago telling his family and friends about his initial contact with Tanzlora and Arcmyrin."

The room fell silent as the weight of her words settled over them. Ridge finally broke the tension with a resigned sigh.

"Alright," he said. "Let's say we go to Pluboria. What's the plan? How do we even get there, and what are we supposed to do when we arrive?"

Madre's lips pressed into a thin line. "I don't know yet. But I believe the path will reveal itself once we take the first step."

Lincoln crossed his arms, his skepticism giving way to cautious consideration. "It's a gamble," he said. "But if Madre's right, and this is connected to something bigger, can we really afford to ignore it?"

Celia looked around the room, her sharp mind weighing the pros and cons. Finally, she nodded. "Fine. If this is the path you believe you need to take, I won't stand in your way. But I expect updates. Constant updates. And you'd better have a solid plan before you set foot on that planet."

Madre nodded, a flicker of relief in her eyes. "Thank you, Celia. You won't regret this. So, is this everyone saying yes to taking Bronte to Pluboria?"

As the family exchanged wary glances, one by one they nodded their heads in the affirmative. Ridge and Lincoln exchanged reluctant but resigned looks, and even Dr. Marshall Stern gave a curt nod.

"I guess we're doing this," Ridge said, rubbing the back of his neck.

"Looks like it," Lincoln added, his tone laced with a mix of curiosity and caution.

Madre's expression softened as a sense of determination settled over the room. "Thank you, all of you. I know this isn't easy to understand, but I truly believe this is the right path."

Lorinda broke the silence that followed, her voice light but thoughtful. "That still leaves the question of who's going to Washington with Celia."

Celia turned in her chair to face her, her expression softening into a smile. "Dear, would you like to go with me? We could do a lot of wedding planning while we're there."

Lorinda blinked in surprise, then let out a small laugh. "You're asking me to accompany you on an interstellar diplomatic mission *and* plan a wedding? I suppose I'd better brush up on multitasking."

"Think of it as killing two birds with one stone," Celia said with a twinkle in her eye. "Besides, I could use your perspective, not just on wedding details but on the alliance. You've seen both sides—Earth's skepticism and the unity of the sister planets. Your insight would be invaluable."

Lorinda tilted her head, considering the offer for a moment. "Alright, I'm in. But I get to choose the sites we visit and tour for at least one afternoon of our visit. I have never been to Washington DC before and would love to play tourist for some of this trip."

"Deal," Celia replied, her smile growing wider.

Ridge chuckled, his usual seriousness breaking for a moment. "Looks like you've been drafted, Lorinda. Good luck keeping mother out of trouble in Washington."

"Trouble?" Celia shot back, feigning indignation. "I'll have you know I'm the picture of decorum."

The room filled with light laughter, a brief reprieve from the weight of their responsibilities.

As the family regrouped to discuss logistics for both missions, the atmosphere shifted. Though uncertainty loomed over the coming days, the decision to act—whether it was a journey to Pluboria or a trip to Washington—brought a renewed sense of purpose to Sage Manor.

For better or worse, they were moving forward together.

4

The media room of Sage Manor buzzed with activity, a whirlwind of color, sound, and energy. Once a makeshift medical ward during the battle with the Umbralox, it had now been repurposed into a multi-grade classroom for the Beaumonts and their extended family. But despite its best intentions, the room was struggling to meet the demands of such a diverse group of learners.

At one end of the room, Francis Roller sat cross-legged on the floor with Maya, Maddox, and Monica, a pile of colorful construction paper, glue sticks, and safety scissors scattered around them.

"Okay, kiddos," Francis said with a smile, holding up a glue stick like it was a wand. "We're making star constellations today! Think of your favorite constellation, and let's recreate it using these shiny stickers."

"I'm making Orion!" Maddox declared enthusiastically, reaching for a sheet of gold stars.

"Mine's Pegasus!" Monica added, carefully cutting out a horse shape.

Maya, however, frowned, holding up a blue sheet of paper. "I don't want a constellation. I want to make a spaceship!"

"Then you make the best spaceship ever, Maya," Francis encouraged.

The cheerful chatter of the younger children filled the room, their laughter occasionally punctuated by the clatter of scissors or the crinkling of paper.

At the other end of the room, Bethany stood at a long table, administering exams to Waverly and Lynx. The older siblings sat with furrowed brows, their focus strained as they tried to block out the lively commotion.

"Question twelve," Bethany said, her tone professional as she read aloud. "What are the main causes of deforestation, and how does it impact global ecosystems?"

Waverly glanced toward the younger kids, her concentration breaking as Maya giggled loudly at Maddox's attempt to stick a gold star to his forehead.

"Seriously?" Waverly muttered under her breath, her pen hovering over the test paper.

Lynx, equally distracted, sighed and rubbed his temple. "Mom, can we—"

"Hold on," Bethany interrupted, her eyes narrowing as she leaned closer to Waverly's paper. "Did you write 'climate change' twice? You're supposed to explain the causes, not list them."

Waverly groaned, dropping her pen. "I can't focus with all this noise. Mom, can we please finish the test somewhere quieter? Like the library?"

Bethany hesitated, glancing toward Francis and the kids. The younger ones were clearly having a great time, but the room was undeniably chaotic. She nodded after a moment.

"You're right. The library will be better for this," Bethany said. "Gather your things, and we'll finish up there."

"Finally," Waverly muttered as she gathered her test papers.

"Lynx, you too," Bethany added.

Francis looked up from her arts and crafts station as the trio prepared to leave. "What's going on?"

"The library," Waverly replied curtly, already heading toward the door.

Francis grinned. "Ah, the sanctuary of quiet learning. Good luck!"

As the door closed behind them, Francis turned back to the kids, who were now eagerly comparing their creations.

"Alright, who wants glitter?" Francis asked, holding up a bottle with a mischievous glint in her eye.

"Me!" all three children shouted in unison, their voices ringing out like a chorus of joy.

When Bethany, Waverly, and Lynx arrived at the library, they were greeted by yet another hurdle. Madre, Marshall, Ridge, Lincoln, Celia, and Lorinda were comfortably scattered across the room, deep in conversation about Pluboria and the upcoming diplomatic missions.

"Um, excuse me?" Waverly said, standing in the doorway with her arms crossed.

The group looked up, some mid-sentence, their expressions ranging from curious to mildly annoyed.

"What's this about?" Lincoln asked.

"We need the library," Bethany said, her tone polite but firm. "Waverly and Lynx can't focus in the media room, so we're finishing their exams in here."

Celia raised an eyebrow. "And where are we supposed to go? The parlor?"

"Yes," Waverly replied bluntly.

Lorinda chuckled. "Well, at least she's honest."

Madre stood, brushing imaginary dust from her skirt. "Alright, alright. We'll leave you to your academic pursuits. Marshall and I need to speak with Bronte about Pluboria anyway."

Marshall rose, gathering his notes. "I'm sure that conversation will be just as lively as this one."

"I don't envy you," Lynx muttered, earning a smirk from Marshall.

Celia and the others followed suit, rising from their chairs and gathering their belongings.

"I suppose the parlor will do," Celia said, a touch of mock resignation in her voice. "Though I was starting to enjoy the ambiance in here."

"It's temporary, Gran," Waverly said with a faint smile.

Ridge clapped Lynx on the shoulder as he passed. "Don't fail your test, kid. We'll need your brains in case Madre gets us lost on the way to Pluboria."

"Gee, thanks for the vote of confidence," Lynx replied dryly.

As the group filed out of the library, Madre and Marshall headed toward Bronte's room, while Celia, Ridge, Lincoln, and Lorinda made their way to the parlor to continue their discussions.

With the library finally cleared, Bethany, Waverly, and Lynx settled into their seats. The quiet was immediate and welcome, the soft creak of chairs and the faint rustle of paper the only sounds breaking the silence.

"Alright," Bethany said, flipping through her notes. "Let's get back to it. Question twelve—what are the main causes of deforestation, and how does it impact global ecosystems?"

This time, Waverly didn't glance toward any distractions or mutter under her breath. The library's calm atmosphere allowed her and Lynx to focus, their pens moving steadily across their papers. And here, in the peaceful library, the Beaumonts could find the balance they needed to navigate their many roles: students, leaders, and protectors of a galaxy still learning how to find harmony.

Madre and Marshall climbed the stairs to Bronte's room, the quiet hum of the chair lift at the staircase's edge a subtle reminder of the accommodations that had been made to ease Bronte's situation. When they reached his door, Madre knocked lightly.

"Bronte?" she called.

A gruff voice barked from inside. "Come in if you have to."

Exchanging a glance, Madre and Marshall pushed the door open to find Bronte sitting in his wheelchair, facing the window. He stared out at the pond and gazebo below, his shoulders hunched and his hands resting limply on the arms of his chair.

The in-home nursing aide bustled past them, her duties evidently complete. "He's all set for the morning," she said quietly, giving Madre a knowing look before leaving the room.

Madre's gaze drifted to the untouched breakfast tray sitting on a nearby table. Her heart sank. "Bronte, you haven't touched your food," she said softly, stepping toward the tray.

He didn't turn to look at her. "Not hungry," he muttered.

"Not hungry, or not bothering?" she asked, her tone firm but laced with concern. "You've been skipping meals, refusing to come down to the dining room... What's going on?"

Bronte shifted slightly in his chair, but his eyes stayed fixed on the window. "What's the point, Madre? This chair's my life now. You think I'm gonna sit down there with everyone like it's normal? It's not."

Madre glanced at Marshall, who stepped closer and gestured toward the bed. "Mind if we sit?" Marshall asked.

Bronte grunted but didn't object.

The two doctors sat on the edge of the bed, their expressions a mix of empathy and determination. Madre leaned forward, her hands clasped.

"Bronte," she began, her voice steady, "I need to talk to you about something important. It's about my dreams—visions, really. They've been persistent, and they're all about you and Pluboria."

That finally made Bronte turn his head slightly, though his expression remained guarded. "Pluboria? What about it?"

"I've seen you there," Madre said, her tone earnest. "I don't know how or why, but the visions are clear. You, me, Ridge, and Lincoln—we're supposed to go to Pluboria. I believe that planet holds the key to your recovery."

Bronte snorted, his lips curling into a bitter smile. "You're basing my future on dreams? Madre, I've been poked, prodded, scanned, and tested by some of the best minds across three planets, and nothing's worked. What makes you think this... Pluboria is any different?"

"It's not just a dream," Madre insisted. "It felt real—like something, or someone, was guiding me. Bronte, you've tried everything else. What do you have to lose?"

He turned fully toward them now, his sharp eyes narrowing. "What do I have to lose? Time. Energy. What little dignity I have left, traipsing around another planet on a fool's errand. That's what I have to lose."

Marshall spoke up, his voice calm and measured. "Bronte, I understand your frustration. But Madre isn't suggesting this lightly. None of us are. If she believes Pluboria could help, don't you think it's worth considering?"

Bronte let out a long sigh, his head dropping slightly. "You two really think this is gonna work?"

Madre leaned closer, her voice softening. "I don't just think, Bronte. I know. I don't have all the answers, but I believe this is part of something bigger—something that could change everything, not just for you, but for all of us."

The room fell silent as Bronte stared at the floor, his expression unreadable. Finally, he let out a reluctant grunt. "Fine. I'll think about it. But don't expect miracles."

"That's all we ask," Marshall said with a small smile.

Madre reached out and placed a gentle hand on Bronte's arm. "Thank you, Bronte. This means more than you know."

He didn't respond, his gaze drifting back to the window. As Madre and Marshall stood to leave, they exchanged a look that spoke of cautious hope.

"Let us know when you're ready to talk more about it," Marshall said as they reached the door.

Bronte gave a noncommittal grunt, but Madre chose to take it as progress.

As they descended the stairs, Madre's thoughts churned. The road ahead would be difficult, but for the first time in days, she felt a glimmer of hope. Perhaps, just perhaps, Pluboria could offer the healing that no one else could.

5

The parlor of Sage Manor was bathed in soft morning light, the warmth of the sun streaming through the large windows. Ridge, Lorinda, Lincoln, and Celia sat sipping tea and enjoying freshly baked biscuits. The comforting aroma of butter and jam filled the air, but the conversation was anything but lighthearted.

"So, for the trip to Washington," Celia was saying, stirring a spoonful of honey into her tea, "I'll need to ensure I've outlined the key points about Earth's role in this alliance. Lorinda, I'll want your input on how Tanzlora and Arcmyrin might react to the President's concerns."

Lorinda nodded. "Of course. I've been thinking about ways to frame Earth's intentions without making it seem like we're questioning the sister planets' harmony. It's a delicate balance."

Lincoln leaned back in his chair, cradling his teacup. "The real question is whether Earth's leaders are ready to listen. If they come off as condescending, it could do more harm than good."

Ridge, sitting across from him, sighed. "That's what worries me. Earth doesn't have the best track record when it comes to diplomacy—let alone interstellar diplomacy."

Before the conversation could continue, Marshall and Madre entered the parlor.

Everyone immediately looked up, their expressions a mix of curiosity and hope.

"Well?" Celia asked, setting her teacup down. "What did Bronte say?"

Marshall glanced at Madre, who gave a small nod before stepping forward. "He's... considering it," she said.

Ridge raised an eyebrow. "Considering it? That doesn't sound like a yes."

"It's not a no, either," Marshall countered, taking a seat beside Madre. "Bronte's stubborn, as you all know. But I think we planted a seed. He agreed to think about it, and that's more than we had this morning."

Madre sighed, her shoulders relaxing slightly. "He's frustrated, and I can't blame him. This situation has taken a toll on him—not just physically, but mentally. He doesn't want to feel like a burden, and the idea of traveling to Pluboria seems like another gamble to him."

"He's scared," Lorinda said softly.

Madre nodded. "Exactly. And I don't think it's just about the trip or his condition. I think he's afraid of hoping for something that might not work."

Celia reached out and patted Madre's hand. "You've done well to get him this far, Madre. If anyone can convince Bronte to take a leap of faith, it's you."

Marshall smiled faintly. "Let's not discount the rest of us. Ridge and Lincoln, you're coming along for this, too. Your voices will carry weight with him. If we work together, we can help him see this as a real opportunity."

Lincoln sipped his tea thoughtfully. "I suppose we'll need to start planning for the trip, just in case. What's the timeline?"

"That depends on when Bronte decides he's ready," Madre said. "But the sooner, the better. Every day we wait is another day he's stuck in this limbo."

Lorinda leaned forward. "And what about Washington? If Ridge and Lincoln are going to Pluboria, it'll just be Celia and me heading to D.C."

"That's manageable," Celia said firmly. "We'll be a smaller team, but that doesn't mean we'll be less effective. Besides, I think it might help to keep the delegation smaller—less intimidating for Earth's leaders."

Ridge smirked. "And if anyone can handle a room full of politicians, it's you, mom."

Celia chuckled. "I'll take that as a compliment, dear."

The room fell quiet for a moment, the weight of their upcoming missions settling over them. Each person knew the stakes—both personal and cosmic—and the challenges that lay ahead.

Madre broke the silence, her voice soft but resolute. "I know this isn't easy for any of us. But if we've learned anything from the battles we've fought, it's that nothing worth doing comes without risk. Bronte deserves this chance. And so do the sister planets."

Ridge nodded, his jaw tightening with determination. "Then let's make it happen."

As the group continued their discussion, the parlor's cozy atmosphere became a hub of strategy and hope. They knew the road ahead would be fraught with uncertainty, but together, they were ready to face whatever challenges the galaxy had in store.

Footsteps on the parlor floor interrupted their conversation, and Bethany entered, followed closely by Waverly and Lynx. All three carried a mix of relief and exhaustion on their faces, the intensity of their exams evident in their expressions.

"Finally done," Waverly announced, plopping down into an empty chair. "I don't want to write another essay for at least a week."

Lynx flopped onto the couch, rubbing his temples. "Or answer another question about deforestation. I swear, if I hear that word again..."

Bethany smiled warmly as she perched on the arm of a chair. "You both did well, even under the circumstances. I'd say you earned yourselves a break."

Celia poured tea into two waiting cups and handed them to Waverly and Lynx. "You've both worked hard. Have some tea and biscuits —you deserve it."

Waverly took a grateful sip, leaning back and letting the warmth soothe her. Lynx grabbed a biscuit, biting into it with relish.

"This is way better than studying," he said around a mouthful of crumbs.

Just as the room began to settle into a moment of peace, more footsteps interrupted again. Monica stood in the doorway, her small frame outlined by the sunlight streaming in from the hall. Her hands were covered in glue and glitter, the sparkly mess extending up her forearms.

"Lincoln? Bethany?" she said, looking at them with wide eyes. "Francis says you need to come to the media room. It's Maddox, and she said you'd know what to do."

Lorinda's eyes widened as she spotted her daughter's sticky, glittery hands. "Monica!" she exclaimed, jumping up from her chair. "Don't touch anything!"

Monica froze, looking sheepish as Lorinda hurried over to her.

"Honestly, how did you manage this?" Lorinda asked, inspecting the glittery mess. "Never mind. Let's get you cleaned up before you spread sparkles all over the manor."

Lincoln chuckled as he stood, setting his teacup down. "Sounds like Maddox is making things interesting. I'd better go see what's going on."

Bethany followed, laughing softly. "I'll come with you. Between the two of us, we can handle whatever glitter disaster is happening in there."

As Lincoln and Bethany left the parlor, Lorinda gently took Monica's hand, careful not to get glue or glitter on herself. "Excuse me, everyone," she said. "I need to get this one sorted out."

Monica smiled up at her mother. "Sorry, Mama. I was making stars, and the glitter went everywhere."

Lorinda sighed but couldn't help smiling as she led her daughter out of the room. "We'll talk about proper glitter use while we wash your hands."

As the parlor emptied slightly, the remaining family members chuckled at the small chaos that seemed to follow the children.

"Never a dull moment around here," Ridge said, shaking his head with a grin.

"No," Celia agreed, her smile warm as she poured herself another cup of tea. "And thank goodness for that. It reminds us why we do all of this—family, harmony, and a bit of glitter to keep us grounded."

Lincoln and Bethany stepped into the media room, immediately struck by the tense atmosphere. Francis stood near the arts-and-crafts station, her face pale, her hands fidgeting with a piece of glitter-covered paper. Maya sat on the floor, unnaturally still, her wide eyes fixed on her brother Maddox.

Maddox was on his knees in the middle of the room, rocking back and forth. His hands rested limply on his thighs, and his eyes were tightly closed as he repeated a phrase over and over:

"Yes, I can hear you. Yes, I can hear you."

"Maddox?" Lincoln said, rushing to his son's side. He knelt in front of him and gently grabbed him by both arms. "Son, what's going on? Who are you talking to?"

Before Maddox could respond, a shimmering figure materialized in the corner of the room. Mistara, Spirit of Water, appeared in her ethereal, flowing form, her presence immediately commanding the room. The light around her rippled like liquid, and her voice resonated with calm authority.

"Lincoln Beaumont," she said, her translucent figure drifting closer. "You must listen to your son very carefully."

Lincoln turned his head, momentarily stunned. "Mistara? What is this? What's happening to Maddox?"

Mistara's watery eyes softened. "He is not in distress. He is a vessel, open to the energy of the cosmos. There is a message he must deliver—a vital message."

Bethany took a hesitant step forward. "Mistara, what does this mean? Why Maddox?"

"The spirits do not choose lightly," Mistara replied. "His connection is strong, guiding your path."

Lincoln's grip on Maddox's arms tightened slightly, his heart pounding in his chest. "Okay," he said, swallowing hard.

He turned back to his son, his voice steady despite his racing thoughts. "Maddox, I'm here. I'm listening. Who do you hear?"

Maddox stopped rocking. Slowly, he opened his eyes, their usual brightness now tinged with something deeper—an awareness that seemed far beyond his years.

"I hear Galen," Maddox said, his voice clear and calm. "He's telling me how to get to Pluboria."

Lincoln felt his breath catch in his throat. "What?" he whispered, barely able to comprehend what he was hearing.

Bethany crouched beside him, her hand on his shoulder. "Maddox," she said softly, her voice gentle, "can you tell us what Galen is saying about Pluboria?"

Maddox's gaze didn't waver. "He says the path isn't in the stars—it's in the water. A reflection will show the way. You'll know the place when you see the stillness."

Mistara nodded, her form rippling with approval. "Trust in his guidance."

Francis, still standing near the craft table, finally found her voice. "But... what does that mean? What reflection? What stillness?"

Mistara turned her glowing eyes toward her. "The answers will come when they are needed. For now, your part is to trust the message and prepare."

Lincoln's mind raced, the weight of Maddox's words and Mistara's presence pressing heavily on him. "I don't understand why this is happening," he said, his voice tinged with frustration. "Why my son? Why now?"

Mistara's voice was gentle, yet firm. "Because he is attuned to the flow of the cosmos in ways others are not. You must honor his role in this journey, even if it is difficult to comprehend."

Lincoln turned back to Maddox, his son's calm gaze meeting his own. "Maddox," he said quietly, "are you okay? Do you feel alright?"

Maddox nodded. "I'm fine, Dad. Galen just... wanted me to tell you."

"Thank you, buddy," Lincoln said, his voice breaking slightly. He pulled Maddox into a tight hug, feeling the enormity of the moment sink in.

Mistara's form began to fade, her final words lingering in the room. "The journey to Pluboria begins with understanding. Open your hearts, and the path will reveal itself."

As her light dissipated, silence fell over the media room. Lincoln held Maddox close, his mind spinning with possibilities.

Bethany reached out and gently touched Lincoln's arm. "We need to tell the others."

Lincoln nodded, his grip on Maddox unwavering. "Yes. They need to know everything."

As they prepared to leave the room, Maya, still sitting quietly, looked up at her father. "Is Maddox going to be okay?" she asked softly.

Lincoln managed a small smile. "He's going to be just fine, sweetheart. He's just... special. Like you are. You are both very, very special."

They all left the media room, their hearts heavy with uncertainty but bolstered by a newfound sense of purpose. The journey to Pluboria was no longer just a possibility—it was inevitable. And the answers, though shrouded in mystery, were beginning to take shape.

6

The foyer of Sage Manor was a flurry of activity as Lorinda and Monica stepped out of the bathroom, Monica now free of the glitter and glue that had caused her mother to slightly panic earlier. Lorinda was fixing Monica's hair, smoothing down flyaways when the door to the media room swung open, and Francis, Lincoln, Bethany, Maddox, and Maya emerged together, all deep in conversation about what had just transpired with Maddox.

As they moved into the foyer, everyone stopped abruptly, stunned by what they saw.

Bronte Sutton sat in his wheelchair at the bottom of the grand staircase, his expression unreadable as he stared at the room's flurry of movement. For days, he had insisted on staying in his room, avoiding the dining room and much of the family altogether. Seeing him here, out of his self-imposed isolation, was a surprise to everyone.

Before anyone could react, the sharp ring of the phone in the office echoed through the manor.

"I'll get it," Bethany said quickly, handing off Maya's hand to Francis and darting down the hall toward the office.

As the others stood frozen, unsure whether to address Bronte or give him space, Monica stepped forward. The little girl's face lit up with a kind, innocent smile as she approached him.

"Hi, Mr. Bronte," Monica said softly. "Do you need any help? I could push your wheelchair for you if you want."

Bronte's gruff exterior softened slightly as he looked down at Monica, her earnestness impossible to ignore. "You want to push me around, do you?" he asked, his voice low and gravelly but tinged with a hint of amusement.

Monica nodded enthusiastically. "I'm really good at it. Ask Mama—I pushed her shopping cart last week, and it didn't even bump into anything!"

Lorinda, watching from a few feet away, suppressed a smile, her heart warmed by her daughter's determination to help.

Bronte grunted, the corner of his mouth twitching in what might have been the beginnings of a smile. "Alright, kid. Let's see what you've got. Just don't ram me into any walls, okay?"

Monica giggled and carefully took hold of the handles of Bronte's wheelchair. "Don't worry, I won't. Where do you want to go?"

"Parlor's fine," Bronte replied, nodding toward the open doorway.

As Monica began pushing the wheelchair, her small frame surprisingly steady, the others watched in silence, their earlier shock giving way to a mixture of relief and curiosity.

Francis leaned toward Lincoln and whispered, "Well, that's unexpected."

Lincoln nodded. "Yeah, but maybe it's a good sign."

Meanwhile, Maddox watched the scene intently, his expression thoughtful. Maya clung to Francis's hand, looking between her brother and Bronte, sensing something important was unfolding even if she didn't fully understand it.

In the hall, Bethany reappeared, her expression urgent. "That was the Vice President's office," she said, addressing the group. "They're confirming the arrangements for Celia's trip to Washington. They want to finalize the details by this evening."

"Alright," Lincoln said, his focus shifting back to the matter at hand. "Let's get everyone to the parlor. Looks like we have a lot to discuss."

As Monica carefully maneuvered Bronte's wheelchair toward the parlor, the atmosphere in the manor seemed to shift. For the first time in days, Bronte wasn't just an observer—he was present, engaged, and moving forward, even if only in small steps.

The family followed, their steps lighter than they'd been in days, as if Monica's small act of kindness had sparked a glimmer of hope in all of them.

The parlor was alive with energy as the family gathered together, settling into their usual places. The mood was a mix of curiosity, tension, and hope, all swirling around the events of the morning. Bronte's unexpected presence added a layer of intrigue, his wheelchair parked at the end of the room, Monica standing proudly beside him.

Lincoln stood at the center, his expression serious but calm. "I need to tell you all something," he began, his voice steady. "Something that just happened in the media room with Maddox."

All eyes turned to Maddox, who shifted nervously beside Francis.

"Maddox said he heard Galen's voice," Lincoln continued, his tone steady but filled with awe. "Mistara even appeared and confirmed it. Maddox told us Galen was guiding him—telling him how to get to Pluboria."

Celia straightened in her chair, her sharp gaze locking on her grandson. "Maddox, come here, sweetheart," she said gently, holding out her hands.

Maddox hesitated for a moment before standing and walking over to her. Celia pulled him into her lap, her arms wrapping around him protectively. "Tell me more, darling," she said softly, her eyes filled with warmth. "What did Galen say to you? What did his voice sound like?"

Maddox glanced around the room, his small hands fidgeting nervously with the hem of his shirt. "He said the path isn't in the stars—it's in the water. A reflection will show the way. He said we'd know the place when we see the stillness."

The room was quiet as everyone absorbed his words.

"Did his voice sound... unusual?" Celia asked, a thoughtful expression crossing her face.

Maddox nodded. "Yeah. Some of the words he said sounded funny. Like... like he was saying them different than the way we do."

Celia's eyes widened, and then, to everyone's surprise, she smiled. "Oh my stars," she whispered, brushing Maddox's hair back gently. "It really was him. Galen Beaumont, your great-great-great-grandfather. He struggled his whole life with a slight lisp. He was terribly self-conscious about it, and out of respect, no one ever talked about it. But now..." She laughed softly, shaking her head in amazement. "That slight lisp has become the thing that proves it really was him. Maddox, you heard our Galen. I'm absolutely amazed."

Maddox blinked up at her, his nervousness fading into a small, proud smile.

Celia looked around the room, her gaze finally landing on Madre. "I owe you an apology, Madre," she said, her voice sincere. "I've been skeptical of your visions and dreams, but this... this changes everything. I believe you now, wholeheartedly."

Madre, sitting beside Marshall, gave a gracious nod. "Thank you, Celia. I completely understand why you were questioning it all. I might have done the same in your position."

A warm silence settled over the room as everyone took in the enormity of what had just been revealed. The weight of their dual missions—to Pluboria and Washington, D.C.—seemed to grow heavier and more profound.

And then, breaking the stillness, Bronte's gruff voice rang out. "Okay," he said, his tone impatient but tinged with determination. "So when does this trip begin? I want my legs back in action!"

The room erupted into laughter, the tension dissolving for a moment as Bronte's bluntness brought everyone back to the reality of their plans.

"You're nothing if not direct, Bronte," Ridge said with a grin.

"Well, someone's gotta keep this family moving," Bronte retorted, a spark of his old fire returning.

Madre smiled warmly at him. "Soon, Bronte. We'll start preparing right away."

Lincoln sat at the edge of the couch, rubbing his hands together as he looked at his son. "Maddox, can you remember anything else about what Galen told you? Anything specific about where to find the reflection?"

Maddox frowned, his small fingers twisting into the fabric of his shirt. "I just remember the words he said. The stillness. The water. And... it felt peaceful, like a quiet place."

"A still body of water," Marshall murmured, exchanging a glance with Madre. "That could mean anything—an ocean, a lake, a pond—"

"The pond," Bronte said suddenly, causing heads to turn toward him. He was sitting straighter in his wheelchair, his sharp eyes focused on the others. "The one outside this house. It's the place I always go to think. It's quiet, peaceful—still."

Madre's breath hitched. "That would make sense."

Lincoln nodded. "Then that's where we start. First thing in the morning, we'll go to the pond and see if we can find anything."

Celia, who had been quietly listening, finally spoke. "While you prepare for Pluboria, Lorinda and I must finalize our trip to Washington. The Vice President's office is expecting us soon. We'll need to gather everything we need for those discussions."

"Do you think the President and his advisors will be open to what we're saying?" Waverly asked, concern etching her features.

Celia gave a measured nod. "I believe they're open to the conversation, but that doesn't mean they trust Tanzlora and Arcmyrin yet. Earth's leaders are cautious, and they'll need assurances that this alliance is truly in their best interest. That's where Lorinda and I come in."

Lorinda folded her arms, thoughtful. "We'll need a strategy to make them see that formal agreements could actually weaken trust instead of strengthening it."

Lincoln rubbed his chin. "That'll be tricky. Earth leaders are used to dealing in contracts and treaties. If they see an alliance without them as unstable, they'll hesitate."

"It's a delicate balance," Celia admitted. "But we'll find the right words."

Bronte let out an exaggerated sigh. "Alright, so to recap—half of you are heading off to charm the bureaucrats, and the rest of us are about to take a trip to some living planet in hopes that it'll fix my legs." He huffed. "I've been on crazier adventures, but this one's going to be a real story."

A smirk played on Ridge's lips. "Don't worry, Bronte. We'll make sure to get plenty of pictures for posterity."

Bronte rolled his eyes, but there was a flicker of amusement there.

Bethany, sitting with a notepad in her lap, tapped her pen against the paper. "Alright, we need an official timeline. If Celia and Lorinda are expected in D.C. within a couple of days, their departure could be first. But we still don't know how to actually *get* to Pluboria yet."

"Tomorrow," Lincoln said decisively. "We investigate the pond first thing. If we find something, we go from there."

Madre exhaled, feeling the weight of the unknown. "I have no doubt the path will be revealed when we're ready for it."

Silence settled over the room for a moment as the reality of what they were about to do sank in.

Then, Francis, who had been quietly watching the entire discussion, clapped her hands together. "Well, I don't know about the rest of you, but I say we need one last *normal* dinner before we start running off to alien planets and government buildings. Who's hungry?"

A chuckle rippled through the group, breaking some of the tension.

Lorinda smiled. "I'll help set the table."

"And I'll make sure Monica and Maya don't sneak into the dessert early," Waverly added.

As everyone stood and began to disperse, moving toward the dining room, Lincoln pulled Maddox aside and crouched to his level. "You did good today, kid," he said gently. "I know all of this is a lot, but you helped us more than you know."

Maddox nodded, a small but determined smile on his face. "I just told you what Galen said."

"And that might be exactly what we needed."

With a final ruffle of his son's hair, Lincoln stood and joined the others.

Tomorrow, the search for Pluboria's gateway would begin. And soon after, Celia and Lorinda would step into the political battlefield of Washington, D.C.

The family was walking into the unknown. But as they always had, they would face it together.

7

The dining room of Sage Manor buzzed with lively conversation as the family gathered around the long wooden table. The scent of roasted vegetables, fresh bread, and warm spices filled the air, a comforting reminder of the moments of normalcy they clung to amid the chaos of interstellar diplomacy and mysterious planetary summons.

Lorinda passed a bowl of mashed potatoes to Lincoln, who was deep in conversation with Celia about their upcoming trip to Washington, D.C. Bronte sat at the head of the table, idly tapping his fork against his plate, his usual gruffness softened by the decision he had made earlier.

Midway through the meal, Lynx cleared his throat, shifting slightly in his chair. "Uh, I've got some news too," he said, glancing around at the family. "Keelee reached out to me. He's asking for my help on Tanzlora."

Madre looked up from her plate, curiosity flickering in her eyes. "Keelee? What does he need?"

Lynx set his fork down and leaned forward. "Tanzlora's council is still on edge about Earth's hesitations in the alliance. Keelee thinks having me there might help strengthen trust. I'm supposed to work alongside council, sort of as an Earth liaison, to help smooth things over."

Celia nodded approvingly. "That's a wise move on his part. You've been to Tanzlora before, and they respect you. You could be a real bridge between their leaders and Earth."

44

Lynx shrugged, but there was a glint of excitement in his eyes. "I figured it was better than sitting around here waiting for updates."

"You won't be the only one heading off to another planet," Waverly added, setting down her glass of water. "I just got word from Elara—she wants me on Arcmyrin."

Lincoln raised a brow. "You? Why?"

"Elara thinks I can help relay Arcmyrin's concerns directly to Earth. She's hosting me, and I'll be working closely with their council to figure out the best way to communicate Arcmyrin's stance in a way that won't get tangled in Earth's bureaucratic nonsense."

Lorinda chuckled. "Well, that sounds like a diplomatic nightmare."

Waverly smirked. "Oh, it will be. But if it means keeping this alliance together, I'm willing to do it."

Celia, clearly impressed, set her napkin down. "So we're sending representatives to all three planets at the same time—Tanzlora, Arcmyrin, and Earth. It's a bold move."

"More like a necessary one," Ridge added. "The sooner we establish trust between everyone, the better."

Bronte, who had been quiet for most of the conversation, finally grumbled, "Just make sure nobody screws it up. I'm not about to get my legs working again just to find out the whole alliance fell apart while I was gone."

Lynx chuckled. "No pressure, huh?"

Madre smiled, though her expression was filled with the weight of everything ahead. "We've all got our roles to play. But let's not forget—we're stronger together. No matter how far apart we are, we're all working toward the same goal."

Lincoln raised his glass, and the others followed suit. "To unity, to trust, and to whatever madness we're about to walk into."

"To unity," the family echoed, their voices filled with a mixture of resolve and anticipation.

The air around Sage Manor felt charged with an energy that no one could quite name. The family and their guests all gathered by the pond at dawn, the soft golden light reflecting off the still surface of the water. Though the morning carried the scent of damp earth and fresh pine, there was something else—a presence, an anticipation that made the hair on the back of their necks stand up.

Ridge, Lincoln, Madre, and Bronte sat at the edge of the pond, waiting. Maddox stood beside Lincoln, his small hands clenched into fists as he stared at the water, as if he could already see what the rest of them could not.

"It's happening," he whispered, his voice full of knowing.

A ripple moved across the pond—not from wind or movement, but from something unseen. The water remained unnaturally still except for the expanding ring, as if responding to a force from beyond.

Then, a light emerged.

It was unlike any earthly glow—neither golden like the sun nor silver like the moon. It was iridescent, shifting between colors, as if the very essence of the universe had manifested in liquid form. The pond itself became luminous, its depths no longer reflecting the trees but revealing something else entirely.

A gateway.

Inside the liquid mirror, a landscape shimmered into view—unfathomable mountains of glowing crystal, a sky pulsing with nebulae, a city that looked as if it were woven from the very fabric of time.

Pluboria.

Gasps rang out from the family as the gateway expanded, the air vibrating with an unearthly hum.

Then came the voices.

They were melodic yet incomprehensible, resonating not just in the air but in the soul. Words were not spoken so much as felt—welcoming, expectant, calling.

Bronte, despite his usual stubbornness, was struck silent. His hands gripped the arms of his wheelchair, his body locked in a state of awe and uncertainty.

Madre took his hand. "It's time."

Lincoln looked at Ridge, who gave a slow nod. No more hesitation. No more second-guessing.

They lifted Bronte from his chair, one on each side of him and they all stepped forward.

The water lifted from the pond in thin, glowing tendrils, wrapping around each of them—not as a restraint but as an embrace, a guide. Bronte gasped as the light touched his legs, as if his very nerves were awakening from a deep sleep.

"I can feel it," he whispered. "I can feel my legs."

The family stood frozen, watching as their loved ones became engulfed in the luminescent glow. Celia reached out instinctively, though she knew this was beyond her reach. Lorinda held onto Monica and Maya, who stared wide-eyed at the spectacle. Lynx and Waverly exchanged glances, their own missions waiting, but unable to look away from the sheer wonder unfolding before them.

Marshall, Bethany and Francis looked on in awe, with Marshall feeling some guilt at not fully believing his wife before this moment.

Then, in a pulse of radiant light, Ridge, Lincoln, Madre, and Bronte vanished into the gateway, their forms dissolving into shimmering energy.

The pond stilled. The light faded. The forest around them remained unchanged, as if nothing had happened.

But the family knew better.

They had just witnessed the first step into the unknown—a journey that would change everything.

Bethany exhaled slowly, blinking away the images of the dazzling light that had just engulfed Ridge, Lincoln, Madre, and Bronte. The pond had returned to its usual stillness, but the air still thrummed with an energy that hadn't been there before.

She moved quickly, crossing the damp grass to Bronte's now-empty wheelchair, gripping the handles tightly. It felt strange, like a relic of something that no longer belonged to this world.

"Alright, everyone," Bethany said, her voice steady and firm, "we should head back inside. There's nothing more we can do here."

Francis nodded, scooping up Maya while Monica took her hand. Maddox, still staring at the pond as if waiting for more, hesitated.

"Come on, buddy," Bethany said gently, brushing his curls back from his forehead. "They'll be okay. And right now, we've got school-work to do."

Maddox turned to her, his wide, knowing eyes searching hers. "They're safe," he murmured. "Pluboria welcomed them."

Bethany's stomach twisted, but she nodded. "Good," she whispered. "Now, let's go inside."

As she wheeled Bronte's empty chair toward the house, Francis led the children inside, taking them toward the media room, which had once been a medical ward and was now a makeshift schoolroom. Maya and Monica, still giddy from the morning's strange events, chattered excitedly about the glowing water, while Maddox remained quiet, deep in thought.

Bethany lingered just long enough to make sure the children were settled before leaving them in Francis's capable hands. She then made her way to the parlor, where Celia, Marshall, Waverly, Lynx, and Lorinda were already gathering, their expressions reflecting the gravity of the moment.

8

Celia sat near the fireplace, her gaze distant, her mind clearly racing through the possibilities ahead. She turned toward Lynx and Waverly as Bethany entered. "I imagine Keelee and Elara are expecting you both soon."

Lynx, who had been absently rubbing his palms together in thought, nodded. "Keelee is ready for me on Tanzlora. The council is still hesitant about Earth's role in all of this. I think they see us as the unpredictable factor in the alliance."

"They're not wrong," Waverly muttered. "Arcmyrin is feeling the same way. They trust Tanzlora, and they trust each other, but Earth? We're the wildcard. Elara wants me to work with them, but it's going to be a fight to convince the entire council."

Lorinda crossed her arms, frowning. "And the worst part is, Earth's leaders are the ones pushing for formal agreements, while the sister planets don't see the need for them. If we push too hard, we risk making it worse."

Celia leaned forward, clasping her hands. "That's why we have to take this step carefully. Earth's leaders think in terms of laws, treaties, and official documents. Tanzlora and Arcmyrin operate on something deeper—long-standing trust, shared history, balance. Forcing them into rigid agreements will feel unnatural to them."

Lynx sighed. "So what's the approach? How do we convince Earth that a formal treaty might not be the best path forward, while also assuring Tanzlora and Arcmyrin that we're not here to control or exploit them?"

"That's what we need to figure out," Celia said.

49

Bethany sat down beside Lorinda. "Maybe it's not about convincing all three planets of the same thing at the same time," she suggested. "Maybe we have to speak their language—find different ways to appeal to what each world values most."

Lorinda's brow furrowed. "Go on."

"Well, Earth needs structure," Bethany continued, "so we could propose an agreement that feels familiar to them—something diplomatic, something that feels official but isn't a contract in the way they expect."

"A charter," Celia murmured, eyes lighting up with understanding.

Bethany nodded. "Exactly. A declaration of intent, rather than a treaty. A unified philosophy rather than a list of demands."

Lynx leaned back in his chair, considering. "That might actually work. It wouldn't bind Tanzlora and Arcmyrin in ways that feel unnatural to them, but it would still give Earth something tangible to ease their fears."

Waverly tapped her fingers against her knee. "Tanzlora and Arcmyrin care about mutual benefit. If we show them that Earth isn't just looking for a safety net, but that they actually have something to contribute to the balance of the triad, they might be more willing to accept Earth's presence."

Lorinda nodded. "And that's where Lynx and Waverly come in. You're going to be the bridge. They'll trust you more than any Earth diplomat."

Celia sat back, pride flashing in her gaze. "I think we're on the right track."

Bethany, who had been quiet for a moment, finally spoke again. "And what about Pluboria?" she asked softly. "What if Pluboria becomes a part of this alliance too?"

The question sent a ripple through the room.

"We don't know enough about Pluboria yet," Celia admitted. "But if it's as powerful as Madre believes, and if it truly is sentient... we might have to consider it."

The thought sent a thrill of unease and excitement through the group.

Lynx stood, determination in his eyes. "Well, we won't figure it all out from here. Waverly and I need to get to our destinations. Lorinda, you and Gran need to get ready for D.C."

"And we all need to hope Ridge, Lincoln, Madre, and Bronte come back soon," Waverly added.

The group nodded in agreement.

Celia rose from her chair, smoothing her dress. "We're standing at the precipice of something truly unprecedented," she said. "The choices we make now will shape the future of not just one planet, but three—maybe four."

Lorinda exhaled, running a hand through her hair. "No pressure, right?"

As the group remained in deep discussion, the weight of their separate missions settled over them. Celia, ever the strategist, leaned forward in her chair, eyes sharp with thought.

"There's one crucial aspect we cannot overlook," she said. "Each of these planets—Tanzlora, Arcmyrin, and Earth—has its own sovereignty, its own way of life. If we push too hard for unity in a way that disregards that, we'll lose everything before we even begin."

Waverly nodded. "Tanzlora and Arcmyrin have existed in harmony for centuries without treaties or bureaucratic interference. They trust in a natural balance—something Earth struggles with because we tend to control, regulate, and systematize everything. The last thing they want is for Earth to come in with our rules and definitions, demanding they conform to our way of thinking."

"That's exactly what I've been thinking," Lynx added. "They don't want a legal contract. They want to know we understand them, respect them. Tanzlora sees the future through biological and ecological evolution—nurturing their world and their people through organic advancements, strengthening their bond with nature itself. Arcmyrin is similar, but they take it further, focusing on energy harnessing, mind-melding, and expanding their consciousness rather than altering their environment. They're growing in ways we don't fully understand, but they embrace it. And then you look at Earth…"

Lorinda sighed. "And we're focused on artificial progress—technology, mechanization, expansion. Our advancements are external, synthetic. We create machines to do what other species might develop naturally. It's not necessarily bad, but it's different. The risk is in how those different approaches will align… or clash."

Marshall, who had been listening intently, interjected. "If we're not careful, our differences could drive us apart rather than bring us together. Tanzlora and Arcmyrin might see Earth's reliance on artificial technology as intrusive, even dangerous. And Earth might see their biological and energy-based advancements as unpredictable, uncontrollable."

Celia nodded in agreement with Marshall stating, "That's why this alliance has to be built on something stronger than just shared interest. It has to be about balance—about learning from one another. Because if we don't, one side is going to try to dominate the others."

Lynx rubbed his chin. "That's already happening in smaller ways. There's fear on all sides. Tanzlora and Arcmyrin worry Earth will bring its artificial constructs and disrupt their natural advancements. Meanwhile, Earth is terrified that these planets have biological and energy-based technologies beyond our understanding, and that one day, they might see us as irrelevant."

Celia exhaled slowly. "So the key to this isn't just diplomacy. It's trust-building. It's proving that none of these paths have to be in conflict. They can coexist, even enhance one another."

Waverly leaned forward, her expression determined. "That's the message we need to deliver. Tanzlora and Arcmyrin don't want interference. Earth doesn't want to be left behind. If we can establish that Earth's technology can be used to support and uplift rather than control, and that Tanzlora and Arcmyrin's advancements aren't a threat but an opportunity, we have a chance."

Lorinda tilted her head. "But can we? Can we truly align those goals?"

Bethany met her gaze. "I think we have to. Because if we don't, there won't be an alliance at all."

A heavy silence fell over the room as each person absorbed the reality of the situation.

Celia, always the voice of wisdom, finally spoke. "This is the mission ahead of us. Not just to negotiate, but to reshape the way these planets see one another. It won't be easy, and it won't happen overnight. But if we succeed, we won't just be building an alliance—we'll be shaping the future of interstellar cooperation itself."

The enormity of the task weighed on them, but in the same breath, it fueled their determination.

Lynx stood, stretching as he exhaled. "Well, that settles it. Waverly and I need to get to work. Keelee is expecting me on Tanzlora, and Elara has plans for Waverly on Arcmyrin."

Lorinda nodded. "And Celia and I will finalize our trip to Washington."

Bethany took a deep breath and smiled faintly. "And Francis and I will make sure the kids stay on track with school while we hold down the manor with Marshall."

Marshall nodded.

Celia glanced around the room, pride evident in her expression. "Each of us has a role to play. Let's make sure we do it well."

The group dispersed, each preparing for their part in a mission that would determine not just the fate of three planets, but the course of history itself.

Ridge, Lincoln, Madre, and Bronte materialized into a space unlike anything they had ever seen or imagined. They found themselves standing in what appeared to be an endless desert, its sands as pure and white as freshly fallen snow, stretching out in gentle, untouched waves beneath their feet. Above them spread a thick canopy of stars, each point of light shining more brilliantly than they had ever seen, illuminating the desert in silvery hues. The breathtaking expanse of stars was surpassed only by the brilliant, golden portal pulsating right in front of them.

Suddenly, magnificent beings of pure, ethereal light emerged around the outer perimeter of the glowing portal. Their luminous forms shimmered softly, radiating serenity and power. Though more muted now, the melodic voices and celestial music from earlier continued, gently caressing their ears like whispers of comfort.

The beings gracefully motioned for them to move forward. To everyone's astonishment and delight, Bronte stepped forward alongside them, his movements somewhat clumsy but entirely unassisted. His face lit up with joy and astonishment as he took another cautious step, gaining confidence with each stride.

As the group reached the glowing portal and stepped inside, an extraordinary warmth enveloped them. A deep, peaceful feeling blossomed within each of their hearts, filling their souls with a tranquility and harmony unlike anything they'd ever experienced before.

They found themselves suspended in a multilevel chamber, its walls completely transparent—or at least appearing to be. Their bodies felt weightless, their senses overwhelmed by the sheer vastness of their surroundings.Behind the clear surfaces, shimmering, light-formed beings moved gracefully, their shapes barely distinguishable from the waves of illumination that pulsed through the space.

The strangest part?

Total silence.

Not the quiet of an empty room or the muffled hush of deep space. This was absolute.

Ridge turned his head toward Lincoln, his mouth opening instinctively to ask if he was seeing the same thing, but—no sound came out.

Lincoln's eyes widened. He tried again, gripping Ridge's arm in alarm. Nothing.

Bronte, sitting just behind them, lifted both of his hands and stared at them in disbelief. His body felt whole. Strong. Powerful. His legs, which had been lifeless for weeks, now pulsed with vitality. He wanted to shout in triumph—but couldn't.

Madre felt the rising panic in all of them as she touched her throat. No voice. No sound. Only the weight of silence pressing against them.

Then, movement.

9

Four luminous beings—tall, ethereal, their very essence shifting like liquid light—appeared before them. Though there were no distinguishable features, the warmth of their presence washed over them like sunlight breaking through storm clouds.

They reached out, each placing a single glowing touch upon the inner wrist of the four travelers.

Instantly, a flood of warmth surged through them.

Not just warmth—love. Peace. A profound connection to something greater than themselves.

Their panic dissolved as if it had never existed.

And then, they heard it.

Not in sound. Not in spoken word. But inside of them.

"You are safe. You are the beginning. All will be revealed to you."

The words reverberated through their minds, each syllable anchoring them in the strange yet undeniable certainty that they belonged here.

The luminous beings stepped back, their radiance pulsing gently before shifting their attention upward.

Suddenly, a force pulled them.

Not harshly, not violently—but deliberately.

They floated, their bodies completely at ease as they moved toward the upper level, where a portion of the transparent wall was rippling like water on the pond.

Beyond the rippling surface, they could now make out other beings. Some were the same light-formed entities, but two figures stood apart from them.

These two were different.

They wore bright white hooded robes, their faces obscured beneath the glowing fabric. The sheer presence of them sent an overwhelming hum of wisdom and power vibrating through the chamber.

As they floated closer, the room beyond came into view.

In the very center stood a massive circular table—but not just any table.

It was identical to the one in the chamber beneath the gazebo at Sage Manor.

The only difference?

The indentations.

Each space was carved with precision, waiting—expecting.

The moment they reached the shimmering circle in the center of the glass wall, it opened like a giant iris, allowing them to pass through effortlessly.

One by one, they were gently lowered into waiting chairs, each of them automatically adjusting to fit their form.

Their hands—without conscious thought—were drawn to the indentations.

The moment their palms pressed into the grooves, golden shimmering threads tightened around their bodies. Not constraining, not binding—but connecting.

The glow spread across the table, lines of pulsing energy lighting up across the smooth surface, syncing to their presence.

Still, they could not speak.

Still, their voices were locked away.

Yet now, every sound around them was heightened.

The hum of the chamber. The movement of the light beings. The soft vibrations of the air itself. Even the pulsing rhythm of their own heartbeats sounded deafening.

Everything was amplified.

And then—

The two robed figures stepped forward.

For the first time, they heard a voice—not in their minds, not in thought, but in sound.

"Welcome."

It was rich. Layered. As if it carried thousands of voices speaking as one.

Bronte, Ridge, Lincoln, and Madre sat frozen, hearts pounding, as the realization settled in.

Whatever was about to happen—

They were part of it now.

The chamber beneath the gazebo hummed with energy, its crystalline walls pulsing in anticipation of what was to come. The Crystal Gate stood at the far end of the room, glowing in swirling hues of violet and silver, its power amplifying with each moment as it prepared for the dual departures.

Lynx and Waverly stood before it, poised and ready, their respective mixtures in hand—specially prepared elixirs infused with elements from each sister planet to aid in their interdimensional travels.

Bethany and Francis stood nearby, each keeping a careful watch over the children—Maya, Maddox, and Monica—who were clutching hands, their wide eyes filled with wonder. Celia and Lorinda stood on the opposite side, their expressions proud yet cautious, knowing how pivotal this moment was.

This was not just a journey to foreign worlds.

It was the first step toward binding the planets together in a true interstellar alliance.

As if sensing the readiness of the moment, the holographic figures of Keelee and Elara materialized, their shimmering forms appearing in front of Lynx and Waverly.

Keelee's silvery white hair and piercing violet blue eyes made his presence immediately commanding as he faced Lynx. "The Tanzloran Council is expecting you, Lynx. This mission is vital. We need to establish a path forward that preserves our sovereignty while allowing unity. The Tanzloran people will be listening and watching you closely."

Lynx nodded firmly, gripping his vial of the Tanzloran mixture. "I understand. I'll represent Earth's role fairly, but I won't let them feel like we're trying to control the process."

Keelee smiled approvingly. "That is all we ask."

Meanwhile, Elara, the Arcmyrin envoy, stood before Waverly. Her holographic form flickered momentarily before stabilizing, her deep emerald green eyes steady and composed. "Arcmyrin has long been wary of Earth's rapid technological progression, Waverly. Your presence is meant to build trust. The Arcmyrin Council will challenge you, but they must see that Earth is not a threat—nor a force seeking to impose its way of life."

Waverly inhaled deeply and squared her shoulders. "I'm ready for the challenge. Arcmyrin values wisdom and balance. I'll show them that Earth can contribute to that harmony."

Elara gave a measured nod. "Then your path will be smoother than most."

The Crystal Gate surged, its core spiraling with newfound energy.

In that moment, two more figures appeared—Ignissa, the Spirit of Fire, and Ambreela, the Spirit of Air.

Ignissa, with her fiery radiance, moved toward Lynx. "I will accompany you to Tanzlora, guiding you through the portal and ensuring your safe arrival. The fire of diplomacy must be tempered, but it must also burn brightly."

Ambreela's soft, ethereal presence surrounded Waverly. "And I shall be with you, child, as you cross into Arcmyrin. The currents of thought and understanding must flow freely."

Lorinda exhaled, gripping Celia's hand. "They won't be alone."

Celia, watching the scene unfold, smiled proudly. "No, they won't."

The children, standing in awe, held onto one another tightly.

Maddox, who had remained quiet for much of the preparation, suddenly whispered, "They're going to come back different."

Bethany glanced down at him, her hand resting on his shoulder. "What do you mean, sweetheart?"

Maddox didn't look away from the glowing portal. "They won't just be visitors. The planets will leave their mark on them."

Celia overheard and smiled softly. "That is the nature of diplomacy, my dear. They are not just bringing messages; they are forging connections that will change them as much as they change the planets."

The Crystal Gate pulsed, signaling the moment of transition.

Keelee's gaze locked onto Lynx. "Now, step forward and drink the Tanzloran mixture. Your path will open."

Lynx raised his vial, exchanging one last glance with Waverly before drinking it down in a single motion.

The golden liquid immediately reacted, his body shimmering with an iridescent light, attuning itself to the frequency of Tanzlora. The moment he stepped forward, Ignissa's flame wrapped around him, shielding him as he disappeared into the portal.

Simultaneously, Elara nodded at Waverly. "It is time."

Waverly lifted her vial and drank the Arcmyrin mixture, the cool, electric sensation rushing through her veins. A soft gust of wind wrapped around her body, shimmering with the hues of the Arcmyrin sky.

Ambreela's voice whispered, "Go forth with the winds of wisdom."

With a steady breath, Waverly stepped forward—and vanished into the swirling light.

The chamber fell into a hush, the portal pulsing faintly before stabilizing once more.

Celia exhaled, her grip on Lorinda tightening.

Francis turned to the children. "Come on, little ones. Let's go back to the house."

Monica hesitated before turning to Celia. "They're going to be okay, right?"

Celia knelt, brushing a soft curl from Monica's face. "Yes, my dear. They're exactly where they need to be."

As Francis and Bethany led the children away, Celia, Lorinda, and Marshall remained.

"Now," Celia said, straightening her spine, "we prepare for Washington."

The chamber hummed around them. The missions were in motion. The future was unfolding.

And there was no turning back.

10

The house settled into a rhythm again, though there was a noticeable shift in the air—a sense of purpose, of anticipation for what was to come. In the media room, Bethany and Francis resumed their roles as educators, guiding Maya, Maddox, and Monica through their lessons. Though the children had been wide-eyed with wonder after watching Lynx and Waverly disappear through the Crystal Gate, Bethany knew the best way to ease their nerves was through routine.

"Alright, let's refocus," she said, tapping a lesson plan onto the tablet in front of her. "Today, we're learning about planetary ecosystems. Monica, why don't you start by telling us how Tanzlora's plant life is different from Earth's?"

Monica, still fidgeting slightly from the excitement of the morning, tried her best to concentrate. "Well... Tanzlora's plants glow sometimes. Like, they actually give off light. And I remember you saying they don't just grow in soil—they can grow on water, even in the air if they're close to the right kind of energy."

Bethany smiled, nodding. "Exactly. Their plants thrive with symbiotic energy absorption, meaning they can take nutrients from the air and water around them rather than being rooted in soil like ours."

Maddox, resting his chin in his hand, mumbled, "That's kind of like Arcmyrin's energy system, too."

Francis raised an eyebrow. "You're right, buddy. Arcmyrin doesn't rely on artificial power grids like Earth does—they harness ambient energy naturally from the environment."

Bethany saw Maya's hand go up. "So if Tanzlora and Arcmyrin are so natural and connected to the world, why is Earth the one always making machines?"

It was a heavy question for a second grader, but Bethany wasn't surprised. These children were growing up between three worlds, their perspectives far broader than most.

She exchanged a glance with Francis before answering carefully. "Earth's history has always been about innovation through invention. Machines helped us survive in environments that weren't always kind to us. But just because we use technology differently doesn't mean it can't exist alongside other ways of living."

Maddox's gaze flickered toward the window overlooking the pond, a knowing look in his young eyes. "That's what the Triad has to figure out, right?"

Bethany smiled. "Exactly."

As the children returned to their lessons, Bethany and Francis exchanged a knowing glance. They weren't just preparing these kids for everyday knowledge—they were shaping the next generation of those who would understand and protect the balance of worlds.

Upstairs, Celia and Lorinda packed their bags for Washington, D.C., their movements purposeful but filled with quiet reflection. Lorinda neatly folded a deep blue blazer, smoothing out any creases before placing it into her suitcase. "We'll need to be precise with our wording when we present Earth's mission statement," she said, her voice thoughtful. "The Vice President and world leaders will be expecting concrete terms, but we have to make sure we frame it in a way that respects Tanzlora and Arcmyrin's sovereignty."

Celia, carefully tucking an elegant but modest dress into her travel case, nodded. "Earth wants legal assurances. Tanzlora and Arcmyrin want relational trust. Our role is to make sure both sides understand one another—and that neither feels pressured into something that will break that trust."

Lorinda glanced toward her, a small smile forming. "You really were made for this, you know."

Celia let out a soft chuckle, closing her case. "Perhaps. But I never imagined my later years would be spent shaping the diplomatic future of three planets."

Lorinda smirked, zipping her suitcase shut. "I suppose no one really plans for something like this."

Celia gave a fond nod before stepping away. "I'm going to take a moment to myself before we leave."

Lorinda understood immediately. "Of course. I am going to head on downstairs with our luggage to check on the children and I'll be ready when you are."

As Lorinda began wheeling the luggage into the hallway outside Gran Celia's suite, she nearly bumped into Marshall, who was making his way toward the stairs.

"Whoa!" Marshall laughed lightly, sidestepping just in time. "Looks like you might need a hand with those. Let me help."

Lorinda smiled gratefully. "Thanks, Marshall. Are you headed downstairs, too?"

Marshall nodded. "Actually, I was just heading to the library to do some research on Earth's charters. I figured I'd brush up so I can be helpful when the alliance reaches the stage of actually putting words on paper."

Lorinda's eyes brightened appreciatively. "Well, thanks for both kinds of help, Marshall. Honestly, we're lucky to have you."

They each picked up one of the smaller suitcases, pausing briefly when they looked at the largest piece still sitting there, heavy and cumbersome.

Then, Lorinda's eyes lit up with a sudden spark of ingenuity. "Marshall, why don't we use Bronte's chair lift for that one? It would save both our lower backs, and probably time, too."

Marshall grinned widely, impressed. "Wow, brilliant idea, Lorinda! With thinking like that, you're going to do great in DC."

Together they maneuvered the largest suitcase onto the chair lift, sharing a laugh as it smoothly glided down the stairs.

Celia entered her bedroom, closing the door softly behind her. The room was as serene as ever, filled with the familiar warmth of home.

She moved toward the window seat, overlooking the sprawling landscape of Sage Manor—the pond, the trees, the sky, all so still in the wake of the morning's events.

She lowered herself onto the cushioned bench and folded her hands in her lap.

Then, she prayed.

"Origin, Keeper of All, Guide of the Cosmos..."

"I come to You not just as Celia Beaumont, but as a guardian of this family, as a steward of this alliance, as a humble soul seeking wisdom."

"The path ahead is vast and uncertain, but You have given us this role, this purpose. We do not carry it lightly. We do not take it for granted. But we ask for Your blessing as we step forward."

"Bless Lynx as he walks among the Tanzlorans. Let his words bring trust where there is hesitation."

"Bless Waverly as she speaks with Arcmyrin. Let her wisdom be a bridge between their world and ours."

"Bless Ridge, Lincoln, Madre, and Bronte in Pluboria. Let them find what they seek, and may Bronte be healed in ways we cannot yet understand."

"And bless Lorinda and me, as we enter the halls of Earth's leaders. Let our words be strong yet kind, our hearts unwavering yet open."

"May the Triad be forged in harmony, not fear. May we unite not through contracts, but through understanding."

"And may Your light guide us through whatever trials come next."

She sat in silence for a moment, allowing the weight of her words to settle into her soul.

Then, a soft knock came at the door.

"Celia?" Lorinda's voice came gently. "The airport transport is here."

Celia took a deep breath, smoothing the folds of her skirt before standing. "I'm ready."

As she picked up her purse and stepped into the hallway, she felt lighter, more assured.

The Triad's journey was beginning.

And she would not let them falter.

The light surrounding Ridge, Lincoln, Madre, and Bronte gradually softened as the shimmering threads binding them to their chairs faded away. The two robed figures stepped forward, the air around them pulsing with energy, their white robes glowing with a radiant warmth.

Slowly, they lifted their hoods.

The first to reveal himself was Galen Beaumont.

His presence radiated wisdom, his sharp yet kind eyes holding the weight of centuries. Though his body was now purely of light and energy, his features carried the essence of the man he had once been on Earth.

Beside him, the second figure lowered her hood, revealing Victoria Beaumont—her ethereal face ageless and serene, her soft features illuminated by an inner glow.

Ridge and Lincoln exchanged stunned glances.

"...Galen?" Lincoln whispered, his voice thick with disbelief.

Galen smiled. "Yes, my dear great-great-grandson. And I am pleased to finally stand before you."

Madre's breath hitched. "You... you both have been here, all this time?"

Victoria stepped forward, her presence soothing. "Yes, Madre. After our time on Earth ended, our biological bodies ceased, but our spirits endured. Origin gave us a choice—to merge with the eternal flow of creation or to exist as light-beings in a realm where our presence could still matter."

Galen nodded. "We chose Pluboria as our eternal home. It is a place of pure harmony, where we could continue to watch over our family without interfering with the natural course of events."

Bronte, who had been listening with arms crossed, finally spoke up. "So, what's the deal, then? Why now? Why bring us here?"

Galen's expression darkened slightly. "Because while your family has remained benevolent in its relationship with the elemental spirits, there have been those among our bloodline who sought to twist the gift for their own ends."

Lincoln frowned. "You're talking about Gideon."

"Yes," Galen confirmed. "He was part of the bloodline, but he chose the path of darkness. He betrayed not just the family, but Origin itself."

Victoria's eyes saddened. "His actions were not merely selfish—they were malevolent. And because of that, he did not just lose his place among us... he lost his eternal existence."

Ridge narrowed his eyes. "You mean, he's just... gone? No spirit? No afterlife?"

Galen nodded solemnly. "He was erased. When Waverly stopped him on Tanzlora, he was already beyond redemption. His actions forfeited his right to exist beyond his biological form."

Madre shuddered at the thought. "That's... unsettling."

"Yes," Galen agreed. "But thankfully, others in the family—like Waverly, Lincoln, Lynx and Ridge—have counteracted Gideon's evil. Your choices have restored balance where he sought to disrupt it."

Bronte, still skeptical, leaned forward. "So that's it? Gideon's gone, and the family's in the clear?"

A shadow flickered over Galen's expression. "No."

The room chilled slightly.

"There is still one more," he said, his voice heavy with meaning.

Lincoln and Ridge stiffened.

Galen continued, "There is one more in the family who is unbalanced—someone who can still harness their gift for evil. This individual is not on Earth but is believed to be on Arcmyrin."

The words sent a shockwave through the room.

Lincoln's eyes widened. "What? Who?"

Victoria said, "It is your aunt Josephine."

Ridge stepped forward, his brows furrowed. "How is that possible? I thought Gideon was the only traitor."

Victoria's face was sorrowful. "Gideon may have been the true source of darkness, but he did not walk that path alone."

Galen's voice deepened. "Josephine followed him."

Lincoln let out a sharp breath, his mind racing. "That's not possible. How has no one found her? She's human—she would stand out on Arcmyrin."

Galen sighed, shaking his head. "That is where you are mistaken, Lincoln. Josephine possesses the gift of Earth."

Ridge stiffened. "Terraveta's gift?"

"Yes," Victoria confirmed. "Though she has not used it in the way it was intended, she knows how to manipulate the elements, particularly rocks, minerals, and soil. She uses them to alter her appearance, making herself unrecognizable wherever she moves."

Lincoln's jaw clenched. "Then she could be anywhere."

"She is hiding, but she is not lost," Galen assured him. "She is still connected to the family's energy, even if she has chosen a path of deception."

At that moment, a soft gust of wind filled the chamber, followed by the scent of fresh earth and stone.

Two new presences materialized in the space.

11

M istara, Spirit of Water, and Terraveta, Spirit of Earth.
Terraveta's form was deep, rich brown and emerald green, shifting like the layers of the planet's crust. She moved with quiet strength, her energy grounding, steady. Her voice, when she spoke, was a rumble of the earth itself.

"The last time I felt my connection to Josephine," Terraveta said, *"was when Gideon still existed. I could sense his influence twisting her mind, pulling her toward his darkness. But unlike Gideon, Josephine never fully committed. She was... conflicted."*

Mistara's voice, ever fluid, joined in. *"She loved her brother and always followed him. Even as a child, she looked up to Gideon, believing he could do no wrong."*

Ridge shook his head in frustration. "Then why would she stay on Arcmyrin?"

Victoria exhaled. "Because she is torn."

The room fell into silence.

Galen turned to his great-great grandsons, his gaze filled with something deeper than sadness—understanding.

"Your grandfather, Joseph Beaumont, and his wife, Geneva, had four children: Jameson, Garvis, Gideon, and Josephine."

Lincoln and Ridge stiffened. Their father, Jameson, was the oldest.

"Jameson and Garvis served the family well," Victoria continued. "They honored the family's legacy, using their gifts for good, for balance. But Gideon… he was different. A bad seed through and through. He influenced Josephine, and she followed because she could never resist her older brother's persuasion."

Terraveta's form dimmed slightly, as if the memory brought her sorrow.

"Josephine still has a choice. But if she remains hidden, if she uses her gift for deceit rather than truth, she could undo everything the Triad is building."

Mistara's voice became urgent. *"She is not beyond redemption, but she is dangerously close to making a decision that could set her on Gideon's path."*

Lincoln exhaled slowly, his expression unreadable. "And if she makes the wrong choice?"

Victoria's face darkened. "Then, like Gideon, she will forfeit her place—in this family and beyond."

Ridge turned to Lincoln, their thoughts aligned.

They had to find Josephine—before it was too late.

And the only place to start...

Was Arcmyrin.

Ridge leaned back in his chair, his mind racing. "If Josephine is on Arcmyrin, then Waverly's walking into a situation she is not prepared for."

Lincoln nodded grimly. "We need to alert Elara, Rykas and the council about this."

Victoria placed a radiant hand over Lincoln's. "And that is why you are here. You are the beginning of what comes next."

Galen stepped closer, his voice filled with an ancient certainty. "The future of the Triad—Earth, Tanzlora, and Arcmyrin—depends on how this unfolds. You are the ones who must bring balance before it is too late."

Bronte exhaled sharply. "Well. Guess it's a good thing we're here, then."

A knowing smile passed between Galen and Victoria.

"Yes," Galen said simply. "It is."

Madre sat back in her chair, the glow of the room reflecting in her wide, thoughtful eyes. The weight of everything Galen and Victoria had revealed pressed upon her, but there was something else nagging at her mind—a puzzle piece that didn't quite fit.

She turned her gaze toward Galen, then to Victoria, then finally to the luminous being standing just beyond them. Her voice, though steady, held a note of uncertainty.

"I don't understand where Bronte and I fit into all of this," she admitted, glancing toward Bronte, who nodded in agreement. "I thought I understood... I thought Bronte and I were siblings here on Pluboria. That we were connected as starseeds on Earth because of that bond."

At this, one of the light beings—its form shifting and flowing like liquid light—stepped forward. It radiated a profound warmth, its very presence filled with wisdom and clarity.

"Yes, Madre. You and Bronte are indeed siblings from centuries ago," the being's voice resonated, though it spoke not with sound, but through thought, its message flowing directly into their consciousness.

"You chose to manifest back on Earth during this exact timeframe for a singular purpose—to assist the Beaumonts in ushering in the new beginning of the Triad. You were sent to Earth because your connection to Pluboria allows you to guide the balance of these three planets and help ensure that they can coexist in peace and harmony."

Bronte crossed his arms, his expression thoughtful. "So we're like... intergalactic babysitters?"

The light being's glow pulsed in what could have been amusement.

"No, Bronte. You are not babysitters. You are here to be stabilizers—pillars of balance in a time where the Triad could either rise in unity or fall apart in division. Your presence is essential, for without you, the scales may tip too far in either direction."

Bronte let out a slow breath, nodding, though he still seemed skeptical. "Alright. I get that. But here's my next question—will Pluboria ever become part of the interplanetary alliance?"

The chamber went still.

Then, the light being answered.

"No. Pluboria is not a planet for biological lifeforms. It exists as a realm for light spirit entities who have completed their cycles elsewhere and chosen to return here for eternity. It is separate from the laws of the Triad because it does not function under the same constructs as Earth, Tanzlora, or Arcmyrin."

"Your presence here now is a rare exception, a unique occurrence permitted by Origin as a means to set this new beginning in motion. It will not happen again. Once you are returned to Earth, you will not be able to travel back to Pluboria while in biological form. You will only return when your physical bodies reach their end, and at that time, you will have the choice to remain here for eternity or be reborn again elsewhere."

Madre's breath caught in her throat. "So… this is the only time we will ever see Pluboria in our physical forms?"

"Yes."

Bronte looked away, his expression unreadable.

Ridge leaned forward, shaking his head slightly. "I don't understand. If Madre and Bronte were able to come back to Earth for this timeframe to help with the Triad, then why couldn't Galen and Victoria do the same? Or any other spirit, for that matter?"

Galen and Victoria exchanged a look before the light being answered once more.

"Because light beings can return to biological form—but not as their original selves. If they choose to return to the physical realm, they must be born again as a different biological entity, on whichever planet they choose. They cannot simply step back into the world as they once were."

The group fell silent, letting the weight of the revelation settle over them.

"This is what Earth calls reincarnation," the light being continued. *"Tanzlora and Arcmyrin refer to it as Mutradiare—the cycle of existence. When a spirit chooses to re-enter the physical plane, they do so as an entirely new being, with new memories, new experiences. But when their time in that form ends, they may return here, and the cycle begins again."*

Lincoln let out a slow breath, absorbing the enormity of it. "So... Galen and Victoria could return to the physical realm—but only if they started life over as someone else."

"Correct."

The chamber fell into a tense silence.

Lynx stepped forward into the pulsing vortex of the portal, feeling the now-familiar sensation of energy wrapping around him like an invisible force. The moment his foot left the ground at Sage Manor, his body became weightless, his senses stretching beyond what was normally possible.

Ignissa moved beside him, her fiery aura shifting into a steady pulse of crimson and gold. Her presence was warm but not overwhelming, a steady guide through the interdimensional passageway.

Though Lynx had traveled through portals before, this time was different.

For the first time, there was no fear of an ambush. No dark presence lurking between dimensions.

Yet, despite this knowledge, he couldn't shake the nerves creeping in. His past journeys to Tanzlora had been riddled with danger—Umbralox attacks, Abasimtrox infiltrations, interference that nearly cost them everything.

Ignissa must have sensed his unease because she turned her glowing, ember-like eyes toward him, her voice smooth and assured.

"You are troubled, Lynx Beaumont."

He let out a slow breath, feeling the weightlessness of the journey pressing on him. "I can't help it," he admitted. "The last times I came through here... we were attacked. We barely made it out alive. It's hard to trust that this will be different."

Ignissa smiled, her flames flickering in soft amusement. *"You are a warrior in heart and mind, always preparing for battle. But I tell you now—there is no battle to be fought here today."*

Lynx met her gaze, searching for confirmation. "The Abasimtrox and Umbralox are truly... gone?"

Ignissa's flames flared for a brief moment before settling into a steady glow. *"Yes. They have been eradicated, their darkness wiped from existence. The path to Tanzlora is clear. There are no enemies lurking, no shadowed forces waiting to pull you from your course."*

Lynx hesitated, then let out a breath he hadn't realized he was holding. "...That's a relief."

Ignissa tilted her head. *"Then why do you still feel unsettled?"*

Lynx frowned, looking out into the swirling expanse around them. The portal was alive, filled with color and movement, a tapestry of dimensions weaving together in a dance of light and sound.

He had never really looked before.

Not like this.

Every time he had traveled between worlds, he had been too preoccupied—dodging attacks, bracing for impact, anticipating what came next.

Now, as Ignissa's words settled into him, he realized something—he had never allowed himself to experience the journey.

So, this time, he did.

He let himself feel the pull of energy against his skin, like a soft wind guiding him forward.

He listened to the whispering sounds—not voices, but melodies that seemed to exist between time and space.

He opened his eyes fully, taking in the spectacle of colors—indigos and silvers, golds and ambers, swirls of light forming into constellations that flickered in and out of sight.

It was... beautiful.

Breathtaking.

Like a dream made real.

Ignissa smiled as she watched him take it all in. *"See? The journey itself is a gift, Lynx. One must not always rush toward the destination without appreciating the path that takes them there."*

He gave her a small, genuine grin. "You sound like Keelee."

Ignissa laughed softly, the sound like crackling embers in the wind. *"Perhaps that is why you are going to Tanzlora, then."*

Lynx smirked, shaking his head as he turned forward once again. Ahead of them, the portal began to shift.

Ignissa's voice turned firm yet calm. *"Our exit point approaches. It is time."*

Lynx took a steadying breath. This was it.

The swirls of energy before them parted, revealing a shimmering veil of lush green and golden light—the atmosphere of Tanzlora opening to receive him.

With a final nod toward Ignissa, Lynx stepped forward—and through.

Lynx emerged onto the soft, sunlit terrain of Tanzlora, his boots touching the rich, moss-covered ground that pulsed with life beneath his feet.

The air was thick with the scent of flourishing flora, carrying an almost sweet, crisp freshness that immediately settled over him. Sunlight filtered through the crystal-leaved trees, casting golden reflections across the land.

Standing before him were three figures—Keelee, Sanodia, and Callum.

Keelee, his silvery white hair braided back, was the first to step forward, his violet blue eyes bright as he regarded him. "You made it," he said, a small smirk playing at the corner of his lips.

Lynx chuckled, running a hand through his hair. "Yeah. Without getting attacked this time. Feels weird."

Sanodia, ever composed, gave a slow nod. "The times have changed, Lynx Beaumont. There is peace now. You will see that for yourself."

Callum, the warrior who had valiantly helped them fight the Umbralox, grinned. "Which means no excuses for not enjoying yourself while you're here."

Lynx smirked. "I'll keep that in mind."

Ignissa's presence lingered beside him for a moment before she shifted into a streak of golden light, ascending into the sky. Her part in his journey was complete—for now.

Keelee extended a hand toward him. "Come, Lynx. There is much to discuss."

Lynx inhaled the warm, fragrant air of Tanzlora and stepped forward, his mind open, his mission clear.

12

The blacked-out SUV rolled smoothly down the winding road leading away from Sage Manor, its sleek frame blending seamlessly into the remaining mist that still lightly blanketed the forests of Galen Valley. Inside, Celia and Lorinda sat quietly, both women lost in thought as the weight of their mission pressed upon them.

The vehicle's driver, a silent and efficient agent, had not spoken a word beyond his initial greeting, and the security escort sitting in the front passenger seat only occasionally murmured into a discreet earpiece. It was clear that their journey to Washington was of high importance—one that warranted a level of secrecy and caution.

Lorinda glanced at Celia, her fingers idly smoothing the fabric of her deep navy travel suit. "I have to admit," she said, "I didn't expect to be whisked away like some kind of foreign dignitary."

Celia gave a knowing smile. "Well, we are diplomats now, my dear."

Lorinda let out a small chuckle. "I suppose we are."

Within the hour, the SUV pulled into a private hangar at Asheville Regional Airport, where a sleek white and blue government aircraft awaited them. The moment the vehicle came to a halt, their doors were opened by a waiting attendant.

"Welcome, Mrs. Beaumont and Ms. Rooney," the man said, offering them a polite nod. "If you'll follow me, the plane is ready for take-off."

With security detail flanking them, Celia and Lorinda ascended the narrow staircase into the aircraft's cabin. It was a smaller, private jet, undoubtedly arranged for efficiency and security rather than luxury, but the accommodations were still immaculate. Soft leather seats, polished wooden paneling, and a refreshment station stocked with drinks and snacks greeted them.

As they settled into their seats, a well-dressed woman in a crisp gray blazer stepped forward.

"Mrs. Beaumont, Ms. Rooney," she said warmly, extending a hand. "I'm Rachel Timms, Deputy Chief of Staff for Vice President Houston. I'll be your point of contact during your stay in D.C."

Celia shook her hand firmly. "A pleasure to meet you, Ms. Timms."

"Please, call me Rachel," the woman insisted before turning to Lorinda and shaking her hand as well. "The Vice President is very much looking forward to your arrival. We have a full itinerary planned for your visit, including meetings with global leaders on the Council for Interplanetary Relations. The goal is to begin discussions on a mutual agreement for peace, prosperity, and the harmonious sharing of knowledge, resources, and technology between Earth and the sister planets."

At the mention of technology, Lorinda couldn't help but raise an eyebrow. She waited until Rachel had finished before casually glancing at Celia. "At what point," she asked, half amused, half concerned, "are you planning to let the Vice President know that technology isn't exactly a strong suit for Tanzlora or Arcmyrin?"

Celia gave a knowing smile and reached for a cup of hot tea that had been prepared for her. She took a slow sip before replying, her voice calm, composed.

"I'll let things unfold as Origin sees fit."

Lorinda exhaled a quiet laugh, shaking her head. "Of course. Why did I even ask?"

Rachel, oblivious to their exchange, continued with her prepared briefing. "Once we land and get you settled in at your accommodations, you'll be taken to the Vice President's residence. Vice President and Mrs. Houston wishes to personally welcome you before tomorrow's initial round of discussions. The President himself will be joining later in the negotiations this week, but for now, Vice President Houston is handling the preliminary arrangements."

Celia nodded. "That sounds fine, Rachel. We're here to listen, observe, and help guide these talks toward a mutual understanding between all planets involved."

Rachel smiled. "That's precisely what the administration is hoping for as well."

The plane gave a slight lurch as it ascended into the sky, the beautiful Blue Ridge mountains of North Carolina disappearing beneath them.

As Celia stared out of the window, watching the clouds drift by, she clasped her hands together, whispering a silent prayer in her heart.

"Origin, let our words be strong, yet wise. Let us navigate this moment with grace, with patience, and with the understanding that our purpose is not to force—but to unite."

She let out a slow breath, eyes twinkling with quiet determination.

The air within the multilevel chamber of Pluboria shimmered, a place where reality bent to the will of light and energy. Ridge, Lincoln, Madre, and Bronte stood, still absorbing the weight of what had been revealed to them. But now, the conversation turned toward what had been in the back of all their minds—Bronte's healing.

One of the light-body entities, a being of soft golden luminescence, stepped forward, addressing Bronte with a voice that resonated directly into his consciousness.

"Bronte Sutton, you will not return to Earth as you were before. The damage your body sustained at Looking Glass Falls will be undone. Your form will be restored to its true balance, free of limitation, free of pain."

Bronte swallowed, his voice steady but laced with uncertainty. "So... no more chair? No more struggling to move?"

"Correct," the being confirmed.

For a moment, Bronte was silent. Then, a sharp laugh burst from his throat—a laugh of pure, unfiltered relief. "Well, about damn time."

Madre placed a hand on his arm, squeezing gently. "This is why you had to come here, Bronte. Your healing isn't just physical. It's... something deeper."

Bronte looked down at his hands, flexing his fingers as if testing to see if the change had already begun. "And once we go back... it'll stick?"

"Your body will be whole, your spirit aligned. What was taken from you in injury will be restored in full."

Before Bronte could respond, two of the light entities moved toward him and Madre, their forms radiating with a warm, golden glow.

"Come," one of them said gently. *"Your healing awaits."*

Madre glanced at Ridge and Lincoln, giving them a small, reassuring nod before turning back to Bronte. "Ready?"

Bronte gave her a big smile. "I am ready."

With that, the two were led from the chamber into another space—a place where energy pulsed with the power of renewal.

The portal to Arcmyrin pulsed with a soft glow as Waverly stepped through, feeling the familiar rush of energy shift around her. The sensation was both exhilarating and grounding—like stepping through a veil between two realities.

The moment her feet touched the lush, glimmering terrain of Arcmyrin, a sense of peace washed over her. The air was different here—lighter, charged with a gentle hum of energy that thrummed in her very bones.

Waiting for her was Elara, her emerald-hued eyes shimmering with welcome. Her long, flowing robes of deep purple shifted slightly in the soft Arcmyrin breeze as she smiled. "Welcome, Waverly Beaumont. It is good to see you again, this time under peaceful circumstances."

Waverly returned the smile, shaking off the residual energy from the portal. "It feels… different. The last time I was here, we were fighting for survival." She turned her gaze to the sky, which was a mesmerizing blend of soft silvers and deep indigos, streaked with shifting auroras. "But now… it's like the whole planet is alive in a way I didn't see before."

Elara's expression softened with pride. "That is because Arcmyrin has healed."

As they began their walk toward the Council Chambers, Waverly couldn't help but take in the beauty of her surroundings.

The landscape was unlike anything she had ever seen—glowing flora in shades of sapphire and emerald lined the paths, and luminous crystal-like trees pulsed with a gentle radiance. The air itself carried a fragrance so rich, so intoxicating, it was almost dizzying—a mix of sweet nectar, fresh rain, and something floral yet unfamiliar.

She slowed her steps and took a deep breath, inhaling the divine scent of Arcmyrin. "Elara… this is incredible," she murmured, glancing around in awe. "I don't remember these flowers, or the way everything smells so—alive."

Elara smiled knowingly, brushing her fingers across the petals of a blooming violet-and-gold flower, watching as it responded to her touch, glowing momentarily before settling.

"That is because the Abasimtrox had damaged our ecosystem so severely," Elara explained. "When you were here before, our lands were struggling, our connection to the planet disrupted. The Arcmyrin people were diminished because we are deeply connected to this world—when it suffers, so do we. But now, with the darkness gone… the balance has returned."

Waverly ran her fingers along a silver-leafed vine that curled upward as if greeting her. "So, the planet and the Arcmyrins… you're all connected?"

Elara nodded. "Yes. The vibrations and frequencies of Arcmyrin and its people are now aligned once more. You see, Waverly, our world is not just a place we live. It is an extension of us. Its energy flows through our bodies, just as our own energy flows back into it. That harmony was broken during the invasion... but now, it thrives like never before."

Waverly took a deep breath, closing her eyes for a moment. She could feel it—the pulse, the frequency, the gentle hum beneath her feet.

"This is amazing," she whispered. "If only Earth could feel this—if my home could experience this level of peace and balance."

Elara regarded her thoughtfully. "Perhaps it can."

Waverly opened her eyes, blinking in curiosity. "You think so?"

Elara nodded. "It will take time, but harmony is possible anywhere. The key is not forcing nature to bend to your will, but rather... listening. Working with it, not against it."

Waverly thought about Earth—the pollution, the wars, the constant push for technological advancement without balance. Could her people learn from Arcmyrin? Could Earth be restored to balance, the way this world had been?

Hope flickered in her chest.

As they continued their walk, the Council Chambers came into view. It was a breathtaking structure—made not of stone or metal, but of intertwining crystal and light. The building itself seemed to shift in color, adapting with the flow of energy in the air.

Elara turned to her, her expression serious yet welcoming. "It is time for you to meet the Arcmyrin Council of Elders."

Waverly straightened her spine, preparing herself for what was to come.

She had fought for this world once before.

Now, she would fight for its future—for the Triad—in a very different way.

13

Madre and Bronte followed the two radiant light beings through a softly glowing corridor on Pluboria. Each step they took seemed lighter, as if the very air carried them forward. They soon entered a large, circular chamber, its walls gently pulsating with a serene golden hue.

At the chamber's center stood an extraordinary structure—a tube-like capsule resting atop a pedestal, angled precisely at 45 degrees. Its surface shimmered, colors they had never before witnessed swirling and dancing in mesmerizing patterns. The chamber itself was windowless, yet appeared alive, vibrant, filled with an energy both mysterious and comforting.

One of the luminous beings gracefully motioned for Madre to sit in a nearby chair, egg-shaped and cushioned, encircled by colors matching the healing chamber itself. Madre settled into it carefully, marveling at the soothing energy flowing around her.

Bronte approached the healing chamber, guided by the second being. With a gentle wave from the being's radiant hand, the top of the capsule lifted smoothly, revealing a bed inside, layered with white linens that emitted a soft, peaceful glow, reminiscent of Galen and Victoria's luminous robes.

"Lie within," the being instructed softly, its voice a comforting whisper. Bronte climbed in cautiously, easing himself into the welcoming warmth. The fabric beneath him embraced his weary body, instantly calming him.

The other light being returned to Madre's side, holding a softly glowing robe. Tenderly draping it around Madre's shoulders, it instructed her gently, *"When the healing begins, you must lift the hood and cover your face completely."*

Madre nodded, her eyes filled with wonder, as she continued to watch Bronte settling himself. When Bronte was fully comfortable, the lid of the healing chamber began its descent, sealing him gently inside. A final glance passed between Bronte and Madre, filled with trust and anticipation, before he disappeared from view.

"Cover your face," the being reminded Madre kindly. Obediently, she raised the hood, letting its soothing fabric fall lightly over her face. Immediately, the colors intensified, swirling in patterns of profound beauty and complexity. The familiar melodic voices returned, filling the room, blending with the serene, celestial music that now surrounded them entirely.

Both Madre and Bronte felt themselves gently drifting into a deep and restful sleep, each surrendering to the comforting harmony that enveloped them. Their consciousness began to fade into peaceful dreams...

In the dream, they found themselves standing together on a planet that resembled Earth, yet held subtle differences—a sky richer in color, flowers that swayed gently without wind, and grass softer than they'd ever known. All around them were other children, their laughter pure and joyful, a melody unto itself. They were playing freely, running hand-in-hand through fields bathed in sunlight, carefree and happy in a way they hadn't felt since childhood.

The sensation was breathtaking, a perfect moment of innocent joy and connection. For a timeless moment, their souls felt united, their bond stronger and clearer than ever before.

Eventually, gentle hands touched Madre's shoulder, bringing her slowly back to consciousness. The hood was gently pulled away, and she blinked her eyes open, feeling utterly refreshed. Beside her, the chamber opened once again, revealing a peacefully sleeping Bronte. The light beings assisted him from the chamber, his face filled with a quiet awe.

Madre rose, moving swiftly to Bronte's side. They turned toward each other simultaneously, each recognizing the unmistakable truth reflected in the other's eyes.

"You felt it too?" Madre asked softly, barely above a whisper.

Bronte nodded, his usually gruff voice softened by wonder. "The dream...us as children. Playing."

Madre's eyes shone with emotion. "I've never felt so... connected."

Bronte reached out and gently squeezed her hand. "Neither have I."

For a moment, words weren't needed. They simply stood together, absorbing the miracle they had shared, knowing deep within their hearts that their bond had become something extraordinary—a union of souls woven through time itself.

The grand chamber doors opened soundlessly, allowing Waverly to step into a space unlike any she had seen before. The Council Chamber of Arcmyrin was both vast and intimate—a circular room where the walls pulsed with an ambient glow, the material seemingly woven from both crystal and pure energy. The air hummed with an almost musical frequency, as if the very space responded to the presence of those within it.

At the center of the chamber stood six distinguished figures, each exuding an aura of wisdom, power, and grace.

Elara took a step forward, motioning for Waverly to follow. "Welcome to the Arcmyrin Council of Elders, Waverly Beaumont."

Waverly felt the weight of their gazes upon her, but there was no hostility, only curiosity and measured acceptance. She took a steady breath, holding her head high as she walked toward them.

The leader of the Council, Releesia, stepped forward. She was tall and elegant, her flowing robes shimmering in colors that subtly shifted—deep sapphire, then silver, then a quiet shade of violet. Her features were soft yet commanding, her deep emerald eyes holding centuries of wisdom.

"Waverly Beaumont," Releesia greeted, her voice smooth and resonant, like a song carried on the wind. "We welcome you to Arcmyrin, not as a warrior, but as a bridge—a voice to connect our world to the Triad's vision of unity."

Waverly inclined her head respectfully. "Thank you, Council Leader Releesia. I'm honored to be here."

The five other Council members each stepped forward in turn, their expressions welcoming, yet full of scrutiny.

Aduralina, an elder with golden emerald-hued eyes and braided silver-white hair, regarded Waverly thoughtfully. "Your presence here marks a turning point for the Triad. Arcmyrin does not take such matters lightly."

Milestree, the tallest of the group, his form almost luminescent, gave a slow nod. "We have been observing, as have the spirits, and we will ensure that the future of this alliance aligns with Arcmyrin's sovereignty."

Silastoria, with her intricate robes flowing like liquid stardust, clasped her hands together. "We recognize the efforts your family has made to protect our world in the past. Now, we seek to understand how Earth fits into our future."

Lunarcher, whose deep indigo markings along his forehead shimmered slightly, spoke next. "The balance of the Triad depends not just on mutual understanding, but on mutual purpose. We wish to know if Earth is truly prepared for this alignment."

Finally, Ruliana, a quiet but sharp-eyed elder with flowing robes of midnight blue, studied Waverly carefully. "Much has yet to be discussed. But first, you must understand what Arcmyrin expects from this alliance. That will come in time."

Waverly absorbed their words carefully, aware that each of them was analyzing her in their own way—not as an adversary, but as an unknown variable.

She straightened slightly, aware that her every word and action from this moment forward would shape Earth's standing within this alliance.

Before she could respond, she sensed another presence.

Standing slightly behind the council members, his posture rigid and his golden eyes watchful, was Rykas.

The leader of the Arcmyrin warriors.

His gaze met hers, and a flicker of recognition passed between them.

Waverly had fought alongside Rykas in the battle against the Abasimtrox on Arcmyrin and again on Earth against the Umbralox. He had been fierce, unwavering, a true warrior among his people. Though he remained silent now, his presence alone spoke volumes—he was here to ensure that Arcmyrin remained strong, even in diplomacy.

Releesia turned slightly toward Waverly once more. "Your accommodations have been prepared. You will have time to rest, to acclimate to Arcmyrin's energy. The journey between worlds can be disorienting to those not born here."

Waverly nodded, grateful for the consideration. "I appreciate that. And I'm ready to listen. I want to understand what Arcmyrin expects from the Triad."

Releesia's expression softened slightly, though the weight of her leadership never faltered. "Then you will. We will reconvene after you have settled. For now, walk our world, experience its renewal. Let Arcmyrin speak to you before we do."

Elara gestured for Waverly to follow her out of the chamber. As they turned to leave, she cast one final glance back at Rykas.

His gaze never left her.

There was much to learn here.

And even more to uncover.

The black SUV came to a smooth stop in front of Blair House, its stately white façade illuminated by the soft glow of antique lanterns. Even in the evening light, the grand residence exuded an air of historic significance, standing as a symbol of diplomacy, elegance, and tradition.

As the security detail opened the door, Celia and Lorinda stepped out, taking in the sight of the President's guest house—a place where incoming presidents, dignitaries, world leaders, and influential figures had stayed throughout history.

Rachel gestured toward the grand entrance with a warm smile. "Welcome to Blair House, Mrs. Beaumont, Ms. Rooney. This will be your residence during your stay in Washington."

Celia, ever the historian, took a long moment to admire the classic architecture, the ornate windows and stately columns. "It's absolutely stunning," she murmured, stepping forward.

Lorinda nodded in agreement. "It's incredible. I can't wait to see the gardens."

Rachel beamed. "I'm so glad to hear that. The Blair House gardens are one of its hidden gems, and I promise a full tour while you're here."

As they stepped inside, the air changed—rich with history, filled with the echoes of the past.

Rachel led them through a brief but impressive tour, pointing out rooms of significance—the Lee Dining Room, the Library, the intimate Blair Drawing Room. The furnishings were pristine yet timeless, a delicate balance of historic preservation and modern luxury.

Finally, she brought them to their quarters, located in one of the private wings of the residence. "These will be your rooms," Rachel said, opening a beautifully carved door to reveal a suite bathed in warm, golden light.

Celia stepped inside, taking in the deep mahogany furniture, the crisp linens, and the delicate floral arrangements that had been placed with care. It was, as expected, impeccable.

"You'll have time to freshen up before we leave for dinner," Rachel continued. "We'll be dining with Vice President Houston and his wife, Allison, at the Naval Observatory. I'll return for you in about an hour."

Celia nodded appreciatively. "That sounds perfect, Rachel. Thank you."

As Rachel exited, closing the door behind her, Celia turned to Lorinda with an amused smirk. "I must say, this is quite the diplomatic treatment."

Lorinda laughed softly, placing her suitcase on the luggage stand. "Not bad for a couple of women from the mountains, huh?"

Celia chuckled, shaking her head as she began freshening up. "Not bad at all."

An hour later, Celia and Lorinda found themselves in the Jackson Place Sitting Room, an elegant space filled with soft candlelight and antique furnishings. The historic portraits on the walls and elegant curtains gave the room a regal yet inviting warmth.

Celia traced a gloved finger along the edge of an ornate side table, admiring the craftsmanship. "I could spend weeks in this house just learning its stories."

Lorinda sighed, settling onto a wingback chair. "I'd be happy just exploring the gardens. The glimpses I caught through the windows when we arrived were breathtaking."

Rachel entered at that moment, her usual composed smile in place. "I love hearing that you're both so interested in the history of Blair House. It's truly one of Washington's most treasured spaces. I'll make sure to arrange a more in-depth tour during your stay."

Celia turned with a warm smile. "We would love that, Rachel. There's something powerful about standing in a place where so much diplomacy has happened."

Rachel gave a knowing nod. "Speaking of diplomacy, the Vice President is expecting us."

With that, they followed Rachel out of Blair House and into the waiting SUV.

14

The SUV moved smoothly through the streets of Washington, D.C., the city bathed in the glow of streetlights and the towering monuments that defined the capital.

Rachel, seated across from Celia and Lorinda, took the opportunity to check in. "I just want to make sure you both are comfortable with the accommodations. If there's anything you need, please don't hesitate to let me know."

Celia patted Rachel's hand reassuringly. "It's quite opulent and perfect, Rachel. I wouldn't change a thing."

Lorinda nodded in agreement. "Honestly, I'm just excited to see the gardens in full morning light tomorrow."

Rachel's eyes lit up. "I promise, you'll love them. They've been maintained in near-perfect condition since the house was first established as the guest residence."

Celia glanced out the window, watching as the streets of D.C. passed by. "And tonight's dinner… what should we expect?"

Rachel's expression turned diplomatic. "Vice President Houston and Allison prefer a relaxed setting for first meetings. Tonight will be about introductions, getting a sense of expectations on both sides before formal discussions begin tomorrow."

Celia nodded, her mind already preparing for the delicate balance they would need to strike in these negotiations.

The SUV pulled through the gates of the Naval Observatory, the official residence of the Vice President of the United States. The sprawling estate was illuminated beautifully, its historic charm even more apparent in the evening glow.

As the vehicle rolled to a stop, a set of grand double doors opened, and Vice President Charles Houston and his wife, Allison, stepped forward to greet them.

Houston was a tall, broad-shouldered man with a charismatic but thoughtful demeanor. His presence carried the weight of responsibility, but his smile was warm as he extended his hand to Celia first.

"Mrs. Beaumont," he greeted, his deep voice welcoming. "It is truly an honor to have you here."

Celia took his hand firmly, offering a warm smile of her own. "The honor is mine, Mr. Vice President. Thank you for hosting us."

Houston turned to Lorinda next, shaking her hand as well. "Ms. Rooney, welcome. We are thrilled to begin this historic dialogue."

Allison, graceful and poised, stepped beside her husband, her smile bright and genuine. "We are both so excited to hear your perspectives and share our vision for what the Triad could become."

Celia, ever the diplomat, returned the sentiment. "We are looking forward to it as well."

Houston gestured inside. "Please, come in. Let's talk over dinner."

With that, Celia and Lorinda stepped into the Vice President's residence, fully aware that this was more than just a meal.

This was the beginning of Earth's role in the Triad.

The dining room of the Naval Observatory was as elegant as expected—rich wooden paneling, soft golden candlelight, and a perfectly arranged table set for an intimate but distinguished dinner. The aroma of freshly prepared cuisine filled the air, and for the first time since arriving in Washington, Celia and Lorinda felt a moment of relaxed conversation.

Vice President Charles Houston and his wife, Allison, were warm hosts, making sure their guests were comfortable as they settled into their meal.

"So, Lorinda," Houston said as he lifted his glass, "I understand you're a nurse?"

Lorinda nodded, placing her napkin onto her lap. "Yes, I've been in critical care nursing for years, but since everything with the Triad has taken shape, I've been more involved with medical diplomacy—ensuring the integration of healing practices between Earth, Tanzlora, and Arcmyrin."

Allison's eyes lit up. "That sounds fascinating. Have you noticed major differences in medical practices across the planets?"

"Oh, absolutely," Lorinda said. "Earth relies heavily on synthetic medicine and technology, whereas Tanzlora and Arcmyrin have biological and energy-based healing methods that are completely different. It's been an eye-opening experience seeing how they approach medicine so holistically."

Houston nodded in understanding. "That's exactly why these negotiations are so crucial. We can learn from them, and they can learn from us. The Triad alliance could reshape the future of healthcare, technology, and diplomacy."

Celia smiled knowingly. "That's what we're here to ensure, Mr. Vice President."

Houston chuckled. "Please, call me Charles."

The conversation shifted as Allison turned toward Lorinda. "And I hear congratulations are in order? You're recently engaged?"

Lorinda's face brightened. "Yes! Ridge proposed not long ago. We're planning a Tanzloran wedding since his role in the Triad has deepened so much."

Allison clasped her hands together. "That sounds absolutely incredible. And Tanzlora—you've both been there?"

"Ridge has, but I have not yet been there," Lorinda said. "But our family tells us that it's a stunning planet. So much natural beauty, and the people have such a deep connection to it. They say the energy there is unlike anything on Earth."

Celia smiled. "And Ridge—he may be a warrior at heart, but that man is wrapped around Lorinda's finger."

The table laughed, the atmosphere warm and comfortably informal.

But then—the mood shifted.

Rachel entered the room abruptly, her composed expression slightly strained. She moved directly to the Vice President's side and leaned down, whispering something in his ear.

Houston's relaxed posture immediately stiffened. He nodded once, his face darkening.

Rachel straightened and addressed the table. "I'm so sorry to interrupt, but the Vice President is needed immediately. It's an emergency."

Celia and Lorinda exchanged glances.

Houston placed his napkin on the table and stood. "I'm afraid I have to go," he said, his voice level but firm. "Rachel will need to accompany me, but we'll arrange for another staff member to take you both back to Blair House once you've finished dinner."

Allison's smile faltered, concern flashing in her expression.

The Vice President turned to her, touching her shoulder gently. "Can you step outside with me for a moment?"

Allison nodded quickly, following him out of the dining room.

Celia and Lorinda sat in stunned silence, listening to the hushed voices just beyond the door.

Minutes later, Allison returned alone.

Her expression had completely changed.

Gone was the polished ease of the evening—her hands trembled slightly as she took her seat, her breath shallow and unsteady.

Celia and Lorinda watched as the Vice President's motorcade sped away, the flashing lights of security vehicles illuminating the night beyond the dining room windows.

Celia turned back to Allison, her voice gentle but firm. "Mrs. Houston, is everything alright? I understand you may not be able to share details, but..."

Allison didn't answer at first. Instead, she stared down at her lap, gripping the fabric of her dress so tightly that her knuckles turned white.

Then, finally, she shook her head.

When she looked up, her eyes were filled with sadness and fear.

"The President is being rushed to the hospital," she whispered. "He's unconscious."

A heavy silence descended upon the room.

Lorinda's breath caught in her throat. "Oh no…"

Celia sat frozen at the news.

"We will pray he is going to be alright," Celia finally managed to get words out.

The drive back to Blair House was silent.

The weight of what had just transpired at the Vice President's residence clung to Celia and Lorinda like a heavy shroud. The blacked-out SUV moved swiftly through the streets of Washington, D.C., cutting through the city's historic avenues, past monuments that now seemed eerily solemn under the glow of streetlights.

Neither woman spoke, their thoughts too tangled with the gravity of what they had just learned.

The President was unconscious.

Charles Houston was now Acting President.

Lorinda glanced at Celia, her hands clasped tightly in her lap. "I can't believe this is happening," she whispered.

Celia exhaled slowly, her gaze fixed out the tinted window. "Neither can I."

They had left the Vice President's residence soon after Allison Houston had shared the devastating news. The Second Lady had immediately begun making calls, reaching out to the First Lady and gathering her staff to coordinate support efforts.

Now, as the SUV pulled through the gates of Blair House, a new reality settled over them.

Once inside, the staff greeted them with quiet efficiency, offering refreshments and asking if they needed anything. Celia politely declined, her mind elsewhere.

Lorinda let out a long breath. "I feel like we're living in a political thriller," she muttered. "This is all so surreal. We're right here, near the White House, while history is unfolding."

Celia nodded. "Come with me," she said, leading Lorinda toward her private suite. "We need to see what's being reported."

The two women entered the expansive bedroom suite, its elegant furnishings now feeling like an odd contrast to the chaos brewing just beyond the walls of Blair House.

Celia grabbed the remote control and turned on the large flat-screen television mounted on the wall. She quickly flipped to a 24-hour news channel, expecting immediate coverage of the unfolding crisis.

Instead, the screen showed a senator being interviewed about legislation.

Lorinda's brow furrowed. "They're not talking about it?"

Celia frowned. "Either they don't know yet... or they're not allowed to report on it."

The senator on-screen continued discussing the bill, oblivious to the storm brewing behind the scenes.

Lorinda sat down on the edge of a plush chair, shaking her head. "This feels surreal. We're literally a few blocks away from the White House, and yet the world is still going on like normal."

Before Celia could respond, the news broadcast suddenly shifted.

A breaking news banner flashed across the screen in bold red letters:

BREAKING NEWS: PRESIDENT RUSHED TO WALTER REED HOSPITAL

The anchor's voice came in sharply, his tone urgent.

"We interrupt our current programming with breaking news. We have just received confirmation that the President of the United States has been rushed to Walter Reed Medical Center after suffering an unspecified medical emergency at the White House. We do not yet have details on the nature of the emergency, but sources indicate that the President was unconscious when he was transported. At this time, his condition remains unknown."

Lorinda and Celia stared at the screen, unmoving.

"As per protocol, when the President is incapacitated in any way and unable to fulfill his duties, the Vice President assumes the role of Acting President. We now have footage of the Vice President's motorcade arriving at the White House, where Charles Houston, now Acting President, is expected to be briefed by senior officials."

The screen switched to live footage—a convoy of black SUVs and the Vice President's sedan pulling through the gates of the White House. Moments later, Vice President Houston stepped out, his normally composed demeanor appearing tightly controlled yet unmistakably grave.

Rachel Timms was right behind him, followed by several other staff members, all moving quickly into the executive residence.

"We are also learning that all Cabinet members have been briefed, as well as congressional leadership, and that a press conference is expected to take place within the hour. At this time, we do not have confirmation of what exactly happened to the President, only that he was transported to Walter Reed unconscious within the last hour."

The camera panned back to the news anchor, who now looked even more serious.

"We are awaiting updates from the White House and Walter Reed Medical Center, but for now, the nation holds its breath as we await further details on the President's condition."

Celia clicked the mute button, the room suddenly too quiet.

Lorinda let out a slow, shaky breath. "Oh no... I can't believe this is happening."

Celia stood, her hands resting on the back of a nearby chair, her eyes locked on the screen. "This is real," she murmured. "This is actually happening."

The weight of the moment settled between them, the reality of being in Washington, D.C., at the epicenter of a crisis.

Lorinda swallowed hard. "We need to do something."

Celia turned to her, her expression unwavering. "We need to pray."

Without hesitation, she reached for Lorinda's hands, and the two women bowed their heads.

"Origin, Keeper of All, Guardian of the Universe..."

"We lift up this nation, this moment, into Your hands. We pray for the President's healing, for his family's strength. We pray for wisdom for Vice President Houston as he steps into this responsibility. We ask for peace, for guidance, for clarity in uncertain times. Let Your will be done, and may we walk with courage through whatever comes next."

The room was still.

The world outside was changing by the second.

And they could only wait for what came next.

15

The soft glow of Pluboria's ethereal light pulsed gently as Madre and Bronte stepped back into the grand chamber, their presence stirring a shift in the atmosphere. The room, which had moments before been filled with the gravity of Galen and Victoria's revelation about Josephine, now carried a renewed sense of urgency.

Lincoln and Ridge, still reeling from the weight of what they had just learned, looked up as Madre and Bronte approached.

Bronte, now fully healed, moved with a strength and ease he hadn't felt in years. There was no wheelchair, no hesitation in his step—he was whole.

"You're walking strong," Lincoln murmured in awe.

Bronte grinned, stretching his arms. "Damn right, I am. And it feels incredible."

Ridge exhaled a sharp breath, shaking his head in amazement. "Guess that means Pluboria delivered."

Madre settled beside them, her gaze sweeping over the room before landing on Galen and Victoria, who stood at the head of the crystalline table, their luminous forms flickering like candlelight.

Galen's expression was serene but resolute.

"It is time," he announced, his voice flowing into their minds like a gentle current. "You have received what you came for. You are healed, you are enlightened, and now… you must return to Earth."

Victoria's soft, glowing presence warmed the space. "The journey ahead of you is not easy, but it is necessary. You have all been chosen to fulfill the responsibilities Origin has placed before you. You are the bridge, the protectors, the ones who must ensure the balance of the Triad."

Lincoln and Ridge exchanged a look, their hands instinctively clenching into fists.

"We're ready," Ridge said, determination hardening his voice.

Galen's light pulsed in response. "Then it is time to say goodbye."

A moment of silence passed between them.

Madre, her heart swelling with gratitude, whispered, "Thank you."

Bronte, uncharacteristically solemn, simply nodded.

Galen and Victoria raised their hands, their golden radiance intensifying, wrapping the four of them in a gentle, familiar warmth.

"Walk with purpose. Hold true to your path. And remember… the light always prevails."

With that, the golden threads returned.

Soft at first, then growing stronger, weaving around their forms like strands of energy, binding them in a cocoon of shimmering light.

Their voices vanished.

They could not speak, only listen.

Their thoughts, however, remained crystal clear—and the voices of the light beings filled their minds.

"You will return as you were, but changed. Your body, your mind, your soul—they have been touched by Pluboria, and that cannot be undone."

"You will awaken with clarity. But clarity does not mean certainty. You must still make the choices that will shape the future of your world."

"And now… it is time to go."

A sudden pull, a gentle lift, and they felt their bodies rising from the chairs.

Their limbs floated effortlessly as they were guided back toward the glass-like wall that separated them from the outside realm of Pluboria.

The transparent surface began to ripple, a circle forming in the center, widening just enough for their bodies to pass through.

As they moved toward the opening, the world behind them shimmered, fading into light and color.

Then, in an instant—

They were falling.

No, floating.

Downward, through waves of vibrant energy, cascading colors, and rushing sound.

It was as if they were being woven back into the fabric of the universe itself.

A final burst of white light—

And then—

The sensation of grass beneath their bodies was the first thing they registered.

The soft sounds of night—crickets, rustling leaves, the gentle lap of water against the pond's banks— slowly replaced the cosmic silence they had just emerged from.

Ridge blinked, his eyes adjusting to the darkness of Earth's sky.

Lincoln inhaled sharply, the scent of fresh soil and damp earth grounding him instantly.

Madre pushed herself up onto her elbows, feeling the weight of her body again—real, solid, present.

And Bronte—Bronte stood up effortlessly.

No pain. No struggle. Only strength.

They were back.

They were home.

And now, the real work began.

The familiar warmth of Sage Manor greeted them as they stepped through the kitchen patio entrance, the door creaking softly as they entered. The air carried the comforting scent of aged wood, herbs from the kitchen garden, and the lingering remnants of evening tea.

The house was still, wrapped in the hush of midnight.

Bronte, moving with newfound ease, lifted his knees high, one by one as if reveling in the simple motion. "I still can't believe I can do this," he muttered, grinning. "No pain. No stiffness. I feel like a damn teenager again."

Madre chuckled, shaking her head. "Well, don't go testing that theory too hard, Bronte. You may feel young, but I doubt you'll bounce back from reckless decisions any better than before."

Lincoln smirked, leading the way into the library, where a warm glow flickered beyond the cracked door.

Inside, Marshall Stern sat at the large oak table, a thick book spread open in front of him. His reading glasses perched on the edge of his nose, and a half-empty cup of tea rested nearby. He had been deep in study, lost in whatever information he had been sifting through—until he heard the creak of the floorboards.

His head snapped up, his brows furrowing in confusion before his eyes widened in astonishment.

"Well, I'll be," Marshall murmured, a slow smile spreading across his face. "You're back."

Madre barely had time to react before Marshall pushed back from the table, stood up, and pulled her into a strong embrace.

She melted into him, exhaling softly as she relished the familiar steadiness of her husband's arms. "We're back," she whispered against his shoulder.

Marshall pressed a kiss to the side of her head before pulling away just enough to look at her. His hands cupped her face briefly, checking her over as if reassuring himself she was really here. "You okay?"

She nodded, smiling. "More than okay."

Then, Marshall's gaze flickered to Bronte—standing tall, strong, and whole.

Marshall's mouth parted in silent awe.

"Well, well, well" he finally breathed. "Look at you, Bronte."

Bronte chuckled, lifting both knees as if showcasing his new, fully functioning body. "Ain't I a sight?"

Marshall took a step closer, his doctor's instincts kicking in. "How do you feel?"

"Better than I have in years," Bronte said truthfully, his voice almost reverent. "Everything works. No pain. No stiffness. It's like Looking Glass Falls never happened."

Marshall let out a low whistle, shaking his head in amazement. "That's a miracle."

"That's Pluboria," Ridge corrected.

Marshall exhaled, still marveling at what he was seeing. Then, shifting gears, he turned toward Lincoln. "You want to tell me what happened on Pluboria?"

Lincoln stretched his arms over his head, exhaustion finally seeping into his bones. "That depends—how long have we been gone?"

Marshall blinked, then let out a small laugh. "You don't know?"

Ridge rubbed the back of his neck sheepishly. "Time works differently in some places."

Marshall chuckled, shaking his head. "You were only gone from this morning to now, it's about 8 o'clock in the evening." He pointed at the antique clock sitting on a side table.

Lincoln's brows furrowed. "Just hours, not even a day?"

Marshall nodded. "Yeah. You left earlier this morning. After you four were gone, Waverly and Lynx left next. Then Celia and Lorinda left around lunchtime for D.C."

Lincoln exchanged a glance with Ridge, who let out a disbelieving laugh. "Felt like we were in Pluboria for weeks."

Marshall shrugged. "That's interdimensional travel for you."

He continued, moving toward his seat and taking a sip of now-cold tea. "Celia and Lorinda called when they arrived in D.C. and Bethany answered—she said Lorinda only had time for a short conversation before they had to get ready for dinner at the Vice President's residence."

Lincoln sank into the nearest armchair, rubbing his hands over his face. "That means they're still in the middle of that dinner right now."

Marshall checked the clock again. "Or just wrapping it up."

Madre sat beside her husband, exhaling softly. "Everything is moving fast," she murmured. "We're all being pulled in different directions, but for the same purpose."

Marshall nodded. "And that's how you know it's all aligning the way it's meant to."

Ridge leaned against the library door frame, crossing his arms. "Still feels strange, though. We go to an entirely different realm of existence, and come back to find out only a few hours have passed? Meanwhile, Celia and Lorinda are out making Earth's first official diplomatic strides toward interplanetary relations."

Marshall chuckled. "Yeah, and Waverly and Lynx are both on different planets trying to keep the Triad alliance from falling apart before it even starts."

Lincoln shook his head, letting out a wry laugh. "Just a normal week for the Beaumonts, huh?"

Bronte snorted. "Damn right."

Marshall stood, gathering up his books and papers. "Well, as much as I'd love to hear the full Pluboria story, I think you all need to rest."

They had returned home, but their mission was far from over.

Ridge turned, his expression hardened with purpose. "We need to talk before we even think about sleeping."

Madre frowned, taking a seat, Marshall settling back down beside her while Bronte took the next available chair and crossed his arms.

"What is it?" Marshall asked, sensing the tension rolling off both brothers.

Lincoln ran a tired hand over his face before exhaling. "While we were in Pluboria… we found out something that changes everything."

Madre and Bronte nodded in agreement with Lincoln as Marshall sat at attention.

Ridge continued, his voice measured but urgent. "Josephine is alive and seems to be headed down the same road to destruction as Gideon. And she's on Arcmyrin."

Marshall's brow furrowed in confusion. "Josephine... as in your aunt Josephine? I thought Celia said that she disappeared after Gideon left the family. They searched for years and did not find her so they assumed she had died."

"That's what we thought too," Lincoln said grimly. "Turns out, she's been hiding."

Marshall, his jaw tightening, let out a low whistle. "And here I thought one traitorous Beaumont was enough." He sat forward, his fingers tightening around the edge of the table. "How is she hiding on Arcmyrin? She's human—she'd stand out."

Lincoln shook his head. "That's the thing. She doesn't. Josephine has the gift of Earth."

Marshall's eyes widened in understanding. "Terraveta's gift."

Ridge nodded. "She's been using Arcmyrin's natural elements to alter her appearance. She's changing identities, blending in, moving undetected."

Madre's expression darkened. "And what does she want?"

Lincoln hesitated before saying, "We don't know. Not yet."

Ridge picked up where he left off. "Galen and Victoria told us that she isn't like Gideon, not completely. She was influenced by him, followed him, but she struggled with it. She was never as wholly committed to darkness as he was. But that doesn't mean she isn't dangerous."

Marshall suddenly sat bolt upright, eyes wide and incredulous.

"Whoa, whoa, whoa..." he interjected, waving his hand. "Hold up. You saw *Galen and Victoria?* You actually *talked* to them? Face-to-face?"

Lincoln exchanged a glance with Ridge, his face composed and serious. "We did. It was unlike anything we've ever experienced."

Marshall shook his head vigorously, eyebrows drawn together in disbelief. "Wait a second—you're telling me you two had a casual chat with your ancestral founders—who, let me remind everyone, have been dead for generations—how is that possible?"

Madre stood up slowly from her seat, recognizing the familiar look of skepticism and scientific curiosity dawning in her husband's expression. She placed a comforting hand on Marshall's shoulder and gently squeezed.

"Marshall," Madre said soothingly, her voice calm yet urgent. "I understand exactly how you feel. It's a lot to take in—I know that better than anyone."

He turned to her, his expression searching hers earnestly. "Madre, are you telling me you believe this?"

She nodded gently, her eyes steady and clear. "More than believe, Marshall. I was there, remember? But we don't have time right now to dissect this. Waverly is on Arcmyrin, and her safety could be at risk. We have to stay focused."

Marshall's eyes searched Madre's for a long moment. He let out a long sigh, running a hand through his hair, a blend of confusion and acceptance softening his features.

"Okay…okay," he finally conceded, throwing his hands up in surrender. "I trust you. I trust all of you. Just…" He exhaled, shaking his head in mild disbelief. "This is all just so… incredible."

Lincoln gave him a small, understanding smile. "I promise we'll sit down later and go through every detail with you, Marshall. But right now, we need you to trust us. Trust Madre."

Marshall took a deep breath and nodded firmly, the scientist in him momentarily taking a back seat to his wife and friends.

"Alright," he said resolutely. "Tell me what you need. I'm listening."

Madre gave his shoulder one more reassuring squeeze, smiling gratefully. "Thank you, dear. I promise I'll help you make sense of it all later."

Marshall chuckled softly, shaking his head. "Well, you better."

As Ridge and Lincoln exchanged relieved glances, Bronte pushed up from his chair and started pacing slightly. "Ok, back to Josephine, you think she's still got access to her gift?"

"Absolutely," Lincoln confirmed. "Terraveta said that even though she hasn't had a connection to Josephine in years, the gift Origin gave her is still hers to summon."

Madre exhaled sharply, rubbing her temples. "If she's on Arcmyrin, that means Waverly is there right now, completely unaware."

Ridge's jaw clenched. "Exactly. And that's why we need to get to Arcmyrin ASAP."

Marshall stood, already moving toward the hallway. "Then let's get Bethany and Francis. I think they have the children in bed by now and we need a plan—"

"No," Ridge cut in. "We don't have time for that. We need to go down to the gazebo and contact Elara."

Madre nodded in agreement, her eyes flashing with worry. "She needs to know what's happening. She can keep a close eye on Waverly until someone can get to Arcmyrin."

Marshall and Bronte exchanged glances before Bronte sighed and stretched his newly healed legs. "Well, guess there's no rest for the wicked... or for those of us trying to stop them."

Lincoln turned toward Ridge. "Let's go. The sooner we reach Elara, the sooner we can stop whatever Josephine is planning."

They moved quickly, their footsteps urgent but silent as they made their way out of the manor and toward the gazebo.

The night air was crisp, the sky a deep indigo, stars burning like scattered fireflies above them.

16

Madre sighed softly as she stepped out of the library into the hall-way, running a weary hand through her tousled hair. She had already pulled several small pieces of grass out during their earlier conversation, remnants from their abrupt landing beside the pond upon returning from Pluboria. She desperately needed a long, hot shower to wash away the fatigue and confusion from the trip.

As she reached the foot of the staircase, she heard hurried footsteps above her. Glancing upward, she saw Bethany descending quickly, a look of genuine surprise crossing her face as she spotted Madre below.

"Madre!" Bethany exclaimed, nearly missing a step in her shock. "You're back already? Where's Lincoln?"

Madre gave a tired smile, pausing with one hand on the polished wooden banister. "He's headed down to the gazebo to try and contact Elara. It's a long story, but—"

Before Madre could finish her thought, the shrill ring of the office telephone interrupted her.

Bethany hesitated, glancing toward the office and then back at Madre apologetically. "Hold that thought," she said, turning quickly and moving toward the sound of the phone.

Madre stood still for a moment, staring longingly up the staircase toward the promise of a refreshing shower. With another soft sigh, she turned away, deciding that explanations and family came first. Reluctantly, she followed Bethany down the hall toward the office, her steps determined despite the exhaustion settling in her bones.

Madre stepped quietly into the office doorway just as Bethany reached the desk and quickly picked up the phone. Bethany's voice lifted with warmth and surprise, instantly recognizable.

"Lorinda! Good to hear from you. How is DC?" Bethany paused, settling herself into the office chair as she listened, a smile crossing her lips. "The children are doing well; they're asleep. And you won't believe this, but Lincoln, Ridge, Madre, and Bronte are back from Pluboria already!" She blurted it all out in one long breath, her eyes bright with relief.

Madre quietly took a seat next to the desk, watching as Bethany's expression changed suddenly, her brow furrowing deeply with concern.

"Oh no," Bethany murmured, her voice dropping. "I had no idea... we haven't had the TV on at all while getting the children's evening routine done." She exchanged a worried glance with Madre, whose curiosity and concern were now fully engaged.

Bethany listened attentively for a few more moments, nodding in understanding before asking, "Are you planning to stay in DC or are you and Celia coming back home?"

Madre's eyes widened as she mouthed silently, "What happened?"

Bethany held up her pointer finger to Madre, signaling her to wait just a moment longer. "Okay," Bethany finally said into the receiver, her tone calm but clearly concerned. "I'll let everyone know. You ladies keep in touch. Bye."

Hanging up the phone gently, Bethany turned toward Madre, her expression deeply serious.

"Bethany, what's going on?" Madre asked urgently, leaning closer.

Bethany took a deep breath before replying, her voice low and steady. "Lorinda just told me that the President was rushed to Walter Reed Hospital earlier tonight. He was unconscious—something medical, they're not completely sure—but it's serious enough that Vice President Houston is now acting President, at least temporarily."

Madre sat back in her chair, absorbing the unexpected news. "Oh no... this is going to impact everything we've been working toward."

Bethany nodded gravely, her expression solemn. "Exactly. Celia and Lorinda aren't sure yet if they're staying in DC or returning home. Everything's still unfolding."

Madre sighed softly, shaking her head. "We need to inform Ridge and Lincoln immediately. They need to know this right away."

Bethany stood up decisively. "Agreed. Let's go find them."

Madre chuckled wryly, though worry was evident in her eyes. "I was hoping to get in a long, hot shower but that might have to wait a bit longer, unfortunately."

"I'm sorry," Bethany replied, "you can go do that and I will let them know about the President."

"No," Madre said, "this is too important, we need to put all our heads together on how we move forward after this news. Just ignore any grass you see in my hair."

They both laughed and hurried from the office, knowing their night was far from over.

Lynx awoke to the distinct feeling that he was not alone.

His room in the Reficiat Haven, a beautiful and serene lodge built into the natural flow of Tanzlora's landscape, was dimly lit by the faint glow of bioluminescent vines woven into the walls. The atmosphere was peaceful—but something was moving.

A soft rustling.

Then, the barely audible clicks of small feet on the wooden floor.

Lynx's muscles tensed. He remained utterly still, his breathing shallow, his senses stretching outward.

The clicks were faint... deliberate... right at the foot of his bed.

His heart pounded, but he kept his body still, waiting, listening. The sounds didn't match anything overtly threatening, but this was Tanzlora—not Earth. And after everything he had encountered, he knew better than to assume he was alone in a room just because he had locked the door.

Time for a plan.

His mind worked quickly.

If something was at the foot of his bed, he needed to trap it—fast. His woven leaf blanket was thick but lightweight, strong enough to throw over whatever was standing there and give him a few seconds to make a run for the door.

Slowly, he shifted his grip under the blanket, preparing to lunge.

Then—

A melodic chirp.

Lynx froze.

The sound was so familiar that for a moment, he thought his sleep-addled brain was playing tricks on him.

Then he saw it—

A small, quilled silhouette illuminated against the wall.

Lynx's entire body relaxed in an instant, his face breaking into a wide, disbelieving grin.

He sat up abruptly, the blanket forgotten.

"No way..." he whispered, his eyes locked on the small creature at the foot of his bed.

The porcufera.

It was back.

The little creature stood there, its round, hedgehog-like body covered in iridescent quills that shimmered softly in the dim light. Its large, curious eyes blinked up at him, and its tiny paw-like feet tapped against the floor as it tilted its head, chirping again.

Lynx let out a breathless laugh. "You found me again?"

The porcufera chirped once more, stepping closer, its quills flattening slightly in a show of trust.

Lynx didn't hesitate this time. He carefully lowered his hand, palm up, and waited.

The porcufera studied him, then, after a few seconds, it hopped onto his bed, curling up beside him like it had never been gone.

Lynx shook his head in wonder, gently stroking its quills, which shifted beneath his fingers like living silk. "I don't know how you keep finding me, but I'm not complaining."

The porcufera gave another contented chirp, then nuzzled into the blankets, making itself comfortable.

Lynx lay back against his pillows, his grin still wide, warmth filling his chest.

Tanzlora had changed in so many ways since the battle against the Umbralox, but some things—like this unexpected little friendship—remained beautifully the same.

As he drifted back to sleep, the porcufera curled beside him, a tiny guardian in the quiet of the night.

Francis moved quietly down the staircase, glancing around the empty hallway, her brow furrowed with mild confusion. She had expected to find Marshall buried in his books in the library, but the room was empty. Maybe he and Bethany had already moved to the kitchen to prepare their evening tea, she thought, turning toward the back of the house.

Entering the kitchen, she paused at the threshold, surprised to find the room silent and dark. The kettle stood cold on the stovetop, the counters tidy and untouched. No Marshall, no Bethany.

"Odd," she murmured to herself, turning back toward the hallway. As she walked, she noticed the glow of the office lamp spilling softly into the corridor. Curious, she made her way toward it, but the office was empty as well.

Shaking her head, she headed toward the library again—maybe she'd missed something. Pushing the door open, she saw Marshall's books lying open across the desk, notes scattered haphazardly, and a half-finished cup of tea sitting abandoned beside them.

"Marshall?" she called gently, confusion growing into mild worry. Still no response.

Exiting the library, Francis headed toward the parlor, her footsteps light and cautious. A slight chill ran down her spine as she noticed the front door standing ajar, gently swaying with the breeze.

"Oh," she murmured, relieved. "They must be on the front porch."

She pushed open the door and stepped outside onto the porch, but found it deserted, the evening air cool and quiet.

Just as disappointment crept into her chest, Francis's eyes caught a faint light spilling onto the grass, emanating from the staircase that led down toward the gazebo chamber.

With curiosity nudging her forward, Francis carefully descended the porch steps, moving quietly along the stone pathway, the glow growing brighter with every step.

"Marshall? Bethany?" she called softly, quickening her pace as she headed toward the open doorway of the chamber beneath the gazebo, eager to discover what had pulled everyone away from their evening routines.

Lorinda sat at the small antique desk in Celia's elegantly furnished room at Blair House, the phone receiver pressed against her ear, her expression growing increasingly frustrated. After several rings, she sighed and gently hung up the phone, shaking her head at Celia.

"Still no answer," Lorinda said with mild concern. "It keeps going to that old-fashioned answering machine in the office. Maybe they're all gathered in the media room—well, I guess it's really more of a school room now," she added, smiling softly at the thought. "Maybe they have the television on, watching the coverage, and just can't hear the phone."

Celia nodded thoughtfully, though her eyes were clouded with unease. "That's possible, I suppose. I just wish we could get through. I'd really like to talk to Lincoln and Ridge about Pluboria. I still can't believe they're already back."

Lorinda leaned back in her chair, crossing her arms and frowning slightly. "I know—me neither. And honestly, I can't figure out if that's a good thing or a bad thing. Everything about this feels uncertain."

Celia moved closer, placing a comforting hand on Lorinda's shoulder. "I know exactly what you mean. My intuition usually guides me, but right now... it's strangely silent. I just can't get a clear feeling."

Lorinda squeezed Celia's hand gently. "Well, let's wait another twenty minutes or so, and then we'll try again. Maybe someone will have wandered by the office by then."

Celia nodded in agreement, offering Lorinda an encouraging smile, though the worry never left her eyes. "All right. Twenty minutes it is."

Both women settled back, waiting anxiously, each lost in her thoughts about the uncertain situation unfolding at Sage Manor.

Francis descended the staircase into the gazebo's chamber, her footsteps slowing as she took in the scene before her. Seated around the familiar oval table were Ridge, Lincoln, Madre, and—to her utter shock—Bronte, looking remarkably healthy and fully alert. She froze mid-step, eyes wide in disbelief.

"What in the world is going on?" Francis whispered urgently, quickly moving toward Bethany, who was seated on a bench next to Marshall.

Bethany turned toward her, patting the empty seat beside her. "Come, sit down," she said quietly. "It's a long story."

Francis sank onto the bench, casting a confused glance at Marshall, who nodded reassuringly. Bethany leaned closer, her voice gentle yet concerned. "Marshall just explained it to me. Apparently, Lincoln and Ridge were warned that Waverly is in danger on Arcmyrin. They're here trying to summon Elara, to alert her and make sure Waverly stays safe."

Francis blinked, trying to process the information. "Oh," she finally said, still visibly confused. "But... they're back so quickly. What exactly happened on Pluboria?"

Marshall leaned forward, looking past Bethany with a knowing grin. "Bronte got healed," he explained matter-of-factly, "and they saw Galen and Victoria."

Francis stared at Marshall, her jaw dropping in disbelief. "What?!" she gasped, eyes widening even further.

Before Marshall could elaborate, Bronte abruptly pushed his chair back and stood up, stretching dramatically. "Well, if this summoning is going to take all night, I'm heading back to the house," he declared gruffly. "I'm hungry."

Bethany let out a soft laugh, shaking her head as Francis stared at Bronte in bewilderment, astonished by how easily and quickly he'd risen from the table. He moved swiftly past her with remarkable agility, heading toward the staircase.

Francis hesitated only for a moment before quickly rising to her feet and following him. At the very least, she thought, she might finally get some clear answers from Bronte—someone who clearly knew firsthand exactly what was going on.

17

Bronte stepped through the back door into the warm glow of the Sage Manor kitchen, Francis following closely behind him. He paused for a moment, breathing deeply, appreciating the familiar scents of home. Francis immediately moved toward the refrigerator, gesturing for him to take a seat at the table.

"Sit down, Bronte," she said warmly. "We have plenty of leftovers, and I'll fix you a plate."

Bronte didn't hesitate, pulling out a chair and sitting down with a satisfied sigh. "Thanks, Francis. I've worked up quite an appetite traveling through dimensions today."

Francis glanced back at him, eyes sparkling with curiosity as she pulled containers of food from the refrigerator. "You have to tell me about Pluboria," she said eagerly. "I'm dying to know what happened. How did you get healed so quickly?"

Bronte leaned back comfortably, folding his arms and narrowing his eyes thoughtfully. "Well, Francis, it ain't easy to explain, but here goes." He cleared his throat dramatically. "First thing, we landed smack dab in the middle of this white desert—sand as white as snow, stars brighter than I've ever seen. Right in front of us was this big, glowing golden portal."

Francis paused, a spoonful of mashed potatoes halfway to the plate, captivated by Bronte's animated recounting. "A golden portal?" she repeated softly, urging him to continue.

Bronte nodded emphatically. "Yes, ma'am. Next thing we knew, these fancy-lookin' light beings came floatin' out, and we couldn't even talk, not a word. Like my mouth forgot how to make sounds."

He chuckled, shaking his head. "Then they took us to Galen and Victoria."

Francis stopped, her eyes widening in amazement. "You saw Galen and Victoria? The Beaumont ancestors? But how is that even possible?"

Bronte waved his hand dismissively. "Trust me, Francis, I asked the same thing. They looked pretty good for a couple of folks who've been dead all this time." He shrugged, eyes twinkling with amusement. "But there they were, glowing robes and all, plain as day."

Francis placed the plate in the microwave, setting the timer as she listened carefully. "Incredible," she whispered, turning back toward him. "Then what happened?"

"Well," Bronte continued, leaning forward on his elbows, "after some talking, they took me into a room with this big glowing tube-chamber-thing. Laid down inside, next thing I knew I felt as good as new. Woke up back here, fully healed—just like magic."

Francis stared at him, fascinated and slightly incredulous. "And it worked just like that?"

Bronte nodded firmly. "Just like that. But the craziest part—" He leaned even closer, lowering his voice conspiratorially. "—was what Galen and Victoria told us about Josephine."

Francis leaned in eagerly, "Josephine? What did they—"

Before he could finish, the shrill ring of the office telephone interrupted them. Bronte leaped up from his chair with surprising agility, heading quickly toward the hallway.

"Hold that thought," he called back to Francis, "I'd better grab that phone before it wakes up the children!"

Francis stood silently for a moment, still mesmerized by Bronte's tale, the microwave chiming softly behind her. Shaking her head with a small smile, she retrieved his plate, wondering how this extraordinary night could possibly become any stranger.

Lorinda and Celia stood close together near the ornate side table at Blair House, the soft lamplight casting a gentle glow across the elegant furnishings. Lorinda dialed the number again, listening anxiously as the phone rang several times, until suddenly, someone picked up on the other end.

"Anybody there?" came a sharp, abrupt voice. "You got my ear, start speaking."

Lorinda pulled the receiver slightly away from her ear, her eyebrows shooting upward. "Uh...I think it's Bronte," she mouthed to Celia, startled by his manner. "Maybe you'd better talk to him."

Celia quickly took the phone, trying not to laugh. Bronte's voice was unmistakable, loud enough to hear clearly from a distance.

"Bronte? It's Celia," she said, speaking slowly to temper her amusement. "Are you okay?"

"Celia!" Bronte practically shouted into the phone. "I'm better than okay. I'm fantastic! Feel like I could run a marathon."

Celia raised an eyebrow at Lorinda, who was watching intently, trying to follow the conversation. "That's... good to hear, Bronte. You sound remarkably energetic. What exactly happened on Pluboria?"

"Ha! A lot," Bronte replied gruffly, "but I think it's best you get that from your boys directly. Lincoln and Ridge can explain better than me, anyway." He paused briefly, then added bluntly, "Besides, I'm starving, and Francis just fixed me a big plate of food. Priorities."

Lorinda covered her mouth to hold back a laugh, shaking her head as she listened.

Celia smiled gently, deciding not to push further. "Well, Bronte, go eat then. We'll catch up later."

"Sounds good," Bronte replied briskly. "Glad you ladies are safe in DC. Tell Lorinda I said hi. See you soon." The line went abruptly silent.

Celia started to hang up but realized she didn't hear a dial tone and could hear talking in the background. She exchanged an amused glance with Lorinda. "Well, I believe that might be the most Bronte-like conversation I've ever had over the phone. It's not disconnected yet so I am going to hold on here for a minute or two."

Lorinda burst out laughing softly. "Honestly, I didn't know whether to be worried or amused when I heard his voice yelling into the phone."

Celia chuckled, her eyes twinkling. "One thing's clear, Pluboria definitely gave him a new lease on life—maybe even a new sense of humor."

Lorinda nodded, still smiling. "He certainly sounds like he feels better. At least we know something good came out of that trip. But I am still curious about what really happened there."

"Me too," Celia admitted, her expression growing thoughtful again. "Bronte's right, though. We'll just have to wait for Lincoln and Ridge to tell us themselves."

Lorinda sighed softly, nodding in agreement. "You're right. And knowing Bronte, there's no getting anything more out of him once he's set his mind to eating."

Celia smiled gently as she continued holding the phone receiver.

"I think I hear footsteps," Celia said to Lorinda as she held the phone out so both women could listen.

"I got it," Francis said loudly to Bronte as he was returning to the table. Reaching for the phone, she said over her shoulder, "You just eat. I'll handle this."

Bronte nodded as Francis was walking into the office, muttering something about cold potatoes.

Taking a breath, Francis lifted the receiver. "Hello?"

"Francis? It's Celia. Is everything all right? Bronte seems... energetic."

Francis quickly sat down on the edge of the office chair, her heart racing. "Celia, I'm so glad it's you. Things are chaotic here. Lincoln and Ridge are down in the chamber trying desperately to contact Elara—something about Waverly being in danger on Arcmyrin."

There was a brief pause. "Danger? What kind of danger?"

"I don't have the details yet," Francis admitted, her voice tight with concern. "Lincoln and Ridge are urgently trying to reach Elara right now. Everyone's pretty worried."

"Oh, dear," Celia breathed, clearly distressed. "Francis, please have Lincoln or Ridge call us as soon as possible. Lorinda and I need details as soon as you get them."

"Absolutely," Francis assured her quickly. "I promise."

There was a slight pause before Celia continued, her tone cautious. "And Francis, did Bethany mention what's happened here in DC?"

"No, what do you mean?" Francis asked, a sudden feeling of dread washing over her.

"You haven't heard?" Celia's voice softened. "The President was rushed to Walter Reed Hospital tonight. Apparently, he collapsed and was found unconscious. It's been a stressful evening. Lorinda and I are trying to navigate things here."

Francis sank back fully into the office chair, covering her mouth with her hand, utterly stunned. "Oh my goodness... Celia, that's terrible. I had no idea."

"It's been quite the evening," Celia said wearily. "Please just keep us updated, and we'll do the same."

Francis nodded, even though Celia couldn't see her. "Absolutely. I'll tell Lincoln and Ridge as soon as they come back up to the house. You ladies take care up there in DC."

"We will. Goodnight, dear," Celia replied gently, hanging up the phone.

Francis stood for a moment in stunned silence, gripping the edge of the desk for support, trying to process the flood of shocking news. She shook her head, bewildered by the chaotic events of the evening, then turned and quickly headed toward the kitchen.

Bronte looked up from his plate as she entered, raising an eyebrow at her troubled expression. "Well? What now?"

She exhaled sharply. "Bronte, there's been trouble tonight. Not only is Waverly in danger, but the President was rushed to the hospital unconscious."

Bronte stared at her in disbelief, setting his fork down with a clink. "What else can possibly happen tonight?"

Francis shook her head slowly, feeling overwhelmed. "I'm not sure I even want to find out."

Bronte glanced at his plate, considering for just a second, then stood decisively. "Maybe we should take my plate and head into that school room. Turn on the news and catch ourselves up."

Francis nodded with relief, grateful he had suggested it first. "Excellent idea, Bronte. Let's go."

Together they headed toward the media room, the urgency of events propelling them forward.

Lynx stirred as the first golden rays of Tanzloran sunlight filtered through the woven shutters of his room in the Reficiat Haven. The warmth on his face was comforting, and for a moment, he simply lay there, feeling the gentle hum of the planet itself.

Then, a soft rustling beside him brought back the events of the night before.

Lynx turned his head and grinned.

The porcufera was still there.

It lay curled in a small, content ball at his side, its iridescent quills shimmering in the morning light. As if sensing his wakefulness, the little creature uncurled, stretched its tiny legs, and let out a melodic chirp, blinking up at him.

"Still here, huh?" Lynx said with a chuckle, reaching out to run a gentle hand over its quills. The porcufera nuzzled into his palm, its warmth strangely grounding.

A soft knock at his door broke the moment.

"Lynx? Are you awake?"

Sanodia's voice.

"Yeah," he called back. "Come in."

The door opened, and Sanodia stepped inside, her flowing tunic a soft shade of green, embroidered with subtle golden patterns that resembled vines. Her dark curls were braided loosely, framing her deep lavender skin, and her keen violet eyes immediately fell upon the porcufera.

She froze.

Her gaze flickered between Lynx and the tiny creature still comfortably resting beside him. "The porcufera... came back?"

Lynx sat up, stretching. "Yeah. Why?"

Sanodia took a slow step forward, studying the creature with a mixture of curiosity and reverence. "That is... not how they usually present themselves."

Lynx frowned. "What do you mean?"

Sanodia lowered herself onto the woven floor mat at the foot of his bed, her gaze still locked onto the porcufera, which was now watching her just as intently.

"Porcufera are not like ordinary creatures," she explained. "They do not simply appear and attach themselves to one person. They come and go as they please, appearing only in moments of great significance. But for one to seek you out... to stay with you overnight... that is unheard of."

Lynx blinked. "So, what? I'm special?"

Sanodia smirked. "I wouldn't go that far. But... it seems the planet has chosen to trust you."

The porcufera chirped softly, as if in agreement.

Lynx scratched his head, feeling both honored and slightly unnerved. "I don't know what I did to earn that, but I'll take it."

Sanodia stood, smoothing out her tunic. "Come with me. I need to gather today's healing plants, and I'd like you to see something."

Lynx glanced at the porcufera. "You coming too?"

The little creature hopped off the bed and landed gracefully on the floor, trotting after him.

Sanodia shook her head in amused disbelief. "Looks like you have a new shadow."

18

Outside, the Reficiat Haven's gardens stretched in beautiful terraced rows, winding through the landscape like flowing rivers of green and gold. The air was thick with the scent of herbs and flowering plants, their colors more vibrant than anything Lynx had seen on Earth.

Sanodia moved with ease, stepping onto the rich, moss-like ground, which softened beneath her bare feet. Lynx followed, noting how everything around her seemed to react to her presence.

And not just in the way plants normally responded to a light breeze or sunlight.

They actually moved.

As Sanodia walked past a cluster of tall, golden-stemmed flowers, the blossoms tilted toward her, as if reaching out.

A vine that had been draping lazily over a stone pillar lifted slightly, curling toward her like a pet seeking affection.

Lynx stopped walking. "Sanodia... they're moving."

She turned slightly, a knowing smile tugging at her lips. "They are greeting me."

Lynx stared. "You... can talk to them?"

Sanodia crouched beside a patch of blue-leafed plants with glowing silver veins, gently brushing her fingers over their surface. "Not in the way you think. I do not speak, but I listen."

Lynx knelt beside her, watching in fascination as the plants shifted subtly under her touch, their luminescence pulsing as though responding to her energy.

"How does that work?" he asked.

Sanodia looked up at him, her violet eyes warm and patient. "The plants on Tanzlora are deeply connected to the energy of the planet, just as we are. They communicate not through words, but through vibrations. When I walk, when I breathe, when I focus my energy on them… they feel it. And in turn, they respond."

Lynx let out a low whistle, shaking his head. "And you just… understand them?"

Sanodia smiled. "It is not about understanding. It is about harmony."

The porcufera chirped and hopped onto a stone ledge, watching them with what Lynx could only describe as pure amusement.

Lynx glanced around at the lush, thriving world around him, and a thought formed in his mind.

"…Do you think Earth could ever be like this?" he asked.

Sanodia's expression turned contemplative. "If Earth learns to listen, to respect the balance of life rather than bend it to its will… then perhaps, one day, it can."

Lynx exhaled, rubbing his hands together. "Then I hope that's what the Triad is leading us toward."

Sanodia stood, gathering a bundle of soft purple leaves and tying them into a woven satchel. "Come, we have much to do today."

Lynx followed her deeper into the living, breathing garden, with the porcufera trotting at his heels.

He had come to Tanzlora to work on diplomatic relations—but it was becoming clear that he was learning something much deeper than politics.

He was learning about the soul of a planet.

And perhaps, just maybe…

Earth could learn from Tanzlora after all.

The morning light streamed through the tall windows of the Blair House dining room, casting golden hues across the elegantly set breakfast table. The scent of freshly brewed coffee and warm pastries filled the air, mingling with the subtle aroma of citrus from a freshly sliced platter of fruit.

Celia and Lorinda sat across from one another, sipping their coffee as they tried to mentally prepare for the monumental discussions ahead. The tension from the previous night still lingered in the air, but now, in the clarity of morning, they felt a renewed sense of purpose, although they still did not know how this day or the rest of the week for that matter would unfold.

Lorinda spread a small amount of jam onto her toast before glancing at Celia. "I still can't believe how much happened in just a few hours. The President being rushed to the hospital? The Vice President having to step in? The family's return from Pluboria and we still don't know what is happening with Waverly on Arcmyrin."

Celia set down her cup, nodding thoughtfully. "We've seen a lot in our time, but being here in DC—this close to the heart of it—makes everything feel different. More… fragile. I trust Lincoln and Ridge to take care of Waverly."

Before Lorinda could respond, the dining room door opened, and Rachel Timms entered, her professional yet relaxed demeanor firmly in place.

"Good morning, ladies," she greeted, offering them both a polite smile. "I hope you slept well."

Lorinda chuckled softly. "Well enough, considering the news we got last night."

Rachel exhaled, taking a seat beside them. "Yes, it was quite the night. That's actually why I'm here—to update you on everything."

Celia straightened slightly, listening intently. "Go on."

Rachel folded her hands on the table, her expression reassuring. "First and foremost, the meeting with the Vice President and the world leaders is on hold for now, however we anticipate that it will still happen within the next 2-3 days so Vice President Houston is asking you to stay in town if that is possible."

Celia nodded. "That's good to hear that you anticipate it happening which is telling me the President's condition is not as serious as first thought?"

Rachel continued, her tone measured but calm. "The President underwent an emergency appendectomy late last night. Fortunately, the surgery was successful, and his doctors expect a full recovery. He's currently awake, alert, and recovering at Walter Reed Medical Center."

Lorinda let out a breath she hadn't realized she was holding. "That's a relief. So… what happens now?"

Rachel offered a small smile. "Since the President is already awake and recovering, he will be able to resume his duties within the next few days as soon as he is released by the doctors. That means the Vice President will be relieved of his temporary role as Acting President soon."

Celia exchanged a glance with Lorinda before nodding. "That's good news. I imagine Houston will be able to focus entirely on the Triad discussions once that happens."

Rachel confirmed with a nod. "Exactly. And to answer the question I know is coming—yes, several world leaders will be in attendance. They are working from their respective embassies until the conference can be held. They all recognize the importance of this and do not want to go back home without meeting you and Ms. Rooney."

Celia leaned forward slightly, curiosity flickering in her eyes. "I am honored and flattered. How many world leaders will be in attendance? I don't believe we ever received that information."

Rachel glanced down at her tablet, quickly checking the updated list before responding. "About that list, the Vice President planned to review it with you and speak about each leader after your dinner last evening but events got in the way of that plan. Let me see," she said as she continued to scroll her tablet. "Seven, including the Vice President."

Celia tapped her fingers thoughtfully against the table. "That's a good number. Enough representation to be impactful, but not so many that the conversation becomes chaotic."

Rachel nodded in agreement. "The focus will be on establishing a foundation—ensuring that every nation understands what the Triad could mean for Earth and our allies in the stars."

Lorinda took another sip of her coffee. "So... do we know the names of the leaders that will be there?"

Rachel smiled. "That information will be given the night before the conference, but I can tell you that we've brought in representatives who have expressed an open interest in interplanetary relations. Vice President and Mrs. Houston would like to host you both again for an informal dinner so that he can speak with you about the leaders."

Celia sat back, letting the information settle. "That's promising, I like that idea."

Rachel rose from her seat, smoothing the front of her blazer. "One more thing. In the meantime, eat, prepare, and enjoy the gardens if you wish. The Vice President has authorized a car at your disposal for any sight seeing you would like to do or Mrs. Houston's suggestion was maybe use the time to shop for wedding dresses. She asked me to provide you a list of the shops in the area that are highly recommended and frequently used."

Rachel handed the list to Lorinda who took it and said, "This is so gracious of her. How very thoughtful."

Celia smiled knowingly. "Mrs. Allison Houston is a great lady."

Rachel nodded. "Yes. I agree wholeheartedly."

With that, Rachel exited, leaving Celia and Lorinda alone with their thoughts.

Lorinda leaned back in her chair, exhaling. "Well, we just ate an enormous amount of food. Do we walk that off today sight-seeing and shop tomorrow? Sounds like we will have both days to ourselves."

Celia smiled. "Excellent plan, my dear."

They both laughed softly, rising from their breakfast table, ready to face the day.

Night turned into early morning as Ridge and Lincoln waited to hear from Elara. Though they had no sleep since getting back from Pluboria, urgency now replaced any lingering exhaustion.

They needed to get to Arcmyrin.

More importantly, they needed to warn Elara. Lincoln reached for the communicator orb again and asked for Elara to appear stating that it was urgent. The others had long left the chamber to go get some sleep leaving the brothers to wait for Elara to appear.

The chamber itself pulsed with a quiet energy, its walls lined with crystalline formations that glowed faintly in shifting hues of blue and silver. The oval stone table at the center, marked with ancient inscriptions of the Triad, stood as a reminder of the delicate balance between the three planets.

Lincoln ran a hand through his hair, exhaling sharply. "I hope she answers. It is not normal to take this long."

Ridge nodded, stepping forward to the glowing orb in the center of the chamber. He placed both hands on it, feeling the familiar warmth of energy surge beneath his fingertips.

The Crystal Gate, embedded in the far wall, began to hum.

Soft light rippled across its surface, shifting and shimmering.

A holographic projection of Elara appeared before them, her elegant figure poised yet alert. Her emerald-hued eyes flickered with recognition as she took in the two brothers standing before her.

"Ridge. Lincoln," she greeted, her voice smooth but carrying an undertone of concern. "Your return from Pluboria was expected, but not so soon. Why have you called upon me?"

Lincoln didn't hesitate. "We have a situation, Elara. A major one."

Elara's gaze sharpened. "Explain."

Ridge crossed his arms, his stance firm. "We just returned from Pluboria, and Galen and Victoria told us something that changes everything. Josephine is alive."

For a split second, Elara's expression was unreadable. Then, her lips parted slightly, her brows knitting together.

"She is on Arcmyrin, isn't she?" she said softly.

Ridge and Lincoln exchanged glances. "You knew?" Ridge asked.

Elara's expression turned solemn. "No. But... I suspected that someone was hiding among us. A presence that did not belong. The energies of Arcmyrin have felt... slightly misaligned at times. I assumed it was due to completing the healing process from the Abasimtrox attack."

Lincoln exhaled sharply. "That's because Josephine has the gift of Earth. She's been using it to disguise herself. She's been blending in, moving undetected."

Elara's shoulders tensed. "And you believe she is a threat?"

Ridge's jaw clenched. "We don't know for certain what her intentions are, but she's been off the radar for too long. She followed Gideon. She may not have been as ruthless as he was, but that doesn't mean she isn't dangerous."

Elara nodded slowly, processing the information. "And Waverly? She is already here. Rykas and I are protecting her."

Lincoln took a step closer, his voice steady but urgent. "That's why we're contacting you. She doesn't know. We need you to watch over her closer, Elara. Make sure she's protected, maybe add more warriors to the protection detail. If Josephine is still torn between loyalty and destruction, she may see Waverly as a threat to whatever she's planning."

Elara's gaze darkened, and she inclined her head in understanding. "I will see to it that she is protected. She will not be left alone."

Ridge's shoulders relaxed—slightly. "Thank you."

Lincoln frowned, his mind already on the next step. "We need to get to Arcmyrin. As soon as possible."

Elara's holographic form flickered slightly. "You wish to come here?"

Ridge nodded firmly. "Yes. We need to find Josephine. Before it's too late."

Elara was silent for a long moment before she finally spoke. "I will make preparations for your arrival. But be aware—if Josephine has remained hidden for this long, she will not be easy to track."

Lincoln's expression hardened. "Then we'll just have to flush her out."

Elara gave them a measured look. "Very well. I will send word when the gate is ready to receive you. Until then—be ready."

With that, the holographic image dissolved, leaving the chamber bathed in its usual ambient glow.

Ridge let out a breath, rolling his shoulders. "Looks like we're heading to Arcmyrin. I need a shower and to eat . We have not eaten anything since we arrived back from Pluboria."

Lincoln nodded grimly. "Yeah, me too. Something tells me though… that Josephine already knows we're coming."

19

As Ridge and Lincoln entered the house, the familiar scent of freshly baked bread and warm spices from the kitchen greeted them. The soft murmur of Sage Manor waking up filled the air, but before they could even take a breath, the sound of small, excited feet pattering against the wooden staircase caught their attention.

Suddenly, Maya, Maddox, and Monica came bursting down the stairs, their energy infectious as they raced toward the dining room.

"Daddy! Uncle Ridge!" Maya called, her bright eyes shining.

"You're back!" Maddox added, his voice filled with relief.

Monica grabbed Ridge's hand and tugged. "Did you see another world? Did you fly? Did you fight anybody?"

Lincoln laughed, ruffling Maya's hair as she hugged his waist. "I missed you all too."

Maddox looked up at him with a curious expression. "Did you bring anything back?"

Ridge chuckled, shaking his head. "No souvenirs, bud. But trust me, we saw things that can't be put in a bag."

Before the kids could bombard them with more questions, Bethany appeared at the top of the stairs, her sharp eyes scanning the scene below. The mother in her was always attuned to order—even amidst excitement.

"All right, all right," she called down, her voice warm but firm. "Breakfast first, then questions. You three have a full day of learning ahead."

Maya groaned. "But Daddy and Ridge just got back!"

Bethany descended the stairs, her focus shifting to her husband as she approached him. Lincoln could see the relief in her expression, even as she tried to keep it casual.

"I did not get a chance to say it last night, but I am so glad you're home," she said softly, reaching for his hand.

Lincoln squeezed her fingers gently, lowering his voice. "I'm glad to be back."

Francis, meanwhile, had no such restraint. Bounding into the dining room with excitement, she immediately turned her focus on Ridge.

"Okay, spill it! What was Pluboria like? What did you see? Bronte gave me the short version but I need details."

Ridge laughed, shaking his head as he pulled out a chair at the dining table. "You don't waste time, do you?"

Francis smirked. "Not when there's interplanetary gossip to be had."

Lincoln took a seat as well, motioning for the others to join him. "It's hard to explain, Francis. Pluboria isn't like a normal planet. It's not like Earth, not even like Tanzlora or Arcmyrin. It's more... fluid. A place of pure energy and light."

Ridge nodded in agreement, folding his arms. "Time doesn't work the same way there. Neither does space. It's not something you walk on or travel through—it's more like... you exist within it."

Francis's eyes went wide. "That. Is. Amazing."

Before Ridge could elaborate, a sudden hush fell over the dining room.

The reason?

Marshall, Madre, and Bronte had joined them.

And Bronte was walking.

For a long moment, the children were silent, not believing what they were seeing.

The sight of the once wheelchair-bound Bronte striding into the room with effortless ease left Maya, Maddox and Monica completely stunned.

Maya gasped audibly. "You're walking!"

Monica nearly knocked over her cup of milk as she turned fully to stare at Bronte. "I—what—HOW?!"

Bronte, ever the gruff old codger, just smirked, rolling his shoulders as if his miraculous healing was nothing worth fussing over. "Hey kids, let's not make a big deal about it."

Maddox, his eyes wide with wonder, stepped closer. "But you were in a wheelchair! You said your legs didn't work!"

Bronte huffed. "Well, they do now."

Monica tilted her head, "Did someone do magic on you?"

Ridge snorted. "Something like that."

Madre, standing beside Bronte, smiled at the children's reactions. "Pluboria healed him. Completely."

Francis still looked like she was struggling to process it. "I mean—it's amazing! But I don't understand how Pluboria could do it when countless specialists on three other planets could not.

Marshall, stepping forward, adjusted his glasses. "Earth's medicine couldn't. Neither could Tanzlora's or Arcmyrin's. But Pluboria... it doesn't follow the same rules we know."

Monica shook her head in disbelief. "So you mean to tell me that after all this time, Bronte is just... fixed?"

Bronte grumbled, folding his arms. "Don't say it like that. Makes me sound like a damn broken machine."

Maya giggled. "But you were kind of grumpy when you couldn't walk."

Bronte narrowed his eyes at her playfully. "I'm still grumpy, kid."

Maddox ran up and hugged Bronte's waist tightly, grinning up at him. "I'm just glad you're okay."

For a moment, Bronte looked caught off guard, his usual rough exterior faltering just slightly. Then, with a small, reluctant pat on Maddox's head, he sighed.

"...Yeah, yeah. Me too."

Ridge sat back, taking it all in. A home full of life. A home full of miracles.

But beneath the joy, he and Lincoln knew—

It wasn't over yet.

And soon, they would be leaving again. This time, for Arcmyrin.

The early morning air was cool and crisp as Waverly stepped out into the communal gardens near the living pods where she was staying. The sky above Arcmyrin was a stunning blend of soft indigos and silvers, with the planet's two distant moons still faintly visible on the horizon.

As she walked along the stone-paved paths, she could feel the energy of the planet humming beneath her feet. Arcmyrin's land was alive in a way Earth's soil wasn't—not just nutrient-rich, but pulsing with frequencies that seemed to sync with those who lived on it.

Trailing a few paces behind, Rykas followed, his posture relaxed but alert.

He didn't hover, nor did he crowd her—but she knew he was watching. Protecting.

It wasn't something he had to say out loud.

The commander of the Arcmyrin warriors was always on guard.

Waverly pretended not to notice, instead focusing on her task. In her free hand, she carried a woven basket, and at her hip, secured in a sheath of silver and leather, was her elemental dagger—the one infused with Ambreela's power.

The Spirit of Air flitted around her in small, swirling currents of shimmering wind, occasionally brushing past Waverly's cheek like a gentle breeze.

"You are comfortable here," Ambreela whispered in her mind. *"The land welcomes you."*

Waverly smiled softly. "I feel it."

As she entered the garden rows, she saw several Arcmyrins already at work, gathering their own food supplies for the day. Lush leafy greens, deep purple root vegetables, and delicate vines bearing fruit similar to citrus but with a soft, bioluminescent glow—everything was slightly different than what she had known on Earth, yet it all felt familiar.

She greeted each person she passed with a polite nod or a quiet "Morya'ven." A warm Arcmyrin greeting that meant both "good morning" and "may your spirit be full today."

The other gatherers smiled and responded in kind, welcoming her presence as if she had always belonged there.

She reached down, plucking a bundle of long, spiral-shaped greens that smelled faintly similar to Earth's anise and pepper. The soil crumbled between her fingers, cool and rich, humming softly with Arcmyrin's natural energies.

As Waverly moved further into the garden, she felt completely at peace.

Until—

A sudden impact jarred her forward, nearly knocking her off balance.

A woman—an Arcmyrin gatherer—had bumped into her with enough force that Waverly stumbled, barely catching herself before she fell into the soft dirt.

Ambreela whipped around her in a sudden gust, reacting instinctively to Waverly's abrupt movement.

Before Waverly could even process what had happened, Rykas was already at her side.

His strong hand rested lightly on her shoulder, steadying her, but his sharp golden eyes were fixed on the woman.

"Are you hurt?" he asked, his voice low but firm.

Waverly righted herself and turned, expecting to see the woman equally startled—maybe even apologizing.

But instead—

The woman was scurrying away.

Her cloak was pulled tightly around her, her posture tense as she weaved through the other gatherers, not looking back.

Rykas' brows furrowed deeply, his gaze tracking the woman until she disappeared beyond the rows of food-bearing plants.

Something about the interaction didn't sit right with him.

Waverly dusted off her hands and turned to him. "That was... strange."

Rykas' jaw tensed slightly. "Yes. It was."

Waverly shook her head. "I mean, accidents happen. The gardens are a shared space. Maybe she just—"

"That was not an accident," Rykas interrupted, his voice edged with certainty.

Waverly narrowed her eyes. "How can you be sure?"

His golden gaze flickered back toward the path where the woman had disappeared. "Because she didn't even acknowledge you. She didn't look back, didn't apologize. She just... left."

A small chill crawled up Waverly's spine.

Now that he mentioned it... the whole thing did seem off. It was not the Arcmyrin way to just leave and disappear after an encounter like that.

Waverly exhaled and rolled her shoulders. "Well, whatever it was, I'm fine. No harm done."

Rykas hesitated, then gave a curt nod. But the way his muscles stayed taut, the way his hand still hovered near his weapon...

He wasn't convinced.

Neither was Waverly.

But instead of dwelling on it, she bent down, picked up her basket, and continued gathering.

If that had been something, they would find out soon enough.

By the time they left the gardens, Waverly's basket was full, and the tension from earlier had faded—slightly.

Ambreela still swirled around her, unusually active, as if sensing something Waverly could not.

Rykas remained at her side, his pace steady, his presence a silent reminder that he had not forgotten the woman's odd behavior.

As they approached the living pods, Waverly glanced at him.

"You don't have to follow me all the way inside, you know."

Rykas arched a brow. "Yes, I do."

Waverly sighed. "Figures."

As they stepped through the threshold, she set down the basket of fresh food and stretched. "Well, I don't know about you, but I'm ready to cook something."

Rykas didn't respond immediately.

Instead, he lingered by the entrance, his eyes still scanning the distant gardens.

"Rykas," Waverly said gently.

He finally looked at her.

She softened. "I appreciate you watching over me. But I'm okay."

Rykas studied her for a moment before exhaling. "For now."

Waverly shook her head with a small smirk, already moving toward the small cooking space within the pod. "Come on, let's eat. You're always in a better mood after food."

That earned her a rare half-smile from him, but he said nothing as he followed her inside.

Still, Waverly couldn't shake the feeling that Rykas was right to be concerned.

Something wasn't right.

And she had a feeling—

This wouldn't be the last strange encounter she had on Arcmyrin.

20

After breakfast, the morning routine fell into place as usual—Bethany and Francis led Maya, Maddox, and Monica into the media room, which had become their makeshift classroom. The children settled into their seats, ready for another day of reading, writing, and lessons.

For the first hour, things went smoothly. Bethany administered a vocabulary quiz to Monica, while Francis worked with Maya and Maddox on simple math problems using colorful counting stones.

But then, a presence at the doorway shifted the energy of the room.

Bronte Sutton stood there, arms crossed, eyebrows raised, and an expression that was both amused and slightly irritated.

He lingered in the doorway for a good minute or two, just watching.

Bethany was the first to notice him. She paused, setting down the stack of quizzes in her hands before addressing him.

"Bronte," she greeted with a smile, "did you need something?"

Bronte scoffed, shaking his head. "No, not really. Just standing here wondering something."

Bethany tilted her head. "And what's that?"

Bronte stepped inside slightly, his sharp gaze scanning the room. "I never see these kids learning anything outdoors. It's always in here—trapped in four walls, staring at books, writing on those tablets."

Bethany and Francis exchanged glances.

"I mean," Bronte continued, "what kind of education doesn't involve building forts, skipping rocks, or learning how to climb trees?"

Maddox's head shot up, his eyes bright with excitement. "We can build a fort?"

Monica's jaw dropped in delight. "Can we really?"

Bronte smirked. "Darn right you can. I don't know about you all, but I learned plenty outside—how to track animals, how to build a sturdy shelter, how to read the sky to tell time. But you kids? You're cooped up all the time."

Francis lit up at the idea.

"That's a fantastic suggestion!" she said, clasping her hands together. "Bronte, you should be their teacher today! Outdoor classroom day!"

The children erupted in cheers, bouncing up and down in their seats.

Bethany laughed, shaking her head. "Alright, alright, settle down!" She turned to Bronte. "If you're up for it, I think they'd love it."

Bronte shrugged. "Course I'm up for it. Someone's gotta show these young'uns how to properly have fun outside."

Francis grinned. "I'll come with you! I'd love to watch the master at work."

Bronte rolled his eyes but didn't protest.

Bethany held up a finger, addressing the now restless children.

"Alright, listen up," she said. "You are to listen to *everything* Bronte and Francis tell you today. If they say stop, you stop. If they say come back, you come back. No wandering off."

The children nodded eagerly.

Bethany smiled. "Then you're dismissed to the outdoor classroom."

The kids whooped in joy, rushing toward Bronte and Francis, their excitement bubbling over.

Bronte chuckled, rubbing his hands together. "Alright, kids. First lesson—fort-building 101. Let's get to it."

With that, the group poured outside, laughter echoing through the morning air.

And for the first time in a long time, Bronte Sutton was happy.

The scent of spiced root vegetables and fresh greens filled the small but welcoming space of the living pod as Waverly and Rykas prepared their breakfast. The open kitchen was simple, with a stone-hewn cooking station where Waverly had been experimenting with Arcmyrin's ingredients, figuring out which ones tasted closest to Earth's foods.

Rykas, ever the warrior, stood nearby with his arms crossed, watching her with mild amusement as she attempted to slice a twisting, vine-like herb that resisted being cut.

She huffed, adjusting her grip. "This plant does not want to cooperate."

Rykas smirked. "It is alive. It resists when it senses uncertainty."

Waverly scowled at him. "Oh, great, so now I have to be confident for my food to let me cook it?"

Rykas simply nodded, reaching over and plucking the herb from her hands. With one swift motion, he deftly sliced through the stubborn plant, the pieces falling cleanly onto the stone surface.

Waverly narrowed her eyes. "Show-off."

Before Rykas could respond, the door to the living pod slid open with a soft hum, revealing Elara.

The Arcmyrin envoy was, as always, poised and graceful. Her violet robes shimmered subtly in the light, embroidered with golden accents that represented her status. Her expression was warm but focused as she stepped inside, taking in the scene before her.

"I see you have already found a way to test Arcmyrin's flora," Elara said, amusement flickering in her gaze.

Waverly sighed, gesturing to the sliced herb. "Yes. And apparently, I must exude unwavering confidence, or else my food refuses to be prepared."

Elara chuckled. "Arcmyrin's plants are deeply connected to the energy of those who handle them. Much like the planet itself, they respond to balance."

Rykas smirked but remained silent as he continued preparing the meal.

Elara moved toward the small dining space, settling gracefully into one of the curved seats carved from Arcmyrin stone. "I came to join you for breakfast," she said, "and to prepare you for today's council session."

Waverly brightened at that, setting aside the knife and moving to take a seat across from Elara. "I'm looking forward to it," she said sincerely. "I want to learn as much as I can about Arcmyrin so I can share that knowledge with my fellow humans on Earth."

Elara nodded approvingly. "That is exactly what today's session is about."

She reached for a plate of sliced fruit-like orbs, their soft glow pulsing faintly as she selected a piece. "The Arcmyrin Council wishes to ensure that Earth's representatives—especially the Beaumont family—fully understand our world and our history. Today's session will focus primarily on who we are, how we have existed, and why we have remained at peace for so long."

Waverly leaned forward, intrigued. "I'd love to hear more about that."

Elara folded her hands neatly in her lap. "Unlike Earth, Arcmyrin has never had internal wars. There has never been a battle among our people. No factions, no civil conflicts. Our society exists in harmonious cooperation—not because we lack disagreement, but because we have always believed that balance is the key to existence."

Waverly absorbed that, nodding slowly. "That's incredible. Humans... we have struggled with that for as long as we've existed. There's always some conflict—political, territorial, personal."

Elara smiled gently. "You are a young species. You are still learning."

Waverly exhaled. "Yeah... we've got a long way to go."

Elara continued. "The only enemy we have ever known was not of our own making. The Abasimtrox and the Umbralox were the only threats Arcmyrin has ever faced. Their darkness spread into the very fabric of the universe, seeking to corrupt and consume. We fought them not for power, but for the survival of our harmony."

Waverly's fingers traced the smooth edge of her dagger, where Ambreela's essence pulsed faintly. "And you weren't alone in that fight."

"No," Elara agreed. "For centuries, Tanzlora stood with us, and when the Beaumont family rose to their role as protectors, Earth became part of that battle as well."

She inclined her head toward Waverly. "And now, for the first time, we do not prepare for war. We prepare for alliance. With the Abasimtrox and Umbralox annihilated, Arcmyrin exists in a level of peace we have never known before. Now, the question is—how do we move forward?"

Waverly felt the gravity of the conversation settle over her.

The war had been won, but the future was still uncertain.

Arcmyrin had never needed a structured interplanetary alliance before. They had always existed in peace, only forming military strategies when evil forces required them to fight. Now, with those enemies gone, the Triad had the potential to become something entirely new.

A true galactic unity.

Elara tilted her head slightly. "Do you believe Earth is ready for this?"

Waverly hesitated. Then, she gave the most honest answer she could.

"I think Earth wants to be ready. But wanting it and knowing how to achieve it are two very different things."

Elara studied her for a long moment before nodding. "Then today, we will begin the process of helping your people understand our people."

Waverly exhaled, pushing her plate aside. "Then I'm ready."

Elara gave a small, satisfied nod. "Good."

Rykas, who had remained silent but ever watchful, finally spoke. "Then let's get moving. The Council is expecting you."

Waverly stood, adjusting her dagger at her hip.

She was about to walk into a room filled with Arcmyrin's powerful leaders.

But she wasn't nervous.

She was ready to listen, to learn, and to ensure that Earth took this next step forward—not in fear, but in understanding.

And as she followed Elara and Rykas toward the Council Chambers, she knew—

This was just the beginning.

The elegant front door of Blair House swung open precisely at 9:00 a.m., revealing a black, government-issued SUV gleaming in the morning sun. Lorinda and Celia stepped onto the porch, savoring the crisp air that felt invigorating after the uncertainty of the night before. As they approached the car, the driver quickly stepped out and opened the rear door, greeting them warmly.

"Good morning, ladies. Your car is ready," he said with a polite nod.

"Thank you," Celia responded with a gracious smile. She and Lorinda climbed into the spacious vehicle, glancing at each other curiously. To their surprise, a young man dressed neatly in a khaki uniform and forest-green jacket awaited them, a warm, genuine smile spread across his face.

"Good morning!" the young man said cheerfully, extending a hand toward each of them. "I'm Scott Adamson, your tour guide for today. It's an honor to meet you both."

Celia's face lit up at the name. "Adamson? Any relation to General Adamson?"

Scott chuckled, nodding modestly. "Yes, ma'am. He's my grandfather. He mentioned you both very highly."

Lorinda smiled broadly. "Well, it's a pleasure, Scott."

As the SUV began smoothly navigating the city streets, Scott enthusiastically began pointing out the passing buildings, weaving historical narratives with effortless charm.

"Our first stop," Scott explained eagerly, "will be the Lincoln Memorial, then we'll make our way around the National Mall. There's so much history in this city, but I promise I'll keep it interesting."

Lorinda grinned, leaning forward slightly in her seat. "We have no doubt you will."

21

They soon arrived at the iconic marble monument, rising proudly into a sky of vibrant blue. Scott led the women up the steps, his youthful enthusiasm tempered by genuine reverence.

"This memorial was completed in 1922," Scott began, his voice taking on a respectful quietness. "It's one of the most symbolic places in our nation, honoring President Abraham Lincoln, who led the country through the Civil War."

Celia gazed upward, deeply moved by the majestic sculpture of Lincoln. "It's incredibly powerful," she whispered.

"Indeed," Scott nodded. "Dr. Martin Luther King Jr. stood right here, where we're standing, when he delivered his 'I Have a Dream' speech in 1963." His voice held a slight catch, clearly moved himself.

They lingered a bit, taking in the atmosphere before returning to their waiting vehicle.

The next stop was the Washington Monument. Scott led them toward the edge of the Reflecting Pool, where the monument's soaring reflection shimmered in the water.

"Construction began in 1848," Scott explained, "but due to financial issues and the Civil War, it wasn't completed until 1884. If you look closely, you can see the two different colors of marble indicating where construction paused."

Lorinda squinted, then nodded in amazement. "That's fascinating."

Scott smiled warmly, clearly pleased by their genuine interest. "Many people never notice it."

As they reached the Jefferson Memorial, Scott narrated Thomas Jefferson's extraordinary life story, his voice resonating gently through the colonnades.

"Jefferson drafted the Declaration of Independence," Scott said, his tone reverent yet passionate, "and as President, oversaw the Louisiana Purchase, effectively doubling the size of the United States."

Celia listened intently, impressed by Scott's grasp of history. "You clearly love what you're doing, Scott."

He flushed modestly. "It's my passion, truly."

Next, Scott led them toward the somber yet striking World War II Memorial. He explained each symbolic aspect of the monument—the states represented, the meaning of the gold stars, and the fountains symbolizing unity.

Lorinda and Celia paused quietly, each offering silent respect to those honored there.

"This place always humbles me," Scott admitted softly, "it reminds me of the sacrifices our families made."

As their SUV circled closer to the Capitol building, Scott shifted topics, sharing intriguing anecdotes from past administrations. His animated storytelling captivated Lorinda and Celia, causing them to smile despite themselves.

"Did you know the dome itself weighs nearly nine million pounds?" Scott asked enthusiastically. "Yet it was completed during the turmoil of the Civil War—symbolizing the resilience of democracy."

Celia laughed warmly. "You're quite the storyteller, Scott. You should teach history."

Scott blushed slightly, a smile stretching across his youthful face. "Actually, I'm training to be a National Park Service ranger. My hope is to get assigned to Pisgah National Forest in North Carolina."

Lorinda and Celia exchanged a meaningful glance, both surprised and pleased. Celia leaned forward, intrigued. "Pisgah? Then you must know Seth Dixon?"

Scott's eyes lit up eagerly. "I haven't met him personally, but I know his reputation. He's one of the best in the field. Working under him would be a dream come true."

Celia smiled warmly, her expression thoughtful. "We'll see what we can do about that."

Scott looked slightly embarrassed yet undeniably hopeful. "Oh, you don't have to—"

"Nonsense," Celia cut in gently. "I'm certain Seth would appreciate someone with your enthusiasm."

Their final stop was the Martin Luther King Jr. Memorial, its powerful presence standing proudly amidst cherry blossom trees. As Scott recited memorable quotes from King's speeches engraved in stone, Lorinda felt a deep resonance with their current mission—peace, understanding, and unity among diverse peoples.

They stood silently for a moment, absorbing the powerful words:

"Out of the mountain of despair, a stone of hope."

Celia sighed softly, eyes thoughtful. "A stone of hope. That feels fitting today, doesn't it?"

Scott nodded seriously, sensing the weight behind her words. "Indeed, ma'am. It's as true today as it was then."

The ride back to Blair House was quiet, filled with reflection. When the vehicle pulled up, the driver opened the doors, and Scott stepped out first, offering each woman a hand.

As Lorinda exited, she turned toward Scott warmly. "Thank you so much, Scott. Today was wonderful."

Celia took Scott's hand next, holding it a moment longer to look directly into his eyes. "Scott, you're exceptionally talented and knowledgeable. It was a privilege having you guide us today."

Scott beamed, visibly touched. "Thank you, Ms. Celia."

She squeezed his hand gently. "I meant what I said earlier. When we return home, I will personally speak with Seth Dixon. He'll want someone like you on his team."

Scott flushed bright red, clearly overwhelmed. "You have no idea how much that means to me. Thank you both so much."

Lorinda smiled warmly. "We should be thanking you."

Scott stepped back respectfully, raising his hand in farewell. "Have a lovely rest of your day, ladies."

They stood quietly, watching the SUV disappear down the road. Lorinda glanced over at Celia, smiling broadly. "Well, wasn't he impressive?"

Celia chuckled softly, nodding. "Indeed. I'll speak with Seth the minute we're home. Scott Adamson is exactly the kind of young leader we need."

Lorinda laughed, linking her arm with Celia's as they turned toward the elegant entrance of Blair House. "Now, let's see what else this incredible day has in store for us."

As Waverly stepped into the Arcmyrin Council chambers, she was getting ready to get a different history lesson and was immediately aware of the shift in energy. The chamber, grand yet serene, radiated an almost sacred presence. The walls pulsed with an ambient glow, carved from crystalline formations that shimmered in hues of blue, silver, gold and violet. The ceiling stretched high above, resembling the night sky, dotted with softly glowing constellations that seemed to shift and move like living stars.

Rykas walked beside her, his presence steady, his gaze flicking briefly around the chamber before motioning toward a chair set before the Council table.

The chair was unlike any she had seen before—it bore a striking resemblance to the chairs around the oval table in the chamber under the gazebo back at Sage Manor.

Waverly hesitated for only a moment before sinking into the seat.

The instant she did, a gentle warmth spread through her. It wasn't just a chair—it was alive in some way, resonating with her energy.

Her mind became clearer, sharper—her thoughts organizing themselves effortlessly, like puzzle pieces falling into place.

She shifted slightly, placing her hands on the carved armrests, feeling the gentle pulse of energy beneath her fingertips. Leaning toward Rykas, she whispered, "I feel... one with this chair."

Rykas gave her a rare full smile, his golden eyes bright with amusement. "Then enjoy the presentation."

Before Waverly could reply, Councilor Releesia rose from her seat at the long, curved table.

The leader of the Arcmyrin Council was regal in presence, her flowing violet robes embroidered with golden markings representing her lineage and wisdom. Her silver-streaked hair cascaded down her back, and her orange-golden-hued eyes held the depth of centuries.

She offered Waverly a warm nod of respect. "Waverly Beaumont. Welcome to the Arcmyrin Council Chambers."

Waverly straightened, her heart swelling with both pride and humility. "Thank you, Councilor Releesia."

Releesia's voice was calm but resonant. "Today, we will share with you the history of Arcmyrin and our people. We understand that Earth's way of measuring time is different, so we will use Earthling terminologies and references to help you comprehend what you are about to hear."

Waverly smiled, feeling truly grateful. "On behalf of my family and the people of Earth, I want to express our appreciation. The fact that the Arcmyrin Council is open to this intergalactic alliance means so much. And personally—" she paused, letting herself feel the sincerity of her next words, "—though this is only my second time on Arcmyrin, I feel at home here. I love the Arcmyrian people just as I love my fellow humans."

A ripple of pleased murmurs passed through the Council members, and Releesia smiled approvingly. "That is a rare and beautiful thing to say, Waverly Beaumont. Your soul is more attuned to the universe than most."

With that, she began.

Releesia gestured toward a circular platform in the center of the chamber, and immediately, the glowing constellations above shifted—their light refracting into a holographic display of Arcmyrin's ancient past.

"Our people were created over twenty centuries ago, though time here does not flow as it does on Earth," Releesia explained. "Arcmyrins were born from the pure energies of Origin, designed to live in harmony with this world, with each other, and with the Cycle of Existence."

The projection showed Arcmyrin's lush, glowing landscapes, vibrant and teeming with life. The planet had never known war—never experienced internal conflict.

"We have always lived as one," Releesia continued. "Because we do not strive for power or conquest—we strive for balance."

Waverly marveled at the idea. "So you've never fought amongst yourselves?"

Releesia shook her head. "Never. The only enemies we have ever known were not of our own making. The Abasimtrox and the Umbralox sought to disrupt our harmony, but with the help of Tanzlora and your family, we were able to defeat them—time and time again."

She let her words settle before continuing. "But now, those dark forces are gone. And for the first time in our history, Arcmyrin exists in a peace unlike any before. Now, we must look toward the future."

Releesia gestured toward the holographic display, and it shifted again, showing the image of an Arcmyrin body—strong, luminous, pulsing with natural energy.

"The lifespan of an Arcmyrin is between 400 to 500 Earth years."

Waverly's eyes widened. "That long?"

Releesia nodded. "We do not die from illness or natural causes as Earthlings do. All illness is healed naturally, using the plants and minerals that Origin has provided. Every healer knows how to utilize these gifts, and thus, no disease can take us before our time."

Waverly sat back, stunned. "That's… incredible."

Releesia smiled knowingly. "It is the way of our world."

"But," Waverly hesitated, "if Arcmyrians don't die from illness or age, then… how do your lives end?"

Releesia's expression softened. "It is a choice."

The room fell silent.

"Our lifespan is long, but not eternal," she explained. "At some point—between 400 and 500 Earth years—each Arcmyrian feels the call to return to Origin. When that time comes, we do not fear it. It is a celebration, not a sorrowful event."

She glanced at Waverly, ensuring she understood before continuing.

"The process is called Mutradiare—the cycle of existence."

Waverly inhaled deeply. "You mean… like reincarnation?"

Releesia nodded. "Yes, I believe Earthlings call it that. When we choose to leave our biological forms, we return to Origin's embrace, becoming light body entities until we decide whether to be reborn into a new existence or remain in light form."

Waverly could barely comprehend it. A choice. A conscious decision to transition to the next life.

But then, a darker thought struck her.

"…Has there ever been a time when an Arcmyrian's life ended before they made the choice?"

Releesia's expression darkened slightly. "Yes. When we have been attacked by dark forces."

The holographic display shifted again—this time revealing shadowy tendrils of the Abasimtrox creeping toward Arcmyrin figures, consuming them in darkness.

"When an Arcmyrian falls to an enemy of darkness, the soul does not transition freely to Origin," Releesia said, her voice solemn. "Instead, it is trapped."

A chill ran through Waverly. "Trapped?"

Releesia nodded. "When darkness slays one of us, the soul is caught in a void—a prison of shadow. There, Origin must determine if the soul has been corrupted or if it remains pure."

Waverly's stomach turned. "And if it's corrupted?"

Releesia's expression was grave. "Then it is permanently destroyed."

A stunned silence fell over the room.

Waverly's heart pounded. She had always believed in some form of an afterlife, but the idea that an Arcmyrian soul could be erased completely—never to return to the cycle—was horrifying.

She exhaled shakily. "That's... a lot to take in."

Releesia's gaze was filled with understanding. "It is. But knowledge is power, Waverly Beaumont. And you must carry this knowledge back to Earth."

Waverly swallowed hard and nodded.

She would carry it.

And she would make sure Earth understood what was at stake.

22

As Waverly absorbed the profound knowledge that Councilor Releesia had just shared about Mutradiare and the cycle of existence, the chamber remained quiet and still, allowing her time to process.

She had always known Arcmyrin was different, but learning that its people had never experienced war amongst themselves, never suffered from disease, and chose when to return to Origin—it was a staggering contrast to Earth's reality.

And now, there was more to learn.

Seated beside Releesia, Councilor Milestree shifted forward slightly, signaling it was his turn to speak.

Milestree was a tall and broad-shouldered Arcmyrin, his presence calm yet commanding. His deep blue robes shimmered subtly, embroidered with golden patterns resembling interwoven tree branches, symbolic of his role as the Ambassador to Tanzlora. His eyes, a rich amber color, held a depth of understanding that reminded Waverly of Tanzlorans she had met before.

"Waverly Beaumont," he said in a measured, resonant tone, "I am Milestree, the Ambassador to Tanzlora. It is my role to maintain our eternal bond with our twin world—our sister planet."

Waverly straightened in her chair, intrigued. "Twin planet?"

Milestree nodded, lifting his hand. As he did, the holographic projection above them shifted once more, displaying two planets, side by side, mirroring one another.

"Arcmyrin and Tanzlora are twins in creation," Milestree explained. "They were born from the same divine energies at the same

153

time, both nurtured by Origin. We, the Arcmyrins, were placed here to care for this world, to nurture it, to ensure its balance. And so too were the Tanzlorans given the same responsibility for Tanzlora."

Waverly's gaze remained fixed on the projection. Even though she had been to both planets, she had never fully realized how deeply connected they were. "They were created together... to be in harmony?"

Milestree inclined his head. "Precisely."

The projection expanded, showing shimmering energy lines flowing between the two planets, almost like an unseen lifeline connecting them.

"This connection between our worlds is more than just shared existence," he continued. "It is a sacred bond. The same way Arcmyrin provides for its people, Tanzlora does the same. The land nourishes us, and in return, we care for it."

Waverly nodded slowly, her fingers resting on the armrests of her chair. "Tanzlora's forests... its waters... they feel alive in a way that's different from Earth's. I felt that when I was there."

Milestree smiled. "Because they are alive, Waverly. As is Arcmyrin. Our worlds do not merely sustain life; they are life. That is what Origin intended when we were placed here."

The projection shifted again, displaying the lush landscapes of both Arcmyrin and Tanzlora.

Milestree continued. "Just as I am the Ambassador to Tanzlora, Tanzlora has their own Ambassador to Arcmyrin. And you, Waverly, have already met him—Lumorith."

Waverly perked up at the name. "Yes! I know Lumorith!"

She had first met Lumorith during the battle against the Umbralox on Tanzlora, and their interactions had been both insightful and inspiring. Lumorith had been one of the most graceful, wise, and intuitive leaders Waverly had ever encountered.

Milestree nodded approvingly. "Lumorith and I share a unique responsibility—we are the bridge between our people."

Waverly leaned in, eager to hear more. "How often do you see each other?"

Milestree smiled, his golden eyes twinkling. "During times of peace, when there are no threats, and the portal systems are fully operational, Lumorith and I visit each other's worlds frequently. We share knowledge, discuss our people's well-being, and ensure that Arcmyrin and Tanzlora remain in harmony."

Waverly nodded, imagining the ease of such a relationship between two planets. "That must make things much easier when conflict arises."

Milestree's expression darkened slightly, but only for a moment. "Indeed. But when dark forces emerge, we do not meet as often. Instead, we immediately shift into action—ensuring the safety of our people, reinforcing our defenses, and ensuring that neither world falls to the enemy."

He paused for a moment, then added, "But do you know what we have never had to do, Waverly?"

She shook her head, curious.

Milestree's smile returned. "We have never needed to write a treaty. We have never needed contracts, agreements, or paper documentation of our alliance."

Waverly raised an eyebrow. "Not even once?"

Milestree chuckled. "Not once."

She tilted her head. "Then... how do you ensure that both sides hold up their end of the partnership?"

Milestree's expression softened. "Through trust, love, and camaraderie. That is all that is needed."

Waverly's heart clenched slightly at the simplicity of it. No legal documents. No bureaucracy. No mistrust.

Just friendship.

"Earth... doesn't work like that," she admitted, shaking her head. "Every agreement has contracts, laws, clauses—ways to ensure that neither side betrays the other."

Milestree nodded in understanding. "Because your people do not yet live in true harmony. You still struggle with division, with the concept of power, with the fear that one will take more than they should."

Waverly sighed. "Yeah. That's... pretty much it."

"But do not despair," Milestree said gently. "Earth is still growing. Learning. And if this alliance succeeds, perhaps your world will begin to understand that trust is stronger than any written contract."

Waverly let his words sink in.

Could Earth ever be like Arcmyrin and Tanzlora? Could humanity truly learn to live in balance rather than competition?

She wanted to believe it was possible.

And maybe—just maybe—this alliance was the first step toward making it happen.

She looked up at Milestree with newfound respect. "I'm honored to be learning this. And I can't wait to share it with Earth."

Milestree smiled. "Then let us continue. There is still much for you to know."

As Waverly settled deeper into her chair, feeling its energy strengthen her clarity once more, she knew—

This knowledge was going to change everything.

The woods near the pond were alive with the sounds of snapping twigs, rustling leaves, and the happy chatter of three excited children. The morning sun filtered through the trees, casting a golden glow over Bronte Sutton and his eager students—Maya, Maddox, and Monica—as they worked on their fort-building project.

Bronte stood near a pile of freshly gathered tree limbs, his old hunting knife in hand, cutting strips of canvas from what had once been his beloved tent. The thick fabric ripped cleanly, creating sturdy coverings to drape over the wooden frame they were assembling.

Monica, watching him intently, suddenly frowned. "Bronte... why are you cutting up your tent?"

Bronte grunted, giving her a sidelong glance before slicing through another section. "Because, kid, I don't need it anymore."

Monica's brow furrowed. "But... wasn't this where you lived before?"

Maddox, wiping dirt off his hands, nodded. "Yeah, you loved that tent."

Bronte smirked, tossing a piece of canvas toward Maya, who was carefully draping another layer over their growing rustic-looking fort.

"Sure, I did," Bronte admitted. "But I don't live out here anymore. I got a nice room and a bed in the house now, so this ol' tent ain't doing much good just sittin' around."

He gestured toward the fort taking shape around them—a sturdy lean-to style structure supported by thick tree limbs, reinforced with vines, small branches, and layers of the cut canvas.

"But out here?" he continued, dusting his hands off. "It's got a better purpose—teachin' you kids how things were done before you had big houses, electricity, and all the modern luxuries you take for granted."

Maya, standing on her toes to tie one of the canvas pieces to a tree limb, looked at him curiously. "You mean like... way, way before?"

Bronte nodded. "Yeah. Long before your time. Before cars, before phones, before houses were built with bricks and metal. Back when folks had to build shelters like this to survive."

Monica, her hands on her hips, gave the fort an appraising look. "So, like... when cowboys were around?"

Bronte let out a low chuckle. "Even before that. Think back to the first folks who traveled across this country—before it was all towns and roads. People who landed on the shores from England, lookin' for a new life. They had to make forts just like this to survive the first winter."

Maddox's eyes widened. "They didn't have houses already built?"

"Nope," Bronte said. "They had to cut down trees, build everything with their own two hands. No supermarkets, no heaters, no fancy stoves. If they wanted to eat, they had to hunt. If they wanted to stay warm, they had to build fires. And if they wanted to be safe, they needed a fort just like this one."

Monica wrinkled her nose. "That sounds really hard."

Bronte grinned. "That's because it was."

The three children looked around their fort with a new kind of appreciation.

Maya ran her hands over the canvas covering. "So this is kinda like... what those first travelers built?"

Bronte nodded proudly. "Darn right it is. And you built it yourselves."

Maddox straightened his shoulders, grinning. "That means we'd survive out here, huh?"

Bronte snorted. "Don't go getting' ahead of yourself, kid. You still gotta learn how to start a fire."

The children laughed, excitement filling the crisp morning air.

As they finished securing the last pieces of their rustic fort, Bronte leaned back on a tree stump, watching them with a rare softness in his eyes.

He might not have needed his tent anymore, but in this moment, watching these kids build, learn, and connect to the past, he knew...

It had found a better purpose.

Children's laughter filled the crisp air as the newly built fort stood proudly beneath the towering trees. The structure, a rustic masterpiece of tree limbs, vines, and canvas, was both sturdy and inviting, thanks to Bronte's guidance and the eager hands of Maya, Maddox, and Monica.

As the children admired their handiwork, a familiar voice called out from the path leading back to the house.

"Well, well! What do we have here?"

The children spun around, faces lighting up as they saw Francis approaching, her hands on her hips and a wide smile on her face.

Francis stopped in her tracks, her eyes widening with delight as she took in the completed fort. "Look at this! You three really built this?"

"We did!" Maya chirped proudly, her hands still covered in dirt from tying knots and digging out branches.

Maddox, unable to contain his excitement, added, "Bronte showed us how! And he told us all about how people long ago built forts like this when they first came to America!"

Monica, never one to be left out, jumped in. "Yeah! He said they had to make shelters with wood and canvas just like this to survive the winter!"

Francis raised an eyebrow, clearly impressed. "A history lesson and a fort-building project? Well, I'd say you've had quite the morning!"

The children nodded enthusiastically, their faces flushed with pride and excitement.

Francis clapped her hands together. "Alright, little builders, I actually came to tell you—it's lunchtime."

Immediately, a chorus of protests erupted:

"Can we eat in the fort, Francis?" Maya begged, her eyes wide with excitement.

"Please?" Maddox chimed in, clasping his hands together dramatically.

"Yeah! It can be our first meal in our new house!" Monica added, bouncing on her heels.

Francis laughed, holding up her hands. "Well, I suppose that can be arranged!"

The kids erupted in cheers, already imagining their picnic feast inside their masterpiece.

Francis turned to Bronte, her expression warm and full of gratitude. "I'll go up to the house and let Bethany know we need a 'lunch-to-go' special."

As she passed Bronte, she paused, her eyes soft with appreciation.

"Bronte," she said, her voice sincere, "thank you. This—what you did for them—it's special. You'd make a great teacher."

Bronte, clearly uncomfortable with the compliment, grunted, shifting his weight and scratching his beard.

"Not sure about that," he muttered, "I just like being outdoors. Figured they would too."

Francis gave him a knowing smile. "Well, maybe… but it seems to me, they're learning a whole lot more than just building forts."

Bronte didn't reply, but the corner of his mouth quirked up ever so slightly, and his eyes glinted with something that could almost be called… pride.

As Francis headed back toward the house, the children, still buzzing with excitement, began planning where they would sit inside the fort for their grand meal.

And Bronte, ever the gruff teacher-in-denial, stood back and watched them with a quiet satisfaction.

He hadn't set out to teach anything—

But somehow, he had given them a lesson they'd never forget.

23

Waverly sat comfortably in the council chamber, still feeling the gentle hum of energy from the chair beneath her. The glow of the crystal-lit walls cast a soft radiance over everything, and the air itself felt alive, pulsing in rhythm with the planet's energy.

Across from her, Councilor Aduralina spoke with a tone of quiet reverence, her emerald-hued robes shifting like flowing water as she moved.

Aduralina was one of the most knowledgeable council members regarding Arcmyrin's ecology, her connection to the natural world unparalleled even among the elders. Her deep green eyes held wisdom that seemed to stretch across centuries.

"Waverly Beaumont," she began, her voice soothing yet commanding, "it is essential that you understand the very essence of Arcmyrin. Not just its people, not just its history, but all the life that thrives here."

Waverly nodded, leaning forward slightly. "I'd love to learn."

Aduralina's lips curled into a small, knowing smile. "Then let us begin."

She gestured toward the holographic projection hovering in the center of the chamber. With a graceful motion of her hand, the image of Arcmyrin itself came to life.

Waverly watched, completely mesmerized, as the landscape unfolded before her.

Arcmyrin was unlike Earth in so many ways—yet, it pulsed with the same vibrancy, the same interconnected web of life.

"Our world," Aduralina began, "is nourished by two suns and two moons. They move in balance, creating a natural rhythm of day and night that differs from Earth's cycle."

Waverly's eyes followed the twin celestial bodies in the projection.

"The twin suns bathe our planet in constant energy—not just light, but nourishment. Unlike Earth's singular sun, ours do not burn as intensely. Their combined presence provides a gentle, steady warmth, ensuring that our flora never withers, our waters never freeze."

Waverly tilted her head, fascinated. "So… there are no extreme seasons?"

Aduralina nodded. "Correct. There is no winter, no scorching heat. The planet remains in eternal equilibrium, where growth never ceases."

She moved her hand, and the projection zoomed in on a lush forest teeming with bioluminescent trees and vines.

"Our forests," she continued, "are woven with energy, just as Tanzlora's are. Every tree, every plant, every river is connected to the planet's pulse."

Waverly watched as the holographic flora pulsed softly, as though breathing.

"The trees," Aduralina explained, "do not simply grow—they glow. Their roots intertwine beneath the soil, carrying energy much like Earth's mycelium networks. They share nutrients, strength, and even memory with one another."

Waverly's eyes widened. "Memory?"

Aduralina nodded. "Yes. When one tree thrives, the others thrive with it. When one is injured, the others adjust and heal. This is how we have sustained life for centuries—without war, without disease."

Waverly exhaled, taking it all in. A planet that grows in unity. A world that flourishes as one.

The projection shifted again, displaying rivers and ponds that shimmered with luminescent blues and silvers.

"Our water is not like Earth's," Aduralina continued. "It does not simply hydrate—it rejuvenates. It carries the essence of the land, allowing those who drink from it to heal faster, feel stronger."

Waverly stared at the glowing rivers. "Is that why Arcmyrians don't get sick?"

Aduralina gave a knowing nod. "Partly. Origin has blessed us with healing waters, healing lands, and knowledge of how to use them."

Waverly felt a pang in her chest, thinking about Earth's polluted rivers, its declining forests, its struggle to sustain its own people.

"We have never needed to develop modern medicine the way Earth has," Aduralina said. "We rely on what is already here. The plants, the minerals, the energy of the world itself."

She let those words settle before continuing.

"But that does not mean we cannot learn."

Aduralina turned to face Waverly fully now, her expression calm but intent.

"This is why we are interested in the alliance."

Waverly listened closely.

Aduralina continued. "Earth's biological and ecological systems intrigue us. Despite its struggles, despite its imbalance, your planet is abundant. You have species of plants we have never encountered. Your oceans teem with life we have never known."

She gestured, and the hologram changed, displaying images of Earth's vast rainforests, rolling meadows, and towering mountain ranges.

"We wish to understand your ecosystems," Aduralina said. "We wish to exchange knowledge—not just for the benefit of Arcmyrin, but for Earth as well. If your people learn what we have mastered... perhaps they can restore what has been lost."

Waverly's heart pounded.

This wasn't just about political alliances or trade agreements.

This was about life itself.

Aduralina's eyes softened slightly. "Tanzlora feels the same. We know this because we have always shared our knowledge with one another. But Earth is... different. Its people are disconnected from their own world. And that is what concerns us."

Waverly swallowed hard, nodding. "You're right. A lot of humans have forgotten how to live in balance with nature. That's something we have to fix."

Aduralina inclined her head. "And that is something we are willing to help you fix."

The hologram faded, leaving the chamber bathed in silence.

Waverly took a deep breath, feeling the weight of what had just been shared.

Arcmyrin didn't want Earth's political structure. They didn't want technology or power.

They wanted healing.

And they were willing to teach Earth how to do it.

Finally, she met Aduralina's gaze. "I'll make sure Earth understands this. I'll take this back with me, and I'll make sure they know that this alliance isn't just about diplomacy—it's about survival."

A small, approving smile touched Aduralina's lips.

"Then today, Waverly Beaumont, you have taken the first step toward something greater than politics. You have taken a step toward restoration."

Waverly smiled.

For the first time since she had arrived on Arcmyrin, she truly understood her role.

Elara quietly approached Rykas in the Arcmyrin council chamber, placing a gentle hand on his shoulder to catch his attention. "Rykas, may I speak with you outside for a moment?"

Rykas looked up, his calm expression briefly revealing mild curiosity. He nodded respectfully to the council elders and whispered softly to Waverly, "I'll be right back," before standing and following Elara toward the arched entrance of the grand chamber.

Once they had stepped into the quiet hallway, illuminated by the subtle, soothing glow from the crystalline walls, Rykas turned to Elara, concern evident in his eyes. "What is it, Elara? Is something wrong?"

Elara took a slow breath, carefully choosing her words. "I received troubling news from Ridge and Lincoln. While they were on Pluboria, Galen and Victoria warned them that Josephine—Waverly's great-aunt—is here on Arcmyrin. She is dangerous, Rykas. Apparently, she's capable of manipulating the elemental gifts for darkness, just as her brother Gideon did."

Rykas straightened abruptly, his jaw tightening. "Josephine? Here, on Arcmyrin?"

"Yes," Elara confirmed gravely. "She's been disguising herself, altering her appearance with earthen materials, making her extremely difficult to detect."

Rykas's eyes darkened suddenly with realization. "Elara, this morning in the gardens, a woman collided with Waverly. She disappeared immediately afterward. At the time, I was concerned but not enough to report it, but now..."

Elara's heart quickened at this revelation. "That must have been Josephine," she murmured, worry threading through her voice. "It's too great a coincidence."

"I agree," Rykas responded firmly, his eyes narrowing with determination. "We can't risk Waverly's safety. Have you informed the council yet?"

"No," Elara admitted. "But as soon as this session is over, I intend to speak with them. Ridge and Lincoln indicated that they want to come to Arcmyrin as quickly as possible to assist us. However, I'm beginning to think it might be wise to pause the presentations and send Waverly home immediately."

Rykas exhaled, conflicted but decisive. "I share your concerns. If Waverly returns to Sage Manor, my warriors and I could focus fully on locating Josephine. As much as it saddens me to halt the presentations—I know how important this alliance is—I can't justify risking Waverly's life."

Elara nodded gently, placing a reassuring hand on Rykas's arm. "I feel exactly the same. We must protect her at all costs. I'll speak to the elders, and I'm confident they'll agree."

With quiet resolve, they re-entered the council chambers. Inside, Waverly was attentively listening to Councilor Silastoria as he prepared his notes for the next portion of the presentation. Before he could begin, Elara politely stepped forward.

"Pardon me, Elders," she said respectfully. "Perhaps this would be an appropriate time for everyone to take a brief break and refresh themselves before continuing."

Councilor Releesia inclined her head graciously. "Very well. A short pause may benefit us all."

Elara gestured subtly to Rykas, who immediately stepped forward, gently placing his hand on Waverly's shoulder. "Allow me to escort you back to the pod, Waverly."

Waverly hesitated, slightly confused by the unexpected interruption, but she nodded in quiet acceptance. "Of course," she replied, standing gracefully.

As Rykas guided Waverly gently from the chamber, Elara exchanged a meaningful glance with the elders. Their expressions reflected trust, even as questions lingered in their eyes. They knew that she would soon reveal her reason for this pause.

Walking side by side with Rykas along the crystalline path toward the living pods, Waverly studied his thoughtful, guarded expression. "Rykas, what's going on? Why did Elara interrupt?"

Rykas carefully masked his tension with a calm smile. "It's simply a precaution, Waverly. Elara just wants to ensure that everything remains smooth and secure. We'll explain shortly."

Waverly nodded slowly, sensing his attempt to comfort her, but unable to shake the slight unease settling in her chest.

As they reached her pod, Rykas paused, gently placing a reassuring hand on her shoulder. "Rest for now, Waverly. Elara and I will handle everything else."

She looked up at him, grateful for his steady presence. "Thank you, Rykas. I'm glad you're here."

He offered a reassuring smile, determination sparking in his eyes. "You're safe with us. Remember that."

She nodded again, stepping inside as Rykas quietly took position near the entrance, keeping a watchful eye. Inwardly, his heart tightened with concern, knowing that Josephine's shadow loomed dangerously close. But he vowed silently, with unyielding resolve, that no harm would come to Waverly on his watch.

24

Lynx adjusted the strap of his satchel as he walked up the shimmering stone steps leading to the Tanzloran Elders' Chambers, the weight of the moment settling over him.

Beside him, the porcufera trotted along, its iridescent quills shimmering faintly in the warm Tanzloran air. It had followed him faithfully since reappearing in his quarters the night before, chirping and weaving around his feet as if it had never left his side.

Now, as they approached the ancient council hall, Lynx couldn't help but notice how the small creature's presence seemed to ripple through the space.

Two Tanzloran guards at the entrance straightened, their expressions shifting from neutral to outright shock the moment their eyes landed on the porcufera. One of them, a tall, broad-shouldered warrior, even took an instinctive step back.

Lynx frowned. "Everything okay?"

The guard hesitated before nodding slowly. "You… bring the porcufera to the Elders?"

Lynx glanced down at the small creature, which chirped and flicked its glowing quills before scampering forward into the grand chamber.

"Uh… yeah," Lynx said, rubbing the back of his neck. "That a problem?"

The guards exchanged uneasy glances before gesturing for him to proceed.

Something about the way they reacted put Lynx on edge, but he pushed the thought aside and stepped forward into the chamber.

The grand chambers of the Tanzloran Council stood serene and majestic, sunlight filtering softly through the intricate crystal windows, casting a gentle rainbow of colors across the polished stone floors.

Lynx entered the chamber, his footsteps soft but steady, the porcufera trotting happily at his side, its iridescent quills shimmering with every playful bounce.

As he approached the semi-circle of elders, he noticed their expressions—not of alarm, but of warm surprise.

Brakar, the head elder, leaned forward slightly, her violet eyes glinting with curiosity and approval. "Well, well," she said with a soft rumble, her voice laced with both wonder and understanding. "The porcufera has chosen to accompany you once more."

The other elders exchanged pleased glances, their reactions not of concern but of recognition. A rare occurrence, yes—but a welcome one.

It was Lumorith, the eldest among them, whose voice carried the wisdom of centuries, who spoke next. "This is no cause for concern," he said with a knowing smile, his eyes crinkling with warmth. "The porcufera has chosen you this time, Lynx Beaumont, not out of warning—but out of connection."

Lynx, feeling the warmth of the creature's presence, glanced down at the little companion. "Connection?" he asked, curious.

Brakar nodded. "The porcufera senses the heart of those it chooses to accompany. It is drawn to those of pure heart and pure intention. It does not always need to be a dangerous situation."

Another elder, Thaloria, added softly, "You have a light within you, Lynx. The porcufera recognizes this—your goodness, your sincerity. It walks with you not as a guardian, but as a friend."

Lynx felt a subtle warmth rise in his chest, a soft blush of humility and gratitude. "That's... quite the honor," he said quietly, looking down at the little creature, which chirped softly and flicked its quills playfully.

Brakar's expression grew thoughtful, and she folded her hands together. "But the porcufera's presence is not the only reason for your being here, Lynx."

Lynx straightened, sensing the shift in the conversation. "I had wondered," he said, "why I was called to return to Tanzlora."

Thaloria's eyes met his, filled with both kindness and gravity. "We summoned you, Lynx, because you are more than a messenger. You are a bridge."

Brakar continued, her voice rich with meaning. "You are here because we wish you to take something precious and true back to Earth's leaders. Not just an agreement, but our history—our heart, our hopes, and our truth."

Thaloria's voice, soft but powerful, carried through the chamber. "The people of Tanzlora desire only one thing from this alliance—a Triad united in peace, harmony, and balance."

Brakar nodded. "No treaties bound in complication. No greed. No power struggles. Only this: A community where Tanzlora, Arcmyrin, and Earth exist together—not in competition, but in understanding and mutual care."

Lynx felt the weight and beauty of their words settle deeply into his heart. "And you want me to bring this message back to Earth," he said, his voice firm with purpose.

Thaloria's smile softened, and she inclined her head. "Yes. Because we believe you will speak from the heart. And because the porcufera has chosen you, we know your heart is true."

Lynx's gaze swept across the council of elders, feeling their trust, their openness, and their hope.

He looked down at the porcufera, which chirped softly as if in encouragement.

Raising his head, he spoke with quiet conviction.

"You have my word," he said firmly. "I will take your history, your hopes, and your wishes for the Triad back to Earth's leaders. And I will speak with the truth and heart you've entrusted to me."

Brakar's eyes glimmered with pride. "Then, Lynx Beaumont... you are no longer just a visitor to Tanzlora. You are a part of it."

The elders bowed their heads as one in a gesture of respect and gratitude.

The porcufera chirped, rubbing against Lynx's leg, its quills flickering with soft, golden light.

And Lynx felt something settle within him—

Not a burden, but a calling.

Lynx had listened, absorbed, and processed more information than he had ever expected during his meeting with the Tanzloran elders. The depth of their knowledge, their connection to the planet, and their vision for the Triad's alliance had been nothing short of awe-inspiring.

Now, as he prepared to take his leave, something still nagged at the back of his mind.

A question that he needed answered before he returned to Earth.

He paused at the threshold of the council chambers, turning back toward the elders.

Brakar raised an eyebrow. "Is there something you wish to ask?"

Lynx hesitated for only a moment before stepping back toward the center of the room. "Yeah... there is. I need to understand more about the portal system."

A low murmur rippled through the elders, but there was no objection to his request.

Brakar nodded. "A wise question. But you will not find your answer with me."

She turned her gaze toward Draven, the Overseer of the Warriors and the Portal System.

Draven was an imposing figure, taller than most Tanzlorans, with piercing dark eyes that seemed to analyze everything at once. His hair, bound in warrior's braids, was streaked with the silver markings of his rank, and his deep green armor bore the intricate insignia of the planetary defense.

He stepped forward, his presence commanding yet composed.

"You wish to understand the portals?" Draven asked, his voice deep and steady.

Lynx nodded. "Yes. I've used them before. I know they work—but I don't fully understand how they work. Or why they're so essential to life here."

Draven folded his arms, his expression thoughtful.

"Unlike Earth," he began, "Tanzlora and Arcmyrin do not require roads, motorized vehicles, trains, or planes to move from place to place. A portal system is all that is needed."

Lynx listened intently as Draven continued.

"The portals are ancient," Draven explained. "They were not built by Tanzloran hands, nor by Arcmyrin's. They were created by Origin and have existed since the dawn of our civilizations. They are part of the natural energy flow of the planet—woven into its very essence."

Lynx frowned slightly. "I am not sure I fully understand."

Draven paused before continuing, trying to find a better way to explain. "They are planetary conduits, connected through the pulse of Tanzlora's energy fields. Every community, village, and settlement has a portal because they are extensions of the land itself. They do not pollute. They do not disrupt. They are as natural to this world as the rivers and trees."

Lynx exhaled, trying to wrap his mind around the idea.

"So, instead of building infrastructure like roads and vehicles," he said, "you just... step through a portal and arrive where you need to go?"

Draven nodded. "Precisely. Travel is instantaneous. There is no need for fossil fuels, mechanical engines, or transportation networks the way Earth requires."

Lynx could barely fathom it.

"No traffic," he muttered, shaking his head. "No fuel dependency. No pollution. Just... walking through energy pathways?"

Draven smirked slightly. "It is simpler than your world has chosen to make it."

Lynx blew out a low whistle. "That would change everything on Earth."

Draven's expression darkened slightly. "And that is why your world must be ready before such knowledge is shared."

Lynx's brow furrowed. "Why do you say that?"

Draven's gaze locked onto him, sharp and assessing.

"Because Earth does not yet understand balance. You consume, extract, and take, often without thought of consequence. If portal technology were given freely, would your leaders use it wisely? Or would they harness it for power and control?"

Lynx swallowed, feeling the weight of the question.

He couldn't deny the truth of Draven's words.

Earth had always taken advancements and turned them into competition, profit, and war.

Draven studied Lynx carefully before continuing.

"The portals do not only exist within our planets," Draven said. "They also connect Tanzlora and Arcmyrin."

Lynx nodded slowly. "So... Tanzlorans and Arcmyrins travel freely between the two planets?"

Draven exhaled. "Yes—but not always frequently. Our connection is not based on trade or necessity, but on friendship and knowledge. When Tanzlorans go to Arcmyrin, it is to learn, to teach, to share knowledge. The same is true for Arcmyrins who visit Tanzlora."

Lynx ran a hand through his hair. "So there's no... control over who goes where? No customs? No borders?"

Draven arched an eyebrow. "Borders?"

Lynx hesitated. "On Earth, we have divisions between lands, governments, and countries. You can't just... go wherever you want. There are rules. Restrictions. Passports. Politics."

Draven sighed. "That is the way of a world still in conflict with itself. Tanzlora and Arcmyrin do not have such barriers, because we trust one another. We do not seek to conquer, claim, or exploit. We only seek to share."

Lynx let out a slow breath.

It made sense.

Earth had divided itself for so long that the idea of a world without territorial restrictions seemed impossible. But here—on these planets—it was reality.

Draven crossed his arms once more. "Tanzlora and Arcmyrin have always been two halves of the same whole. The portals are a reflection of that—an unbroken connection that ensures we are never truly apart."

Lynx thought about the portals he had utilized, their shimmering lights swirling with a mixture of deep blues, silvers and a myriad of other colors.

The very thing Earth struggled to achieve—unity, sustainability, and trust—already existed here.

And now, it was his job to take this knowledge back.

To try and make Earth see what was possible.

Lynx turned back to Draven, nodding firmly. "Thank you. I understand now."

Draven's expression softened slightly. "Then you are ready to return home. Go with this knowledge, Lynx Beaumont—but be careful who you give it to. Some truths are meant to be earned, not taken."

Lynx felt the weight of those words settle in his chest.

He would be careful.

Because the fate of the Triad alliance—and perhaps Earth itself—depended on it.

25

R idge paced restlessly beside the oval table within the chamber beneath the gazebo, tension evident in his stiff movements and troubled eyes. Lincoln, seated but equally tense, repeatedly glanced toward the screens, waiting impatiently for Elara's holographic appearance.

Lincoln sighed sharply, breaking the heavy silence. "How long has it been? We should've heard something by now."

Ridge paused, turning to face his brother. "I know. This waiting is maddening. I can't help but wonder if they're taking this seriously enough."

A sudden ripple of gentle energy filled the chamber, quickly silencing their frustrations. On the screen nearest Lincoln, the graceful form of Mistara, Spirit of Water, appeared, her voice gentle but firm.

"*Your impatience betrays your trust, Lincoln. Ridge.*" Her voice carried softly but resonantly throughout the chamber. "*Have you forgotten all that you have learned alongside Elara and Rykas?*"

Terraveta, the wise Spirit of Earth, manifested beside Mistara, her eyes warm but unyielding. "*Your quick reactionary impatience arises from a deeper place—one of mistrust, fear, and uncertainty. It is this very consciousness within humanity that limits your people's growth and development.*"

Lincoln lowered his eyes, realizing the truth in her words. Ridge shifted uncomfortably, a flush of embarrassment creeping up his neck.

Mistara continued calmly, compassion filling her tone. "*Tell me, Ridge, Lincoln—do you not trust Elara and Rykas to protect Waverly? After all that you have faced together?*"

Lincoln hesitated, swallowing hard before speaking. "It's not that we don't trust them, it's just... the danger feels so close. It's difficult not knowing."

Terraveta nodded sympathetically. "*But remember, your bond with Arcmyrin and Tanzlora was forged through bravery, mutual sacrifice, and trust. Elara and Rykas fought side by side with you when the Umbralox threatened your world, just as you fought to protect theirs. Have they ever given you reason to doubt?*"

"No," Ridge replied quietly, shame softening his voice. "Never. They have always been true friends."

"*Precisely,*" Terraveta agreed. "*The Beaumont family has carried the mantle of trust and friendship across generations. Gideon and Josephine chose betrayal, but that is not the legacy your ancestors intended.*"

Mistara spoke again, her voice gentler now, offering wisdom and reassurance. "*Earth's leaders are looking to you, Lincoln and Ridge, to set the example. If you embody mistrust or impatience, they will follow suit. Your responsibility extends far beyond yourselves.*"

Both brothers fell silent, absorbing the profound weight of her words.

Finally, Lincoln looked up, humility in his expression. "You're right. We've allowed fear and uncertainty to cloud our judgment. It was never a lack of faith in our friends, only fear for Waverly."

Ridge stepped forward, meeting the spirits' gazes with sincerity. "We apologize. We understand now. Trust and patience must guide us. Our family's example must rise above doubt and fear."

Mistara smiled softly, her gentle energy radiating serenity. "*You see clearly now. Trust is not passive; it is courageous. It is rooted in the knowledge that those you rely upon share your same commitment.*"

Terraveta added, a reassuring tone entering her voice, "*All is not lost. You both have the power to restore balance, to demonstrate unwavering faith in your friends on Arcmyrin and Tanzlora. Humanity has great potential, and the alliance you seek can indeed become reality—when all parties embrace balance, harmony, and genuine trust.*"

Lincoln felt relief washing over him. "Thank you for reminding us. We'll not forget again."

Mistara inclined her head gracefully. *"You have taken an important step today."*

Terraveta's expression grew softer. *"And remember, your ancestors—Galen and Victoria—understood deeply what you are learning now. Trust was their greatest power."*

The chamber fell silent again as Mistara and Terraveta faded gently, leaving a lasting warmth behind. Lincoln looked across at Ridge, the weight on their shoulders lighter now, replaced by newfound clarity.

"I can't believe we let our fear take hold like that," Ridge murmured, shaking his head regretfully.

Lincoln rose from his chair, clasping his brother's shoulder warmly. "It happens, Ridge. But we won't make that mistake again."

Ridge smiled slightly, determination returning to his eyes. "No, we won't. From here forward, we trust our friends. Waverly is safe with them."

Lincoln nodded firmly. "Agreed. It's time we live the trust we preach."

Elara quietly stood before the Arcmyrin Council of Elders, sensing the elders' curious eyes upon her.

Councilor Releesia, sensing the gravity of Elara's expression, spoke gently. "Elara, you wished to address us urgently. What is it?"

Elara bowed her head respectfully. "Honored Elders, I bring troubling news from the Beaumont family on Earth. Ridge and Lincoln have returned from Pluboria, carrying an urgent warning regarding Waverly's safety."

The elders exchanged quick glances, their expressions growing immediately solemn.

"Please explain," said Milestree softly, leaning forward slightly.

Elara took a measured breath, her voice steady and clear. "Galen and Victoria revealed to the Beaumonts that Josephine—the sister of Gideon—is currently hiding here on Arcmyrin. Josephine possesses the gift of Earth, using it to manipulate and disguise herself. She is dangerously powerful, having embraced the darkness as her brother did."

Councilor Silastoria's eyes narrowed, clearly disturbed. "Josephine? Gideon's sister? Is she as dangerous as her brother was?"

Elara nodded gravely. "Yes. Perhaps even more so, because she has vengeance fueling her now. Elders, we believe Josephine specifically seeks revenge against Waverly."

Releesia's brow furrowed deeply. "Why target Waverly specifically?"

Elara hesitated slightly, her voice gentle yet direct. "Because Waverly was the one who destroyed Gideon—who went by the name Patereon while here on Arcmyrin. It was only through his destruction that we could eradicate the Abasimtrox. Now, Josephine seeks retribution for her brother's permanent removal from existence."

The chamber fell into tense silence. Each elder visibly absorbed this information, their faces reflecting varying degrees of concern and sorrow.

Ruliana leaned forward, shaking her head sadly. "Such bitterness only breeds darkness. We cannot allow Josephine's vengeance to threaten our alliance—or Waverly's safety."

Councilor Aduralina, who typically remained quiet during such discussions, spoke firmly. "We must make a swift and decisive choice. Protecting Waverly must be our priority, but capturing Josephine swiftly is equally urgent. Her presence here endangers all."

Milestree nodded slowly, deep in thought. "Increasing Waverly's protection here could drain resources vital to locating Josephine."

"Agreed," Ruliana said. "Our warriors' attention would be divided between protection and pursuit. This could weaken both efforts."

Releesia held up her hand gently, bringing order back to their discussion. "Then perhaps our wisest course is clear: we must return Waverly safely to Earth immediately. It removes the target from Josephine's grasp, giving our warriors space to focus entirely on finding her."

The elders nodded in consensus, quietly murmuring agreement.

Releesia turned calmly toward Elara. "Elara, inform the Beaumont family at once of our decision. Please prepare Waverly for her return home. Additionally, instruct Rykas to choose two of his most capable warriors to accompany her through the portal. We must not risk her safety."

Elara bowed deeply, grateful for their decisive wisdom. "I understand, Elders. Your guidance is wise, and I thank you."

Releesia offered a compassionate nod. "Our alliance with Earth and Tanzlora is vital, Elara. The Beaumonts have proven their courage and trustworthiness repeatedly. It is now our turn to protect and support them."

With a respectful bow, Elara withdrew quietly from the council chambers, her heart heavy with responsibility yet encouraged by the elders' clear and compassionate decision. She hurried toward the pods, knowing that Waverly must be prepared swiftly, and that the Beaumonts needed reassurance of their daughter's imminent return.

26

The afternoon sky over Arcmyrin was beautiful soft hues of lavender and amber, calming Elara as she walked to Waverly's living pod. The pod's door opened softly, and Elara stepped in, her serene presence instantly filling the room.

Waverly sat comfortably at the table with Rykas, both quietly sharing a meal of freshly gathered vegetables, fruits, and warm grain-like bread. The aromas filled the small, cozy pod, making the atmosphere feel inviting and peaceful after the intensity of the morning's events.

Waverly smiled warmly, relieved to see her friend.

"Elara, come join us," Waverly said, gesturing toward the small table where an extra place setting waited. "Rykas and I fixed enough food for you, hoping you'd join us."

Elara inclined her head graciously, returning Waverly's smile. "Thank you both. It is greatly appreciated."

As Elara moved gracefully across the room to gather her plate, she spoke gently but urgently. "Waverly, Rykas—I've just met with the elders about an urgent matter. There's been a development."

Waverly paused mid-bite, exchanging a quick glance with Rykas, whose body had instantly tensed. "What happened?" she asked softly, setting down her utensil.

"Lincoln and Ridge have been in contact," Elara continued calmly, filling her plate thoughtfully. "They brought news from Pluboria—disturbing news regarding your safety."

Waverly felt a sudden tightness in her chest, her meal now forgotten. "What kind of news?"

Elara turned toward them, her expression gentle yet serious. "The elders and I have learned that Josephine, Gideon's sister, is here on Arcmyrin. Lincoln and Ridge were informed on Pluboria that Josephine is dangerous and we believe that she seeks revenge against you specifically, Waverly, for Gideon's death."

Rykas straightened immediately, a protective edge sharpening his eyes. "We also believe it was Josephine that caused the incident in the gardens earlier."

Waverly shuddered, memories flooding back. "The woman who bumped into me?"

Elara nodded slowly, concern etched across her face. "It is very likely that woman was Josephine herself. Lincoln and Ridge urgently requested that we increase your protection or return you to Earth immediately. After lengthy discussion, the elders agree: It is safest to send you home."

Waverly stared blankly, her heart heavy with a confusing mix of fear and frustration. "But—but the alliance discussions—"

Elara offered a reassuring smile, stepping closer to gently touch Waverly's shoulder. "Your safety is far more important. The elders deeply value your presence, but not at such risk."

Rykas nodded firmly. "Your well-being is our highest priority, Waverly."

Waverly released a shaky breath, feeling both relief and disappointment. "All right. If the elders believe this is best, I trust their decision. When do I leave?"

"As soon as possible," Elara replied gently. "Rykas and two trusted warriors will escort you through the portal personally."

Waverly nodded quietly, trying to absorb the sudden shift in her journey. Her eyes drifted back to her meal, now feeling completely drained of her appetite.

Elara gently moved toward the basket holding the remaining food, intending to fill her plate and join them. But as she reached out, her hand froze midair, her body abruptly rigid.

Her eyes widened, her golden gaze locked upon a small object partially hidden in the basket—a pendant dangling over its edge.

"Waverly," Elara whispered, her voice strained and wary. "Where did you get this pendant?"

Waverly followed Elara's gaze, "I found it in my basket after that woman collided with me in the gardens. I was planning to return it to her if I saw her again. But, now—"

"Do not touch it," Elara warned quickly, stepping back cautiously. "That pendant carries malevolent energy. I've seen it before—Lincoln showed it to me during our communications in the gazebo's chamber. Josephine likely planted it, hoping it would harm or corrupt you."

Rykas immediately stood, his hand reflexively moving toward his weapon. "How could we have missed this?" he muttered, frustrated.

Waverly stood up quickly, stepping away from the basket. "I—I didn't realize. I would have never—"

"We know," Elara reassured her gently. "Josephine is cunning. She knew precisely what she was doing. But it didn't harm you—your own pure energy shielded you."

Waverly exhaled, feeling slightly reassured but still shaken. "What do we do with it?"

"The elders are aware," Elara assured her. "They'll destroy the pendant safely. We must not touch it ourselves."

Rykas stepped protectively closer to Waverly. "Then we should move quickly. The sooner Waverly returns to Earth, the safer she'll be."

Elara nodded. "Agreed. Gather your belongings swiftly. We must move quickly now."

Waverly nodded resolutely, grabbing her small satchel and carefully placing a few items inside, her hands trembling slightly. Rykas watched protectively, his expression fiercely determined. "I will personally ensure you safely reach Sage Manor."

"Thank you, Rykas," Waverly whispered gratefully.

Elara moved gracefully to Waverly's side, gently squeezing her hand. "Everything will be alright, Waverly. Your family awaits your safe return."

With that reassurance, they hurried out of the pod, the presence of danger heightening their urgency. Elara stayed a step behind, alert and vigilant, her mind racing with protective plans and silent prayers.

As the trio moved swiftly toward the portal chamber, Elara silently vowed she would do everything within her power to shield Waverly, the alliance, and the peace of their worlds from Josephine's dark ambitions.

Following their leisurely lunch, Celia and Lorinda found themselves at the entrance to Blair House's main hall, where they were greeted warmly by a woman whose gentle presence and meticulous attention to detail immediately put them at ease.

"Good afternoon, ladies," she said kindly, her hands clasped together gently. "I'm Margaret Alston, Chief Curator here at Blair House. I look after all the historical artifacts and ensure their preservation."

Celia's face lit with delight, her curiosity piqued. "It's a pleasure, Margaret. Lorinda and I are fascinated by history, especially when presented firsthand."

Margaret smiled warmly, clearly pleased. "Then you're in for a treat."

She began guiding them gracefully through the elegantly furnished corridors, each step revealing new treasures and stories from the past. They admired exquisite portraits, gleaming chandeliers, antique furniture dating back centuries, and original paintings whose colors had been carefully preserved.

"How do you keep everything so pristine?" Lorinda asked, clearly impressed as she studied a beautifully carved mahogany table.

Margaret's eyes sparkled with enthusiasm. "Each piece requires very specialized care. We maintain strict climate controls, regular restorations, and, of course, gentle handling. Our job is to preserve history so that future generations can appreciate and understand the heritage of our nation."

Celia nodded appreciatively. "What a wonderful responsibility. You must be very proud."

Margaret smiled modestly. "I am indeed. History should be cherished, not forgotten."

After exploring several grand rooms, Margaret gestured gently toward a set of glass doors overlooking a verdant landscape beyond. "Would you like to see the gardens? They're especially lovely at this time of day."

"Oh, yes, please!" Lorinda said eagerly. "I've been waiting for that."

Margaret chuckled softly, leading them out into the expansive garden, where vibrant blooms were expertly arranged along manicured paths. Lush greenery surrounded them, interspersed with delicate fountains whose trickling waters enhanced the peaceful atmosphere.

Two gardeners worked carefully nearby, gently pruning rose bushes and examining flower beds. One, a middle-aged woman with a friendly face, looked up and smiled warmly as the trio approached.

"Afternoon, Margaret," she called softly. "Who do we have here?"

Margaret introduced them warmly. "This is Mrs. Celia Beaumont and Ms. Lorinda Rooney. They're guests from North Carolina and very interested in our historic gardens. Ladies, this is Helen, our head gardener, and Timothy, her assistant."

"It's wonderful to meet you," Lorinda greeted warmly, admiring the meticulous precision of their work.

Celia stepped closer, gently touching a nearby bloom. "This garden is extraordinary. How long have you worked here, Helen?"

Helen smiled proudly. "Going on fifteen years now. It's quite special. Many First Families have enjoyed this very garden."

Timothy nodded earnestly, his enthusiasm shining. "And we're especially proud of maintaining varieties planted decades ago—some even dating back to when President Truman stayed here."

Celia's eyes widened with interest. "That's remarkable. Do you use heirloom plants exclusively, or mix in newer varieties?"

Helen carefully set down her pruning shears, happy to engage further. "Primarily heirloom, to respect the historical integrity, but occasionally we'll introduce new varieties chosen specifically for their compatibility with the existing garden."

"Fascinating," Lorinda said thoughtfully. "What about maintenance? Is it particularly challenging to keep the gardens so pristine?"

Timothy chuckled softly. "Sometimes. But it's worth every bit of effort. The trick is to care consistently, season to season. Nature responds to patience and attention, much like preserving history indoors."

Margaret nodded approvingly. "Helen and Timothy are invaluable here. Their passion and knowledge ensure this garden remains a living artifact."

Celia glanced warmly at Lorinda, admiration clear on her face. "It certainly feels that way. It's rare to experience a place where history feels alive both inside and outside."

Helen smiled gratefully, her eyes shining with pride. "That's exactly our goal. We believe history shouldn't feel distant—it should be alive, accessible."

After thanking Helen and Timothy warmly, Margaret led Celia and Lorinda along a shaded pathway lined with blooming lilacs, their fragrance drifting gently around them.

"Thank you so much for sharing all of this with us," Celia said, turning to Margaret with genuine appreciation. "I feel I've learned so much today—not just about Blair House, but about the dedication required to preserve history."

Margaret smiled warmly. "It's truly been my pleasure. I'm delighted that you appreciate it as deeply as we do."

Lorinda squeezed Celia's arm gently, gazing around the garden one last time, savoring its beauty. "This has been a wonderful escape from everything else going on."

Margaret inclined her head gently, her expression understanding. "I'm glad we could provide a moment of peace for you. History has a way of offering comfort and clarity, especially during challenging times."

As they moved back toward Blair House, Celia paused thoughtfully, turning back to Margaret with a gentle smile. "You've done a remarkable job here, Margaret. Thank you again for giving us this experience. I'll remember it fondly."

Margaret's eyes warmed, clearly touched by the sincerity of Celia's words. "That means a great deal, Mrs. Beaumont. Thank you."

Arm in arm, Celia and Lorinda slowly made their way back into the historic home, hearts lighter from the beauty they'd just experienced. They both felt a renewed sense of peace—and perhaps a fresh perspective on their mission ahead.

27

Inside the chamber beneath the gazebo, Lincoln paced back and forth, occasionally casting anxious glances at Ridge, who sat quietly at the oval table, his eyes fixed expectantly on the softly humming screens. They had been patiently awaiting word from Arcmyrin for what felt like hours, nerves worn thin by the weight of uncertainty.

Suddenly, the gentle hum intensified. The screen in front of them began shimmering faintly, and Elara's graceful figure materialized in holographic form, her golden eyes serene but serious.

"Lincoln, Ridge," she spoke, her voice clear and calming, "I come with news from the elders."

Lincoln stopped pacing immediately, stepping closer to the table, visibly bracing himself. "Is Waverly safe, Elara?"

A gentle smile softened Elara's features. "Yes, Waverly is safe. But after careful consideration, the Arcmyrin elders has decided it's best for her to return to Sage Manor immediately. We can better protect her by removing her from Josephine's reach."

Relief flooded Lincoln's face, his shoulders relaxing noticeably. "Thank goodness," he murmured.

Ridge rose from his chair, nodding firmly in agreement. "We completely trust the elders' decision. How soon will she arrive?"

"Very soon," Elara answered reassuringly. "Rykas and two of our most trusted warriors will personally escort her. We will begin preparations now, so please ready yourselves to welcome them."

Lincoln's eyes shone with gratitude and relief. "Elara, we can't thank you enough for everything you've done—for protecting Waverly and always standing by our family. Please, pass along our sincere gratitude to the elders."

Elara inclined her head gracefully, sincerity glowing in her gaze. "Your family is our family, Lincoln. Arcmyrin and Tanzlora stand with the Beaumonts, now and always."

The brothers exchanged appreciative looks, moved by her words.

"We'll be waiting," Ridge assured her. "On the front porch, ready to greet them."

Elara smiled warmly. "Then I shall see to it. We will begin the journey immediately." With a gentle nod, her image gradually faded from the screen, the soft humming quieting back to its usual soothing tone.

On Arcmyrin, Elara turned gracefully, stepping towards the chamber entrance where Waverly, Rykas, and two warriors stood ready. She handed each of them a small vial filled with a shimmering herbal mixture. "Drink, quickly now. It will aid you during the journey."

Waverly nodded quietly, taking the vial from Elara's gentle hand. She glanced briefly at Rykas, feeling comforted by his calm strength. Silently, they all drank their mixtures.

"Good," Elara said softly, smiling warmly at Waverly. "Step into the portal without fear. You'll be home soon."

Waverly smiled gratefully. "Thank you, Elara."

Elara nodded, placing a reassuring hand briefly on Waverly's shoulder. "Go safely, dear one."

Rykas moved protectively beside Waverly as the portal began glowing brightly before them, its crystalline energy swirling gracefully. "We should move," he advised gently, stepping forward into the brilliance. Waverly and the two warriors quickly followed, enveloped instantly by the portal's warm, gentle embrace.

At Sage Manor, Ridge and Lincoln waited anxiously on the manor's expansive porch, eyes trained expectantly toward the distant gazebo and pond. Marshall and Bronte had joined them, hearts filled with anticipation and hope.

Suddenly, a vibrant burst of golden-white light erupted near the gazebo, the soft hum carrying across the grounds. Figures emerged from the brilliance, stepping carefully onto the lush grass.

Waverly stood for a brief second, looking around at the familiar comforting sight of home. Her heart surged with emotion and relief as she spotted her family on the porch. Without hesitation, she started running swiftly across the lawn.

Lincoln hurried down the steps, meeting her halfway. They collided in a heartfelt embrace, Lincoln lifting her slightly from the ground as tears of relief blurred his eyes. "Waverly," he breathed into her hair, "thank goodness you're safe."

"I'm okay, Dad," she whispered, hugging him tightly. "I'm home."

Ridge stood close by, emotion evident in his eyes. As Lincoln released her, Ridge stepped forward, enveloping Waverly in a warm, comforting hug. "You had us all worried, kiddo," he teased gently.

"Sorry, I had no idea," she replied softly, feeling grateful for their comforting strength. "But now that I do, I'm glad to be home."

Nearby, Rykas and his warriors stood respectfully, quietly observing the emotional reunion. As Ridge and Waverly released their embrace, Lincoln turned immediately toward Rykas, stepping forward and clasping his hand firmly. "Rykas, thank you for protecting my daughter. You have my deepest gratitude."

Rykas inclined his head humbly. "You're most welcome, Lincoln. It was my honor. But I must return swiftly to Arcmyrin. Josephine remains a threat, and we must find her."

Lincoln nodded, understanding the urgency. "Please be careful. We're here if you need us."

"Thank you," Rykas responded sincerely, stepping toward Waverly. The brief moment that passed between them was subtle, yet full of meaning. He gently took her hand, meeting her gaze directly. "Take care, Waverly."

Her voice softened. "You too, Rykas. Please be safe."

Their shared look lingered just a heartbeat longer than normal. Ridge, observing closely, raised a curious eyebrow at this brief exchange, sensing more to their friendship than possibly they even realized, yet wisely choosing to remain silent.

With a final, reassuring nod, Rykas reluctantly let go of Waverly's hand and stepped back to his warriors, giving the signal to depart. Within moments, they disappeared toward the portal, leaving the Beaumont family standing quietly on the lawn.

Lincoln wrapped a gentle arm around Waverly, guiding her toward the manor. "Let's get you inside, sweetheart. I know your mom and siblings can't wait to see you."

As they moved slowly toward the warmth and safety of Sage Manor, Waverly glanced back briefly toward the gazebo, gratitude filling her heart.

The brilliant Tanzloran suns shone softly through emerald-hued leaves, casting intricate patterns of shadow and light upon the smooth stone pathways winding gracefully toward the Reficiat Haven. Keelee and Lynx walked side by side, the porcufera trotting contentedly between them, occasionally chirping softly as if joining their conversation.

Keelee turned a gentle smile toward Lynx. "You handled yourself admirably in the council session today. The Elders were very impressed."

Lynx felt warmth spread through him at the praise, though he couldn't fully suppress his lingering curiosity. "There's so much I still want to understand," he admitted openly. "But some of the questions didn't seem right to ask in front of everyone."

Keelee nodded knowingly. "Wisdom often grows best in quiet moments shared between a few. There will be other opportunities for—"

A voice interrupted him, smooth and cheerful, from the pathway ahead. "Perhaps one of those opportunities might be now?"

Both Lynx and Keelee looked up, slightly startled to see Sylvaris approaching with a welcoming smile, his golden robes flowing behind him in the gentle breeze.

Sylvaris paused a respectful distance away, offering a slight bow of greeting. "Keelee, Lynx, pardon the interruption. But I overheard your conversation, and I thought perhaps Lynx might appreciate a less formal environment to continue our discussions."

Keelee regarded Sylvaris thoughtfully, then turned toward Lynx with an encouraging expression. "It's your choice, Lynx. Sylvaris is a respected elder; an informal conversation with him could provide valuable insight."

Lynx hesitated, but Sylvaris spoke again, warmly reassuring. "Lumorith will also be joining us. He is quite eager to speak with you further about Tanzlora, as well as your own home on Earth. We sense you have many questions, Lynx—questions easier asked over a comfortable meal."

Lynx glanced down at the porcufera, which chirped brightly. He looked back at Keelee, nodding slowly. "I'd be honored to accept, Sylvaris."

Keelee smiled gently, placing a reassuring hand briefly on Lynx's shoulder. "Very good, Lynx. I'll inform Sanodia so she doesn't prepare your midday meal—or the porcufera's."

Sylvaris's expression shifted slightly, briefly calculating before returning to its usual warmth. "Ah, yes. Of course, the porcufera—I nearly forgot. Don't worry; I have something appropriate for it."

Keelee nodded approvingly. "Very thoughtful, Sylvaris. Lynx, I'll see you again this evening. Enjoy your time."

As Keelee gracefully walked away, Lynx turned fully toward Sylvaris, feeling a bit nervous but reassured by the Elder's calm confidence.

28

"Come," Sylvaris said gently, gesturing toward the nearby dwelling. "Lumorith is already waiting for us. He's been quite eager to speak with you."

Lynx followed closely, the porcufera padding happily at his side. Sylvaris led him through winding pathways bordered by vividly colored blooms that perfumed the air sweetly. They soon approached Sylvaris's elegant home, its walls entwined with delicate flowering vines that shimmered slightly in the sun.

Lumorith stood waiting at the doorway, his smile broad and genuine. "Welcome, Lynx!" he greeted warmly, stepping forward. "It's wonderful you could join us. Sylvaris and I greatly value the chance to discuss more openly."

"Thank you," Lynx responded gratefully. "I've been looking forward to learning more."

Lumorith ushered them inside, where a cozy dining area awaited, filled with tantalizing aromas of fresh herbs, fruits, and baked grainbreads. The porcufera settled comfortably beside Lynx, softly humming with contentment.

As Sylvaris busied himself briefly at the far counter, Lumorith leaned forward, his expression openly curious. "I confess, Lynx, I find Earth's complexity fascinating. And I believe there's much our planets can learn from each other."

"I agree," Lynx said eagerly, relaxing into his chair. "Tanzlora's harmony with nature feels deeply special to me—so different from Earth."

Sylvaris approached quietly, setting out plates of food and pouring shimmering blue juice into their glasses. He placed a small dish of brightly colored fruits in front of the porcufera, who immediately began nibbling contentedly.

"Exactly," Sylvaris interjected, seating himself comfortably. "Your observations are insightful, Lynx. Earth has developed many technologies to compensate for its distance from nature. Tanzlora chose a different path. We are eager to understand how we might harmonize these two approaches for mutual benefit."

Lynx considered this carefully, thoughtfully choosing his next words. "On Earth, technology can sometimes overshadow our respect for nature. But our cultures have also thrived in other ways—art, music, history."

Lumorith nodded with genuine enthusiasm. "Precisely why we desire an open exchange. Knowledge shared freely strengthens bonds, fosters understanding, and perhaps can heal wounds we didn't even realize were there."

Sylvaris offered a smile, but there was an edge to it—so subtle that Lynx nearly missed it. "And such healing is vital, wouldn't you agree?"

Lynx felt a slight flutter of unease but quickly dismissed it. "Of course. Trust, openness, understanding—they're essential."

"Indeed," Sylvaris agreed, raising his glass. "Then let us enjoy this meal together, building that trust among us."

Lumorith raised his glass in agreement, and Lynx did likewise, smiling warmly. As they ate, Lynx found himself relaxing, engaged in genuine and deep conversation, asking questions he hadn't dared voice earlier and receiving thoughtful responses in return.

Yet, beneath the ease of conversation, Lynx could not entirely shake an intuitive whisper, a gentle warning that something unseen lurked behind Sylvaris's friendly eyes.

The porcufera, seemingly sensing Lynx's subtle tension, briefly pressed against his leg reassuringly. Lynx relaxed again, pushing aside any lingering doubts. The conversation was productive, illuminating, and he was grateful for the insights.

Sylvaris leaned back in his chair with a friendly smile. "I believe this delightful conversation deserves an equally delightful ending," he said, his tone smooth and inviting. "Would you two be willing to try the most delicious sweet dish I have ever tasted?"

Lynx exchanged a quick glance with Lumorith, whose expression brightened eagerly. "Certainly," Lumorith replied warmly. "Your hospitality is most generous."

Sylvaris stood up, his robes flowing gracefully behind him. "Excellent. The village woman who helps me prepare my meals created it, and honestly, I can't get enough of it." He stepped away toward the kitchen, leaving Lynx and Lumorith in relaxed silence.

A few moments later, Sylvaris returned, expertly balancing three delicate plates filled with golden-hued treats. In his other hand, he held a small bowl for the porcufera, carefully placing each item down on the table.

"I inquired about the ingredients," Sylvaris said reassuringly as he sat down, catching Lynx's questioning glance toward the bowl placed before the porcufera. "My cook assured me it was absolutely safe for our spiked friend to enjoy."

Lynx nodded appreciatively. "Thank you. I know it'll enjoy it."

The porcufera chirped curiously, sniffing the bowl enthusiastically before starting to nibble eagerly. Lynx lifted his spoon, scooping a small portion of the dessert into his mouth. The texture was silky, the sweetness perfectly balanced. Lumorith seemed equally impressed, offering Sylvaris a sincere nod of approval.

"This truly is exceptional," Lumorith praised, savoring another bite.

Sylvaris's smile deepened slightly. "I knew you'd find it remarkable."

As Lynx ate, a subtle heaviness gradually began to settle over him. At first, he attributed it to the rich sweetness of the dessert or perhaps his long day of intense conversations, but the heaviness intensified. His vision blurred slightly, and he struggled to keep his eyelids from drooping.

He glanced at Lumorith, noticing with rising alarm that the elder appeared equally affected, blinking slowly and slumping slightly in his seat.

"Sylvaris?" Lynx murmured sluggishly, his words slow and thick. "I... feel strange..."

Sylvaris made no move to respond. Instead, he calmly sat back, observing them closely, his eyes now devoid of warmth or kindness.

Lynx fought against the encroaching darkness, panic rising faintly beneath his exhaustion. His eyes dropped downward, landing on the porcufera. His heart sank as he saw it lying on its back, tiny paws lifted helplessly in the air, unmoving.

"No," Lynx managed weakly, his head swaying. "Sylvaris...what have...?"

But his words faltered as he saw Lumorith slowly tilt sideways, his entire body falling from the chair as though in a surreal, slow-motion scene. Lynx struggled to stay conscious, desperate to fight against the betrayal, but it was no use. The room spun gently, his vision dimming further as his limbs grew impossibly heavy.

The last thing Lynx saw before succumbing completely to unconsciousness was Sylvaris leaning forward slightly, his expression shifting into something darkly triumphant.

Late-afternoon sunlight streamed through the windows of Blair House, bathing the historic rooms in a soft, inviting glow. Celia and Lorinda sat comfortably in a cozy sitting area, sipping tea, when Lorinda glanced at the ornate clock above the fireplace.

"Celia," Lorinda began, setting down her cup, "we've got a few hours to spare before dinner. Maybe we could check out one or two of the bridal shops from Mrs. Houston's list—at least the ones closest to us?"

Celia's face brightened immediately. "Oh, I love that idea! There's no sense in wasting the afternoon just sitting here."

Lorinda grinned, rising quickly and retrieving the list from her handbag. "I'll go find our drivers."

They stepped outside to find their two assigned drivers leaning casually near the black SUV, chatting quietly. As the women approached, the men straightened immediately, polite smiles on their faces.

"Excuse me," Lorinda said warmly, "we wondered if it would be possible for you to take us to a couple of nearby bridal shops? We've got a little free time before dinner."

The lead driver smiled amiably, giving a small nod. "Of course, Ms. Rooney. Wherever you'd like to go."

Minutes later, Lorinda and Celia were settled comfortably in the SUV, heading smoothly toward the first bridal boutique. As the vehicle pulled up to a chic-looking storefront, Lorinda's excitement grew—until she stepped inside.

She froze briefly, blinking in shock at the elegant showroom filled with breathtaking gowns shimmering beneath tasteful lighting. Taking a hesitant step forward, she reached out to glance at a price tag and immediately recoiled, her eyes wide.

"Oh my word, Celia," Lorinda whispered urgently. "Have you seen the prices on these dresses?"

Celia chuckled softly, joining Lorinda at the rack. "Lorinda, dear, when's the last time you actually went shopping for clothes?"

Lorinda sighed sheepishly, shaking her head. "It's been a while. You know I wear scrubs most of the time, and everything Monica and I wear on weekends comes from the big department stores—usually at bargain prices. But..." She paused thoughtfully. "I did visit one of the boutiques in downtown Galen Valley a few months ago, when my mother came to visit. I remember thinking how expensive everything was there, too. We looked, admired, then promptly left empty-handed."

Celia smiled knowingly. "Which shop was it?"

"Valley Vogue," Lorinda replied with a rueful smile. "They have gorgeous clothes, but honestly, who can afford those prices? And who can afford these bridal gowns?" She lifted another tag briefly and winced visibly. "Certainly not me—not on a single mom's nursing salary."

Celia gently squeezed Lorinda's arm, smiling knowingly. "You do know that the sheriff's wife, Kathryn Bowen, owns that shop, right?"

Lorinda's eyebrows rose in surprise. "No, I had no idea."

"Oh yes," Celia continued, eyes sparkling. "Kathryn is originally from New York City. Before she met and married Marshall and moved to Galen Valley, she was deeply embedded in the fashion world."

"Whoa," Lorinda responded, amazed. "I can only imagine her culture shock, going from the big city to our little town."

"Yes," Celia said with a nod. "Which is probably why Marshall put three mortgages on his house to help her start her boutique. But she's been very successful with it. It's been open for years now. Kathryn graduated from the Fashion Institute of Technology in New York City and worked as an intern at Vogue before becoming one of the lead buyers at Bergdorf Goodman."

Lorinda's eyes widened with newfound admiration. "That's impressive!"

"Marshall said she cried for days when she turned in her notice," Celia explained gently, her voice filled with sympathy. "It broke his heart to have her give up all she had worked for to move for him. But, I suppose love wins out in all things, and he made sure she still kept herself involved in fashion."

Lorinda shook her head with a soft smile. "What a good man our sheriff is, Celia. I had no idea about any of this. You really are just a walking history book of Galen Valley."

Celia laughed warmly, gently guiding Lorinda toward the fitting rooms. "Come on, let's try some dresses on you."

"But Celia," Lorinda protested, eyes widening with panic again, "I can't afford these dresses!"

"Don't worry about the money," Celia said reassuringly, her tone confident and serene. "I have a feeling things will be taken care of."

Lorinda paused, giving Celia a puzzled, slightly suspicious look. "What exactly does that mean?"

Celia just smiled mysteriously, gently pushing Lorinda forward. "Trust me, Lorinda. Let's just enjoy ourselves. You're only a bride once!"

Lorinda smiled tentatively, allowing herself to relax slightly under Celia's warm guidance. Still uncertain, but buoyed by Celia's calm confidence, she allowed herself to imagine the possibilities, trusting that somehow things really might work out.

29

Rykas stepped swiftly through the glowing portal, his warriors trailing just behind him. They headed directly to the Arcmyrin council chambers. Without pause, he crossed the expansive hall, his golden eyes scanning the room and landing immediately upon Elara, who was standing beside Lunarcher and Milestree, deep in conversation.

Elara turned quickly at his approach, relief clear in her gaze as she stepped forward to greet him.

"Waverly?" she asked immediately, concern evident.

Rykas nodded reassuringly. "She's safe at Sage Manor, Elara. Lincoln and Ridge are with her, as is the rest of the family. She will be protected there."

Elara exhaled a quiet breath of relief. "Good. That is one burden lifted."

Milestree and Lunarcher stepped closer, their expressions serious yet relieved by Rykas's news.

"However," Rykas continued gravely, "we must now direct our focus toward finding Josephine. The warriors must immediately spread out across the villages and begin searching—particularly keeping watch on anyone who has shown themselves to be a loner or an outlier in their community."

Lunarcher exchanged a quick, troubled glance with Milestree, then turned solemnly back to Rykas.

"There's been a development, Rykas," Lunarcher began carefully. "As soon as you departed for Earth, we implemented exactly the strategy you've outlined. The warriors began searching the villages immediately, and within moments, we received alarming news."

Rykas narrowed his gaze sharply, instantly alert. "What kind of news?"

Milestree took a step forward, his voice tense with worry. "One of our villagers—a healer from Eldavia—reported seeing a woman, someone who'd always been considered rather strange, running hastily through one of our secondary portals to Tanzlora."

Rykas stiffened, momentarily stunned. "Josephine? You think she's escaped to Tanzlora?"

Milestree nodded gravely. "It's possible. Likely, even. I've been attempting to contact Lumorith on Tanzlora to verify this, but..." He hesitated, visibly troubled. "He hasn't responded to my summons."

An icy dread settled in the pit of Rykas's stomach. "Lumorith hasn't answered?"

"Not yet," Milestree confirmed, clearly disturbed. "I planned to give him a few more moments, and if he still doesn't respond, I intend to summon Brakar immediately. This situation has become too perilous to delay further."

Realization struck Rykas sharply, dread turning to urgency. "Lynx is on Tanzlora," he said firmly, voice edged with alarm. "If Josephine truly made it there, he could be in danger. We cannot wait."

Elara paled, instantly understanding the gravity of the situation. "Lynx! I'd nearly forgotten—he's still there, under Keelee's care."

She turned quickly to Lunarcher and Milestree. "I agree with Rykas. We cannot risk waiting even another moment. Summon Brakar now. Immediately."

Lunarcher exchanged a swift look with Milestree, who nodded firmly. "We'll go at once," Lunarcher said decisively. "Brakar and the Tanzloran council must be warned immediately."

As Lunarcher and Milestree hurried from the chamber, Elara quickly turned back toward Rykas, her expression grave yet determined. "I must inform Keelee. He might be with Lynx right now, and they have no idea Josephine could be among them."

Rykas nodded sharply, his gaze intense and focused. "Good idea, Elara. Reach him as soon as possible. Warn him. Lynx's safety could depend upon it."

Without another word, Elara swiftly moved to activate the communication portal to Tanzlora, her fingers trembling slightly with urgency. Rykas watched intently, tension radiating from his poised figure as the chambers filled with the hum of energy. He could feel the clock ticking down, each second now critical.

The quiet calm that normally permeated the Arcmyrin council chambers had vanished, replaced instead by an unyielding sense of urgency and danger.

Elara quickly moved to the chamber's communication screen, her graceful fingers swiftly activating the holographic link to Keelee. Within seconds, Keelee's serene form appeared, his expression calm and attentive.

"Elara," Keelee greeted warmly, sensing the urgency in her posture. "What news from Arcmyrin?"

"Keelee," Elara began quickly, her voice tight with anxiety, "there's been a serious development—too much to tell right now but Josephine, long lost Beaumont sister and dangerous like her brother Gideon, may have used the portal system and is believed to be on Tanzlora. We have been attempting to contact Lumorith, but he's not responding. We are very concerned about Lynx's safety."

Keelee, familiar with both of those names and their negative connotations, raised his hand soothingly, offering immediate reassurance. "Elara, you need not fear. Lynx is quite safe. In fact, he's here at the Reficiat Haven—or was moments ago. He's currently with Sylvaris and Lumorith, enjoying a midday meal and discussing Tanzloran history in Sylvaris's home."

Elara visibly exhaled, tension easing from her shoulders. "Oh, that's a relief to hear."

"Yes," Keelee continued, smiling gently. "They're having quite a friendly discussion. Lumorith himself was looking forward to speaking informally with Lynx, and Sylvaris kindly offered to host."

Elara nodded slowly, feeling reassurance spread through her. She turned toward Rykas, who had moved closer during the exchange, listening intently.

"Lynx is safe," she informed him, her tone lighter with evident relief. "He's with Sylvaris and Lumorith at Sylvaris's home, having an informal lunch."

Rykas's expression softened slightly, but his warrior instincts immediately surged forward again. "That's great news to hear—but perhaps we shouldn't let our guard down too quickly. It might still be wise to alert Pazlun, so he can assign protective warriors to Lynx until Josephine is located." He paused briefly, then added decisively, "Or better yet, send Lynx back home to Sage Manor immediately, where his family can watch over him."

Elara nodded firmly, understanding and agreeing with Rykas's cautious suggestion. Turning back to Keelee, she said gently but with determination, "Did you hear him, Keelee?"

Keelee's holographic form nodded calmly, though his gaze sharpened with seriousness. "Yes, clearly. I agree wholeheartedly. We'll inform Pazlun immediately and arrange for a protective detail. I'll also talk with Lumorith once the luncheon concludes and have arrangements made to return Lynx home if we feel any further danger is imminent."

Rykas gave a relieved nod, grateful for Keelee's swift agreement. "Thank you, Keelee. Stay vigilant."

"Always," Keelee replied with a reassuring smile. "I'll keep you informed of any changes."

With that, Keelee's image slowly faded from the screen, leaving Rykas and Elara standing quietly in the council chamber, relief interwoven with lingering unease. They shared a brief glance, silently acknowledging the delicate balance between reassurance and vigilance.

"Let's hope this caution is unnecessary," Elara whispered quietly, glancing toward the window, where Arcmyrin's golden sunset now gave way to gentle twilight.

Rykas placed a firm, comforting hand on her shoulder. "If Josephine is indeed there, they'll find her. We'll end this before it begins."

Elara nodded firmly, drawing strength from his confidence. "Yes. We have to."

Together, they stepped away from the council chambers, prepared to confront whatever lay ahead, their determination unwavering, their hearts united by purpose and resolve.

The late afternoon sun cast warm, golden rays across the expansive front lawn of Sage Manor. Lincoln, Ridge, Waverly, Marshall, and Bronte stood on the front steps, quietly discussing their recent experiences when the front door swung open, and Bethany, Madre, Francis, and the children spilled eagerly outside to join them.

Bethany's eyes widened with relief when she saw Waverly standing safely next to her father. She didn't hesitate, rushing forward and wrapping Waverly in a fierce, loving "mom" hug. "Oh, my sweet girl!" Bethany breathed, squeezing her daughter tightly. "I'm so relieved you're back safe."

Waverly hugged her mother back, emotions bubbling up inside her. Before she could respond, a chorus of excited voices erupted behind them.

"Waverly!" Maddox and Maya shrieked in unison, barreling into their older sister and gripping each of her legs tightly.

Waverly laughed as she staggered backward, nearly losing her balance as Bethany steadied herself, still gripping her firmly. "Whoa!"

Waverly exclaimed through a blend of laughter and tears. "I missed you too! Give me a second to breathe, guys!"

Lincoln chuckled softly, his eyes warm as he watched the happy reunion. Ridge placed a comforting hand on his brother's shoulder, quietly relieved himself.

Bethany finally released her hold slightly, stepping back but keeping an affectionate grip on Waverly's shoulders. Her eyes searched her daughter's face carefully, a mix of love and concern evident. "You really are okay, aren't you?"

Waverly nodded, wiping joyful tears from her cheeks. "Yes, Mom, I promise. I'm fine."

Before the conversation could continue, Maddox and Maya wrapped themselves tightly around Waverly's legs again, giggling joyously.

"Oh!" Waverly laughed, stumbling slightly as she struggled to stay upright. "Easy, you two!"

Monica, noticing her friends' exuberance, joined the chorus, tugging eagerly at Waverly's sleeve. "We have something to show you!"

Francis smiled indulgently, reaching out to steady the excited trio. "They've been waiting anxiously for you to get back. Bronte and I took them outside today, and he's been teaching them—"

"Forts!" Monica interrupted, her eyes sparkling with excitement. "We built a fort!"

"A fort?" Waverly asked curiously, glancing from Monica to Bronte with amused surprise.

"Yep," Bronte said, folding his arms across his chest with pride. "Built it with branches and even cut up my old tent. Taught 'em a little about history, too."

"Come on!" Maddox shouted, pulling insistently at Waverly's hand. Maya wrapped herself around the other leg again, urging, "Please, Waverly, please!"

Waverly smiled helplessly at the gathered adults, shrugging dramatically. "Well, I guess I'm going to see this famous fort."

Bronte chuckled and stepped down from the porch, following closely behind as the children began excitedly leading Waverly toward their masterpiece.

They had made it about halfway across the lawn, filled with laughter and cheerful chatter, when Waverly abruptly stopped in her tracks, her face suddenly turning serious. She turned around slowly, staring at Bronte, her expression incredulous.

"Wait...," Waverly murmured slowly, eyes wide in shock. "Bronte... you're walking."

Bronte paused, looking down at his legs in mock astonishment. "Would ya look at that? Reckon I am."

"How on earth did I not notice that?" Waverly asked, shaking her head incredulously. "You're—you're walking, Bronte! You're not in the wheelchair anymore!"

Bronte chuckled deeply, eyes twinkling with amusement. "Well, you were too busy being hugged to death and nearly knocked over by the little ones here." He motioned affectionately toward the children. "Don't worry—I almost forgot myself when I first realized I could walk again."

"Wait, how—?" Waverly began, astonishment clear in her voice.

Francis stepped forward gently, giving Waverly a reassuring smile. "Bronte had quite the extraordinary trip to Pluboria, Waverly. Let's just say miraculous things happened."

Waverly took a moment to absorb this revelation, her eyes still wide with amazement. Slowly, a broad smile spread across her face. "Miraculous indeed," she murmured softly. "I'm so glad, Bronte."

He gave her a gruff nod, clearly touched but hiding his sentimentality. "Alright, enough of all this mushy stuff," he said gruffly, gesturing toward the children who were tugging at Waverly's hands impatiently. "We got history to teach. And a fort to see."

Waverly laughed brightly, giving Bronte a nod of affectionate understanding. "Yes, I guess I better go see this fort before the kids revolt."

The group moved forward again, the children leading the way, their voices bright with excitement as they described every detail of their new creation. Bethany, and Madre watched fondly from the porch, their smiles matching the warmth of the late afternoon sun.

Lincoln leaned toward Ridge with a relieved sigh. "After all that's happened recently, it feels good to see them smile again."

Ridge nodded slowly, eyes never leaving Monica, who was laughing and chasing after Maya and Maddox in circles around the yard. "Yes. We all needed this moment of peace."

Marshall quietly joined the men, his gaze thoughtful. "I couldn't agree more. Times like these remind us why the alliance is worth fighting for. Moments of pure joy and love—like what we're seeing right now—this is what matters most."

They stood together in silent agreement, watching as Waverly finally reached the fort, expressing exaggerated admiration that drew delighted squeals from the kids. The afternoon air carried their laughter and voices clearly, reaching all the way back to the porch steps.

Ridge smiled gently, meeting Lincoln's gaze again. "I just wish it could always be this easy—this peaceful."

Lincoln sighed, his expression softening as he watched his family playing happily on the lawn. "It can be, Ridge. Someday, maybe it will be. This is what we're fighting for. This exact moment."

Marshall placed a reassuring hand on Lincoln's shoulder. "And this," he said firmly, his voice strong and hopeful, "is exactly why we won't give up."

The three men stood in quiet agreement, absorbing the warmth of family laughter drifting across the lawn. The afternoon breeze carried the children's delighted voices to them, promising that no matter how uncertain their future might seem, these moments of joy were worth every challenge that awaited them.

30

A damp coolness brushed Lynx's skin, pulling him from an uneasy sleep. Groggily, he opened his eyes, but the room remained a blurry mess of colors and shadowy forms. As his mind gradually surfaced, a jolt of confusion swept through him: Where am I?

He could just barely make out the unfamiliar face hovering above him, a deep violet skin tone with large, searching eyes—someone he did not recognize. He flinched slightly, disoriented, as the stranger applied something wet and cold to his forehead.

Voices filtered into his consciousness, distant and muffled at first. Gradually they sharpened—two distinct voices, a female and a male.

"…must hurry. We have to leave immediately." The male voice held a tense urgency that raised alarms in Lynx's muddled mind.

"Almost done," the female voice replied, calm yet focused. "Get yourself changed. I'll finish up here."

Lynx's senses sharpened further as the sound of footsteps moved quickly away. Blinking hard, his vision cleared enough to see the violet-faced woman staring intently at him. She moved closer, speaking softly but sternly.

"Sit up now. Good, you're awake. Try to stand—you should be able to. I didn't put too much in your dish."

A rush of fear surged through Lynx. Dish? What had she done to him?

Fighting dizziness, Lynx sat upright. His muscles trembled as he slowly rose, gripping the table to steady himself. Immediately, his eyes darted around the unfamiliar room, desperately searching until they landed on a small shape lying motionless in the far corner.

His breath caught painfully. "The porcufera... Is it okay?"

The woman glanced over her shoulder, giving a slight shrug of irritation. "Unfortunately, yes. And now it must come with us."

Lynx's eyes widened, horrified. He tried to protest, but his voice was weak, barely more than a rasp. Relief that the creature was alive mixed uneasily with dread of what would come next.

Before Lynx could say another word, the male figure returned, towering over him. The man leaned down, glaring directly into Lynx's face. Lynx's heart froze, recognizing Sylvaris instantly. But the once gentle Tanzloran elder now had dark, lifeless eyes devoid of kindness or compassion.

Anger and confusion flooded Lynx, granting him a brief burst of defiance. "What did you do to us, Sylvaris? Why—?"

Sylvaris' sharp voice silenced him abruptly. "No, boy. You don't run this conversation—I do." His words were ice-cold, devoid of feeling. "You will do exactly as the lady here instructs you, and quickly, or your little friend in the corner will surely die."

Lynx's gaze flicked helplessly to the porcufera again. The creature's chest rose weakly, barely moving. He swallowed painfully, heart aching. He returned his gaze to Sylvaris and saw nothing but empty, soulless darkness staring back. A cold dread settled in his stomach. He had no choice. His body was weak, and resistance at this moment could cost the porcufera its life.

Defeated, Lynx lowered his head, chin dropping to his chest as a wave of despair washed over him. He clenched his fists, fighting down a wave of nausea and anger. Patience, he thought desperately. Stay calm.

Sylvaris nodded with grim satisfaction. "Good," he sneered. "Get his robes on, and let's go. We're running out of time."

The violet-skinned woman moved swiftly, draping a hooded robe roughly over Lynx's shoulders and pulling the hood forward to obscure his features. Lynx's mind raced frantically, searching for some way out of this nightmare, but he was too disoriented and weak to do anything but follow along for now.

As he shuffled toward the doorway, his eyes lingered one last time on the helpless porcufera. The little creature looked toward him with dim eyes, quietly whimpering. Lynx's chest tightened painfully.

"I'll get us out of this," he whispered faintly to the porcufera, though he barely believed the words himself.

Sylvaris, impatient, shoved him harshly toward the door. "Move!"

Stumbling forward, Lynx stepped out into the cool air of Tanzlora's twilight, feeling utterly helpless, but his resolve growing steadily stronger beneath the cloak of darkness now surrounding him.

The three robed figures moved silently along the winding road, keeping close to the shadowed edge of the forest. Lynx walked unsteadily between Sylvaris and the violet-faced woman, his heart heavy and his mind racing desperately for a way out. Their hurried pace matched the urgency in Sylvaris's harsh whispers.

"Move faster," Sylvaris hissed, his dark eyes darting constantly, searching for possible danger or discovery. "Stay close to the trees and avoid attention. We must get there unnoticed."

Lynx obeyed silently, his weakened legs struggling beneath him. Every so often he stole glances at the woman who walked slightly behind him, noticing that she carried something small wrapped within the folds of her robes. Before he could make sense of what it was, she suddenly let out a sharp, startled cry.

"Ouch! Damn thing bit me!" she shouted, stumbling to a stop.

All three froze as a small form dropped from her arms, landing with a thump on the road directly ahead of them. Lynx's heart leaped in astonishment and relief—the porcufera!

The creature quickly righted itself, quills bristling and eyes blazing defiantly. It hissed fiercely at the woman, then turned swiftly, scrambling into the dense, protective shadows of the woods.

Lynx couldn't help the small smile of triumph that flashed across his face. Run, little friend!

The violet-skinned woman growled in irritation, clutching her hand as small drops of red-hued blood oozed from her finger. "Great! It's getting away," she hissed angrily. "Now what do we do?"

Sylvaris's face darkened in annoyance, but he maintained his icy composure. "We keep heading to Erevelle," he growled, his voice tight. "The porcufera can't talk. No one will be able to understand where we're headed just from that thing's screeching."

He shot a venomous glance at Lynx, who was still staring hopefully after the escaped creature. Reaching forward abruptly, Sylvaris grabbed Lynx by the back of the neck, his grip iron-like. Lynx gasped as pain shot down his spine, the pressure nearly bringing tears to his eyes.

"Pick up those feet, boy!" Sylvaris snarled, shoving Lynx roughly ahead. "We need to get a move on. Now."

Lynx stumbled forward, wincing but regaining his footing as Sylvaris roughly pushed him along the path. He knew better than to protest. Behind him, the woman wrapped her injured hand in a piece of her robe, muttering curses under her breath, clearly furious at the porcufera's unexpected rebellion.

Yet deep within, a spark of hope ignited in Lynx's chest. If the porcufera was free, there was a chance—however small—that help might come. He focused on that fragile hope as the trio quickened their pace, pressing deeper into the shadows toward Erevelle. The ruins he thought he would never return to.

As darkness descended fully upon Tanzlora, Lynx silently vowed that no matter what happened next, he would remain strong. Help was coming—he was certain of it.

Late afternoon sunlight spilled through the windows of Blair House as Celia and Lorinda stepped inside, their arms heavy with bags from their bridal gown adventure. Lorinda let out a satisfied sigh, smiling warmly at Celia.

"That was unexpectedly wonderful," Lorinda said, placing her bags gently onto the ornate sofa. "Even if those dresses were outrageously priced, it was fun dreaming for a little while."

Celia chuckled affectionately, her eyes twinkling. "Well, I'm glad you finally loosened up and enjoyed yourself. But right now, we need to freshen up and get ready for dinner."

As Lorinda reached for her handbag, a flicker of longing crossed her expression. She paused and turned toward Celia.

"You know," Lorinda began softly, "before dinner, I'd love to call Sage Manor. I miss Monica so much already—I just want to hear her voice."

Celia gave her a gentle smile. "That's a wonderful idea, dear. I'm missing them all myself. Let's check in."

Lorinda eagerly reached for the phone, swiftly dialing Sage Manor's number. After a few rings, Bethany's warm, familiar voice came on the line.

"Sage Manor, this is Bethany."

"Bethany, it's Lorinda," she said with relief in her voice. "Celia and I just got back from bridal dress shopping and wanted to check in. How is everyone?"

"Oh, everything is good here," Bethany reassured cheerfully. "The kids are outside with Waverly and Bronte, running around like wild things. Bronte has really taken charge of them today—it's a wonderful sight, actually. Everyone else is relaxing on the porch."

Celia's ears perked up at Bethany's mention of Waverly. She leaned toward the phone and asked quickly, "Wait—Waverly is there? She's back safely?"

"Yes, thankfully," Bethany said, relief evident in her voice. "Rykas and his warriors just brought her home from Arcmyrin. She's doing well—safe and happy to be home."

"Thank goodness," Celia breathed, closing her eyes briefly. Then she hesitated, anxiety creeping into her tone. "And... Lynx? How is he doing? Have we had any updates?"

Bethany paused, the hesitation in her voice unmistakable. "Honestly, Celia, we haven't heard anything yet. There's been no word since Lynx left for Tanzlora."

Celia exchanged a worried glance with Lorinda, whose face registered concern.

"Perhaps someone should check with Keelee," Celia suggested firmly. "We can't let ourselves become complacent, especially considering recent events."

"You're right," Bethany agreed immediately. "I'll talk to Lincoln right now and ask him to head down to the chamber under the gazebo. He and Ridge can contact Keelee and find out about Lynx."

"Please do," Celia urged gently.

Bethany asks, "How is everything going in DC? Are they taking good care of you?"

Celia smiled softly, sensing Bethany's effort to soothe the tension. "Oh yes, everyone has been so kind. We're just waiting now—to meet with the leaders, and hopefully, we'll see meaningful progress. Lorinda and I spent the day exploring a little. You'll be happy to hear we managed to find some potential bridal gowns."

Bethany laughed gently. "That's wonderful. You both deserved a little enjoyment."

Lorinda leaned closer to the phone, voice filled with longing. "Bethany, please tell Monica I called. I miss her so much and can't wait to see her again."

"Of course," Bethany replied warmly. "I'll have her call you back tonight before bed. She misses you too, Lorinda, more than you know."

"Thank you," Lorinda whispered gratefully.

After a few more exchanges, Lorinda hung up the phone, sharing a worried glance with Celia. "I hope Lynx is okay," Lorinda murmured softly, her anxiety clear.

Celia squeezed her hand reassuringly. "Lincoln and Ridge will take care of it. Let's trust them to get to the bottom of things."

31

Back at Sage Manor, Bethany stepped onto the porch, feeling the gentle breeze carrying laughter from the yard. Lincoln sat with Ridge, Marshall, and Madre, quietly talking, their eyes warm as they watched the children play.

"Lincoln," Bethany called softly, approaching him. He glanced up immediately, sensing the seriousness in her tone.

"What's wrong?" he asked gently.

"I just spoke to Celia and Lorinda. They're worried about Lynx—we all are," Bethany explained. "Can you and Ridge go down to the chamber and try contacting Keelee? We haven't heard a thing since Lynx left for Tanzlora."

Lincoln stood quickly, concern sharpening his features. Ridge rose beside him, nodding solemnly.

"We'll do that right away," Lincoln assured her. "We'll get answers. Don't worry."

Bethany gave him a grateful nod, watching as Lincoln and Ridge walked quickly down the steps, heading purposefully toward the gazebo. She exhaled slowly, trying to soothe the lingering anxiety that tugged at her heart, and turned her gaze back to the children, praying silently that the news from Tanzlora would bring reassurance instead of more worry.

Keelee ascended the polished stone steps leading toward the grand Tanzloran council chambers, his thoughts heavy with concern over Elara's urgent message. Before he'd reached halfway, Brakar and

Draven emerged hastily from the entryway above, their faces tense with urgency. Recognizing their distress, Keelee fell immediately into step beside them.

"Brakar, Draven," Keelee began swiftly, matching their brisk pace, "Elara has reached out from Arcmyrin. They're deeply concerned—Josephine Beaumont has been corrupted and may have crossed over to Tanzlora."

Brakar's gaze met Keelee's, worry etched clearly into her features. "Yes, we received a similar message from Milestree and Lunarcher. Josephine's presence here could pose an imminent threat. Lumorith isn't responding to our summons, so we're going directly to his home to check on him."

Draven nodded sharply, his voice firm with authority. "Pazlun, Callum, and a squad of warriors have already been dispatched there. They'll be waiting for us."

Keelee felt his pulse quicken. "Lynx was also at lunch with Lumorith and Sylvaris," he informed them, concern deepening his tone. "We need to confirm his safety immediately."

"Agreed," Brakar responded, voice strained. "Lumorith's home first. We must find out why he isn't responding."

Together, they hurried down the stone-lined path, their footsteps urgent yet graceful. As Lumorith's dwelling came into view—a modest home nestled peacefully among lush foliage—Keelee's eyes fixed on the two figures standing alert at the front entryway: Pazlun and Callum.

Brakar quickened her pace, calling out sharply as they approached. "Pazlun! Have you found Lumorith?"

Pazlun turned swiftly, frustration and worry clear on his face. "No. We've pounded on both front and back doors, called out repeatedly, and peered through the windows. No response, no signs of movement inside. We hesitated to breach an Elder's private residence without authorization."

Without hesitation, Draven stepped forward decisively. "You have my authorization—go in immediately and search the premises."

Pazlun and Callum exchanged quick nods before Pazlun pushed open the heavy door and entered cautiously, Callum and the warriors following close behind. Draven, Keelee, and Brakar stood anxiously outside, tension palpable.

Minutes later, Pazlun returned swiftly, shaking his head in frustration. "It's empty—no sign of Lumorith or anyone else."

"Impossible," Keelee murmured anxiously. "Maybe they're still at Sylvaris's home. They were having lunch together there earlier. Let's move quickly."

Without another word, the group made their way to Sylvaris's dwelling nearby. Approaching the neatly constructed home, Draven immediately pounded heavily on the front door. "Sylvaris!" he called out, his voice resonating sharply. "Lumorith! Lynx!"

Silence was their only reply.

Draven's expression hardened. With a swift nod of authorization, he said, "Enter. Quickly."

Pazlun pushed the door open, stepping into the dimly lit home. Keelee, Draven, and Brakar followed closely, cautiously scanning the interior for signs of life. A tense stillness hung in the air, oppressive and unnatural.

Suddenly, raised voices erupted from somewhere deeper inside. Without hesitation, Keelee, Draven, and Brakar rushed toward the commotion, hearts pounding anxiously.

Rounding the corner into Sylvaris's kitchen, they came to an abrupt halt, eyes wide with shock.

Pazlun and Callum stood protectively over a figure lying on the kitchen floor, struggling weakly against tight bindings that secured his wrists and ankles. A gag muffled his protests, his eyes wide and desperate as he recognized them.

It was Lumorith.

Brakar quickly moved forward, voice filled with concern and disbelief. "Lumorith! What happened?"

Draven knelt down swiftly, removing the gag from Lumorith's mouth. Lumorith gasped desperately for air, relief washing over his features as he found his voice.

"Sylvaris," he rasped, voice hoarse. "Sylvaris betrayed us—he drugged our food. I collapsed immediately, but before I lost consciousness, I saw him approaching Lynx. There was another figure—a woman I didn't recognize—waiting in the doorway. They took Lynx, Draven. They've taken him somewhere."

Keelee felt dread pooling sharply in his chest. "Josephine," he whispered bitterly. "She must have allied herself with Sylvaris."

Lumorith nodded weakly, his expression tortured. "Yes. It was her—she's here. I recognized her from long ago before she started painting her face. And Sylvaris... he's lost to darkness. The eyes of our friend are no longer his."

Draven stood sharply, his voice firm, his authority unquestionable. "We must locate Lynx immediately and apprehend Sylvaris and Josephine. Pazlun, Callum, gather every warrior available. Begin searching the villages, forests, and pathways near Sylvaris's dwelling. They can't have gone far yet."

As Pazlun and Callum immediately sprang into action, Brakar knelt carefully beside Lumorith, gently untying the remaining bindings. "Rest, friend. We'll get you help."

Lumorith shook his head urgently, reaching weakly for Brakar's arm. "No—no rest yet. I must help. While they thought I was still unconscious, they spoke of Erevelle. Sylvaris was adamant they must hurry there. You must go quickly."

Keelee felt cold fear seize his heart. "Erevelle... Why there?"

Lumorith's eyes darkened with urgency. "I fear they mean to reclaim something powerful—something hidden there. Perhaps they believe the Triadorne was returned to that place. You must hurry, or everything may be at stake."

Draven turned decisively toward Keelee, eyes hard with determination. "Alert the Arcmyrians. We will need Elara and Rykas, possibly others. This betrayal runs deep, and we must stand united."

Keelee nodded sharply, understanding the gravity of the moment. "I will inform them immediately."

Brakar stepped forward, her voice resolute, filled with strength. "Draven and I will lead the warriors directly to Erevelle. Keelee, after you've contacted Arcmyrin, join us with reinforcements. We will not lose Lynx or our peace."

Keelee quickly clasped Brakar's forearm. "May Origin guide your path."

"And yours," she replied earnestly, her eyes blazing with determination.

With the swift decisiveness of true leadership, Draven turned, signaling Pazlun and Callum forward. "To Erevelle—immediately. Sylvaris and Josephine must not succeed."

As the Tanzlorans moved swiftly into action, Keelee turned back briefly, his eyes lingering on the weakened form of Lumorith, his heart heavy yet determined.

A great betrayal had struck Tanzlora from within for the first time in their history—but they would not let it shatter them.

And Lynx would be found—he had to be.

The twilight deepened as Sylvaris led Josephine and Lynx abruptly away from the main path, guiding them into the depths of a tangled forest. Lynx's heartbeat quickened; the paths looked familiar yet different, overgrown and wild from when he had faced the Umbralox. Thick foliage surrounded them, branches interlacing like fingers, blocking out what little remained of the fading daylight.

As they pressed deeper into the woodland, Lynx racked his mind desperately, searching for a way to leave a trail or slow their progress. He glanced at Josephine, whose strange behavior earlier had rattled him deeply. Her violet skin glistened oddly, the coloration strangely inconsistent and patchy, almost like paint melting beneath the heat. Sylvaris moved silently ahead, relentless in his urgency.

Gathering his courage, Lynx slowed his pace slightly, intentionally stumbling over roots and rocks. He needed a moment—just one brief pause to leave some sign of their direction. But Sylvaris quickly noticed.

"Pick up the pace, boy!" Sylvaris barked harshly. "Stop your pathetic games!"

Lynx ignored him, stumbling even more dramatically, falling to his knees in the soft moss. As he collapsed, gasping for breath, he noticed droplets of strange purple-hued sweat falling onto the ground. He blinked, confused—his sweat had never looked like that before.

"What's your problem now?" Sylvaris snapped irritably.

"I—I can't breathe properly," Lynx rasped, exaggerating slightly but genuinely alarmed at the difficulty he felt in catching his breath. He glanced up at Josephine, who was now leaning against a nearby tree, gasping and breathing heavily as well. Her violet-hued face was streaked with sweat, revealing patches of an entirely different color beneath.

Lynx stared at her openly, unable to conceal his confusion.

Josephine noticed his gaze and scowled fiercely. "What are you looking at?"

Lynx hesitated, feeling an odd surge of defiance despite his weakened state. "Who...who are you, really? And why does your skin look so strange—so streaky? I've never seen a Tanzloran look like that."

Josephine pushed off the tree angrily, striding swiftly forward until she loomed directly over Lynx, her eyes burning with resentment. "That's because, foolish boy, I'm not a Tanzloran."

Sylvaris stepped toward her, voice tight with warning. "Josephine—stop. This isn't the time—"

"No!" Josephine hissed, spinning to confront Sylvaris sharply. "It's past time. He should know exactly who he's dealing with."

She turned back to Lynx, crouching down so her face was just inches from his. Lynx shrank back slightly at the bitterness radiating from her eyes.

"You see, boy, I am your family—though I'd rather not admit it. I'm your great-aunt Josephine, Gideon's sister. Of course, you've never heard of me. Your precious family would never reveal the truth—not after what your wicked sister did."

Lynx's pulse thundered painfully in his chest as icy chills crept down his spine. "Gideon...sister? My sister... Waverly?"

Josephine sneered, her expression twisted in hatred. "Yes. Your so-called hero sister Waverly destroyed my brother. Gideon was forced into oblivion, wiped from existence—by your sister's hand."

A wave of nausea overcame Lynx, dread settling heavily in his gut. "You're...my family?"

Josephine laughed bitterly, coldly. "Was your family. I've kept my name, unlike Gideon. But I refuse to be recognized as a Beaumont in any shape, form, or fashion. Not after everything they did."

Lynx's mind spun. He could barely process what Josephine was saying. A hidden aunt? Gideon? His family had kept this dark history from him completely. Anger and fear warred within him.

Sylvaris, losing patience, stepped forward abruptly. "Enough of the family reunion," he barked harshly. "We must continue. Erevelle awaits, and our time is limited." Sylvaris pulled two small vials from the folds of his robes and thrust them at Josephine and Lynx. "Drink this. Both of you. It will keep you breathing easier long enough to reach the ruins."

Josephine grabbed her vial first, uncorking it immediately and drinking deeply. Lynx hesitated, eyeing the vial suspiciously.

Sylvaris saw Lynx's reluctance, grabbing him roughly by the shoulder. "Drink it now, or I promise, boy, you will collapse and die right here."

Reluctantly, Lynx swallowed the herbal mixture, grimacing slightly at the bitter taste. Yet his breathing immediately eased, strength flowing back into his limbs.

Sylvaris leaned in close, eyes cold and merciless. "I hope your memory of Erevelle is sharp. You'll either help us or die in those ruins. The choice is entirely yours."

With another harsh shove, Sylvaris forced Lynx forward. Josephine quickly adjusted her hood, hiding her oddly streaked face once more, clearly angered by revealing more than she'd intended. As they continued, Lynx stole glances at her, a sinking dread settling deep in his heart.

His great-aunt Josephine was alive, vengeful, and desperate. And she had allied herself with Sylvaris, a Tanzloran traitor. The realization filled him with fresh determination. He had to stay alert and wait for his chance. He would not let Josephine's bitterness poison the future, nor allow Sylvaris to harm Tanzlora or Arcmyrin.

As Lynx stumbled along, he reached up to wipe the heavy beads of sweat from his forehead. Pulling his hand away, he was startled to see streaks of the strange purple paint now coating his fingers. Glancing quickly toward Josephine and Sylvaris, ensuring they were too preoccupied with their path to notice him, he deliberately pressed his stained palm against the rough bark of a nearby tree, leaving a vivid purple handprint clearly visible against its pale surface.

Lynx exhaled quietly, heart pounding with cautious hope. If Keelee or the Tanzloran warriors came looking, they would have a trail to follow. Determined now, he continued onward, discreetly brushing his hand against tree trunks as he passed, leaving subtle yet unmistakable signs to guide any rescue party straight to Erevelle.

32

Lincoln paced restlessly in front of the large oval table, his nerves now frayed by every passing second. Ridge sat silently, eyes fixed intently on the screens, quietly willing them to come alive. Each minute of silence deepened the tension between the brothers, amplifying the uncertainty they both felt.

"Why didn't we worry about not hearing from Lynx?" Ridge muttered impatiently, breaking the heavy silence. He glanced at Lincoln, whose worry-filled expression mirrored his own.

"Because we were so focused on Waverly," Lincoln replied.

Ridge sighed heavily, tapping his fingers anxiously on the table's cool surface. "Keelee needs to know about Josephine just in case and possibly put more protection on Lynx."

At that moment, the screens flickered briefly, filling the chamber with gentle white light. The familiar holographic image of Keelee appeared, his normally serene features lined with worry. Lincoln and Ridge both moved quickly toward the table.

"Keelee, thank goodness, we just wanted to check in on Lynx" Lincoln breathed in relief, though his relief quickly evaporated as he registered the grim look on Keelee's face. "What's happened?"

Keelee's voice was calm, yet held unmistakable urgency. "Lincoln, Ridge—I'm sorry. Things have escalated quickly here. Lynx has been taken."

Lincoln immediately stepped forward, gripping the edge of the table tightly. "Taken? By who?"

"Sylvaris," Keelee confirmed gravely. "And your aunt Josephine. They drugged Lumorith and kidnapped Lynx during a meal. We've

222

just found Lumorith alive, but Lynx is still missing. They're taking him to Erevelle. Pazlun and the warriors, along with Draven, Brakar, and myself, are mobilizing now."

Lincoln's face drained of color. "We have to come through right away. We can help you search—"

Keelee interrupted swiftly, shaking his head firmly. "I'm sorry, Lincoln, but that won't be possible. The council has ordered the immediate shutdown of the portal system, including your Crystal Gate, to prevent Josephine and Sylvaris from escaping off-planet again."

"No, Keelee—wait!" Lincoln pleaded desperately, eyes wide with alarm. "You can't shut it down now! We have to help Lynx—please, just wait!"

As Lincoln spoke, Keelee turned away briefly, his expression troubled. Suddenly, the chamber around Lincoln and Ridge plunged into darkness, the glowing hum of the Crystal Gate abruptly silenced. Lincoln's heart dropped into his stomach as he exchanged a panicked look with Ridge.

"It's already done," Keelee explained solemnly, turning back with deep sympathy in his eyes. "I'm truly sorry. The gate is dark; the system has been shut down."

"Then how can we help him?" Lincoln demanded, anguish straining his voice. "We can't just sit here and do nothing!"

Keelee's tone softened, attempting reassurance. "You're not helpless, Lincoln. Before Lunarcher shut down the portals, Rykas and a squad of Arcmyrian warriors passed through to assist us. They arrived safely and are joining us now. I promise you, we will do everything in our power to find Lynx quickly."

Lincoln exhaled shakily, taking some comfort from Keelee's confident words. "You know where they're headed for certain?"

"Erevelle," Keelee confirmed, determination blazing in his eyes. "We're moving fast. Josephine and Sylvaris have a lead, but they cannot evade us forever. We'll find them—and we'll get Lynx back safely. You have my solemn word."

Lincoln and Ridge exchanged another tense glance, weighing Keelee's sincerity and resolve.

"Keep us informed, Keelee," Lincoln said quietly, his voice steady but edged with worry. "Every step of the way. Please."

"I will," Keelee assured firmly. "Trust us. We'll bring Lynx home."

With a final nod, Keelee's holographic image flickered and faded, leaving Ridge and Lincoln alone in the chamber, enveloped in the oppressive darkness.

Lincoln collapsed into the nearest chair, burying his face in his hands. Ridge placed a steadying hand on his brother's shoulder, feeling his own heart twist with worry.

"We have to trust them, Lincoln," Ridge said gently. "Keelee, Draven, Rykas—they won't fail us."

Lincoln nodded slowly, lifting his head. His eyes shone with fierce determination. "I know. But waiting...the waiting might just kill me."

Ridge squeezed his shoulder firmly, silently echoing Lincoln's sentiment. All they could do now was hold onto hope, praying that Keelee's next update would bring good news—and that Lynx would be returned safely to Sage Manor soon.

The path into Erevelle felt like stepping into a forgotten scar of time. The air was cold and wrong, thick with the echoes of the past. Towering trees, their trunks twisted and gnarled, loomed overhead, their branches clawing at the sky. Crumbling structures—once homes, once life—stood broken and skeletal, their stone frames devoured by moss and time.

The soft crunch of the trio's boots against the overgrown path was the only sound. Lynx's pulse quickened as they entered the heart of the abandoned village. He remembered this place—

The broken towers, the shattered wells, and the skeletal remains of homes—they had once been his battlefield.

The last time he stood here was during the fight against the Umbralox—a fight where he had come face-to-face with darkness and death, and had helped save Tanzlora alongside his family.

As they reached the center of the ruins, where the remains of the old communal hall crumbled like ancient bones, they stopped.

The air grew heavy, and Lynx felt his body tense with an instinctual chill.

Then—

"You should know... you were my second choice," Josephine hissed.

She began to circle him, her twisted form moving with an unsettling grace. "Oh, how I longed for your sister." Her voice twisted with cruel longing. "I wanted to rip her from her precious connection to the elements—to take her life and power for myself."

Her face darkened with malice. "For what she did to Gideon—" She snarled his name, her eyes flashing with grief and rage. "For murdering my brother—my Gideon—and destroying everything we were building."

Lynx's fists clenched. "Gideon was a monster. Waverly saved lives by stopping him."

Josephine's lips pulled back in a snarl. "She stole from me. My brother. My family." Her voice cracked with a bitter agony.

"But... your sister—" Her tone sharpened with frustration. "—That fool, Rykas, never leaves her side." She sneered. "So I couldn't get to her."

Her eyes narrowed, glittering with malice. "But then... dear Sylvaris here"—she gestured to the elder standing stiffly beside her—"offered me something sweeter."

Her voice dropped, venom thick. "You."

She smiled coldly. "And when I kill you, Lynx... your precious sister will feel a pain she can never escape—" Her eyes burned with vengeance. "The same pain I felt when Gideon was taken from me. She will mourn you... forever."

At Josephine's words, the Porcufera—showing up out of nowhere—chirped loudly, a sound filled with warning and challenge. Its faint glow brightened, the soft pulse of its life force beginning to gather again—a small shield, a tiny, pure defiance against the dark.

But Sylvaris's eyes, cold and emotionless, flicked to the creature—and with swift, brutal cruelty—

He kicked the Porcufera—hard—away from Lynx.

"NO!" Lynx screamed, his voice raw with terror as the Porcufera's small body flew—

—and collided with a crumbling stone pillar with a sickening thud.

The pillar, weakened and decayed by time, didn't stand against the impact—

Instead, it disintegrated into a cloud of ancient dust, cascading down over the small creature like a curtain of gray ash.

The Porcufera's cry—high and sharp—cut through Lynx's heart like a blade.

His voice broke as he lunged forward, "No! No, no—" His knees hit the ground hard as he reached for the creature, his hands trembling with fear.

But beneath the soft layer of stone dust—

A faint, glowing pulse.

The Porcufera's little body shuddered—its glow flickering, but still there—

Still alive.

Josephine chuckled, her eyes watching Lynx's agony with malicious pleasure.

"Oh, the pain in your eyes, dear boy," she cooed mockingly. "It's... delicious."

But as Lynx's hand closed protectively over the small, warm body of his companion—

The terror in his chest began to burn—

Burn into something cold—

Something sharp. Something ready.

His voice, low and steady, cut through the dust and darkness:

"You made a mistake, Josephine."

His eyes lifted, burning with a fury as pure as the stars.

Because he wasn't just a boy.

He was a Beaumont. And they had no idea...

They were already standing on the edge of their own destruction.

Lynx's heart pounded, but his mind was sharp and clear.

Without hesitation—he ran.

His boots slapped against the moss-covered stone, his body moving swiftly through the shattered remains of Erevelle. The air felt electric, charged with danger, but Lynx felt something else—

Control. Purpose. He knew exactly what he was doing.

From behind him—"Get back here, boy!" Josephine's voice cracked with venom.

And from Sylvaris—"You little fool! You can't escape us!"

But Lynx grinned. That was exactly what he wanted. Chase me. Follow me. You won't like where you end up.

The crumbling ruins blurred around him, but Lynx was navigating by memory, his feet finding familiar paths—

This wasn't his first time here. He had fought here before. He knew what they didn't.

Suddenly—there it was. The entrance—a gaping, dark maw beneath a collapsed archway. The entrance to the underground chamber, once a place of power—and peril. The place that once held the Triadorne.

Lynx skidded to a stop just inside the entrance and quickly knelt, placing the trembling Porcufera on the cool stone floor.

His voice was soft but urgent, his hand brushing over its glowing quills—

"Stay close. Stay very close."

The Porcufera chirped softly, a sound of fear and trust, and its tiny body pressed against his boot.

The sound of pursuit thundered behind him—Sylvaris and Josephine, their footfalls fast and sharp, closing the distance.

As Lynx took the first steps downward, the cold, rough stone damp beneath his boots, he heard Sylvaris's voice—

A cold, cruel laugh.

"You absolute fool." His voice was dripping with malice. "There are no underground tunnels in Erevelle. You've trapped yourself!"

Lynx's lips curled into a smirk they couldn't see.

"That's what you think."

The air grew colder as Lynx reached the bottom of the stone staircase. The space was pitch black, but he didn't need light—he remembered every inch.

The chamber was large and circular, the stone walls crumbling, but there was one key feature—

A massive, bottomless void in the very center—where the vessel that powered the elemental daggers rose up to them. Once that vessel was taken, it left a trap waiting for the unwary in the center of the chamber.

Lynx quickly scooped the Porcufera into his arms, holding it close to his chest. The little creature's body shivered against him, its soft glow barely illuminating his hands.

With slow, careful steps, he plastered himself against the rough, cold wall, pressing so tightly that the stone scraped his back.

Then he began to side-step, inching his way around the chamber's perimeter—staying on the only safe ground, the solid perimeter of stone that surrounded the vast opening.

Above him, the sound of footsteps—fast, relentless.

Then—

The first one descended.

Sylvaris was the first to reach the chamber floor, his form emerging from the darkness, his voice full of mockery:

"No escape now, boy. You're cornered."

But then—

The air shifted—

And—

"AAAAAGHHHHH—!"

With a single, misplaced step—

Sylvaris vanished.

One moment he was there—

The next—

His body plunged into the abyss.

His scream, sharp and raw, echoed against the stone—

Growing fainter—

And fainter—

Until—

Only a distant, fading cry.

Then—silence.

Josephine, just behind him, saw nothing—only blackness.

Her reaction came too late—her voice, shrill and furious—

"Sylvaris—?! Where—"

But She Was Moving Too Fast—

"No—NO!"

Another Plunge—Another Scream

Her form, barely a shadow in the dark—

Suddenly—

Gone.

Her scream tore through the chamber—

Longer, louder—

And it did not stop.

Lynx, holding his breath, felt his heart pounding in his throat—

Because—

The screams didn't fade.

Josephine's voice—

It continued. Twisting. Echoing. As if falling forever.

Her shrieks of rage and agony—endless.

The Porcufera trembled violently in his arms, its tiny body quivering from the chaos and terror.

Lynx whispered softly, his voice low and soothing against the tiny creature's tremors—

"It's okay… It's over. They're gone."

The Porcufera's glow flickered weakly—then brightened, a soft pulse of relief and trust.

But then—Footsteps Above

Suddenly—

The sound of many footsteps above—

Lynx's heart froze—then leapt—

A Voice—A Familiar Voice—

"LYNX!!"

Keelee—

Lynx's heart surged—

"Down here!!" he shouted, his voice echoing up the stairwell.

Clutching the Porcufera tightly, he began to carefully retrace his path, his back still to the wall, moving with calculated precision.

Step by Step—

His feet found the first stair—then the next—

And then—

He ran—

33

Lincoln and Ridge moved swiftly up the path from the gazebo toward the warmly lit kitchen of Sage Manor, dread churning heavily in each step. Ridge, sensing Lincoln's growing anxiety, placed a reassuring hand on his brother's shoulder. "We'll get through this," Ridge said quietly, attempting to steady his brother.

Lincoln nodded wordlessly as they reached the kitchen door. He pushed it open, stepping into the warm, inviting room. Immediately, Bethany turned from the stove, smiling softly until she registered the somber expressions of her husband and brother-in-law.

Her brow furrowed. "Lincoln? Ridge? What's wrong?"

Lincoln hesitated, heart tightening painfully as he struggled to find words gentle enough to deliver the devastating news. Ridge, sensing his brother's struggle, stepped forward.

"It's Lynx," Ridge said carefully. "We finally heard from Keelee. Josephine has him. She's working with Sylvaris, and they've taken him toward Erevelle."

Bethany's face paled instantly, her body swaying as she reached blindly for the countertop to steady herself. "Taken? How—what do you mean taken?"

Ridge gently guided Bethany to a chair at the kitchen table, his voice soothing. "Sylvaris betrayed Tanzlora, Bethany. He took Lynx, and Josephine is involved. Keelee and Draven are tracking them right now."

Bethany's breath caught sharply, tears instantly filling her eyes. "No—oh please, no..." Her voice shook as her fingers trembled, gripping Ridge's arm tightly. "Not Lynx..."

231

Lincoln knelt beside his wife, pulling her into a protective embrace. "Bethany, Keelee and the Tanzlorans, and even Rykas from Arcmyrin—they're doing everything possible to find him."

Bethany shook her head, anguish clear on her face. "I need to be there, Lincoln! I need to help!"

"Beth, we have to trust Keelee—"

"I can't just sit here!" Bethany exclaimed, her voice breaking into tears. "He's our son, Lincoln! He needs us!"

As her voice echoed through the kitchen, Lincoln pulled Bethany into a comforting embrace, holding her tight as silent sobs shook her shoulders.

Ridge, his jaw tense with sorrow and frustration, took out his phone and dialed the number Lorinda had given him for the Blair House, stepping aside to give Bethany and Lincoln a moment of privacy.

Celia answered immediately, sensing the tension from Ridge's tone. "Ridge, what's wrong?"

"It's Lynx," Ridge said, voice heavy with regret. "Sylvaris betrayed the Tanzloran elders and abducted Lynx. Josephine is involved. Keelee and Draven are tracking them, but it's serious. We don't have him back yet."

"Oh no," Celia gasped, her voice thick with worry. "How's Bethany taking it?"

Ridge glanced back, noting the tears streaming down Bethany's face as Lincoln held her close. "Not well. She's devastated, mom."

Celia's voice wavered slightly, filled with resolve. "I'm coming home."

"No," Ridge interjected firmly, his tone leaving no room for debate. "You're needed in DC. Keelee and Draven will find Lynx—we need you there to help Earth's leaders navigate an alliance proposal. Please, trust me."

After a long pause, Celia exhaled shakily. "Fine, Ridge. But the second you have news, you call me."

"We promise," Ridge assured her gently. "The moment we hear anything."

As Ridge hung up, Francis, Madre, and Marshall entered the kitchen, concern evident in their eyes. Francis stepped forward cautiously, sensing the heaviness in the room. "Is everything alright?"

Lincoln sighed heavily, looking up. "Lynx has been taken. Josephine and Sylvaris."

Madre gasped softly, covering her mouth. Marshall stood rigid, his jaw clenching in anger.

Just then, the front door burst open, voices filling the air. Monica and Maya bounded into the kitchen, giggling, with Maddox trailing just behind. The children's laughter faded as they noticed the room's tension. Monica immediately ran to Francis, sensing something wrong, and Maya lingered hesitantly by the door.

Maddox, however, moved straight toward his mother. He reached out, taking Bethany's shaking hand in his tiny grasp, his dark eyes full of an intensity far beyond his years. Gently, he began to pat his mother's shoulder, as though he were the parent offering comfort. Bethany, still trembling, looked down into Maddox's serious face and tried to compose herself.

"Maddox, sweetheart, you should go play with Maya and Monica," Bethany said softly, trying to muster a reassuring smile.

"No," Maddox said firmly, his voice calm but determined. "I'm staying right here."

Bethany stared at her son, seeing a sudden maturity in his gaze that took her breath away.

Then, with quiet certainty, Maddox looked up at Lincoln. "Lynx is fine."

The room fell silent as every eye turned toward Maddox.

"What did you say?" Lincoln asked gently, kneeling to meet his son's gaze.

Maddox's voice was unwavering. "He's fine, Dad. He's taken care of them."

Lincoln knelt slowly beside Maddox, eyes searching his son's face with confusion and hope. "What do you mean, Maddox? How do you know this?"

Maddox tilted his head thoughtfully, as if hearing something far off. "Galen," he said quietly. "He just told me. Lynx is scared, but he's smart. He's already taken care of things. You don't have to worry."

Lincoln and Ridge exchanged stunned, uncertain looks.

Ridge stepped closer, gently placing a hand on Maddox's shoulder. "Galen spoke to you again, Maddox?"

"Yes," Maddox said with absolute clarity. "He said Lynx is safe now. You can ask Keelee. Keelee will know."

Lincoln's heart hammered with a mix of hope and fear. He turned quickly to Ridge, urgency flooding through him. "We need to check this—right now."

Ridge nodded decisively. Without another word, the two brothers rushed back outside, down the path toward the gazebo chamber.

Bethany watched them go, speechless, tears still fresh in her eyes, but now shimmering with cautious hope. She turned slowly to Maddox, cupping his small face gently between her hands. "Are you certain, Maddox?"

Maddox smiled warmly, patting her hand again reassuringly. "Yes, Momma. Galen never lies."

She felt warmth blossom in her chest. Gently pulling her son into her arms, Bethany hugged him fiercely, the tears still falling but softened by renewed hope.

"Galen, huh?" Bronte asked quietly, sitting back in his chair, watching carefully. He chuckled softly to himself, shaking his head. "Guess Pluboria was right about more than just my legs."

Maddox smiled gently at Bronte, nodding knowingly, as if sharing a secret between them alone. Then, together as a family, they waited, clinging to hope and trusting in the wisdom of a child—and the spirit who had reached across worlds to speak.

Celia paced restlessly around her bedroom suite at Blair House, tension evident in every movement. She cast frequent glances toward the antique clock sitting on the mantle, its ticking marking each uncertain second. Lorinda sat quietly on the elegant chaise, observing Celia's unease.

Finally, Celia stopped pacing and reached for the phone. "Lorinda, I'm calling Rachel Timms," she said decisively. "We need clarity about how much longer this is going to take. If we have to rush back to Sage Manor for Lynx, I need to know how we can do it without offending the leaders here."

Lorinda nodded, understanding completely. "Do it. We need answers, Celia."

Celia quickly dialed Rachel's number, placing the call on speakerphone as it began ringing. Rachel answered almost immediately, her voice pleasant and professional.

"Rachel Timms."

"Rachel, this is Celia Beaumont. I'm sorry to call unexpectedly, but something urgent has come up."

Rachel's tone immediately shifted, concern evident. "Of course, Celia. Is everything all right?"

Celia drew in a calming breath. "To be honest, no. There's an emergency on Tanzlora involving my grandson Lynx. It's a complicated matter, and we're waiting for more information—but if it escalates, Lorinda and I might need to leave DC immediately."

There was a brief silence on the line as Rachel processed this information. Finally, she spoke softly and carefully. "I see. I'm so sorry, Celia. Is there anything immediate we can do from here?"

"No, thank you," Celia replied gently. "But I do need to ask—how soon can we expect Vice President Houston to bring everyone together for the conference? We truly don't wish to inconvenience the world leaders who've remained here to meet with us, but we need to know a timeline."

Rachel answered swiftly, her voice steady and reassuring. "Actually, Celia, I was preparing to come over to Blair House within the hour to update you on that. An informal dinner at the Vice President's residence—the Naval Observatory—has been scheduled for tomorrow evening, allowing everyone to socialize and discuss matters informally before the formal conference at the White House the following day. The President's recovery is progressing quickly, and he anticipates hosting that meeting himself."

Celia exhaled quietly in relief, feeling slightly reassured by the timeline. "Thank you, Rachel. That information helps us tremendously. I believe Lorinda and I will simply have dinner and turn in early tonight, then. There's no need for you to come over—we appreciate your consideration, truly—but we'll see you at the VP's residence tomorrow evening."

Rachel's voice warmed appreciatively. "Understood, Celia. If anything changes, or if you require assistance, please don't hesitate to call me directly."

"Thank you, Rachel," Celia said sincerely. "We'll keep you updated."

As the call ended, Celia placed the phone down carefully, turning to Lorinda with a thoughtful expression. "At least we have a firm timeline now."

Lorinda nodded, giving Celia a gentle smile. "Let's just hope we don't get worse news from home."

"Yes," Celia whispered quietly. "Let's pray for that."

<h1 style="text-align:center">34</h1>

Lynx stumbled wearily up the stone stairs, gripping tightly to the weakened porcufera against his chest. His muscles trembled from exhaustion, his breath shallow from adrenaline and fatigue. When his eyes finally cleared the edge, he stopped abruptly, surprised to see Keelee, Brakar, Draven, Pazlun, and Callum anxiously waiting at the top.

Keelee moved swiftly forward, relief washing visibly across his face. "Lynx, thank Origin you're safe!"

Pazlun and Callum immediately stepped toward the stairway, determined to descend into the darkness, weapons at the ready. But Lynx reacted instantly, his voice sharp and desperate. "No, no, no! Don't go down there! You have to seal it off now!"

Brakar frowned deeply, stepping closer. "Lynx, what is down there? What happened to Sylvaris and Josephine?"

"There's a massive hole in the center of the chamber—it's pitch black, and there's no bottom," Lynx explained, breathless, his voice trembling from lingering shock. "Sylvaris and Josephine chased me, and they fell. They're gone forever."

"Gone forever?" Draven echoed skeptically. "A hole? How could—?"

Keelee and Pazlun exchanged a knowing look, realization striking both of them simultaneously. Keelee turned to Brakar. "He's right. When the Umbralox was attacking Tanzlora, the Triadorne descended from the chamber's ceiling, and the vessel to energize the elemental daggers rose from below. With the vessel removed, a void likely remained. It could be dangerously unstable."

Pazlun nodded gravely. "It's true—I remember clearly now. A bottomless pit opened beneath where the vessel had been. If Sylvaris and Josephine fell in, they will never return."

Brakar considered their words carefully, turning her steady gaze back to Lynx. "You are absolutely certain?"

"Yes," Lynx answered without hesitation, his tone resolute. "They fell straight into it, and Josephine's screams just faded into silence. Trust me—there's nothing anyone can do for them now."

Draven's eyes narrowed with determination. "We still must confirm this. Pazlun, Callum, take warriors and torches. We need to see this for ourselves—but carefully. Stay along the perimeter walls, heed Lynx's warning."

Several warriors immediately moved, lighting torches and preparing themselves to descend. Draven instructed firmly, "Stay alert. Keep your footing secure and remain along the outer edges."

As the warriors began their cautious descent down the stone stairway, Keelee stepped toward Lynx, studying the weakened boy closely. He carefully examined the porcufera, noticing its trembling form nestled protectively against Lynx's chest.

"The porcufera?" Keelee asked softly, voice filled with concern.

"He's alive," Lynx said, his voice breaking slightly with emotion. "But he's weak. Sylvaris hurt him."

Keelee gently placed his hand on the creature's quivering fur. "It's breathing—that's good. Sanodia will know how to heal it. But we must get both of you back to Reficiat Haven quickly."

Lynx exhaled shakily, relieved. "Thank you, Keelee."

Keelee motioned urgently to Pazlun and Callum, now reemerging from the cavern's stairway. "Prepare another vial of herbal mixture. Lynx needs strength to walk back. And fashion a sling—he must carry the porcufera safely."

Within moments, a fresh vial was placed into Lynx's hand, and the warriors quickly fashioned a sturdy sling from strips of woven cloth. Lynx gently settled the porcufera into the sling, comforting it quietly.

"Hang on, little buddy," Lynx whispered softly. "We're going home now."

Brakar stepped forward, placing a gentle hand on Lynx's shoulder, her usually stern eyes softened with gratitude. "Your bravery saved Tanzlora and Arcmyrin from further harm, Lynx. We will forever honor your courage."

Lynx flushed slightly at the elder's praise, murmuring a modest thank you. His legs felt stronger with the fresh herbal mixture, allowing him to stand a bit taller.

Keelee instructed Pazlun clearly, "Get Lynx and the porcufera safely back to the Haven. Protect them both, no matter what."

"Consider it done," Pazlun responded firmly.

With Callum carefully helping to secure the sling around Lynx's shoulders, the group prepared to leave. Yet just as they stepped onto the path leading away from Erevelle, a familiar voice called out to them. Rykas appeared through the foliage, flanked by several Arcmyrian warriors, their expressions hardened yet relieved upon seeing Lynx alive.

"Rykas!" Lynx exclaimed, smiling with genuine relief.

"Lynx!" Rykas rushed forward, quickly assessing the young man's condition. "Thank Origin you're safe."

Keelee stepped up, swiftly briefing Rykas. "Sylvaris and Josephine fell into a void in one of the ruin's cavern. Lynx cleverly lured them into a trap. The immediate threat is gone, but we still need to seal the area and confirm they're both truly gone."

Rykas nodded sharply. "I'll help Draven and his warriors. Pazlun, you and Callum get Lynx safely back to Reficiat Haven. Take warriors with you to ensure there are no other dangers."

Before they departed, Rykas stepped toward Lynx, placing a supportive hand gently on the boy's shoulder. "You have done something extraordinary today, Lynx. Your family would be proud of you—I know I am."

Lynx felt warmth rush through him at Rykas's words, though exhaustion made his limbs heavy. "I just did what I had to," he said modestly.

Rykas gave a knowing nod, pride evident in his golden gaze. "That's precisely what makes you special."

Rykas stepped aside, signaling the warriors to begin their trek back to the Haven. Lynx took another sip of the herbal mixture, feeling strength gradually return. With renewed determination, he held tightly onto the sling, feeling the soft heartbeat of the porcufera against his chest.

"Let's get you home, my friend," he whispered to the porcufera gently, his voice quiet but resolute.

With Pazlun and Callum leading the way protectively, the group moved swiftly along the forest paths. Lynx glanced upward at the towering trees, grateful for the safety they now symbolized. The nightmare he'd endured was nearly over, and soon he would return safely to the Reficiat Haven—and eventually to his family at Sage Manor.

As they continued, Callum walked close beside Lynx, his presence a steady reassurance. Lynx looked up into his face, gratitude mingling with admiration. "Thank you, Callum. For everything."

Callum smiled warmly, the usual sternness of the warrior softening for a moment. "I'll always be there when you need me. Arcmyrin, Tanzlora, and Earth—our planets are forever bound."

Lynx nodded silently, feeling the weight of that bond deep in his heart.

Yet even as they walked swiftly along the forested path, Lynx's mind drifted to his family. He thought of his parents, of Ridge and Waverly, Gran Celia, Bronte, and little Maddox and Maya. He wondered what they were doing, and if they knew yet what had happened to him.

He smiled gently to himself, confident that somehow, even now, they were feeling his thoughts. He knew in his heart that his family's strength was always with him.

At his chest, he felt the porcufera's soft breathing slowly steady, and Lynx felt a wave of relief. He would soon be back safe at Reficiat Haven, thanks to courage, friendship, and the unity of all their worlds.

He glanced upward again, whispering a quiet thank you to Origin for watching over them all.

"Almost home," he reassured himself, stepping firmly forward with renewed strength.

35

Lincoln and Ridge stood anxiously in front of the shimmering holographic image of Elara in the chamber beneath the gazebo. Her graceful presence radiated calm, even through the screen, yet both men felt an undercurrent of urgency in her demeanor.

"Elara, thank you for responding so quickly," Lincoln said, stepping forward. "We need to know what's happened with Lynx. Maddox told us he was fine—but how could he possibly know that?"

Elara's expression softened, a gentle smile crossing her lips. "Maddox was right. Lynx is safe. He showed extraordinary courage and quick thinking today in Erevelle."

Lincoln exhaled deeply, visibly relieved but still shaken. "What exactly happened? Please tell us everything."

Elara nodded solemnly, her eyes gentle yet serious. "Sylvaris betrayed the Tanzloran Council and allied himself with Josephine. They intended to use Lynx as bait to seek revenge against your family—particularly Waverly. On their way to Erevelle, Josephine revealed her intentions clearly."

Lincoln stiffened, anger flickering in his eyes. "What intentions?"

Elara continued carefully, her voice reassuring yet firm. "Josephine intended harm, revenge for Gideon's defeat. However, Lynx outsmarted them both. He remembered Erevelle from the Umbralox battle, specifically the chamber beneath where the Triadorne had once been held."

Ridge raised an eyebrow, astonished. "That's incredibly quick thinking for someone his age. What did he do?"

Elara's holographic image brightened, pride evident in her golden eyes. "He deliberately led them into the chamber, knowing a large void had been left behind after the elemental daggers vessel rose from the ground. It was dark, and he stayed along the edges, guiding them directly toward that dangerous pit. Sylvaris and Josephine fell into the darkness, permanently removing their threat. Lynx's bravery and intellect saved both himself and the Triad from potential disaster."

Lincoln shook his head slowly in disbelief, pride mingling with astonishment. "My son did that?"

"Yes," Elara affirmed with absolute certainty. "Lynx has grown stronger, wiser. He demonstrated today he is every bit a Beaumont."

Ridge smiled quietly, glancing at his brother. "We always knew it, didn't we?"

Lincoln gave a shaky laugh, tension visibly leaving his body. "I suppose we did. It's just hard to see your own children grow into warriors before your eyes."

After a pause, Ridge shifted his expression to one of curiosity. "Elara, about Maddox. How could he possibly know Lynx was okay?"

Elara's gaze deepened thoughtfully. "That is something else important we need to discuss. I believe Maddox is developing Tanzloran visionary gifts. His intuitive sense—particularly sensing Lynx's safety—is remarkably similar to abilities Sylvaris once possessed."

Ridge's brow furrowed slightly. "Sylvaris's visionary gifts? Are you sure that's a good thing?"

Elara gave a gentle nod, her tone reassuring. "Visionary gifts, like any gift from Origin, can be used for good or evil. Sylvaris chose darkness, but many others on Tanzlora have these abilities and use them wisely. Maddox's extraordinary connection is almost certainly due to his birth and upbringing on Tanzlora among our people. His visionary talents have clearly awakened."

Lincoln's expression shifted to a mixture of pride and caution. "What does this mean for Maddox? Should we be worried?"

"No," Elara said quickly, her voice firm. "You should be proud—and watchful. Maddox's gift can greatly benefit not only Tanzlora, but Earth and Arcmyrin as well. His visions may provide guidance and insight for the entire Triad. As he grows older, it will be important for his talents to be cultivated carefully, to guide him so he understands his responsibility."

"How do we do that?" Ridge asked, clearly concerned for his nephew.

Elara paused, choosing her words carefully. "When Maddox reaches his early teens, it may become necessary for him to return to Tanzlora for training. His connection is deep, rare, and precious. He needs mentorship, someone to help him understand and control this gift—someone to help him use it wisely, for the good of all three worlds."

Lincoln glanced at Ridge, uncertainty lingering in his expression. "You think he should return to Tanzlora permanently?"

"No, not permanently," Elara clarified gently. "But training and guidance are critical during those formative years. He will learn much among our people, and then bring those gifts home to Sage Manor and Earth. It is a blessing for both your family and for our planetary alliance. The Tanzloran and Arcmyrin councils must be informed of Maddox's unique connection, especially his ability to communicate with Galen on Pluboria. This is unprecedented and should not be taken lightly."

Ridge's eyes widened slightly. "You think his gift comes from his connection to Galen?"

"Yes," Elara said firmly, warmth coloring her voice. "Maddox's ability to hear Galen—especially considering Galen's lisp confirms it—is deeply significant. It links Earth, Tanzlora, Arcmyrin, and now Pluboria in ways we never imagined possible. Maddox represents a new level of unity, a bridge between worlds."

Lincoln rubbed his forehead thoughtfully, absorbing this information. "You're saying Maddox might be the key to the future unity of the Triad?"

Elara's expression softened, her voice sincere and gentle. "Yes. Maddox, along with your family, may guide all our peoples toward true interstellar harmony. It's vital we nurture his gifts wisely."

A solemn yet hopeful silence settled over the chamber. Lincoln finally nodded slowly. "Then we will do everything in our power to make sure he's ready."

Ridge stepped forward, eyes bright with resolve. "We understand, Elara. We'll prepare him carefully—and we'll lean on you and the councils for support."

Elara smiled warmly. "You will always have it. Tanzlora and Arcmyrin stand by your family, as always. For now, celebrate your son's safety and his bravery. Then, together, we'll prepare Maddox for the future ahead."

Lincoln exhaled deeply, releasing lingering fears. "Thank you, Elara—for everything."

With a gentle nod and a comforting smile, Elara's holographic image faded, leaving the brothers alone. Lincoln glanced at Ridge, quietly processing the magnitude of all they'd just learned.

"It's a lot," Ridge admitted softly.

Lincoln nodded, turning toward the stairs that led back to Sage Manor. "But our family has always faced challenges head-on. This is no different. Come on. Let's share the news with Bethany—and Maddox. He deserves to know."

As they ascended the staircase, the soft pulse of the communicator orb behind them intensified. Ridge and Lincoln paused mid-step and turned around to see Keelee's shimmering form materializing holographically at the base of the stairs.

"Keelee!" Lincoln said in relief, quickly stepping back down. "Thank goodness you're here—we just spoke with Elara."

Keelee's calm presence steadied the brothers. "I'm glad. Elara has relayed everything accurately. Lynx was incredibly brave and is now safely at Reficiat Haven. Sanodia is tending to both Lynx and the porcufera. He is weak but recovering quickly, and as soon as he regains sufficient strength, I promise to bring him home."

Lincoln visibly relaxed, tension easing from his shoulders. "Thank you, Keelee. You don't know how much that means to us."

Keelee offered a gentle nod. "Your gratitude is appreciated, but it was Lynx's own courage that ensured his safety—and ours. He's an extraordinary young man."

Ridge stepped forward, concern etched on his face. "Keelee, Elara told us about Sylvaris's betrayal. What does this mean for the alliance? Will this endanger everything we've built?"

Keelee hesitated, choosing his words carefully. "I'll be honest with you: Sylvaris's betrayal has sent a shockwave through both councils. Some elders are now more hesitant than ever to discuss an alliance with Earth. Gideon's and Josephine's actions had already deeply damaged trust. Now Sylvaris's involvement—one of our own, a trusted visionary—has shaken that trust to its foundation."

Ridge bristled slightly, frustration clear in his voice. "But Gideon and Josephine were traitors in our own family. They betrayed Earth just as Sylvaris betrayed Tanzlora. How can the elders blame humanity entirely, without placing equal responsibility on Sylvaris?"

Keelee gave a solemn nod, understanding Ridge's frustration. "That very discussion is ongoing among our council now. Some believe Josephine influenced Sylvaris, using human methods—particularly what they describe as her womanly wiles—to corrupt his heart. Betrayal of this kind has never occurred before, neither on Tanzlora nor Arcmyrin. Our elders are struggling to process this deeply personal violation of trust."

Ridge shook his head, his expression both sympathetic and exasperated. "Well, Keelee, in that case, maybe Earth is exactly the partner you need. We deal with betrayal, lies, and political corruption every single day. Honestly, it's practically part of our culture."

Lincoln swiftly shot Ridge a reprimanding look. "Keelee, I think I understand my brother's sentiment, though perhaps I can phrase it better." He paused, gathering his thoughts before speaking again carefully. "The truth is, we deeply acknowledge the hurt and betrayal your elders feel. Humanity has faced it repeatedly from our own leaders. Our elected officials have broken promises, acted selfishly, and betrayed the trust placed in them countless times. Unlike your elders, however, our leaders only remain in positions of power briefly—until we choose to replace them. But even so, betrayal hurts us deeply, and recovery is never simple."

Lincoln continued earnestly, meeting Keelee's gaze steadily. "The difference here is the depth of your elders' bonds. They remain in their positions for decades, growing close and relying on absolute trust. Earth cannot fully understand that depth, but we empathize deeply. This betrayal wounds your people profoundly, far beyond simple politics."

Keelee listened carefully, his gentle eyes reflecting both pain and gratitude. "I appreciate your words, both of you. Ridge, I truly understood your meaning as well, and sadly, you're correct—Earth has considerable experience with betrayal and dishonesty in leadership. Perhaps your world can indeed guide us through this difficult time, helping us navigate our recovery."

Keelee paused, sorrow evident in his gentle voice. "Still, it will not be easy. Trust, once fractured, takes great care to mend. Sylvaris was one of our wisest, most gifted elders. To discover such darkness in his heart is not just shocking—it is deeply painful."

Ridge's tone softened immediately, regret coloring his voice. "Keelee, I didn't mean to minimize your pain. I spoke rashly out of frustration. We truly grieve with you, for what Sylvaris's actions have done to your people."

Keelee offered Ridge a gentle smile. "I understand completely, Ridge. Your words came from a place of sincerity and a desire to help. It is difficult for both our peoples, but we will move forward. In fact, the very act of us speaking openly like this, with honesty and compassion, is proof the alliance still has hope."

Lincoln stepped closer, his tone steady yet reassuring. "Then let us help rebuild that trust, Keelee. Our family and your people—we've stood together through battles, darkness, and victories. Allow us to stand together now, through this pain."

Keelee's eyes warmed, gratitude clear on his face. "Your sincerity means more than you know, Lincoln. The elders will hear your message. It may take time, but healing will come. And perhaps, with patience and compassion, our alliance will grow even stronger."

Lincoln exhaled deeply, relief and hope filling his heart. "Thank you, Keelee."

Keelee nodded gently, beginning to fade. "Rest easy tonight, knowing Lynx is safe, and remember that your family's sincerity and loyalty has always been the foundation of our friendship. Trust may have been shaken, but it can be rebuilt."

As Keelee's image slowly dissipated, leaving Ridge and Lincoln standing in contemplative silence, Ridge finally turned to his brother, sincerity heavy in his voice.

"I'm sorry I spoke so carelessly, Lincoln. I didn't mean to minimize their pain."

Lincoln rested a comforting hand on Ridge's shoulder. "I know. And so does Keelee. Betrayal is complicated, painful. But they'll heal—and maybe, with our help, even faster."

Ridge nodded thoughtfully. "You're right. This alliance is worth every effort. For us, for Tanzlora, Arcmyrin… and for our children."

Lincoln smiled softly, turning again toward the stairs leading back to Sage Manor. "Exactly. Let's go share the good news about Lynx with Bethany. After that, we need to have a talk with Maddox. The future of the Triad depends on him, too."

36

After dinner, Ridge and Lincoln quietly gathered Bethany, Waverly, Francis, Bronte, Marshall, and Madre into the warmth of the parlor. A comforting fire crackled gently in the fireplace, casting a soft glow around the cozy room. The children were safely tucked into bed, sleeping peacefully upstairs, oblivious to the serious discussion unfolding below.

Ridge carefully dialed Celia's number, placing his mobile phone on speaker in the center of the coffee table, its faint glow adding another layer of gentle illumination. The ringtone echoed softly in the tense silence, and everyone relaxed slightly when Celia's familiar voice came clearly through the line.

"Hello, Ridge, Lincoln—everyone. Lorinda's here with me. Is everything okay?"

Lincoln leaned forward, his voice steady and reassuring. "Mom, first, I want to assure you that Lynx is okay. He's safe, recovering, and Keelee promises he'll be home soon."

A collective sigh of relief swept around the room, though Celia's soft exhale was particularly audible through the speaker. "Thank goodness," she breathed. "That's wonderful news."

Ridge exchanged a meaningful glance with his brother before gently continuing. "There's something else, though—something important you both need to hear before your meetings tomorrow."

"Go on," Celia urged, sensing his hesitation.

Lincoln took over, his voice carefully measured but forthright. "We spoke with Keelee and Elara. Due to Gideon, Josephine, and now Sylvaris's betrayals, the councils on Tanzlora and Arcmyrin are un-

249

derstandably shaken. Both planets are now very hesitant about moving forward with alliance discussions involving Earth. They're afraid, Mom. Afraid of further betrayal."

There was a moment of stark silence, broken only by the faint crackling of the fire. Celia's voice finally emerged, heavy with disappointment. "Oh, Lincoln. That's heartbreaking news."

Lorinda's gentle voice quickly followed, full of quiet concern. "How serious is it? Do you think they'll withdraw completely?"

Lincoln sighed, leaning back against the sofa. "Not yet. But trust has been deeply fractured. It's going to be very difficult for them to agree to any formal negotiations right now. Keelee didn't sugarcoat it. It's bad, Lorinda."

Ridge added quietly, "They've never experienced betrayal at this scale before—especially not from within their own trusted leadership. Sylvaris's involvement, combined with Josephine and Gideon's actions, has left both councils doubting humanity itself."

Francis shook her head slowly, her eyes wide with sorrow. "I can't blame them. That level of betrayal would devastate anyone."

Bethany shifted closer to Lincoln, clasping his hand firmly. "How do you think we can help them rebuild trust?"

Lincoln shook his head thoughtfully. "I don't know exactly, but honesty, transparency, and patience will be crucial. We have to recognize their pain and acknowledge our own part in this, even if it was Josephine and Gideon acting alone."

Bronte, never one to mince words, leaned forward abruptly. "Maybe it's time these Earth leaders finally get a taste of their own medicine. Let them see what it feels like when no one trusts you."

Marshall gently placed a hand on Bronte's shoulder, attempting to calm his fiery temperament. "I understand what you're saying, Bronte, but we need this alliance. Punishing leaders isn't the answer—healing trust is."

Celia spoke again, her voice firm yet compassionate, from miles away in DC. "Tomorrow evening, Lorinda and I have that informal meeting at the Vice President's residence. The following day is the official conference at the White House, where the President is expected to join us after his recovery. How am I going to explain this situation to them?"

Lincoln sighed heavily, voice full of empathy. "I wish I knew exactly what to tell you, Mom. I completely understand their hesitation, but the leaders here—they might not. Ridge made a point earlier to Keelee. Here on Earth, we've become accustomed to betrayal and broken promises by our leaders. It's sad, but we've grown numb to it. Arcmyrin and Tanzlora haven't. Their sense of betrayal cuts far deeper."

Celia replied thoughtfully. "I understand, Lincoln. The Vice President and the world leaders might struggle to comprehend the depth of the sister planets' pain, but it's vital they understand. I'll do my best."

At that moment, Bethany reached out, gently placing her hand on the phone's edge, her voice warm with conviction. "Celia, if anyone can make them see reason and empathy, it's you. There's no better diplomat in the world to navigate this delicate situation."

Madre's soft voice murmured agreement from beside Marshall, who nodded silently but with profound sincerity.

"Yes," Madre affirmed. "Celia, your strength, compassion, and sincerity will bridge this gap. We all believe in you."

Marshall spoke up, "Bethany's right. There's no one more capable of explaining Earth's perspective—and the depth of Tanzloran and Arcmyrin hurt—than you, Celia."

In DC, Lorinda reached out instinctively, gently patting Celia's hand, a reassuring smile lighting her face. Celia briefly closed her eyes, touched by the overwhelming support of those she loved. She took a deep breath and opened her eyes again, determined.

"I appreciate your confidence, all of you. I promise I'll do everything in my power to help the Earth leaders understand just how significant this breach of trust has been. If our planet is ever to join the Triad in genuine harmony, we must first fully acknowledge and respect their pain."

"That's exactly right, Mom," Lincoln said, pride clear in his voice. "I knew you'd understand."

Waverly, who had been quietly listening and leaning against the doorway, finally spoke up gently. "Gran, it's okay to remind the Earth leaders that unity, harmony, and peace come from mutual understanding. Our family learned that from Arcmyrin and Tanzlora. Maybe now it's our turn to teach that lesson back here on Earth."

Celia's voice softened. "You're wise beyond your years, Waverly. Thank you, sweetheart. That's exactly the message I'll carry tomorrow."

Lorinda squeezed Celia's hand warmly, her eyes brimming with quiet pride. "You've got this, Celia. And you'll have me by your side the whole way."

There was a moment of gentle silence. Finally, Lincoln spoke again, more optimistic and resolute than before. "We'll be here at Sage Manor, waiting for your update. And when Lynx comes home, we'll be ready to support whatever comes next."

Bethany, still nestled close to Lincoln, added softly, "Just keep reminding them of our shared humanity. It's what makes us vulnerable, yes, but it also makes us capable of extraordinary forgiveness and understanding."

Celia smiled warmly, even though they couldn't see it. "Thank you, Bethany. Thank you all. Lorinda and I will do everything possible, and we'll call again soon. Give my love to the children. I miss you all very much."

Lorinda, squeezing Celia's hand gently, spoke up cheerfully. "Especially give Monica a big hug from me. Tell her I can't wait to come home and hear all about her fort adventures!"

Everyone laughed softly, the moment of gentle humor breaking through the heaviness.

"Consider it done," Ridge said warmly. "We'll talk again tomorrow. Goodnight, Mom, Lorinda. Love you both."

"Goodnight," Celia said, her voice soft yet determined. "Love you all."

Ridge ended the call, and the family sat quietly for a moment, absorbing the weight of the conversation.

Bronte eventually broke the quiet, rising with a loud grunt. "Well, I'm going to make some tea. All this diplomacy has given me a headache."

Smiling softly, Marshall stood as well. "I'll join you. We could all use something calming."

As the room slowly returned to normal, Lincoln watched Bethany carefully, reassuring himself she felt steadier now. He leaned back, eyes thoughtful, feeling profoundly grateful for the family's bond that remained strong even in uncertainty.

At that moment, despite all that had occurred, an overwhelming feeling of hope and unity filled Sage Manor, reaching all the way to Celia and Lorinda in DC, binding their hearts in purpose and determination.

37

The breakfast dishes were cleared away from the table, and the soft chatter that usually accompanied the family's morning meal faded to gentle silence as Francis gathered Maya and Monica.

"Alright, ladies," Francis said cheerfully, holding out her hands to the girls. "Let's head to the classroom and see what fun craft Waverly and Bronte have planned for today."

"Yay!" Monica cheered, bouncing with excitement, while Maya grabbed Francis's hand, waving at Maddox, who remained seated at the table.

Bethany leaned over, gently brushing a stray hair off Maddox's forehead. "Maddox, sweetheart, we'd like to talk to you about something special. Is that okay?"

Maddox glanced up curiously, his deep, expressive eyes flicking from his mother to his father and uncle. "Sure," he said with a shrug, slightly uncertain.

Lincoln leaned forward, a reassuring smile on his face. "How about we talk in the fort you built? You did such a great job with it, and I know you really love being out there."

At that, Maddox's face brightened immediately. "Yes! I love the fort!"

Bethany laughed softly, relieved by her husband's thoughtful suggestion. "Perfect, then. Let's head out there and have a little talk."

Maddox eagerly jumped up from the table, leading the way out the kitchen door and down the gentle slope toward the woods where the fort stood proudly. The morning sun danced through the trees, casting soft patterns on the ground as the group walked together in comfortable silence.

When they reached the fort, Maddox proudly ducked under the canvas flap, ushering his parents and uncle inside. He beamed at Lincoln. "Do you like it, Dad?"

Lincoln's eyes sparkled with pride. "You did a fantastic job, buddy. Did you build this all by yourself?"

Maddox puffed up his small chest proudly. "Bronte helped me and Monica and Maya. But I did a lot of it myself."

Ridge reached up to tap the sturdy branches, nodding appreciatively. "I can see that. You really know what you're doing."

Bethany gently nudged the conversation toward the reason they'd come. "Maddox, yesterday you told us you heard Galen. Can you talk to us a bit more about that?"

Maddox's cheerful expression shifted slightly, becoming thoughtful, serious even, for someone so young. He shrugged his small shoulders lightly. "I just hear him sometimes."

Ridge leaned in a little closer. "When you hear Galen, does it feel different? Do you notice anything right before it happens?"

Maddox nodded earnestly, looking down at his hands as if trying to visualize it. "Yes, I hear loud ringing right before Galen talks to me."

Bethany exchanged a look with Lincoln, whose face mirrored her intrigue. Lincoln spoke up gently, "Do you ask him questions, and then he answers you?"

Maddox immediately shook his head. "No, that's not how it works."

Bethany's curiosity intensified. "How do you know that's not how it works?"

Maddox tilted his head thoughtfully. "I just know."

Lincoln and Bethany exchanged another startled glance. Lincoln softly cleared his throat. "Was the first time you heard Galen the day in the classroom, when you told us how to get to Pluboria?"

"No," Maddox answered calmly, matter-of-factly.

Bethany's voice wavered slightly. "No?"

Maddox shook his head again, eyes bright and serious. "No. I've heard him since I was little. Even before I came to live at his house here at Sage Manor."

Bethany caught her breath, stunned, and exchanged another look with Lincoln, her voice almost a whisper. "Maddox, are you saying Galen spoke to you before you even lived here?"

Maddox's small face remained steady, confident. "Yes. He told me I would come here and live. That this was where I belonged."

Ridge leaned closer, softly placing a comforting hand on Maddox's shoulder. "Did Galen tell you anything else, Maddox? Something important that he wants you to know?"

Maddox hesitated for a brief moment before responding slowly, carefully choosing his words. "He's told me lots of things, but I only tell you what he wants me to. The other things are just… for me. They help me get ready."

Ridge's curiosity deepened. "Ready? Ready for what exactly, Maddox?"

Maddox's gaze shifted from Ridge to his parents, then back to Ridge again, his voice steady, almost eerily wise for his age. "My purpose."

Bethany felt her heart tighten in her chest, gently laying a hand over Maddox's. "Did Galen tell you what your purpose is, sweetheart?"

"No." Maddox shook his head seriously, his young eyes locked onto his mother's. "Origin told Galen it's not time for me to know yet."

All three adults went completely still, a stunned silence hanging in the small enclosure of the fort. Maddox, unaware of the depth of their reactions, began to fidget, restless and suddenly eager to end the conversation. "Can I go inside now? I wanna see what craft we're doing with Francis today."

Lincoln quickly regained his composure, softly ruffling his son's hair. "Of course, buddy. Let's head back inside."

They stepped out of the fort, Maddox already bounding ahead toward the house. Ridge, Lincoln, and Bethany followed a little more slowly, processing everything they'd just learned.

Bethany sighed softly, still slightly shaken. "Did we just hear our son say he's been talking with our ancestor Galen since before he even lived here?"

Lincoln nodded slowly, watching Maddox run ahead. "I'm still processing it, but yes, it seems so. It's remarkable."

Ridge cleared his throat, thoughtfully adding, "It explains a lot, though. His calmness, his wisdom for someone his age... It's like he's been guided all along."

Bethany nodded, eyes moistening. "Yes, but how do we help him handle something so big?"

Lincoln put his arm gently around her shoulders as they walked. "We do what we always have—we support him, protect him, and nurture him. Maddox is special, but he's still our little boy. Nothing changes that."

Ridge smiled warmly at his brother and sister-in-law. "Exactly. And as a family, we'll all figure this out. Together."

Bethany squeezed Lincoln's hand tightly, reassured by the support. "You're right. One step at a time."

Ahead of them, Maddox burst through the front door, excitement radiating from him as he rushed toward the classroom, already calling out eagerly for Francis.

Bethany smiled, the heaviness in her heart lifting slightly. "For now, let's just let him be a kid."

Lincoln chuckled softly, opening the door for them. "Agreed."

They walked back inside Sage Manor, hearts and minds buzzing with questions yet oddly comforted by the strength and mysterious wisdom held within their young family member.

Celia sat in the elegant sitting area of her suite at Blair House, her eyes occasionally drifting toward the phone, waiting for the call from Vice President Houston. She felt a sense of urgency and unease about the news she needed to deliver. While not devastating, it was certainly troubling and could influence the trajectory of interplanetary relations. She trusted Houston deeply, and blindsiding him before world leaders tonight would violate that trust.

A gentle knock drew Celia's attention back to the present as Lorinda stepped into the room, self-consciously smoothing the skirt of the first gown she'd selected. The ivory fabric hugged her figure gently, adorned with long, elegant sleeves, a delicate crystal belt accentuating her waist, and a soft sweep of fabric flowing to the floor.

Celia smiled warmly, genuinely admiring Lorinda's natural beauty. "Oh, Lorinda. You look lovely."

Lorinda turned, catching a glance of herself in the antique mirror. "Do you really think so?"

"Of course," Celia assured her gently. Then she paused, her expression thoughtful. "But… is it glamorous enough for a Tanzloran crystal cathedral wedding?"

Lorinda glanced down at the simple gown, nervously fingering the crystal belt. "There are crystals in the belt…" she offered weakly.

Celia's eyes twinkled affectionately. "Hmmm… so there are." Her gentle teasing was laced with warmth, yet the slight hesitation told Lorinda what she needed to hear without being too harsh.

Lorinda sighed softly, her shoulders slumping slightly. "Maybe you're right. I just thought—I mean, I'm older now, and this is my second marriage. I didn't want something overly extravagant or expensive. And definitely nothing lacy or with a long train. That feels like a young bride's dream, not mine."

Celia stood, walking over and gently placing her hands on Lorinda's shoulders, meeting her gaze tenderly. "Lorinda, your age, or it being a second marriage, shouldn't limit how special your dress is. The gown you wear should reflect the joy and the importance of the occasion—and this occasion is spectacular, historic even. It's about you and Ridge, yes, but also a symbol of hope and unity among the sister planets. Your gown should reflect that."

Lorinda absorbed Celia's words, a soft smile forming on her lips. "Maybe you're right. But I guess I felt selfish or vain even thinking about something grander or more elaborate. I never wanted anyone to think I was trying to be something I'm not."

"Nonsense," Celia said firmly, gently squeezing her shoulders. "No one would ever think that. You're exactly who you need to be. You deserve a gown that matches your radiant heart and the significance of this moment."

A gentle blush rose to Lorinda's cheeks. "Okay," she said quietly, a hint of excitement returning to her voice. "Let me show you the other two dresses. They're both still simple, but maybe one of them will stand out a bit more."

Celia smiled encouragingly. "I'd love to see them."

Lorinda left the room quickly, feeling lighter and more confident. As she walked next door into her bedroom suite, she reflected on Celia's words. Maybe she'd been unfairly downplaying the significance of her own wedding, assuming that a more reserved dress would somehow fit expectations better. She glanced at the remaining two dresses, both carefully draped over the ornate armchair. Reaching out, she selected the second gown, holding it up thoughtfully.

This dress was a delicate ivory satin, with a fitted bodice, an off-the-shoulder neckline edged by tiny shimmering crystals, and elegant, subtle ruching that accentuated her slender frame. The skirt flowed down in graceful layers, each one softly cascading like petals. It was understated yet decidedly elegant.

As Lorinda slipped into the gown, she felt a quiet rush of delight. It was comfortable and undeniably beautiful. When she re-entered Celia's suite, she moved a little more confidently, her chin lifted slightly as she smiled.

Celia turned from the window, and her eyes widened in admiration. "Oh, Lorinda... this one is stunning."

Lorinda's cheeks flushed softly as she stepped closer. "You think so?"

Celia nodded enthusiastically, clasping her hands together in delight. "Absolutely. Turn around for me."

Lorinda obliged, gracefully turning. Celia continued, her voice filled with excitement. "This one truly captures something special. It's still understated, but there's a sophistication and grace here—exactly right for you. The off-the-shoulder neckline is elegant, and those little crystals sparkle beautifully."

Lorinda smiled wider, clearly relieved. "It feels right. Still simple, but maybe special enough to honor the occasion?"

"Yes," Celia said definitively, "this is much closer. But humor me—let's still see the third dress."

Lorinda laughed softly, feeling more confident now. "Alright, you convinced me. I'll be right back."

As Lorinda disappeared again, Celia's eyes drifted toward the phone, hoping Rachel's call would come soon. But she refocused her attention immediately when Lorinda returned moments later, wearing the final gown.

This dress had a more dramatic flair—a gentle A-line silhouette of soft ivory silk chiffon with a beautifully draped, cowl neckline that framed Lorinda's face gracefully. Small, crystal-beaded floral embellishments cascaded subtly from the neckline down one shoulder. The skirt flowed delicately around her legs, pooling softly at her feet, creating the barest suggestion of a small train. It was elegant yet quietly breathtaking, not flashy, but undeniably special.

"Oh, Lorinda..." Celia whispered, a heartfelt warmth in her voice, her eyes brightening. "This is it. This gown was made for you."

Lorinda felt her heart flutter, a blush blooming on her cheeks as she caught her reflection in the large antique mirror nearby. "You think so?" Her voice was barely above a whisper.

Celia stood and approached, eyes shimmering with emotion. "Lorinda, look at yourself. You are radiant. This gown is understated but regal. Elegant but not pretentious. It's perfect for you—and exactly right for a Tanzloran wedding."

Lorinda's eyes softened with gratitude. "I feel like myself—but maybe the best version."

"That's exactly how your wedding dress should make you feel," Celia smiled tenderly.

At that precise moment, the phone rang, causing both women to startle slightly.

Celia quickly walked over and answered, immediately recognizing Rachel's voice. "Celia, the Vice President has a window now—he's just stepped into the car. He can give you exactly ten minutes."

"Thank you, Rachel. I'm ready to speak with him." Celia nodded reassuringly at Lorinda, who quietly stepped aside to give her privacy.

Lorinda stood near the doorway, her heart pounding—not just from excitement over the perfect dress, but also from nervousness about the call. What Celia was about to reveal could significantly impact their mission here in DC.

Celia squared her shoulders, holding the phone firmly. "Hello, Mr. Vice President. Thank you for making time. I promise to keep this brief..."

As Celia spoke in calm, authoritative tones, Lorinda leaned against the wall, taking a deep breath and gazing down at the gown she now knew would become a part of one of the most memorable days of her life.

She just hoped the journey toward that day wouldn't become any more complicated.

<h1 style="text-align:center">38</h1>

Celia steadied herself, holding the phone firmly as she took a breath. Her tone was composed, but a quiet urgency underscored her words.

"Mr. Vice President," she began calmly, "I need to inform you about a very troubling development on Tanzlora. It's crucial that you hear this now, rather than tonight in front of the other leaders."

"I understand," Houston responded, instantly recognizing the gravity in her voice. "Go ahead, Celia. What's happened?"

Celia drew another measured breath before proceeding. "We've just learned there has been a betrayal within the Tanzloran council itself. One of their elder council members, Sylvaris, deceived the council and went so far as to poison another elder named Lumorith, as well as my grandson, Lynx, during what was supposed to be a friendly meeting. Thankfully, both Lumorith and Lynx have recovered, but the repercussions of this incident are severe."

She paused, gathering her thoughts as she heard the Vice President's sharp intake of breath.

"My goodness," he murmured, clearly shaken by the revelation. "This is... deeply troubling news. Is your grandson alright?"

"Yes, Lynx is safe now, but there's more to this," Celia continued. "Unfortunately, Sylvaris did not act alone. He had assistance from a member of my own family—Josephine Beaumont. She has been estranged from us for many years and was thought missing. It turns out, she was corrupted long ago by her brother Gideon. Josephine aided Sylvaris in his treachery, and both of them intended to bring harm not just to my grandson but to sabotage our entire alliance."

There was silence from the Vice President's end for a moment. When he spoke again, his voice had a somber intensity. "This... family member of yours, Josephine, what happened to her?"

"She's gone," Celia responded quietly. "Both she and Sylvaris perished when their own treachery backfired. It was a terrible outcome, but sadly their choices led them down that path."

Charles Houston exhaled heavily. "Celia, this situation is deeply unfortunate. But why would Sylvaris turn against his own people, his own council?"

"That's precisely the point I must stress to you," Celia explained firmly. "Nothing like this has ever happened before on Tanzlora or Arcmyrin. Both planets have existed in uninterrupted peace and harmony for centuries. This betrayal is unprecedented, and its timing—so soon after opening themselves up to Earth—is not lost on their councils."

"I see," Houston said thoughtfully, clearly processing the magnitude of what she was revealing. "You're saying that Earth's involvement is being directly associated with this breach of trust?"

"Yes, Mr. Vice President, that's exactly the concern. To the councils of Tanzlora and Arcmyrin, the betrayal isn't simply about two corrupted individuals—it's tied directly to their interactions with humanity. Both Gideon and Josephine were humans who brought this corruption into their peaceful worlds. While the councils understand intellectually that two individuals do not represent all of humanity, emotionally and culturally, this betrayal has shaken them deeply. They are understandably hesitant to move forward with any communication or negotiations toward an alliance right now."

Houston's voice was serious but empathetic. "Celia, I appreciate you informing me of this immediately. You're right to think this could drastically affect tonight's dinner, not to mention tomorrow's meeting. I assume Tanzlora and Arcmyrin have made no decision to formally end discussions—only to pause?"

Celia replied carefully, "Correct. It's not a final decision. Both councils are hurt, wary, and cautious. This has deeply wounded their sense of trust. What they need is time to process what's happened and to reassess their feelings about continuing the alliance discussions."

The Vice President took another brief pause, clearly troubled yet determined to stay calm. "Celia, what do you suggest we do now?"

She felt a surge of relief and gratitude at his immediate willingness to collaborate rather than criticize. "Transparency," she said decisively. "I strongly believe we must openly inform the other world leaders about this tonight, before tomorrow's conference at the White House. If we attempt to conceal or minimize this incident, it will only deepen the distrust felt by Tanzlora and Arcmyrin. Our best hope to salvage any possibility of an alliance is total honesty."

Houston agreed immediately. "You're absolutely right. Honesty is our only credible option. Tonight, when we gather, I'll give you the opportunity to present the details yourself. It's your story to tell, and your perspective as the Beaumont family leader will be essential in helping the others understand."

"I appreciate that greatly," Celia replied, her voice steady despite the weight on her shoulders. "And thank you for listening. I truly believe this alliance could still be possible, but it will require patience, sincerity, and probably most of all, empathy toward Tanzlora and Arcmyrin's unique experience."

There was a brief pause, and then Houston said sincerely, "I agree completely. We'll move forward carefully, Celia. Thank you again. And please give my best to your grandson—I'm relieved he's safe."

"I will. Thank you," she said warmly, hearing the faint background noise of the Vice President's driver announcing their arrival at their next appointment.

As Celia replaced the phone gently into its cradle, she exhaled deeply, the tension in her shoulders easing just a bit. Lorinda, who had been silently listening near the doorway, approached her softly.

"How did he take it?" Lorinda asked gently, laying a comforting hand on Celia's shoulder.

"Better than I'd hoped," Celia admitted. "He understands. Now, we just have to hope the other leaders will, too."

Lorinda nodded, placing a reassuring hand on Celia's back. "They will. You made me see reason about my wedding dress—I'm confident you can make a room full of world leaders see reason about this."

Celia smiled, appreciating Lorinda's attempt to lighten the mood. "Well, I'm glad you feel that way. By the way, have you decided which dress you'll choose yet?"

Lorinda chuckled softly, shaking her head. "No, not yet. But your insights gave me plenty to think about."

"Good," Celia replied, her eyes softening affectionately. "Because despite everything else happening, you deserve the perfect dress for your special day."

Lorinda squeezed Celia's arm softly. "Thank you. And you deserve to feel good about tonight's meeting."

"I'll try," Celia admitted, standing straighter with renewed determination. "Now, let's finish deciding on your dress—then we'll face this head-on, together."

The Tanzloran council chamber was bathed in gentle golden sunlight streaming through the expansive crystalline windows, casting prisms of color across the smooth, polished surfaces. Lynx entered quietly, cradling the porcufera in his arms, the small creature still a bit weak but alert enough to chirp softly, curious about its surroundings. The familiar comfort of the council chamber did little to settle the nerves fluttering in Lynx's stomach. So much had changed since his last visit.

Lumorith stood at the far end of the room, awaiting Lynx's arrival. The Tanzloran elder's face lit up as he approached, opening his arms in a gesture entirely uncharacteristic of the reserved, formal council meetings. Lynx paused briefly in surprise before stepping into the elder's embrace, warmth and gratitude washing over him.

"Thank you, Lynx," Lumorith murmured, releasing him gently. "I owe you a deep debt. We all do."

Lynx smiled softly, overwhelmed by the elder's sincere emotion. "I'm just glad you're alright."

Brakar stepped forward, her typically stoic expression softened considerably. "Lumorith speaks for all of us. Today, formality has little place here. What you endured, and your bravery in facing such betrayal, deserves nothing less than our full gratitude."

One by one, the Tanzloran council elders rose and approached Lynx, each offering a heartfelt embrace and quiet words of thanks. Keelee held him tightly, whispering, "You have proven once again that you carry a heart stronger than any warrior's blade." Draven, usually so stern, simply grasped Lynx's shoulder firmly, his expression conveying more than words could express.

Once everyone returned to their seats, Brakar gracefully gestured toward the large table in the center of the room. "Lynx, please take your seat. And you may place your companion here beside you if you'd like."

Lynx carefully positioned the porcufera on a plush, intricately woven cushion next to him. The small creature purred contentedly, nuzzling Lynx's hand as he took his seat.

Brakar stood, raising a hand gently. "This meeting is now officially open. Under normal circumstances, our guest from Earth would not witness what we are about to discuss. However, considering recent events, the council unanimously agrees Lynx Beaumont has earned this privilege."

She paused, looking around at the other elders, each nodding in solemn agreement.

"As all are aware, the betrayal of Sylvaris leaves our council incomplete. For Tanzlora's healing and growth, we must quickly choose someone worthy of this sacred responsibility. We must restore harmony, stability, and trust."

She glanced toward Lynx. "This process involves choosing a respected Tanzloran known widely for integrity, wisdom, and the strength of character necessary to rebuild the trust we have temporarily lost."

Lumorith spoke next, his voice calm yet resolute. "The chosen elder must bring fresh vision but also a deep reverence for our planet's history and values. Tanzlora has always thrived on unity, not division. This choice is critical."

Brakar stood regally and took a deep breath, her gaze shifting briefly toward Lynx before she continued, her voice rising with authority. "Elders, please place the name of your chosen Tanzloran upon your selection stone using the stem of the Iridis flower, as our customs dictate. When ready, please bring your stones forward and lay them within the Electus Patera."

Each elder bowed their head slightly in acknowledgment of Brakar's instructions. Lynx watched in wonder as the elders each selected the vibrant, violet Iridis flowers carefully placed before them. With serene movements, they dipped the stems delicately into a silver basin filled with a shimmering liquid, allowing the stem to take on a gentle luminescence.

The chamber grew quiet, reverent, as each elder carefully etched a name upon their smooth selection stones. Keelee sat quietly beside Lynx, his eyes thoughtfully cast downward, the first time he had ever participated in an elder selection ceremony.

After several minutes, each elder rose one by one, solemnly stepping to place their stones into the Electus Patera—a beautifully carved crystal basin etched with symbols representing Origin's wisdom and guidance. Brakar stood calmly beside the Electus Patera, waiting patiently until each elder had returned to their seats.

When all the elders had settled back down, Brakar gracefully extended her hands over the basin. Her voice, gentle but resonant, filled the chamber. "Origin, grant us your wisdom. Illuminate for us the Tanzloran best suited to help heal and restore harmony to our council, our planet, and our Triad. Guide us in our choice, that our path forward is clear, just, and filled with your eternal light."

She paused, letting her words hang in respectful silence, before gently reaching into the basin to retrieve the first stone. Lynx held his breath, his gaze fixed on Brakar.

39

Brakar turned the stone slowly in her fingers, a gentle smile appearing on her serene face as she spoke clearly, "Keelee."

Lynx felt his heart skip a beat. He glanced quickly at Keelee, whose eyes widened in surprise, his expression a mixture of awe and disbelief. Keelee remained perfectly still, as though processing this unexpected honor.

Brakar carefully placed the first stone upon the table before retrieving the next, turning it carefully in her fingers. Her voice resonated warmly once again. "Keelee."

Keelee's eyes glistened, the gentle wonderment on his face deepening as he looked down humbly at the table. Lynx watched Keelee's reactions carefully, emotions rising within himself at the sight of such genuine humility and gratitude from someone he admired so deeply.

The chamber held its breath as Brakar continued. The third stone, once more, carried Keelee's name. "Keelee," she said warmly, placing it gently next to the others.

With each subsequent stone, the same name rang gently throughout the chamber—Keelee. By the fourth and fifth stones, Keelee was visibly moved, his composure trembling softly as quiet tears filled his eyes.

Brakar smiled softly as she read the final stones. Each and every stone, without hesitation, had Keelee's name etched clearly upon its surface.

"Keelee," Brakar announced quietly, placing the last stone carefully beside the others. She looked across at the gathered elders, all smiling warmly in serene approval.

269

Keelee's gentle tears had spilled softly down his cheeks, though his gaze was fixed upon the table, unable to lift his eyes in the face of such overwhelming acknowledgment from his peers.

Lynx felt his own throat tighten with emotion, his eyes burning softly as he fought back tears himself. He wanted so desperately to jump up and embrace Keelee in celebration, but Lynx held himself steady, sensing the sanctity and respect required of this moment.

Brakar stepped around the Electus Patera, approaching Keelee gently. She placed one hand warmly on his shoulder, causing him to lift his gaze slowly to hers.

"Keelee," she said softly, her voice filled with reverence and warmth. "The council has spoken with unanimous heart and clarity. It is you who have been chosen to fill the seat left empty by betrayal, for in your spirit resides strength, compassion, humility, and unyielding dedication to our people. We trust you completely."

Keelee swallowed hard, his voice rough with emotion when he finally spoke. "I—I am deeply honored by your faith in me," he managed softly, his voice shaking slightly. "I vow to serve Tanzlora and our sister planets with unwavering loyalty and integrity."

Lumorith rose, smiling warmly toward Keelee. "We have no doubt, Keelee. Your spirit has long been a beacon among us."

One by one, each elder stood, nodding respectfully toward Keelee, their warm expressions further solidifying their approval. Lynx watched this deeply moving display, pride swelling within him for his dear friend.

Finally, Brakar raised her hands in quiet authority. "It is official. Keelee, please stand and join us at your rightful seat among the elders."

Keelee rose slowly, his movements careful but filled with dignity and grace. He crossed to the vacant seat once occupied by Sylvaris. The moment Keelee settled into the elder's seat, a sense of peace and completeness filled the chamber. The pain from Sylvaris's betrayal felt lighter already, the wounds of mistrust beginning their healing as Keelee took his place.

Brakar turned gently toward Lynx, smiling with warmth. "Lynx, you have witnessed a rare and sacred moment today. Tanzlora owes you our deepest gratitude not only for your bravery but for your wisdom, humility, and friendship."

Lynx nodded respectfully, his voice quiet with sincerity. "Thank you, Brakar. It is an honor to be here and to see Keelee receive such deserved recognition."

Brakar bowed her head graciously. "The honor is ours as well. You have served Tanzlora with courage, and the bond you have forged will not soon be forgotten."

Lynx could only smile, blinking back tears, his heart full. He stroked the porcufera softly, feeling the little creature's reassuring warmth beneath his fingers, its quiet chirping echoing his own feelings of relief, gratitude, and hope.

Brakar stood gracefully, her serene voice bringing the council meeting to a close. "Now that our council is complete once more, we find ourselves in need of a new envoy to represent Tanzlora. Let us take some time to properly attire Keelee in the robes of an elder. When we reconvene shortly, our next task will be to discuss the envoy position and determine who among us will best serve Tanzlora in this role."

The elders nodded in agreement, murmuring softly amongst themselves as they began to rise and quietly depart the chamber. Lynx watched as Keelee stood slowly, still somewhat awed by the honor that had just been bestowed upon him. Keelee met Lynx's eyes, a gentle gratitude still shining in his own.

"You earned this," Lynx whispered quietly to Keelee as he passed by, the porcufera chirping softly in agreement.

Keelee placed a gentle hand on Lynx's shoulder, squeezing it lightly. "Thank you, my young friend. Your support means more than words can express."

Lumorith approached Keelee, a warm smile on his face. "Come, Keelee. It is time for you to don the elder's robes."

Keelee nodded humbly, and the two elders left the chamber side by side, followed closely by the other council members. Brakar approached Lynx, her expression warm and appreciative. "Lynx, you may join us in the gardens as we wait. Sanodia is there and has some food and refreshments to restore your strength. We will summon you again shortly."

"Thank you, Brakar," Lynx replied softly, bowing slightly. He cradled the porcufera protectively as he stood, turning toward the open archway that led outside.

Stepping into the sunlight, Lynx took a deep breath, savoring the peace and quiet of the gardens surrounding the council chambers. He felt relief washing over him, grateful for this brief moment of calm and reflection as he awaited the council's decision on their next envoy.

The formal dining room in the Vice President's residence was bathed in soft, warm light emanating from an elegant chandelier overhead. At one end of the long, polished table sat Vice President Charles Houston, flanked by his wife, Allison, whose presence provided a reassuring calm. Across from them, Celia Beaumont and Lorinda sat poised, attentive, quietly awaiting reactions from the assembled world leaders seated along either side of the table.

After Celia concluded the troubling news regarding the shocking betrayal of Elder Sylvaris on Tanzlora, a respectful, somber silence hung briefly in the air. Vice President Houston gently set down his glass, breaking the silence. "Thank you, Celia. I think I speak for everyone here when I say that we are deeply saddened by what Tanzlora is facing."

Murmurs of agreement filled the room as the world leaders exchanged knowing glances. The German Chancellor, Jurgen Klein, cleared his throat and spoke first, addressing Celia directly. "Mrs. Beaumont, on behalf of Germany—and I believe I speak for my colleagues as well—let me express our sincere condolences for this tragic betrayal. Unfortunately, each of us has known similar heartbreak within our own governments. We understand that Tanzlora requires grace and time to heal."

Nods echoed around the table in acknowledgment, the British Prime Minister, Charlotte Hughes, leaning forward slightly. "Indeed. Betrayal at the highest levels can shake an entire nation. Rest assured, we respect the Tanzloran's need for pause and recovery. However," she continued cautiously, "when Tanzlora feels prepared to reopen communications, we humbly suggest establishing a small delegation composed of selected leaders from around the globe. This delegation could travel to both Tanzlora and Arcmyrin to solidify trust and demonstrate our sincere intention for friendship, balance and harmony."

The French President, Daphne Laurent, spoke next, her voice compassionate yet confident. "In return, it may also be beneficial if a delegation of Tanzlorans and Arcmyrins visits Earth. Mutual exchange is crucial—not only to restore trust but also to lay a foundation for stronger ties in the aftermath of such upheaval."

The Japanese Prime Minister, Akio Yamaguchi, nodded thoughtfully. "This gesture of openness may help reassure our allies of our genuine commitment. Healing from betrayal is difficult, but shared dialogue and interaction will foster deeper understanding."

The Saudi leader, King Rami Kedar, interjected gently, "Indeed. This relationship must remain rooted in transparency and cooperation. Betrayal teaches us painful but valuable lessons, reminding us to nurture trust carefully."

Across the table, the Chinese General Secretary, Bai Zeng, added thoughtfully, "We have all seen the consequences when trust is compromised. As Earth extends its patience and support, we ask Tanzlora and Arcmyrin to consider our suggestions as steps toward strengthening our bonds, once they feel ready."

The Russian President, Lev Voloshin, regarded Celia carefully, choosing his words with deliberation. "As we've learned, rebuilding after betrayal requires openness to new ideas and the willingness to reestablish ties carefully. I trust Tanzlora will appreciate the same."

At the opposite end of the table, Lorinda spoke calmly but firmly, "Your understanding means a great deal. Tanzlora and Arcmyrin value your respect during this difficult period. Once the immediate wounds have begun to heal, I'm confident they will welcome a structured, thoughtful exchange."

Vice President Houston's wife, Allison, who had listened attentively, now offered a reassuring smile. "And we will ensure, from our end, that the delegation reflects the sincerity and good intentions behind this renewed commitment."

Prime Minister Yamaguchi nodded solemnly, "Perhaps through this tragedy comes an opportunity for deeper understanding between our worlds. Betrayal can either divide or unite; let us ensure it does the latter."

Vice President Houston straightened, his tone resolute and hopeful. "Then it's settled. While Tanzlora recovers, we'll allow them space to heal. And when they're ready, we'll propose a delegation exchange. Mutual trust and sincere understanding must be the cornerstone moving forward."

Celia, visibly moved, addressed the leaders warmly. "I want to express my heartfelt gratitude for the opportunity to meet with each of you tonight. It has truly been an honor, and I sincerely hope this will be the first of many meaningful conversations we share together. Even in the face of tragedy, I believe we're taking an important first step toward lasting unity."

Her earnest words prompted nods of appreciation from around the table.

Daphne Laurent, the French President, thoughtfully leaned forward. "Perhaps it would be beneficial if each of us wrote a personal letter to the Tanzlorans and Arcmyrins. These letters, delivered through the Beaumont family, could express our solidarity during this difficult time and extend our best wishes. Such gestures of goodwill might comfort them and reassure them our doors remain open when they're ready to resume communications."

Chancellor Klein from Germany enthusiastically agreed, "I think that's an excellent suggestion. Personal messages would clearly demonstrate our sincerity and solidarity."

Celia smiled appreciatively. "I think that would mean a great deal to them. Your personal support, especially now, could truly strengthen our bond and reassure them that Earth understands their struggle."

Chancellor Klein nodded, "And would we simply address the letters through your family?"

"Yes," Celia replied confidently, "My family will ensure each letter reaches Tanzlora and Arcmyrin safely."

King Kedar of Saudi Arabia interjected softly, "But should these letters be written in English, or must we arrange translations beforehand?"

Celia offered a reassuring smile, "Translations won't be necessary. Each of you can write in your own native languages. The Tanzlorans and Arcmyrins will understand perfectly. Their language capabilities far surpass ours; in fact, they comprehend languages no longer spoken or understood on Earth."

Her words hung in the air, stunning everyone present.

40

King Kedar of Saudi Arabia shook his head in mild disbelief. "Remarkable," he murmured. "Even with advanced technology, we still struggle greatly with accurate interpretations and communication."

A ripple of astonishment spread through the leaders as they exchanged amazed looks, silently acknowledging the extraordinary nature of this revelation.

Vice President Houston took a thoughtful breath, offering a wry smile. "Well, this certainly underscores how much we stand to gain from their friendship and knowledge. Perhaps we need this alliance more than we fully appreciate." He lifted his glass, signaling everyone else to follow suit. "Let's toast, then, to Tanzlora's healing and swift recovery."

Around the table, glasses were raised solemnly, a chorus of agreement resonating in the quiet elegance of the dining room.

For the first time since the discussion began, Celia felt a small sense of relief. The atmosphere around the table was shifting from cautious concern to genuine empathy and cautious optimism. Perhaps, she thought, from this painful moment, Earth, Arcmyrin and Tanzlora might finally build the lasting alliance they had always imagined.

The evening sky over Arcmyrin was tinged with shades of twilight lavender and fading gold, yet the scene in front of the small, humble pod stood in stark contrast to that beauty. Elara stood at the edge of the dwelling, her expression somber yet resolute as she addressed the circle of elders gathered around her. Beside her, Rykas stood protectively watchful, while several warriors quietly offered support from nearby.

The Arcmyrin elders formed a solemn semi-circle, their faces lined with the wisdom of centuries, their eyes carefully appraising the modest structure before them. Nearby, villagers murmured anxiously, casting wary glances toward the pod.

Stepping forward, Elder Releesia spoke gently to reassure them. "We appreciate your cooperation and patience during this troubling situation. Before we proceed, tell us—has anyone here entered or disturbed anything inside this structure?"

A young Arcmyrin villager stepped forward, eyes wide. "No, Elder Releesia. After that woman disappeared, no one dared approach the pod. It felt..." She hesitated, searching for the right word, "wrong somehow. Dark."

Elara nodded in confirmation. "Your instincts served you well. Upon inspection, Rykas and I immediately sensed a disturbing energy emanating throughout the entire space."

Elder Aduralina raised an eyebrow curiously. "You discovered something specific inside?"

"We did," Elara replied gravely. "Directly within the front entrance, there were a few artifacts placed strategically. They radiated a darkness unlike anything we've encountered in recent times. We made certain not to touch them."

A ripple of discomfort passed among the elders, their expressions darkening in concern.

Elara took a breath, steadying herself. "Furthermore," she continued, her voice quieter, "the flooring beneath those artifacts—its pattern was very familiar to me. I've seen it once before when I was on Earth, in the Crystal Gate chamber at Sage Manor."

A collective hush fell upon those gathered, broken only by Elder Releesia's troubled exhale. "That is disturbing," she repeated slowly.

"This cannot be a coincidence. Are the floors in that chamber the same?"

"It isn't," Elara said calmly. "I saw this exact floor in a display in the chamber, one that Keelee showed me when Lorinda Rooney's home was attacked by the Umbralox. A corrupted mirror was placed in her home and now I suspect Josephine did that utilizing the open portal system"

Rykas continued the story, "Keelee contacted Elara about a pendant and shrouded figure he saw on the display when he asked to be shown the conduit for the mirror and that is when the flooring was shown."

"Correct," confirmed Elara, "and that floor is a summoning circle, but altered. It has markings that correspond to elemental symbols—earth, water, air, fire—but they're inverted. That brings forth very dark forces and this strongly supports our suspicions about Josephine's involvement. We believe she was instrumental in facilitating Elder Sylvaris's betrayal on Tanzlora and that he summoned the Umbralox to his own planet. The signs are unmistakable."

Several villagers gasped audibly, turning to each other with widened eyes. Elder Ruliana shook her head in quiet sorrow, her voice tinged with both anger and grief. "How tragic that one living amongst us harbored such darkness."

Elder Aduralina placed a gentle hand on her arm, offering comfort. "It seems betrayal knows no borders. Earthlings have faced this often and now Tanzlorans. It is imperative now that we face this openly, without fear."

Ruliana's eyes narrowed, resolute. "Then we must purge this dark energy immediately. It must not remain here, threatening our harmony."

Releesia gestured to a group of Arcmyrin warriors standing nearby, their weapons sheathed but ready. "Prepare to safely dismantle and remove the artifacts first. Once that is done, we will destroy the structure entirely. The village and this planet must be cleansed of its darkness."

A villager hesitantly stepped forward, his expression troubled yet determined. "Forgive me, Elders. Josephine was strange, withdrawn, and rarely spoke to anyone. But we had no inkling she meant harm—only solitude. I assure you, none among us knew of this."

Elder Ruliana nodded gently. "There is no blame placed upon you or your fellow villagers. You are not responsible for the choices that woman made. We are grateful you have been spared direct harm."

The gathered villagers murmured quietly amongst themselves, their expressions shifting from anxiety to relief.

Elder Releesia spoke softly yet with certainty. "Let us proceed carefully now, with caution and compassion."

As preparations began to carefully remove the tainted artifacts, a heavy silence settled over those gathered. Elara stood solemnly beside Releesia, Lunarcher, and Milestree—her golden eyes reflecting the gravity of the moment. Next to her, Rykas stood with arms folded, a look of grim determination on his face as he directed his warriors.

Josephine's small living pod, a once-innocent dwelling hidden near the edge of the village, had become a stark symbol of darkness and betrayal. Although unassuming from the outside, its walls concealed corrupted artifacts, malevolent charms, and a lingering aura of destructive intent.

"Begin," Rykas commanded softly.

At his word, four Arcmyrian warriors stepped forward, forming a tight circle around the structure. Each held small vials filled with a glowing, vibrant blue liquid. As one, they poured the liquid onto the base of the pod. The solution shimmered briefly, then seemed to seep into the very fibers of the structure, illuminating it from within.

A gentle hum arose, and the villagers watched with wide, curious eyes, clinging to each other for reassurance. The warriors stepped back, and Rykas held up a hand to indicate a pause.

"May Origin cleanse this place of darkness," Releesia said quietly, her serene voice strong and steady. Her words seemed to ripple outward, echoing softly through the gathering.

The pod began to pulse, first faintly, then brighter and stronger. Suddenly, a brilliant flash of golden-white light burst forth, enveloping the structure entirely. Those gathered shielded their eyes, instinctively stepping back as warmth and purity washed over them.

As the light faded, all that remained was a small mound of ash-like particles, glowing faintly with residual energy. No trace of Josephine's corrupted artifacts or dark symbols remained.

"It is done," Lunarcher murmured softly, relief evident in his aged voice. "The corruption is gone."

Rykas nodded to the warriors, his approval clear. Releesia stepped forward, gently placing a hand upon his shoulder in quiet gratitude. Turning to the other elders and the watching villagers, she addressed them with compassion and strength.

"The destruction of this dwelling marks not only the end of that woman's darkness but a new beginning for Arcmyrin," she stated confidently. "Let this moment remind us all of the strength we possess when unified, when protecting the peace and harmony we cherish."

The villagers began murmuring softly in agreement, nodding to each other as the elders stepped forward to join Releesia, forming a circle of quiet strength.

Releesia raised her hands gently, speaking once more. "Now, let us move forward, wiser, stronger, and with our hearts united in the light."

41

Celia was carefully folding her clothes, setting them neatly inside her suitcase, while Lorinda sat on the edge of Celia's bed, eyes glued to the television screen.

Lorinda's voice held a note of concern as she turned up the volume. "Celia, come listen to this. They're saying something about Tanzlora on the news."

Celia immediately stopped packing, quickly crossing the room to stand beside Lorinda. The two women watched anxiously as a reporter stood in front of the White House gates, the familiar backdrop illuminated by mid-afternoon sunlight.

"Thank you, David," the reporter said, her tone steady but tinged with curiosity. "We have just received confirmation that the first official meeting scheduled for President Logan since his recent hospitalization has been abruptly cancelled. White House staff members are citing an unexpected situation involving the planet Tanzlora."

Lorinda gasped slightly, looking over at Celia. "How in the world did the media get wind of this already?"

Celia shook her head, her brow furrowing in concern. "I don't know."

The reporter continued, glancing briefly at her notes. "Initial speculation suggested a potential health-related relapse for President Logan, but sources inside the White House have strongly denied that possibility. Instead, they are pointing to what they're calling 'an unfortunate situation' on Tanzlora, one of the recently confirmed sister planets."

The camera shifted to footage of various world leaders entering limousines and SUVs after last night's dinner, their expressions tense and guarded, as the reporter's voiceover continued, "We are now seeing other world leaders who had gathered here in Washington for this groundbreaking conference departing the Vice President's residence last night. Reportedly, the Vice President and his wife hosted an informal dinner for all of the leaders and representatives of the Beaumont family to acquaint themselves before today's conference. With that conference now cancelled, we are being told that each of those leaders are returning to their own countries immediately."

As Celia sighed deeply, crossing her arms and looking thoughtfully at the screen, the phone rang, cutting through the weighty silence of the room. Both women exchanged a glance before Celia quickly reached for the receiver.

"Hello?" she answered.

"Mrs. Beaumont, it's Rachel Timms," came the familiar voice on the other end. "I hope I'm not interrupting."

"Not at all, Rachel," Celia said as Lorinda moved closer to listen. "What's going on?"

Rachel's tone held a note of urgency, though it remained professional. "Vice President Houston has requested that both you and Ms. Rooney accompany him to a meeting with President Logan. The President would like to personally speak with you both regarding last night's dinner before you depart D.C."

Celia's eyebrows lifted in mild surprise, but she quickly straightened. "That would be an honor," she said, already shifting her mindset into one of diplomacy. "We were just finishing our packing."

"Good," Rachel replied. "Once your meeting at the White House concludes, you'll be taken directly to the airport for your flight back home."

"That's much appreciated," Celia said. "I assume things are a tad tense over the situation with Tanzlora?"

Rachel hesitated before answering. "Yes. There's a lot of uncertainty right now. This meeting will give the President a chance to hear from you both directly, which I think is important for him to fully comprehend the situation."

Celia nodded, though Rachel couldn't see her. "That makes sense."

Rachel's voice softened slightly. "I'm sure you're both eager to get home."

"Yes, very much so," Celia agreed, glancing at Lorinda. "Especially Lorinda—she's been missing her daughter, Monica, terribly."

Lorinda smiled faintly at Celia's words, a warmth filling her heart despite the heaviness of the situation. "Yes, I have."

"I completely understand," Rachel said sympathetically. "I'll make sure everything is in place for a seamless trip home. In the meantime, go ahead and finish packing, and I'll ensure your transport brings you to the White House at 11 AM."

"Thank you, Rachel," Celia said sincerely. "We'll be ready."

As the call ended, Celia exhaled slowly and placed the phone back on the receiver. "Well, I certainly didn't expect that," she admitted, turning toward Lorinda. "Meeting the President before we leave?"

Lorinda smiled. "Neither did I, but it makes sense. He wants to hear directly from us about how things stand with the alliance before making any public statements."

Celia nodded, running a hand over her neatly folded clothes. "I just hope we can give him something reassuring."

"We'll do our best," Lorinda said. "That's all we can do."

With that, the two women returned to their packing, folding their final items into their suitcases when Lorinda suddenly gasped, her eyes widening as she pressed a hand to her forehead.

"Oh my goodness, Celia—the bridal gowns! We need to get those returned back to the store!"

Celia, in the middle of zipping her suitcase, stopped abruptly and let out an exaggerated sigh. "Oh my stars, Lorinda, I completely forgot about them. Have you made a decision on one yet?"

Lorinda nodded quickly. "I really like that third one I tried on."

"It did look beautiful on you," Celia agreed with a warm smile. "Very elegant and timeless."

"I am almost done with my packing, how about you?" Lorinda asked.

"Yes, I'm completely packed," Celia said, dusting off her hands. "And we don't leave for the White House until probably around 10:30, which gives us over an hour if you want to go back to that boutique."

Lorinda exhaled in relief, placing a hand over her heart. "Oh, I would love to. I really want to go back and talk to them about that dress and return the others in person. I know they said they would arrange to pick them up, but I want to inquire about purchasing that third one."

"Then let's go, dear," Celia said, grabbing her purse. "No sense in waiting."

Lorinda beamed as they both gathered the garment bags, carefully draping them over their arms before heading toward the door.

As they stepped into the hallway, they nearly collided with one of their security detail members, who had been passing by. The man stopped in his tracks, glancing between the two women and the bundle of gowns they carried.

"Ladies?" he asked, raising an eyebrow. "You're not scheduled to leave for another hour."

"Yes, about that," Celia said with a charming smile. "Is there any way we can take a quick trip back to the bridal boutique? We have a little errand to run."

The driver exchanged glances with his partner, then nodded. "Of course. Let's get you in the vehicle."

Within minutes, they were on their way, the familiar sights of Washington, D.C., passing by the car windows as excitement bubbled in Lorinda's chest.

As the SUV turned onto the street where the boutique was located, she glanced at Celia, shaking her head with a small laugh. "I can't believe I'm doing this. Buying a wedding dress in D.C. This trip wasn't supposed to be about me at all."

Celia chuckled. "Sometimes, life has a way of sneaking in joyful moments when you least expect them. And if there's anything worth celebrating, it's love." She patted Lorinda's hand. "Besides, Ridge is going to be absolutely speechless when he sees you in that dress."

Lorinda's cheeks warmed. "I sure hope so."

As the SUV came to a stop in front of the boutique, the associate from the previous day spotted them through the window and greeted them at the door with a bright smile.

"Ms. Rooney! Mrs. Beaumont! Welcome back," she said, ushering them inside. "Did you need more time to decide?"

Lorinda smiled as she unzipped the garment bags and handed back the two dresses she wasn't keeping. "Actually, no—I've made my decision. I'd love to purchase this bridal gown."

The associate clapped her hands together in delight. "A wonderful choice! Let's get you taken care of right away."

As the final transaction was completed, Celia watched the excitement on Lorinda's face, feeling deeply happy for her. This was more than just a wedding dress—it was a symbol of a fresh start, of love rekindled, of a future filled with hope.

With the dress safely packed up and the receipt in hand, they returned to the waiting SUV. As they settled back in, Celia glanced at her watch. "Perfect timing. We'll be back just in time to freshen up before we head to the White House."

Lorinda sighed contentedly, hugging the garment bag to her chest. "One more thing checked off the list. Now all I need is to get back home to Monica and start planning."

Celia grinned. "And what a grand wedding it's going to be."

As the SUV pulled away from the boutique, the energy of the city buzzed around them, but Lorinda's heart was already set on home—on Ridge, on Monica, and on the incredible journey that lay ahead.

42

The Tanzloran Council Chambers gleamed with the soft glow of the crystal sconces that lined the vast circular room. The air was thick with anticipation as villagers, warriors, and esteemed members of Tanzloran society gathered to witness a pivotal moment—the appointment of the new Tanzloran envoy.

At the head of the chamber, Brakar stood in her stately Elder robes, her presence commanding yet calm. To her right, Keelee, now in his regal Elder robes for the first time, sat among the other elders. The deep indigo fabric shimmered under the chamber's soft light, the silver embroidery denoting his new position as a guiding force for Tanzlora.

Seated among the honored witnesses, Lynx glanced around at the gathering, taking in the solemn but reverent expressions. Beside him, Sanodia, ever the healer, sat with hands folded in her lap, her sharp eyes observing every nuance of the ceremony. Callum and several warriors stood near the back, their posture disciplined, ready to witness history.

Brakar cleared her throat, the subtle sound immediately silencing the murmurs in the chamber. She swept her gaze across those gathered before she spoke.

"We gather here today in a time of healing and transition, in the wake of a betrayal that shook our very foundation. But Tanzlora does not waver—we endure, we learn, and we rise stronger than before. And now, it is time to fill the role that ensures our connection with our sister planets. A name has been spoken many times, a name that carries trust, wisdom, and unwavering service to our people."

She paused, her eyes warm as they settled on one individual among the gathering.

"Pazlun, will you please step forward to face the elders."

A ripple of approval hummed through the chamber as all eyes turned toward the seasoned warrior. Pazlun, who had long served as a steadfast protector of Tanzlora, hesitated only for a fraction of a second before stepping forward with quiet dignity. His imposing frame, clad in his warrior's tunic, was contrasted by the measured grace with which he moved. His piercing violet eyes met Brakar's with both humility and strength.

Lynx watched as Pazlun walked toward the elders, his respect for the warrior deepening. He had fought alongside Pazlun, witnessed his loyalty firsthand, and seen the unshakable commitment he held toward Tanzlora. There was no better choice.

As Pazlun reached the center of the chamber, he knelt briefly before rising to meet Brakar's gaze.

"Elders," Pazlun said, his voice steady but laced with the weight of the moment. "I am honored to stand before you and that my name is first to be considered for this highly important position. However, I am a warrior at heart, and if you will accept my declination of this honor respectfully, I would like nothing more than to remain the Commander of the Tanzloran warriors."

A hush fell over the chamber. The Elders, along with the gathered witnesses, exchanged surprised glances. The role of Envoy was a deeply respected and highly sought-after position, one that required strength, wisdom, and diplomacy—qualities Pazlun had demonstrated throughout his years of service. But his words carried the weight of truth.

Brakar regarded him carefully, her violet-hued gaze thoughtful. "Pazlun, your loyalty to Tanzlora is unquestionable. The council recognized your leadership and chose you because we believed you would serve with honor. But if your heart remains with the warriors, we must consider that, for no Tanzloran should be placed in a position they do not feel called to."

Keelee nodded from his new seat among the Elders. "A warrior who knows where he belongs is an invaluable asset to Tanzlora. And though you would have made a formidable Envoy, I believe your path as Commander of the Warriors remains essential, now more than ever."

Murmurs of agreement rippled through the chamber. Lynx exhaled slightly, feeling a sense of admiration for Pazlun's decision. He knew firsthand what kind of leader the Tanzloran warrior was—strong, fair, and deeply protective of his people. If anyone could lead their warriors into the uncertain future ahead, it was Pazlun.

Brakar stepped forward, her expression unreadable. "You have spoken your heart, Pazlun, and we respect your decision. You will remain Commander of the Tanzloran warriors."

A chorus of hums, the traditional gesture of respect, filled the air. Pazlun bowed deeply to the Elders before stepping back into place beside Callum and the other warriors.

Brakar took a breath before turning back to the council. "With Pazlun's respectful declination, we must now look to another for this role. We will take a brief recess before continuing the selection of our new Envoy."

The Elders nodded, and Brakar lifted her hand to dismiss the gathering for a moment of reflection. Lynx, still seated among the witnesses, couldn't help but wonder—who would the council choose now?

As the elders exited the chamber for deliberation, the air remained charged with anticipation. Lynx, Sanodia, Pazlun, and the other gathered warriors and villagers murmured quietly amongst themselves, exchanging theories about who the council might choose next. Lynx glanced at Sanodia, who appeared deep in thought, her fingers absently twisting the hem of her sleeve.

"Do you have an idea who they'll choose?" he whispered.

She shook her head, though there was something knowing in her expression. "I do not, but I trust that Origin will guide them to the right one."

Minutes later, the grand doors of the chamber swung open again, and the elders re-entered with a purposeful stride. Brakar took her seat and looked out over the gathered witnesses. The chamber fell into silence as she raised her hand.

"After careful consideration, we, the Elders of Tanzlora, have come to a decision," she announced. "Callum, step forward."

A collective intake of breath filled the chamber as all eyes turned to Callum. Sanodia gasped softly, her hands flying to her mouth. Lynx watched as Callum, momentarily stunned, processed what had just been asked of him. Then, after a brief moment, he squared his shoulders and stepped forward with quiet confidence.

The elders watched him intently as Brakar continued. "Callum, you have spent time on Earth. You have lived among its people, learned their ways, and returned with insight that few Tanzlorans possess. Given the recent events that have tested the trust between our worlds, we believe you would be an invaluable bridge—one who can restore what was lost and build something even greater."

She paused, then added, "Do you accept this role, knowing the responsibility it carries?"

Callum stood tall before the council, his expression one of solemn pride. He clasped his hands together and bowed deeply in the traditional gesture of respect before meeting their gazes.

"Elders," he said, his voice steady but filled with emotion, "I accept this honor with humility and gratitude. I hope to bring pride to Tanzlora and to mend any misunderstandings that may exist between our people and the humans of Earth."

His eyes swept across the room, taking in the gathered witnesses, his fellow warriors, and finally, his sister, whose face was streaked with tears of joy.

"I have lived among the humans," Callum continued, "and I have seen their kindness, their love for their families and their people. They are not all like Gideon and Josephine. We must not let the actions of two corrupted souls poison the future that we, the Triad, are meant to build together."

A wave of silence followed his words, the weight of them sinking deep into the hearts of all present. And then, a single clap echoed through the chamber.

Keelee, newly adorned in his regal Elder robes, had risen to his feet. With his hands clasped together, he began applauding. One by one, the other elders joined him, and soon, the entire chamber was on their feet, their applause ringing through the grand hall.

Lynx turned to Sanodia, whose eyes shone with pride, tears spilling freely down her cheeks. "He will be great," she whispered, her voice trembling with emotion.

Lynx smiled and placed a comforting hand on her shoulder. "Yes, he will."

As the applause continued, Brakar lifted her hands for quiet. When silence fell once more, she nodded approvingly.

"Then it is decided. Callum of Tanzlora, from this moment forward, you shall serve as our Envoy. May you walk in wisdom, truth, and honor, and may Origin guide your every step."

A final chorus of respectful hums echoed through the chamber. Callum, standing tall and proud, bowed once more.

Tanzlora had a new elder and envoy, and a new chapter had begun.

43

Ridge and Lincoln stood in the chamber beneath the gazebo, their expressions serious as they activated the communicator orb. A soft hum filled the room, and the swirling blue mist within the orb began to coalesce into the familiar flickering light of an incoming connection. They expected Keelee to appear at any moment, but as the image began to take shape, they exchanged confused glances.

The figure before them was not Keelee.

As the image solidified, both Ridge and Lincoln leaned forward in astonishment.

"Wait a minute..." Ridge murmured, squinting at the figure before realization struck.

Lincoln's eyes widened as he finally recognized the face staring back at them. "Callum?"

"In the flesh, so to speak," Callum responded with a huge grin, his holographic form standing tall and composed.

Ridge let out a laugh, shaking his head. "It's been a long time, brother. What are you doing answering this call?"

Lincoln, still processing, crossed his arms. "Yeah, last we heard you were still a warrior. No offense, but the clothing you're wearing looks like you're standing in a pretty high-ranking spot."

Callum chuckled looking down at his envoy tunic, but his expression turned serious as he nodded. "Much has happened since we last spoke. Tanzlora has undergone an unexpected shift in leadership."

Both Ridge and Lincoln straightened at this.

"What do you mean?" Ridge asked.

"First, Keelee is now an Elder," Callum informed them, allowing the weight of the statement to settle in.

Lincoln and Ridge exchanged a stunned glance. "Keelee? An Elder?"

Callum nodded. "Yes. After Sylvaris' betrayal, the council came together to select his replacement, and Keelee was chosen unanimously."

Lincoln let out a low whistle. "Well, if anyone deserves it, it's Keelee."

"Agreed," Ridge added. "But what about you? Why are you the one answering this call?"

Callum exhaled, glancing around at his surroundings before looking back at them. "Because I am now Tanzlora's Envoy."

Silence stretched for a moment as Ridge and Lincoln processed this revelation.

"You?" Ridge finally said, a grin breaking across his face. "You're the new envoy?"

"That is correct," Callum replied, amusement twinkling in his eyes.

Lincoln, still slightly in shock, rubbed the back of his neck. "Wow. That's... unexpected, but honestly, I can't think of anyone better for the role."

"Thank you," Callum said sincerely. "I know you both have a lot of questions, but I'll catch you up later. Right now, there's something more important we need to discuss."

Ridge and Lincoln immediately turned serious. "What is it?" Lincoln asked.

Callum's expression darkened slightly. "Pazlun, myself, and several warriors are preparing to bring Lynx home within the next Earth hour."

"Lynx is coming home?" Ridge repeated, relief washing over him.

Lincoln exhaled, nodding. "That's the best news we've heard all day. We'll be ready for him."

Callum hesitated briefly before adding, "He's bringing a friend with him. One that requires special care."

Lincoln and Ridge exchanged confused looks.

"What do you mean, special care?" Lincoln asked, his brow furrowing.

Ridge suddenly sat up straighter as a thought hit him. "Wait a second... Could it be... the Porcufera?"

Callum's expression softened with a small smile. "It seems you already know. Yes, Lynx refuses to leave the Porcufera behind, and from what we've seen, the creature feels the same about him. It's been through a lot and will need healing once it arrives."

Lincoln shook his head in disbelief. "That boy... he's bringing a legendary creature back to Earth."

Ridge let out a chuckle, running a hand through his hair. "Honestly, I'm not even surprised. Lynx and that Porcufera were inseparable. It was only a matter of time before he found a way to bring it home."

"Then make preparations," Callum instructed. "We will arrive soon."

Lincoln nodded. "We'll be ready. And Callum... it's really good to see you again, brother."

Callum gave them a small, knowing smile. "Likewise. See you soon."

The connection flickered and then faded, leaving Ridge and Lincoln standing in stunned but excited silence.

"Welp," Ridge finally said. "We better get ready. We're about to have an unexpected guest."

Lincoln smirked. "And an even bigger story to tell the family."

With that, the two brothers turned and hurried up the stairs, preparing to welcome Lynx—and his mysterious companion—back home.

Vice President Charles Houston walked briskly down the grand hallway of the White House, flanked by Celia and Lorinda. The air was charged with anticipation as they made their way toward the Oval Office. Both women had spent a lifetime in important rooms, but this was the first time either of them would be stepping into the very heart of the United States government.

Celia kept her composure, but Lorinda could feel her pulse quickening. Meeting the President and First Lady was an honor, but under these circumstances, the gravity of the conversation ahead made the experience even more surreal.

"President Logan wanted to meet you both personally before you head back to North Carolina," Houston said as they approached the iconic wooden doors. "He was deeply interested in hearing your thoughts on last night's dinner and, of course, the recent developments on Tanzlora." He turned his head slightly, his voice lower. "Just be direct. The President appreciates honesty over pleasantries."

Celia nodded. "That won't be a problem."

A moment later, a uniformed staff member opened the door, and they stepped inside.

The Oval Office was a stunning sight—the golden drapes framing the windows, the grand desk positioned at the far end, and the rich blue carpet beneath their feet. The room exuded history and power, but Celia's focus was immediately drawn to the man standing near the Resolute Desk.

President Donovan Logan turned from where he had been speaking quietly with his wife, First Lady Gillian Logan. His presence was commanding, yet warm. He extended a hand first to Celia.

"Mrs. Beaumont, a pleasure to meet you. I've heard a great deal about you."

Celia shook his hand firmly. "Thank you, Mr. President. It's an honor."

He turned to Lorinda. "And Ms. Rooney, welcome to the White House."

Lorinda smiled as she shook his hand. "Thank you, sir. I never imagined I'd be here under circumstances like these."

The First Lady, elegantly dressed in a soft lavender suit, approached with a kind smile. "Celia, Lorinda, I'm so pleased to meet you both. My husband and Charles have told me about your work on this interplanetary alliance. It's fascinating."

"Thank you, Mrs. Logan," Celia responded, ever composed. "We're hopeful about what this could mean for the future of not just Earth, but the entire Triad."

The President gestured toward the seating area. "Please, have a seat. Let's get right to it."

As they settled onto the cream-colored sofas, Houston took a seat beside them while the First Lady perched gracefully near her husband. A steward entered, quietly setting down a tray of coffee and tea before exiting.

"I know you both must be eager to get home," President Logan began. "I appreciate you taking the time to meet with me before you leave. Charles briefed me on the dinner with the world leaders last night, but I'd like to hear your impressions directly. Was there real interest in this alliance?"

Celia folded her hands in her lap. "Yes, there was interest, but there were also hesitations. It's a concept that's never been done before, and many of these leaders are approaching it with caution, which is understandable."

Lorinda nodded. "They were receptive, but we also got the sense that they need more time to trust the idea fully. Many of them don't even fully trust each other, let alone two planets they've never visited."

Logan sighed, rubbing his temple. "I expected as much. It's hard enough getting nations to work together—throw in extraterrestrial alliances, and we're in uncharted territory."

Houston leaned forward slightly. "And now, with what's happened on Tanzlora, that caution will only increase."

The President's expression darkened. "Yes. That's what I really wanted to talk to you about." He glanced at Celia. "Charles said you had concerns about Tanzlora stepping back from the alliance?"

Celia took a breath. "It's more than just concerns, Mr. President. We've spoken with our contacts on Tanzlora, and they've made it clear that trust has been deeply shaken by what transpired. One of their most respected elders, Sylvaris, turned against them, poisoning another council member and even plotting against my grandson, Lynx. And the worst part? He was aided by a human."

The President exchanged a look with the First Lady before nodding. "I understand that person was an estranged member of your family, a woman named Josephine."

"Yes," Celia confirmed. "Our own family. And that has made the Tanzlorans and Arcmyrins second-guess whether opening themselves up to Earth was a mistake."

Lorinda added, "The alliance isn't lost, but it's fragile. We need to act carefully moving forward if we want to repair the damage."

The First Lady, who had been listening attentively, finally spoke. "From what I understand, both Tanzlora and Arcmyrin have lived in peace for centuries, correct?"

"Yes," Celia affirmed. "That's part of the issue. This level of betrayal is unheard of for them. It's never happened before."

The President sighed. "And now they're questioning whether humanity is worth the risk."

Celia nodded gravely. "Exactly."

A heavy silence settled over the room as the weight of the situation sank in.

Finally, Logan leaned back, his fingers steepled. "We have to show them that the actions of two people don't define all of humanity. That's our way forward."

Houston nodded in agreement. "I believe that's what the other world leaders need to understand as well. This alliance won't be built overnight, but if we can prove that Earth is committed to peace, we may still have a chance."

Celia smiled slightly. "That is my hope as well."

The President tapped his fingers on the armrest. "I'd like to set up a special delegation—one that will continue these talks even if the other planets remain hesitant for now." He looked at Celia. "And I want you involved, Mrs. Beaumont."

Celia's eyebrows lifted slightly. "Mr. President, I'd be honored."

Logan smiled. "Then let's start making plans. When you get home, stay in touch with Charles and keep the conversations going with Tanzlora and Arcmyrin. We'll find a way forward."

The First Lady reached for Celia's hand, giving it a warm squeeze. "You've already done so much. I have faith in you."

Celia nodded, deeply moved. "Thank you, Mrs. Logan."

The President stood, signaling the end of the meeting. "I appreciate you both coming in today. Safe travels back to North Carolina, and give my best to your family."

As Celia and Lorinda rose, the Vice President walked them to the door.

"We'll be in touch," Houston assured them.

As they stepped out of the Oval Office, Celia exhaled, her mind already working on the next steps. Lorinda glanced over at her and smiled.

"That went well," Lorinda said.

Celia smiled. "Yes. Now let's just hope we can convince Tanzlora and Arcmyrin of the same."

With that, they headed back toward their waiting car, ready to return home to Sage Manor.

44

The golden hues of late afternoon cast a warm glow over Sage Manor as the entire family gathered on the front porch, their eyes fixed on the gazebo in the distance. A palpable sense of anticipation filled the air. Lincoln stood with his arm around Bethany, while Waverly sat on the steps with Maya, Maddox, and Monica, the three children fidgeting with excitement. Ridge, Francis, and Bronte leaned against the porch railing, engaged in quiet conversation, while Madre and Marshall stood side by side, soaking in the peaceful evening.

Then, the moment they had been waiting for arrived.

A radiant glow spilled from the chamber beneath the gazebo, golden beams of light cascading over the surrounding lawn. The familiar hum of the Crystal Gate activation resonated through the air, a sound that signified interplanetary travel was taking place.

Maya gasped, gripping Waverly's hand. "They're here!"

Monica bounced on her toes. "I see them! They're coming up the lawn!"

Everyone straightened, their gazes locked on the figures emerging from the gazebo and stepping onto the tranquil grounds of Sage Manor.

At the forefront, Lynx walked steadily toward them, carrying a sling wrapped securely around his chest. His face bore signs of exhaustion, but his expression was one of relief and quiet triumph. Nestled in the sling, the Porcufera rested, its tiny quills twitching slightly as it nestled close to Lynx's body.

Beside him, Callum strode confidently, his posture reflecting the newfound responsibility of his envoy position. On Lynx's other side,

Sanodia, her kind eyes full of warmth, walked with measured grace. Flanking them, several Tanzloran warriors moved in silent formation, their presence a reassuring sign of strength and security.

As the group approached the house, the children couldn't contain their excitement.

"Lynx! Lynx!" Maddox yelled, dashing down the steps, Maya and Monica right behind him.

Lynx barely had time to brace himself before all three of them collided into him in a group hug.

"Whoa, careful, careful," Lynx laughed, shifting slightly to keep the Porcufera protected in its sling.

Monica's eyes widened as she spotted the small creature. "Is that the Porcufera?"

Lynx nodded. "Yeah, but we have to be really gentle. It's been sick and needs time to heal."

Maya tilted her head, mesmerized. "Can we pet it?"

Lynx crouched down slightly, adjusting the sling to reveal more of the creature's soft quills. "You can, but only gently. It's still weak."

The children reached out hesitantly, their fingertips brushing the creature's fur with featherlight touches. The Porcufera let out a soft, melodic chirp, a sound that made everyone smile.

"It likes you," Lynx told them, glancing at Maddox, who was staring at the Porcufera with fascination.

Lincoln finally stepped forward, resting a firm hand on his son's shoulder. "You're home, son." His voice was thick with emotion. "And I couldn't be prouder of you."

Lynx met his father's gaze, nodding, the weight of his journey settling in. "It's good to be home."

Bethany came forward next, pulling him into a tight hug despite the sling, pressing a kiss to his forehead. "You scared us, Lynx."

"I know, Mom," he murmured. "But everything's okay now."

Ridge clapped him on the back. "You did well, kid. Real well."

Francis, Bronte, and Madre all greeted him warmly, while Marshall gave him an approving nod. "You've had quite the adventure, haven't you?"

Lynx chuckled. "That's putting it lightly."

Sanodia spoke up, her melodic voice soothing. "Lynx showed great wisdom and bravery. He has done a great service for all three planets."

Lincoln turned to Callum, shaking his hand firmly. "Thank you for bringing him home, Callum. We're grateful."

Callum returned the handshake with a confident nod. "It was my honor. Lynx has proven himself to be stronger than he realizes."

Lynx gave Callum a smirk. "Don't make me sound too impressive. I was just trying to survive."

Callum laughed, but Sanodia's eyes twinkled knowingly. "Sometimes, survival is the greatest act of strength."

Bethany exhaled, still holding onto Lynx as if she couldn't quite believe he was standing in front of her. "Alright, enough standing around. Let's get inside and get everyone fed."

Lincoln grinned. "Agreed. We've got a lot to talk about."

As the group made their way up the porch and into the warmth of the manor, Waverly fell into step beside Lynx.

"You've been through a lot, huh?" she asked.

Lynx gave her a side glance, smirking. "You have no idea."

Waverly gave Lynx a knowing look, her eyes twinkling with curiosity. "We'll talk later," she said as they stepped into the welcoming warmth of Sage Manor. "I want to hear everything—what happened, how you outsmarted Sylvaris and Josephine, and what the Tanzloran council was like. Then, we can compare notes on our experiences with each council. I need details, if you're up for it."

Lynx let out a breathy chuckle, shaking his head. "I'll tell you, but let's just say it wasn't exactly the grand diplomatic experience you had." He glanced down at the Porcufera nestled in his sling. "It was more… survival-oriented."

Waverly smirked. "Figures. You always manage to get caught up in the craziest situations."

Lynx raised an eyebrow at her. "Me? Look who's talking. You had to take out Gideon yourself."

Waverly huffed, nudging him playfully. "Yeah, but at least I had a plan. You, on the other hand, I imagine just winged it."

Lynx grinned. "You'd be surprised how much 'winging it' works out when your life's on the line."

Bethany, overhearing their conversation as she led the way into the dining room, turned back and shook her head with a tired smile. "Alright, enough war stories for now, you two. Let's get everyone fed, then you can talk all night if you want."

Lynx glanced over at Waverly. "Deal?"

Waverly nodded. "Deal. But don't think you're getting out of anything. I expect the full story."

As they made their way to the long dining table, Ridge pulled out a chair for Lynx, gesturing for him to sit. "You can start by telling us how you managed to stay one step ahead of them. From what I've heard, that was no small feat."

Lynx lowered himself into the chair with a sigh, feeling the weight of everything settle in. "It wasn't," he admitted, adjusting the Porcufera's sling before picking up a fork. "But I had some help."

Marshall, seated across from him, leaned forward. "From who?"

Lynx hesitated, then gave a small, knowing smile. "I think I'll let Waverly go first. She got to have a proper council experience while I was running for my life."

The room filled with a mixture of laughter and understanding as plates were passed around, the aroma of home-cooked food filling the space.

Waverly smirked at him. "Fine. But after dinner, your turn."

Lynx nodded, finally allowing himself to relax. "Fair enough."

For the first time in what felt like ages, he was home.

The black SUV rolled to a smooth stop in front of Sage Manor, the headlights illuminating the grand porch as Celia and Lorinda gathered their things. The two drivers, the same men who had escorted them to the airport days before, stepped out to open their doors.

"Ladies, welcome home," one of them said with a polite nod as Celia stepped onto the porch, followed by Lorinda.

"Thank you both," Celia said warmly. "We appreciate you getting us back in one piece."

Lorinda, still clutching the garment bag with her carefully chosen wedding dress, sighed with relief. "Yes, thank you. It's been a long trip, and this moment feels like heaven."

The drivers gave them a small salute before climbing back into the SUV. The engine purred as the vehicle pulled away, its red taillights glowing in the night before disappearing down the winding road.

Celia turned to Lorinda, looking down at the neatly stacked luggage at their feet.

"Well," Celia mused, hands on her hips, "let's hope someone is home to help us lug all this inside."

Lorinda, still holding the garment bag over one arm, gave Celia a smirk. "All I know is that I have my dress, and that's all I care about." She lifted the bag slightly for emphasis.

Celia chuckled. "As you should, my dear. That dress is the star of the show."

She reached for the front door, giving it a gentle push, and it swung open with ease. A wave of warmth greeted them, along with the irresistible aroma of home-cooked food filling the air.

Celia inhaled deeply, savoring the scent of freshly baked bread, roasted meat, and something sweet lingering in the air. "Oh my... I think they're having dinner," she murmured, stepping into the inviting glow of the entryway.

Lorinda followed, sighing in delight. "Good," she said fervently. "And I pray they've made enough for us, because it smells delicious."

Celia laughed softly. "If they haven't, I'm sure we can convince someone to whip up a plate or two."

Lorinda set her luggage against the wall and stretched her arms above her head. "That's all the convincing I need. Let's go find the food."

The two women exchanged knowing smiles before making their way toward the dining room.

The dining room of Sage Manor was alive with the sounds of clinking silverware, warm conversation, and the occasional burst of laughter but as Celia and Lorinda stepped into the room, a hush fell over the table for only a brief second before it erupted into a flurry of motion.

Monica, who had been sitting beside Ridge, let out an excited squeal and practically leaped from her chair, sprinting across the room to throw her arms around her mother.

"Mom! You're back!" Monica squeezed her tightly, burying her face against her shoulder.

Ridge followed right behind, wrapping both arms around Lorinda and Monica, pressing a kiss to Lorinda's temple. "Welcome home, sweetheart."

Lincoln had already risen from his seat and strode toward Celia, enveloping her in a firm but loving embrace. "Mom," he murmured. "It's good to see you."

Celia exhaled, allowing herself to melt into her son's familiar strength. "Oh, I missed you all," she said, her voice laced with relief and warmth.

Across the table, Francis and Bethany were already pushing back their chairs, both smiling warmly.

"Glad to have you ladies home," Bethany said as she stood. "Let's get you some plates—there's plenty of food left."

Francis nodded in agreement. "And you're going to want to eat. Bronte and Marshall outdid themselves tonight."

Celia chuckled, patting her stomach. "Oh, that's music to my ears. It smells divine."

Her eyes finally fell on Pazlun, Callum, and Sanodia, seated among the family, their presence a pleasant surprise. She immediately made her way toward them, her expression radiating warmth.

"Well, well, well," she said, her voice full of affection. "Look at who's at my dinner table!"

She first reached for Pazlun's hand, giving it a firm squeeze. "It is so good to see you again, Commander."

Pazlun, ever stoic but with a gleam of genuine appreciation in his eyes, inclined his head. "And you, Miss Celia."

She then turned to Callum, beaming. "I hear congratulations are in order, Envoy Callum."

Callum chuckled, standing to embrace her in a quick but heartfelt hug. "I couldn't have done it without Lynx and Keelee's support. It's good to see you, Miss Celia."

Finally, she stepped toward Sanodia, her voice softening. "Sanodia, dear, I am so pleased you are here." She took Sanodia's hands in hers, giving them a gentle squeeze.

Sanodia smiled, her eyes shimmering with warmth. "Thank you, Miss Celia. It is an honor to be in your home."

Lorinda, now settled into the room, looked around at all the familiar faces. "I feel like we've been gone forever, and it's only been a few days!"

Ridge chuckled, his arm still draped around her shoulders. "A lot has happened, but right now, what matters is that everyone is home safe, and we can all sit down together."

Bethany and Francis returned with two heaping plates of food, placing them at the now-cleared seats at the table.

"Come on, ladies," Bethany urged, "sit down and eat before Bronte starts grumbling that his food is going cold!"

A familiar gruff voice piped up from the other end of the table. "I heard that!" Bronte said, earning a round of laughter from everyone.

Celia and Lorinda finally took their seats, grateful to be back among their family, their friends, and the warmth of home.

<h1 style="text-align:center">45</h1>

Outside the patio doors off the kitchen of Sage Manor, Lynx, Waverly, Maddox, Maya and Monica stood huddled together, their eyes fixed on Sanodia as she gently knelt down and carefully placed the porcufera onto the lush green grass. The creature, still recovering from its ordeal, had been treated with Sanodia's herbal mixtures back on Tanzlora, but this was the first time it had ever set paws on Earth.

The group watched in anticipation, their breath almost held in collective suspense. Would it react well to Earth's environment? Would it be frightened? Confused?

For a brief moment, the porcufera stayed still, its small quills twitching slightly, its tiny paws pressing into the unfamiliar texture of the Earth's soil. Then, suddenly, it scampered forward with a delighted chirp, rolling onto its back and wriggling happily in the grass.

The children burst into laughter.

"It likes it!" Monica exclaimed, bouncing on her toes.

Maya clapped her hands. "Look at it roll around!"

Maddox, ever observant, tilted his head. "It's smelling everything."

The porcufera didn't just stop at the grass—it soon rolled upright and started moving toward them. One by one, it nibbled at their feet, its tiny teeth barely grazing their shoes and ankles.

Maddox let out a small gasp, pulling his foot back slightly. "It tickles!"

Monica let out a giggle, but when the porcufera reached Maya, she instinctively stepped back. "Lynx, is it supposed to do that?"

Lynx, who had been watching the porcufera carefully, nodded reassuringly. "It's trying to get used to your scent. Stay still, don't move too fast, and let it get familiar with you."

The children followed his instructions, standing as still as they could while the porcufera continued its exploration.

Waverly smirked. "This is like getting a new puppy."

Lynx chuckled but shook his head. "Yeah, except this isn't a puppy. It's a porcufera, and it's going to need more care than a puppy."

Sanodia nodded solemnly, her violet-hued eyes flickering with seriousness. "That is correct, my friends. The porcufera is unlike any creature on Earth. It will need time to adjust, and its health must be monitored closely. We do not know how it will react to your atmosphere long-term."

Monica's smile dimmed slightly. "You mean... it might get sick again?"

Sanodia offered a warm, reassuring smile. "Not necessarily, but we must be cautious. We will watch over it, ensure it is comfortable, and give it the care it needs."

Maddox crouched down, his small fingers hesitating just above the creature's soft quills. "Does it have a name?" he asked.

Lynx and Sanodia exchanged a glance.

"On Tanzlora," Sanodia said thoughtfully, "they do not have names like you Earthlings give to your companions. But perhaps it is time for this one to have a name of its own."

The children perked up immediately.

"Can we name it?!" Monica asked excitedly.

Lynx smirked. "I don't see why not. But let's see if the porcufera actually responds to anything before we decide."

Maya crouched next to Maddox, her eyes filled with curiosity. "What about... Star?"

The porcufera kept rolling around in the grass, seemingly oblivious.

Monica tried next. "How about Quillie?"

The porcufera paused, twitched its ears, and let out a tiny chirp.

Lynx raised an eyebrow. "Well, that got a reaction."

Maddox grinned. "I like Quillie!"

Sanodia smiled softly. "Then Quillie it is."

The newly named porcufera chirped again, then darted back toward Lynx, circling his feet before nuzzling against his leg.

Waverly folded her arms, grinning. "Looks like it still knows who it's favorite Earthling is."

Lynx rolled his eyes but smiled anyway, reaching down to gently stroke Quillie's back. "Yeah, yeah. Guess I'm stuck with you, huh?"

The porcufera chirped happily.

And just like that, Quillie the porcufera had officially become a part of the Sage Manor family.

As the dining room bustled with movement, Celia and Lorinda helped Francis and Bethany clear the table, stacking plates and gathering silverware. The warm aroma of freshly baked fruit tarts and cream-filled pastries wafted from the kitchen, signaling the start of dessert.

Celia carried a stack of plates toward the kitchen, but as she stepped through the doorway, she stopped mid-step, blinking in mild surprise.

Three Tanzloran warriors sat at the breakfast table, their backs straight, their hands resting lightly on the smooth wooden surface after finishing their dinner. Their violet-hued skin gleamed softly in the dim kitchen light, and their eyes tracked her entrance with quiet respect.

Celia tilted her head. "I didn't realize you were here."

The warrior closest to her, Drexel, the same warrior who had helped protect Sage Manor alongside Callum, inclined his head. "We did not wish to intrude, Miss Celia."

She frowned, glancing between them. "You're not intruding. We're about to eat dessert—come join us in the dining room."

Drexel's expression remained polite but firm. "No, Miss Celia. That would be inappropriate."

Celia arched a brow. "Inappropriate? Who told you that?"

Drexel hesitated, exchanging glances with the other two warriors before replying, "It is not our place to dine alongside your family during a private meal."

"Nonsense," Celia placed a hand on her hip. "I will not allow you three to sit in here alone while the rest of us enjoy dessert. That's not how we do things at Sage Manor."

Before they could argue, Celia turned back toward the dining room and raised her voice just enough to be heard over the chatter.

"Pazlun, do you see a problem with your warriors joining us for dessert?"

All conversation halted for a brief moment as the Tanzloran commander lifted his gaze. He met Celia's eyes across the room, then glanced toward Drexel and his fellow warriors in the kitchen. His answer was simple and direct.

"No, Miss Celia."

Celia flashed a triumphant smile as she stepped back into the doorway. "See?" She gestured toward them with a slight wave of her hand. "Come on, Drexel, you and your fellow warriors come in here."

The three warriors hesitated for only a second, but then, seeing Pazlun's lack of objection, they rose to their feet in perfect unison. As they passed by Celia, she suddenly realized just how much they towered over her.

Her gaze trailed upward, taking in their sheer size.

"Wait a second," she said, curiosity sparking in her voice. "Just how tall are you?"

Drexel, already aware of Earth's measurement systems, replied smoothly. "In Earth measurements?"

"Yes," Celia confirmed, craning her neck to look him in the eyes.

Drexel tilted his head in thought. "Probably around 6'8."

Celia let out a soft "Wow", watching as they carefully took their seats at the dining table.

The once-serious warriors looked slightly out of place amid the warm, familial atmosphere, but as soon as Francis and Bethany began serving plates of fruit tarts and cream, the tension eased.

Madre leaned toward her husband with a grin. "I think Sage Manor just adopted three more family members."

Marshall chuckled, shaking his head. "Seems that way. After all, we have been here for months now."

And with that, the dessert gathering became a new shared experience, bridging the worlds of Earth and Tanzlora over laughter, conversation, and the simple joy of a meal shared among friends.

46

The peaceful hum of conversation in the dining room was suddenly interrupted by the sound of footsteps pounding across the wooden floors.

Waverly, Lynx, Sanodia, Maya, Maddox, and Monica came bursting through the doorway, all talking at once, their voices overlapping in a chaotic yet joyful frenzy.

"You won't believe it!" Maddox exclaimed, eyes wide with excitement.

"It was rolling all over the grass!" Monica added, practically bouncing on her toes.

"And nibbling at our feet!" Maya giggled, her cheeks flushed from the evening air.

Waverly laughed, grabbing onto the back of a chair to steady herself as she tried to catch her breath. "It's adjusting so well to Earth! I don't think I've ever seen the porcufera this happy!"

Lynx nodded, grinning at the kids' enthusiasm. "It's like it knows this is home now."

Sanodia, ever the gentle caretaker, smiled softly. "It will take time, but it's clear the porcufera is already bonding with your land and your people."

The adults watched the flurry of energy, their own laughter bubbling up as they listened to the kids' rapid retelling of the porcufera's antics.

After a few minutes, Bethany clapped her hands lightly, a knowing smile on her face. "Alright, alright—deep breaths, everyone."

The children immediately quieted, but their eyes still sparkled with excitement.

Bethany gave them a pointed look. "Now, as much as I love hearing all about your new little friend, I think it's time for baths and bed."

The groans were instant and loud.

"Noooo!" Maddox whined.

"But we're not even tired!" Maya argued, crossing her arms dramatically.

Monica, looking to her mother for support, turned big pleading eyes on Lorinda. "Can't we stay up just a little bit longer?"

Lorinda laughed, shaking her head. "Oh no, don't try that look on me—I invented that look." She let out a playful yawn, stretching her arms. "Besides, it's actually past my bedtime too."

The kids looked betrayed, their shoulders slumping.

Bethany reached down and gently tousled Maddox's curls. "Come on, you three. I promise you'll have plenty of time tomorrow to play with the porcufera."

Reluctantly, the kids began trudging toward the hallway, though their grumbles of protest didn't go unnoticed.

Sanodia chuckled. "They remind me of the younglings on Tanzlora. There is always resistance to bedtime, no matter what planet you're from."

Lynx grinned, stretching his arms behind his head. "That's a universal truth if I've ever heard one."

As the kids were led upstairs, their footsteps echoing on the wooden staircase, Waverly turned to Lynx with a smirk.

"You know," she teased, "if you'd told me a few weeks ago that you'd be bringing a porcufera to Earth and that our biggest concern would be convincing the kids to go to bed, I would've thought you were crazy."

Lynx chuckled, shaking his head. "Yeah, well... life is full of surprises, isn't it?"

The evening air was crisp and filled with the lingering warmth of family and friendship as the Beaumonts and their guests walked together down the stone path toward the gazebo. The towering oaks whispered in the night breeze, their leaves rustling like a gentle farewell song.

The Tanzlorans, some adorned in their flowing robes and tunics, others in their warrior uniforms, walked with quiet reverence, their presence both majestic and comforting. Sanodia, Callum, Pazlun, and the warriors had spent enough time at Sage Manor to feel a true connection again to Earth and its people. Now, it was time to return home.

As they reached the gazebo, the light from the chamber that housed the Crystal Gate portal spilled out onto the lawn, beckoning them home.

Sanodia turned to Celia, pressing a folded parchment into her hands.

"This is the list of herbal mixtures I spoke of," she said. "These will help the porcufera continue to acclimate to Earth."

Celia studied the list, grateful for Sanodia's knowledge. "Thank you, dear. I'll make sure we follow this carefully."

Sanodia smiled warmly, her eyes full of sincerity. "I will check on it weekly, and if there is any trouble, I will return."

Callum grinned from beside her. "And I will happily escort her anytime. I think you all know by now that I love Sage Manor and will use any excuse to visit."

Celia let out a warm laugh, stepping forward to hug Sanodia. "Dear, none of you need an excuse to visit. You come to Sage Manor anytime you want—we are family now."

Sanodia's eyes shimmered with emotion, and she nodded.

At that moment, Callum's keen ears caught Celia's quiet confession to Sanodia.

"As a matter of fact," she mused aloud, "I would love to visit Tanzlora. My family has been many times, but I have never been off Earth."

Callum whipped around, eyes wide with enthusiasm. "Oh my stars, Miss Celia! We need to change that immediately."

Lincoln chuckled, shaking his head as he saw Callum's excitement building.

"Maybe it's time we planned for you to visit," Callum continued, "to see the places your family talks about and meet the elders in person."

Celia tilted her head, considering it seriously. "I would love that."

Callum placed a hand over his chest, his expression full of conviction. "Then I will work on making that happen and let you know soon."

Celia beamed. "I look forward to it."

Pazlun stepped forward, offering a firm nod. "It has been an honor to be here. Your home is filled with warmth and strength, and we are grateful for your hospitality."

"And we are grateful for your friendship," Lincoln responded.

Final embraces were shared, promises of reunions made, and then the Tanzlorans turned toward the chamber.

Callum looked back once more. "Till we see each other again."

With that, they descended the stone stairway to the Crystal Gate.

The Beaumont family watched in reverent silence, their faces illuminated by the familiar, brilliant light that spilled outward as the portal started activating.

The air hummed, the light pulsed, and then in an instant—the light flashed a brilliant white.

The family turned to walk back toward the house, the night wrapping around them. But Celia and Lincoln lingered, their gazes still fixed on the gazebo.

"I really do want to visit Tanzlora," Celia murmured, "and Arcmyrin, too."

Lincoln placed a hand on her shoulder, his voice steady with certainty. "And you will, Mama. Callum, Elara, and I will see to that."

The air in the parlor of Sage Manor was thick with the rich aroma of brewed herbal tea, mingling with the faint scent of old books and polished wood. A fire crackled gently in the hearth, adding to the cozy atmosphere of the late evening gathering.

The children had been tucked into bed, their laughter still echoing faintly in the halls as the house settled into a peaceful quiet. Now, the adults had gathered in their cherished evening ritual—tea and conversation.

Celia sat in her favorite armchair, stirring her tea thoughtfully as she surveyed the room, her heart full at the sight of her family and dearest friends reunited once again. Lincoln and Bethany sat together on the couch, with Waverly perched on the armrest, occasionally sneaking glances at Lynx, who was seated on the floor with the porcufera curled up against his side. Ridge and Lorinda sat close together, her hand resting comfortably in his. Bronte, Francis, Madre, and Marshall had each found their places around the ornate tea table, where Francis was busy pouring tea for everyone.

Celia took a sip of her tea and then set it aside, leaning forward slightly. "All right, I've waited long enough—I want to hear everything about Pluboria. I mean every detail, especially about Bronte's healing."

All eyes turned to Bronte, who sat leaned back in his chair, his arms crossed over his chest as he exhaled through his nose in amusement. "Well," he grumbled, "I suppose I should start by saying I didn't die, even though I sure as heck felt like I had been floating between worlds like that."

Francis rolled her eyes affectionately, nudging his shoulder. "Try again, Bronte. Give her the real story."

Bronte sighed dramatically but then leaned forward, his expression softening slightly as he met Celia's gaze. "It was unlike anything I've ever experienced, Celia. Pluboria... it's not a place you can describe with earthly words. It's pure light and energy, but also—somehow—it feels like home. Like we had all been there before."

Madre nodded beside him, her eyes distant as she reflected. "The colors were unlike anything I've ever seen. The air felt different, charged with something I can only describe as... peace."

Bronte tapped his fingers on the table and continued. "The healing chamber, though—that's what I can't stop thinking about. When the light beings led me inside, there was this golden, pulsating tube-like chamber. It wasn't metal, it wasn't glass—it was something else entirely. It hummed, almost like it was alive."

Celia, fascinated, leaned forward. "And that's where the healing happened?"

Bronte nodded. "Yeah. I climbed inside, and the second that thing closed around me, I felt it. I could hear... singing? Voices? I don't know how to explain it, but it was like a melody wrapping around me, sinking into my bones. And then—I started dreaming."

Madre interjected, her voice soft with wonder. "I had the same dream as Bronte. A place that looked like Earth but wasn't. We were children, running through fields, laughing with others."

Celia's breath hitched. "Could it have been Pluboria in another time? Maybe a past life?"

Bronte scratched his chin. "Could be. All I know is when I woke up, I felt... whole. Like I hadn't spent the last several months trapped in this broken body."

Francis shook her head in amazement. "When I saw you walking again like it was nothing, Bronte. I couldn't believe it."

Celia smiled warmly. "It's truly a miracle."

Bronte huffed, trying to mask the emotion creeping into his voice. "Well, I'm still me, don't go expecting me to start dancing around the house."

Laughter rippled through the room, breaking the weight of the moment.

Madre squeezed Bronte's arm. "We don't expect you to start dancing, Bronte. We just expect you to keep living."

A comfortable silence followed, filled only by the sound of tea being sipped.

After a moment, Celia turned to Lynx, who had been quietly stroking the porcufera's quills. "Now, Lynx, I need to hear about what happened on Tanzlora if you are up to telling us, I don't expect you to relive it now if you don't want to."

Lynx exhaled sharply, exchanging a glance with Waverly, who gave him an encouraging nod.

"You have no idea," he muttered.

Waverly chuckled, nudging him. "We'll talk later and compare our experiences with each council. But I also need details of what happened to you in Erevelle—if you're up for talking about it."

Lynx hesitated for a moment, then nodded. "Yeah... I think I need to talk about it."

As the fire crackled behind them, the family leaned in, ready to listen, knowing that this night—filled with revelations, reunions, and quiet moments of healing—was just another step in the ever-unfolding journey of their lives.

47

Sage Manor had settled into a quiet rhythm since Bronte, Francis, Madre, and Marshall had returned to their respective homes. With only the Beaumont family remaining, the grand estate felt slightly emptier.

The mid-morning sun filtered down the stone stairway of the chamber beneath the gazebo, casting shadows across the stone walls. The seed vault smelled earthy and fresh, a mixture of dried herbs and aged parchment, as Waverly and Celia worked together.

Waverly carefully lifted bundles of dried herbs from their storage compartments, placing them into a wooden bowl beside her. Celia thumbed through a leather-bound journal, making notes as she glanced at the stacks of herbs.

"We're going through this faster than I anticipated," Waverly murmured, adjusting the sleeves of her soft linen blouse. "We need to plant more if we want to have enough time to harvest and dry them before we run out completely."

Celia nodded in agreement, tapping her pen against the journal's pages thoughtfully. "Yes, we'll need to start planting tomorrow. The soil is still rich from the last harvest. I'll have Lincoln and Ridge prepare the plots this afternoon."

As Waverly set down another bundle of dried Asteris root, the communicator orb in the central chamber suddenly pulsed—a soft glow radiating through the arched entryway of the seed vault.

Both women froze.

Celia straightened, brushing her hands off on her apron. "Who could that be?" she asked, exchanging a glance with Waverly.

Waverly's brows knitted together. "We weren't expecting a call."

Without hesitation, Celia brushed past Waverly, striding into the central chamber where the orb sat atop the pedestal, its light swirling in slow, rhythmic pulses.

Waverly followed, her heart beating a little faster as Celia reached for the orb.

"Well," Celia said, inhaling deeply before pressing her palm to the orb's cool surface, "let's find out."

The holographic glow of the communicator orb intensified as Elara's image fully materialized in front of Celia and Waverly. The Arcmyrian envoy's golden eyes sparkled with warmth, her familiar presence immediately filling the chamber with a sense of connection across the vast distance between their worlds.

"Waverly, Celia," she greeted warmly, a radiant smile spreading across her face. "It is so good to see both of you."

Celia clasped her hands together. "Elara! What a wonderful surprise. How are things on Arcmyrin?"

"Peaceful and calm—exactly as we want it," Elara replied, her tone serene yet full of meaning. "But we are missing the Beaumonts and would like to invite you to visit Arcmyrin."

Waverly's eyes widened slightly, exchanging a glance with Celia. "All of us?" Celia inquired, a slight tilt of her head.

"Yes, all of you, including any of your house guests."

Waverly chuckled softly. "They've all gone home, so it would just be our immediate family now."

Elara nodded with understanding. "That works just as well. The Council of Elders would like to continue the presentations we had prepared before Josephine's disruption. Now that the danger has passed and the threat is no more, we feel it is time to resume what was put on hold. We also believe your entire family would benefit from hearing this."

Celia's expression turned thoughtful. "That is a lovely idea, Elara. And I am happy to accept on behalf of the family."

Elara's smile widened. "That is wonderful news."

"When would you like us to arrive?" Celia asked, already mentally listing the preparations that would need to be made.

"We are prepared to receive you at any time," Elara responded smoothly. "The only delay will be on your end, ensuring your herbal mixtures are prepared for safe travel and acclimation to our atmosphere. Lynx, of course, can bring the porcufera as well—it will acclimate to Arcmyrin just as it has on Tanzlora."

Waverly's gaze flicked toward Celia. "Should we continue giving it the same herbal mixtures before we leave?"

"Yes," Elara assured them. "Follow Sanodia's instructions up until you depart. However, once you arrive on Arcmyrin, there will be no need for those herbs. Our environment will sustain it naturally."

Celia exhaled in pleasant surprise. "Well, that makes things even easier! And what about our own herbal mixtures? Will we need to bring those?"

Elara shook her head. "No need. Everything will be provided for you here."

Celia's face lit up with excitement. "I can't wait to tell the family about this special invitation."

Elara's image shimmered slightly as she clasped her hands together. "Then let us prepare for your arrival, my friends. We will be awaiting you with open hearts."

As the holographic connection faded and the orb's glow dimmed, Celia turned to Waverly, her mind already racing with details. "I better go find Lincoln and Ridge. We need to gather everyone and start making arrangements."

Waverly grinned. "Arcmyrin... It's been too long. I can't wait to go back."

The Crystal Gate pulsed with vibrant energy, its glow illuminating the stone chamber beneath the gazebo. The entire Beaumont family stood together, anticipation thick in the air as they each held their herbal mixture vials, ready to drink at Celia's command.

The swirling portal of golden and silver light grew more defined, shimmering like liquid glass. The faint hum of its activation filled the chamber, resonating in their bones.

Celia, standing at the front of the group, watched the portal solidify into its full power. When she was sure it was ready, she turned to face her family. "Drink up," she commanded with a firm but excited voice.

The sound of uncorking vials and the soft gulping of liquid echoed through the chamber as Bethany and Lorinda helped the children with their mixtures, making sure every last drop was consumed. Maddox wrinkled his nose but swallowed quickly, eager to begin their journey. Maya and Monica followed suit, their small hands gripping their parents' fingers in excitement and awe.

Once the mixtures were finished, Lincoln tightened his grip on Maddox's hand, keeping his son close. Bethany reached for Maya, while Ridge took Monica's hand in one and Lorinda's in the other.

Celia took a deep breath, the glow of the portal reflecting in her eyes. "Let's go," she said with quiet reverence, stepping forward first.

One by one, the family followed, their steps steady but full of wonder. Waverly and Lynx brought up the rear, the porcufera snug against Lynx's chest in its protective sling. As soon as their feet touched the edge of the glowing threshold—

The elemental spirits appeared.

A burst of energy rippled through the portal as Mistara and Terraveta emerged on one side, their presence sending a cool breeze and an earthy warmth through the air. On the opposite side, Ignissa and Ambreela took their places, the flickering of soft flames dancing beside the rush of gentle, swirling air.

For those traveling the portal for the first time—Lorinda, Celia, and Monica—it was mesmerizing. Their eyes widened as glittering light wove through the energy of the portal, wrapping them in an ethereal glow.

"Look at them!" Lorinda whispered breathlessly, her gaze locked on the elemental spirits as they moved with effortless grace.

Monica, eyes full of wonder, reached toward Ambreela, watching as the spirit of air swirled around her fingers playfully, responding to her curiosity. Maddox stared at Mistara, his connection to the spirit of water already forming in ways he didn't fully understand.

"They're beautiful," Celia murmured, her voice full of awe as she watched Terraveta send golden tendrils of light spiraling along the path.

The elemental spirits watched them just as intently, amused and delighted by their reactions. Ignissa's flames twirled in midair, pulsing as if laughing softly at their amazement.

Lincoln glanced at Ridge, sharing a knowing look. They had seen this before—but seeing their family experience it for the first time made it feel new again.

The warmth of the portal enveloped them fully now, its light stretching forward like an endless path, pulling them toward Arcmyrin.

As they stepped deeper into the portal, time and space blurred—and the journey truly began.

After what seemed like only a few minutes, Lincoln's voice cut through the radiant tunnel of swirling light. "The exit for Arcmyrin is up ahead—get ready to walk through. You may have to be forceful," he instructed, his tone steady.

He turned his head slightly. "Waverly, help your Gran. Lynx, you may need to assist Ridge with Monica and Lorinda."

As the portal exit widened before them, shimmering with golden edges, Lincoln hoisted Maddox into his arms without hesitation and stepped forward, breaking through the threshold first.

Bethany followed suit, scooping Maya up effortlessly and walking through right behind him.

Ridge, seeing their movements, lifted Monica securely, ensuring she wouldn't stumble. Lynx steadied Lorinda, gripping her arm firmly as they moved forward, while Waverly took Celia's arm, keeping her balanced for the transition.

The elemental spirits drifted alongside them, their forms radiant in the shifting energy. Mistara's cool mist wrapped around them in an embrace, Terraveta sent a wave of warmth through the ground, Ignissa's flames flickered with excitement, and Ambreela's whispers of wind carried them effortlessly onto the planet.

As they stepped through the threshold, the blinding radiance of the portal dimmed—and suddenly, the breathtaking expanse of Arcmyrin stretched before them.

Celia stopped in her tracks, her breath catching in her throat.

The sky above was unlike anything she had ever seen. Two suns hung high, casting a shimmering, iridescent glow across the landscape. The hues of the world were not quite like Earth's—soft pastels blended seamlessly with rich, deep colors that pulsed with life. Everything seemed to glow faintly, as if the land itself was humming with energy.

The air was thick with a soothing scent—floral, crisp, and strangely familiar despite never having been here before.

Her gaze swept across the rolling hills, the crystalline rivers winding through lush fields of plants that glowed with their own bioluminescence. The trees had a strange, translucent quality, their leaves catching the twin sunlight and refracting it like prisms.

She was utterly speechless.

Lorinda, standing beside Lynx, placed a hand over her heart, her eyes wide with astonishment.

She looked at Ridge, who was still holding Monica, and said, " No wonder you all love this place so much."

Maddox, nestled in Lincoln's arms, was the first to giggle in excitement, his little hands reaching out toward a floating luminescent flower drifting lazily on the breeze.

Monica and Maya, sensing something magical in the air, giggled with excitement, their earlier fatigue from the portal journey instantly forgotten.

Then—

"Welcome."

The voice was smooth, familiar.

They turned toward it and saw Elara and Rykas standing just beyond the portal's edge, watching them with amused expressions.

Rykas stood tall, arms crossed, his sharp golden eyes surveying the travelers with approval. Elara's expression was warm but knowing, clearly enjoying Celia's reaction to her first moments on Arcmyrin.

"I see Arcmyrin has left quite the impression already," Elara mused, stepping forward gracefully.

Celia tore her eyes away from the stunning landscape long enough to face them, her voice barely above a whisper. "I don't even have words. It's... it's beyond beautiful."

Elara smiled gently. "Welcome, Celia Beaumont. Welcome, all of you... to Arcmyrin."

Ridge looked around, taking in the breathtaking landscape of Arcmyrin's glowing flora, twin suns, and shimmering rivers. He let out a slow breath and shook his head. "I don't know how to act being here with nothing to battle."

Rykas let out a rare laugh, his golden eyes glinting with amusement. "You could try just enjoying yourself, Ridge."

Waverly rolled her eyes and smirked. "Uncle Ridge, don't jinx us."

Ridge scoffed. "I don't believe in that nonsense, Waverly, and you know it."

Lincoln, standing with Maddox still in his arms, grinned. "I, for one, am ecstatic to be here as a tourist and can't wait to explore this beautiful land."

Bethany nodded eagerly. "Same here! I want to take it all in—this place is unlike anything I've ever imagined. Reminds me of Tanzlora but different."

Elara's smile widened. "Then let's get you all settled into your living pods. Once you're comfortable, we will all join the elders for a welcome feast."

Lynx clapped his hands together. "Now that sounds amazing—I am all about a feast!"

The whole family laughed at his enthusiasm, the tension from the long journey melting away as they followed Elara and Rykas down the iridescent pathway toward their living quarters.

As they walked, the bioluminescent plants lining the path pulsed with soft light, shifting colors with each step. Small, floating glowbloom petals drifted through the air, carried by the gentle breeze, and in the distance, a majestic crystalline spire shimmered against the horizon.

Celia glanced at Lincoln and Ridge, her heart swelling with gratitude. "I think this will be an experience none of us will ever forget."

"Agreed," Lincoln said, squeezing Maddox's shoulder.

Rykas led the way, his warrior's stance still ever-watchful but noticeably more at ease. "Welcome to Arcmyrin, Beaumont family. Consider this your second home."

48

Lorinda and Celia stood in stunned silence, taking in the innovative beauty of the Arcmyrin living pods.

The lush gardens surrounding and weaving through the structures were unlike anything they had ever seen. Vibrant climbing vines and glowing flora intertwined with the very walls of the pod, their roots disappearing beneath the floors.

"How is this even possible?" Celia finally breathed, turning in a slow circle, overwhelmed by the seamless blend of nature and function.

She stepped further inside and gasped. "Look at this, Lorinda! The kitchen and dining area are literally part of the garden. It's like the entire floor is a living, breathing ecosystem!"

Lorinda ran her fingers along a soft, leafy herb growing beside the cooking area. "You can just turn and gather your vegetables and herbs while you cook."

Elara smiled at their amazement. "Yes, these are designed much like the Elders' living pods. Not all homes on Arcmyrin have this level of integration, but every pod is built with self-sustaining gardens beneath and adjacent to them. Food is always plentiful, and the land continues to thrive."

Elara gestured toward the path. "Half of you will stay here, and the rest in the living pod just beyond it, near the crystalline river."

Celia, eager to see more, followed the path toward the second pod. When she rounded the corner, she stopped in her tracks.

The pod was nestled beside the shimmering crystalline river, its waters glowing softly under the twin suns.

A slow smile spread across Celia's face. "I am staying right here. I want to fall asleep tonight listening to that water gently flowing by."

Lincoln, having caught up, chuckled. "We may fight over that, Mama."

From behind them, Lynx's voice rang out. "Welp, Ridge—here's your battle you were looking for."

Laughter rippled through the group, and even Rykas—ever the stoic warrior—let out another rare chuckle.

Waverly, standing beside him, grinned. "I love your laugh, Rykas. You should do it more often."

Rykas turned his golden gaze on her, and for the briefest moment, his expression softened. He flashed her a rare, genuine smile, one that was warm and unguarded.

Their eyes locked—a moment just a bit longer than necessary.

The conversation around them faltered, a charged silence falling over the group.

Bethany arched a brow at Ridge, who smirked knowingly. Lincoln glanced between Waverly and Rykas, then at Celia, who had an amused twinkle in her eyes.

Lynx, ever the instigator, elbowed Ridge. "Well, I guess that battle isn't the only thing brewing."

Waverly rolled her eyes. "Oh, hush Lynx."

Rykas cleared his throat and straightened, the moment gone—but not forgotten.

Elara, ever graceful, ignored the exchange entirely. "Now we will leave you to get settled in and we'll be back in about an hour to get ready for the welcome feast. You will all experience Arcmyrian hospitality at its finest tonight."

Elara and Rykas walked side by side along the smooth, iridescent path that led back toward the Council Chambers, the twin suns casting a warm glow over the land. The air carried the scent of glowing blossoms from the nearby gardens, but neither of them were focused on the beauty surrounding them.

Elara's mind lingered on the scene back at the living pods—the look that had passed between Rykas and Waverly. She had seen the way his gaze softened, the way he lingered just a moment too long. It had unsettled her, not just because it was unexpected, but because it reminded her of something else—something dangerous.

She broke the silence first.

"Rykas… what was that back there between you and Waverly?"

Rykas, caught off guard, hesitated for a second before responding. He hadn't expected Elara to bring it up so directly, and truthfully, his thoughts had been tangled since that brief moment with Waverly.

"I… I don't know, to be honest," he admitted, rubbing the back of his neck. "But I will admit I've thought a lot about her since she left. And my heart—" he exhaled sharply, as if even saying it aloud was difficult, "—my heart was very happy to see her again."

Elara tilted her head slightly, studying his expression.

"And how do you plan to deal with that?" she asked carefully.

Rykas shook his head. "I don't know. I don't even know if it's right to feel this way about an Earthling. But I can't help it."

Elara sighed, relieved to hear his honesty.

"I'm glad you told me the truth, Rykas," she said sincerely. "But listen to me—please, discourage any more moments like that. We cannot have another Sylvaris and Josephine situation."

Rykas froze.

His entire body went rigid, his footsteps halting abruptly.

Elara walked a few more steps before realizing he was no longer beside her. She stopped and turned back to face him, frowning at the way his golden eyes narrowed in disbelief.

"What?" she asked cautiously.

But Rykas just stared at her.

The look in his eyes wasn't anger—at least, not entirely. It was hurt. And when he finally spoke, his voice was low and sharp.

"I cannot believe you would put either of us—me, or especially Waverly—in the same thought as those traitors."

Elara's heart sank.

"Rykas, I didn't mean it that way," she said quickly, stepping toward him. "Please don't be offended—"

"Well, I am." His tone was clipped, and his jaw was tight. "I am offended for myself, and I am offended for Waverly."

Before she could say anything else, he turned sharply on his heel and strode past her, his strides long and purposeful.

Elara reprimanded herself silently and quickened her pace to catch up.

"Rykas, please," she urged. "I didn't mean to insult you—I only meant that I fear how this would be perceived by the Elders. Both of our councils would find a romantic relationship between you and Waverly... complicated."

Rykas didn't slow down.

"Well, don't worry," he said flatly. "It won't be happening."

He lengthened his strides further, reaching the grand entrance of the Council Chambers and stepping inside without another word, leaving Elara standing outside, shaking her head.

She sighed, frustrated with herself for how she had phrased things. She hadn't meant to upset him, but she knew the truth of her words.

This was not going to be simple.

And somewhere deep inside her, she couldn't shake the feeling that the situation was far from over.

As the Beaumont family stepped into the Arcmyrin Council Chambers, their eyes widened at the stunning sight before them. The grand chamber, usually a place of diplomacy and discussion, had been transformed into a breathtaking banquet hall.

A long table, carved from a translucent stone that shimmered with faint iridescent hues, stretched across the center of the room. Golden platters and crystal bowls overflowed with vibrant Arcmyrin delicacies, from steaming root vegetables to exotic fruits that glowed faintly in the dim candlelight. Pitchers of luminous blue juice sat beside goblets made of a material that seemed both stone and glass at the same time. The scent of roasted meats and fragrant herbs filled the air, making even those unfamiliar with Arcmyrin cuisine eager to taste.

Surrounding the table were the elders of Arcmyrin, their regal presence commanding quiet respect, along with Elara, Rykas, and several warriors and villagers, all gathered to officially welcome their guests in celebration and fellowship.

"Now, this is what I call a welcome," Ridge said, taking in the elaborate spread with an approving nod.

Lincoln chuckled, wrapping an arm around Bethany as Maddox and Maya squirmed excitedly between them. "I agree, brother. I think we're going to enjoy this a lot."

Waverly, standing beside her grandmother, felt a mix of emotions—excitement, wonder, and a tinge of nervousness. This was a significant moment for their family and their relationship with Arcmyrin.

Elara watched the family's reaction and was truly enjoying it except for one thing.

Originally, when arranging the seating, Elara had chosen to place Waverly and Rykas side by side—a decision meant to encourage familiarity and comfort between the Arcmyrin commander and the Earth envoy.

Now, she regretted it.

After what she had witnessed earlier between them and her follow-up conversation with Rykas about it, she wanted nothing more than to separate them—but the seating was already assigned. It was too late.

Elder Releesia, the wise and respected leader of the council, stepped forward, her luminous golden robes trailing softly behind her. Her warm eyes landed on Celia, then Lincoln, Ridge, Bethany,

Waverly, Lorinda, Lynx and finally the little ones—Maya, Maddox, and Monica.

"Beaumont family," Releesia said, her voice smooth and welcoming. "It is a great honor to have you here in our chambers, to share in our customs and, more importantly, in our unity."

She gestured to the council members.

"Before we feast, I would like to formally introduce you to the Elders of Arcmyrin."

One by one, she announced their names—Aduralina, Milestree, Silastoria, Lunarcher, and Ruliana—each elder stepping forward to offer a graceful nod or warm words of welcome.

"Please," Releesia continued, "allow us to escort you to your seats."

One by one, the elders led each Beaumont to their designated places at the long table.

Celia was escorted by Releesia herself, given the place of honor near the head of the table.

Lincoln and Bethany, along with Maddox and Maya, followed next, seated near Celia.

Ridge, Lorinda, and Monica took their places across from them.

Lynx was guided by Ruliana and seated between Bethany and Lorinda.

Waverly felt a gentle hand brush against her arm, guiding her forward.

"Waverly," Elder Silastoria said warmly, "this way, dear."

Waverly followed, but as she reached her seat, her stomach fluttered.

There it was.

Her seat.

Right beside Rykas.

She forced herself not to react. She had not been able to forget that look he had given her earlier. So many unspoken words behind it, yet so much meaning to it.

She could feel his gaze on her as she carefully took her seat. This is going to be awkward.

Her pulse quickened as Rykas slid into his seat beside her. She glanced at him out of the corner of her eye, and to her surprise, he looked just as tense as she felt.

For a brief moment, neither of them spoke.

Then, as if sensing the weight of the moment, Rykas cleared his throat and finally turned to her.

"I hope you're hungry," he said, his voice even but softer than usual.

Waverly met his gaze, holding it for just a second longer than necessary.

"Famished," she replied, forcing a small smile.

Across the table, Elara's gaze lingered on Waverly and Rykas, their discomfort palpable even across the table. She had seen Rykas in countless battles, unshaken and composed, a warrior without fear. But now? Now, he looked as though he were sitting on a blade's edge.

And Waverly wasn't faring much better.

Elara watched as Waverly kept her hands carefully folded in her lap, only moving when necessary—her posture was too straight, too forced, and the conversation between the two of them was nonexistent.

They were both determined to ignore whatever had happened earlier.

Elara sighed softly but let it go. Now was not the time to address it.

Just then, Releesia stood, the soft shimmer of her robes catching the warm glow of the chamber's lights. All conversation quieted as every Arcmyrin, including the warriors and the elders, turned their full attention to their leader.

"Before we begin," Releesia said, her voice steady and full of reverence, "we must give thanks to Origin, who sustains all life, who grants us this bounty, and who has guided our people in peace and harmony since the dawn of our existence."

The room remained silent as all Arcmyrins, including Elara, bowed their heads, placing their hands over their hearts in a gesture of gratitude and connection.

Releesia continued.

"Tonight is special. We are not merely breaking bread with friends, nor are we simply sharing our table with honored guests. We are standing in the midst of a new era, one of unity, one of understanding. The Beaumont family, who have fought beside us, suffered with us, and triumphed with us, are more than visitors. They are part of the fabric of what we are building. They are a part of us."

Elara saw Celia straighten slightly, touched by the words, and Lincoln incline his head in deep respect. Ridge gave a small approving nod, and Bethany's expression was warm as she squeezed Maddox's hand beneath the table.

Even Waverly looked affected by the words.

Releesia lifted her hands in a gesture of finality.

"Let us eat. Let us celebrate. And let us look toward the future, together."

With that, the feast officially began.

Elara shifted her attention back to Waverly and Rykas, who both reached for their drinks at the exact same moment, as if they had planned it.

Waverly gripped her goblet tightly, bringing it to her lips as if it were the only thing tethering her to reality.

Rykas, ever disciplined, drank in calculated sips, keeping his gaze firmly on his plate.

The silence between them was so loud Elara could almost hear it.

This is painful to watch she thought to herself.

Both Waverly and Rykas focused intently on their food, carefully eating, barely speaking. They were pretending nothing was there—pretending a moment hadn't passed between them earlier that neither of them knew how to handle.

49

As the feast continued, the hum of lively conversation filled the Arcmyrin council chambers. Laughter rang out from different parts of the table, and for the first time in what felt like ages, there was no talk of evil forces, no discussions of betrayal—only warmth, unity, and the enjoyment of one another's presence.

At the head of the table, Celia found herself deep in discussion with Releesia.

"Your journey to Earth's leadership sounds like it was quite the experience," Releesia said, her golden eyes alight with curiosity. "I would love to hear more about the leaders you spoke with and how they received the idea of a Triad alliance."

Celia smiled, grateful for the genuine interest. "It was a delicate process," she admitted. "I knew going in that I needed to be both honest and tactful. Earth leaders are cautious by nature—our planet has seen far too much war, too much division. But despite that, there was an undeniable curiosity about Tanzlora and Arcmyrin. They were eager to learn more."

Releesia nodded in understanding. "Caution is wise, but curiosity is what fuels progress. And what did they say about visiting our worlds?"

Celia leaned in slightly, her excitement evident. "That was perhaps the most promising part of our conversation. During the dinner at Vice President Houston's residence, several of the world leaders expressed their interest in an eventual exchange of delegations. They see value in direct interaction, in immersing themselves in the cultures of Arcmyrin and Tanzlora rather than just hearing about them from us."

Releesia's expression brightened. "This is wonderful news, Celia. I had hoped for such openness, but to hear it confirmed is reassuring. We, too, have long desired to visit Earth. There is much we wish to learn, to understand."

Celia tilted her head, intrigued. "What interests you the most?"

Releesia's eyes took on a dreamlike quality, as if she were envisioning something far beyond the walls of the chamber. "The oceans," she said with a reverent tone. "We have lakes, rivers, and crystalline streams, but we do not have vast, endless waters like those on Earth. I have heard from Waverly and Lynx of the sheer size and power of your oceans. To witness that—to feel the energy of something so alive—would be unlike anything we have ever known."

Celia smiled at this. "I have no doubt that you would be amazed. I grew up visiting the ocean every summer, and I still find myself in awe of it. The way the waves move, the way the water shifts from calm to stormy—it's a force of nature that never loses its mystery. And I would be honored to be the one to take you to see it."

Releesia reached out and gently took Celia's hand in hers, a rare and deeply meaningful gesture among the Arcmyrin people. "Then let us make it happen. Not just for ourselves, but for the future of our worlds. If our people are to trust one another, then they must experience one another's lands, customs, and ways of life firsthand."

Celia squeezed Releesia's hand in return, feeling a true bond forming between them. "I couldn't agree more. And I will make sure our leaders understand how important this is."

Releesia smiled. "Then we move forward, together."

As they released hands, Celia felt something stir deep inside her—a certainty that this alliance was meant to be. That no matter the setbacks, no matter the challenges ahead, they were on the right path.

And for the first time in a long time, she truly believed that unity, harmony and balance between Earth, Arcmyrin, and Tanzlora was not just possible.

It was inevitable.

Lincoln, Bethany, Maya, and Maddox sat comfortably in their smooth stone seats enjoying their meal. Silastoria, the elder responsible for education and knowledge preservation, sat across from them, her serene expression filled with warmth and patience. A few Arcmyrin children were seated amongst the villagers that had been invited to the feast and the young Beaumont children had been observing them.

Bethany had just finished explaining how schools operated on Earth—how children sat in classrooms, learned from books and teachers, and how subjects were divided into specific areas of study. Silastoria listened intently, nodding with interest before offering her own insights.

"Our approach to education is much different than yours," Silastoria began. "We do not have 'schools' in the way Earth does. Instead, learning is woven into our daily lives. From the moment a child can walk and talk, they are paired with a group of mentors—healers, warriors, artisans, historians, or those who commune with the elements. Their lessons take place through experience, observation, and active participation rather than sitting in a single place to be taught."

Maddox's brows furrowed in thought. "So you don't have a school building?"

Silastoria shook her head. "Not as you do. We have communal learning spaces where young ones gather, but their learning is not confined there. They explore, they build, they create. They learn about history by sitting with the elders and listening to their stories, and they learn mathematics through the rhythms of nature—by measuring the cycles of the moons, the patterns of rivers, the growth of crops. Science is not something read in a book; it is lived."

Maddox sat up, intrigued. "Do you make forts?"

Silastoria blinked, then smiled. "Forts?"

Maya giggled. "Yeah! On Earth, we build forts out of sticks and blankets, and we pretend we have our own little houses or castles.

Bronte helped us build one back home before we came here. It's the best!"

Silastoria's golden eyes shimmered with amusement and understanding. "Ah, I see! Yes, our young ones build shelters, particularly as part of their survival training. From a young age, they are taught how to construct protective dwellings from natural materials—branches, woven leaves, crystalline stones. They learn how to sustain themselves in the wild, how to recognize safe places for shelter, and how to work together to build something strong."

Maddox's eyes widened. "So... they build real forts? Like, ones you can actually live in?"

Silastoria nodded. "Precisely. And it is not only practical, but a rite of passage. Young Arcmyrins must build a structure that can withstand the elements, proving their understanding of nature's balance and their ability to work as a community."

Bethany smiled. "That's incredible. It sounds like your children are encouraged to be independent and resourceful from a very young age."

"Yes," Silastoria agreed. "But never alone. Community is essential. We guide them, but they must take their own steps forward."

Maya, still fascinated, leaned forward. "What about games? What do Arcmyrin kids do for fun?"

Silastoria chuckled. "Oh, they play many games. Some involve speed—racing through the forests and across the streams, leaping between crystal formations. Others are games of skill and precision, like testing how well they can balance glowing stones or guiding wind currents through small circular hoops."

Maddox's jaw dropped. "You can control the wind?"

Silastoria laughed gently. "Not in the way you might think. But with focus, movement, and an understanding of how the air flows, one can learn to move with the wind, rather than against it. It is a skill, a game, and a form of meditation all at once."

Maya clapped her hands together. "That sounds amazing! Can we try?"

Bethany chuckled. "I think you two would fit in very well here."

Silastoria beamed. "I would be delighted to arrange for you to experience these games firsthand. Learning through play is a fundamental part of growing."

Lincoln, who had been listening intently, finally spoke. "It seems to me that Arcmyrin children are raised with a very deep connection to their world. They don't just learn about it—they *live* it. It's a beautiful way to teach."

Silastoria inclined her head respectfully. "Thank you, Lincoln. We believe that knowledge should never be separate from the world it exists in. Perhaps Earth and Arcmyrin can one day exchange more than just diplomatic ties—perhaps your young ones and ours can learn from one another."

Maddox looked up at his father. "Dad, can we come back for school?"

Lincoln laughed and ruffled his son's hair. "We'll see, buddy. But I have a feeling this won't be your last trip to Arcmyrin."

Silastoria smiled warmly at them all. "Then let us plan for that future."

Once the feast was concluded they all gathered in the serene garden adjacent to the Arcmyrin council chambers. Milestree stood with his hands clasped behind his back, his presence regal as he faced Ridge, Lorinda, Monica, and Lynx. The glow of the twin suns bathed the crystalline foliage in soft iridescence, casting a peaceful ambiance over the group.

"Lynx," Milestree began, his voice gentle yet commanding. "How are you and the Porcufera doing since your ordeal on Tanzlora?"

Lynx, standing with his hands resting on the sling where the Porcufera was nestled comfortably, nodded. "We're both getting better, thank you. The herbal mixtures Sanodia prepared helped a lot, and being back with my family has been the best thing for me. The Porcufera is still adjusting to Earth's environment, but it's strong."

Milestree gave a small nod of approval. "I am pleased to hear this. I have spoken frequently with Lumorith since the incident, and he seems to have recovered well. His strength of spirit is remarkable."

Lynx let out a breath, relieved. "I was worried about him. He didn't deserve what happened. Sylvaris betrayed him, just like he betrayed all of us."

Milestree's expression darkened momentarily before softening. "Yes, his betrayal was unexpected and deeply painful for many, but Lumorith is resilient. He holds no bitterness, only wisdom from the experience. He hopes to speak with you again soon, Lynx. He sees you as an ally and friend."

Lynx smiled faintly. "I'd like that."

Milestree then turned his attention to Lorinda and Monica, his sharp yet kind eyes resting on them. "And how are you both enjoying Arcmyrin so far?"

Monica's eyes lit up with excitement. "It's amazing! Everything glows, and the buildings are like something out of a fairy tale. I love it here."

Lorinda chuckled, brushing a strand of hair behind her ear. "It's breathtaking, truly. It's hard to believe places like this exist beyond Earth."

Milestree smiled. "And yet, you and your family are no strangers to extraordinary things."

Ridge, who had been standing quietly with his arms crossed, finally spoke. "You've got that right. But it's nice to be here without the threat of a battle hanging over our heads."

Milestree let out a low hum of agreement. "It is rare for us to enjoy camaraderie with your family without the shadow of conflict. This is a first and why we must cherish these moments and nurture them for the future. The alliance between our worlds depends on trust, cooperation, and understanding."

Lorinda nodded thoughtfully. "That's why I'm so eager for these exchanges of delegations. If we can create a real alliance, one built on more than just necessity, it could change everything—for all of us."

Milestree gave her a warm look of approval. "You have a strong spirit, Lorinda. You and your family embody the kind of integrity that could bridge the gaps between our worlds."

Monica beamed up at her mother. "See, Mom? You're awesome."

Lorinda laughed and kissed the top of Monica's head. "Well, that's quite the endorsement."

Milestree's gaze swept over all of them, lingering briefly on Lynx. "I look forward to watching your family's journey continue to unfold. The Triad will be stronger because of you."

Ridge smirked. "No pressure, right?"

Milestree chuckled. "Only the weight of history."

Lynx exchanged a glance with Monica, who grinned up at him. "Sounds like we have some pretty big shoes to fill," he murmured.

Milestree nodded solemnly. "Indeed. But I have no doubt you will rise to the occasion and not let your ancestor Galen down."

The gentle wind stirred the leaves around them, shimmering with the same quiet strength that seemed to echo in Milestree's words. The future was uncertain, but in that moment, they all felt a sense of hope—a belief that, together, they were shaping something new and extraordinary.

50

The soft murmur of conversations and laughter slowly faded as the gathering dispersed, leaving behind the warmth of the evening's feast. Elara stood among the remaining villagers, ensuring all were content before her gaze landed on Waverly, sitting alone near a flowering archway.

That was unusual.

Waverly was never one to remove herself from a group, especially after such a momentous occasion of unity between the Beaumont family and the Arcmyrins. Yet, there she was, off to herself, her expression lost in thought.

Elara knew why.

With quiet steps, she moved toward Waverly and gracefully settled beside her on the stone bench. She said nothing at first, simply allowing the silence to stretch between them as the cool night air carried the faint scent of Arcmyrin's luminous blossoms. Finally, she reached over and gently touched Waverly's hand.

"You look very sad," Elara said softly, her golden eyes filled with quiet understanding. "On such a joyous occasion as this first-time feast of unity, why do you sit here alone with such weight upon your heart?"

Waverly startled slightly, as if she hadn't realized she'd been noticed. She turned to Elara and offered a small, wavering smile—one that didn't quite reach her eyes. She squeezed Elara's hand in return, blinking rapidly as if trying to hold back unshed tears.

"I know," Waverly admitted with a quiet chuckle, shaking her head at herself. "I'm terrible. I should be mingling, learning more about

Arcmyrin from the villagers, enjoying this moment. Yet here I am, mourning for something I know I can't have."

Elara's brows lifted slightly in surprise. "What are you speaking of, Waverly?"

Waverly took a steadying breath, then turned fully to face Elara. She took both of her hands, her grip firm but trembling slightly. There was no hesitation in her gaze, only a deep, raw honesty that Elara wasn't sure she had ever seen in her before.

"Rykas," Waverly said, her voice barely above a whisper.

Elara's heart clenched. She had suspected it, but hearing Waverly say it aloud made it all the more real.

"I know you witnessed that moment between us today," Waverly continued, searching Elara's face for understanding. "It's not the first time I've felt that connection with him. And rest assured, it has never gone past lingering gazes, but... without words, we both know what it means."

Elara exhaled slowly, her expression unreadable.

"And what does it mean, Waverly?" she asked carefully.

Waverly swallowed hard, looking up at the sky for a long moment as if searching for the right words among the stars. Then, with quiet resolve, she turned back to Elara.

"That it can never happen," she said, her voice steady now. "It wouldn't be wise."

Elara studied her for a moment, weighing her words, feeling the sincerity in them.

"Why do you believe that?" she asked, though she already knew the answer.

Waverly let out a soft, broken laugh. "Because I am an Earthling, and he is Arcmyrian. Because I know how much our worlds have at stake right now. Because it would be selfish of me to allow my heart to interfere with the alliance my family has worked so hard to build."

She shook her head and looked down at their joined hands. "If I were to act on this connection, if Rykas were to act on it, it would raise questions neither of our worlds are ready to answer. There's too much history, too much hesitation, too much risk."

Elara let out a slow breath, nodding. "You are wise, Waverly. But let me ask you this—if the risk were not there, if our worlds were already united without doubt or hesitation, would your feelings remain the same?"

Waverly's lips parted slightly as if to answer, but then she hesitated. For the first time, her confidence wavered.

Finally, she exhaled and whispered, "I don't know."

Elara gave her a knowing look. "Then perhaps this is not the time for absolutes. The future is always shifting, always evolving. And while I do not have all the answers, I do know this—denying the truth of one's heart never leads to peace. You do not have to act, Waverly. But do not bury what you feel. Let it be, let it breathe, and let time determine what is meant to be."

A tear slipped down Waverly's cheek before she could stop it. She quickly wiped it away and nodded, forcing another small smile. "Thank you, Elara."

Elara squeezed her hands gently, then stood. "Come, let us return. The feast may be winding down, but there is still time to celebrate the connections that already exist."

Waverly took a deep breath, composed herself, and stood as well. "You're right," she said, casting one last glance toward the garden's glowing blossoms. "Let's go."

As they walked back toward the gathering, Elara cast one last glance at Waverly. The young Earthling was strong—stronger than she realized. But there was a battle waging inside her heart, one that had only just begun.

And Elara knew that no matter how much Waverly tried to deny it... this was far from over.

Laughter rang through the shimmering Arcmyrin garden as the Beaumont children and their new Arcmyrin friends raced around the soft, iridescent grass, their joyful cries filling the air. They leaped and twirled, their tiny hands grasping at the floating crystal blossoms that darted around them like playful fireflies. The blossoms, catching on the gentle wind, sparkled under the setting twin suns, dipping and weaving unpredictably just beyond reach, teasing the giggling children into an endless chase.

A crowd of Arcmyrin villagers and the Beaumont family had gathered around, watching with amusement as Maya, Maddox, and Monica—alongside a group of Arcmyrin children—jumped and squealed, determined to catch the elusive blossoms.

"Almost got one!" Maddox shouted, stretching his arms as high as they would go.

"Try spinning first!" one of the Arcmyrin children advised with a mischievous grin.

Maya immediately took the advice, twirling on her toes and laughing as a blossom danced just above her head. Monica, never one to be left behind, did the same, determination set on her little face.

Around the circle, adults chuckled at the sight, the warmth of the moment bringing a deeper sense of peace and unity than words ever could.

As Waverly and Elara approached the group, they were greeted by the radiant smile of Elder Ruliana.

"They are bonding beautifully," Ruliana observed, her eyes alight with happiness. "It is a joy to see our young ones playing with yours, free of hesitation. This is how the future of the Triad will be shaped—with openness and laughter, not fear and distrust."

Waverly nodded, her heart swelling with gratitude at the sight before her. "Yes, Elder Ruliana, we are so grateful for this invitation and the time to bond with you and your people. This experience will harness a great future for the Triad. I can already feel it."

Ruliana's expression softened, clearly pleased with Waverly's words. She placed a gentle hand on Waverly's shoulder. "We were sorry to have to abruptly pause our presentations with you, but having your entire family here, together, has been a greater opportunity than we could have imagined. This is going better than any of us dared to hope."

Waverly smiled, glancing back at the children still playing. "There was a time I worried that the bond between our planets would always carry hesitation, that trust would take years to build. But seeing this? Seeing my little brother and sister and Monica, so freely embraced by your people? It means everything. This is the future we've all been working for."

Elara, who had been listening closely, nodded in agreement. "We have overcome much, and there is still more work to do, but moments like this remind us why we continue forward."

The conversation paused as a triumphant shout erupted from the center of the circle. Maddox, his face lit with sheer excitement, held up a captured crystal blossom in his small hands.

"I got one!" he declared, jumping up and down.

The Arcmyrin children and the Beaumont siblings cheered loudly, clapping and congratulating him. The blossom, sensing its capture, pulsed once before releasing a gentle shimmer of light, a final playful trick before fading into the air.

Maddox gasped in wonder, looking up at Waverly with wide eyes. "Did you see that?"

She laughed, ruffling his hair. "I did! That was amazing, little man."

The celebration continued as more children took turns trying to capture a blossom, the game weaving through the garden as the bonds between them strengthened with every laugh and cheer.

As Waverly turned back to Ruliana, the elder's expression was filled with pride. "This is what true unity looks like," she said quietly. "And it is only the beginning."

Waverly nodded, her heart filled with the same certainty. "Yes, Elder Ruliana. Only the beginning."

The morning sun cast a warm, golden glow through the crystalline windows of the living pod, illuminating the kitchen area where the Beaumont family was gathering for breakfast. The scents of fresh-baked grain cakes, spiced root vegetables, and a variety of Arcmyrin fruits filled the space, blending harmoniously with the peaceful hum of the flowing river just beyond the walls.

Lincoln stretched as he walked into the kitchen, his movements relaxed from one of the best nights of sleep he'd had in years. He inhaled deeply, the rich aromas making his stomach rumble. His mother, Celia, was already seated with a steaming cup of morning tea in hand, looking as serene as ever.

"How did you sleep, Mama?" Lincoln asked as he moved to pour himself a drink.

Celia smiled warmly. "Like a baby. That water flowing by my open window put me into a gentle slumber within seconds of my head hitting the pillow. Honestly, I think I slept the best I have in decades."

Lynx strolled in behind him, stretching his arms over his head. "Me too," he chimed in, his voice still heavy with lingering sleep. "Slept like a rock."

Lincoln chuckled, taking a sip of his drink before turning toward Waverly, who was already at the food spread, silently loading her plate. "And you, Waverly? How did you sleep?"

She didn't respond.

Instead, she continued selecting her food, her expression unreadable, her movements slow and methodical as though lost in thought.

Lincoln frowned, casting a glance at Bethany, who had just walked in with Maddox and Maya. Bethany picked up on his confusion immediately and turned to Waverly.

"Waverly, darling, did you not hear your father?"

Waverly blinked, as if suddenly pulled from another world, and turned to look at Bethany. "What?" she asked, clearly disoriented. "I wasn't paying attention."

Lincoln raised an eyebrow. "I just asked how you slept."

"Oh." Waverly quickly looked away, turning back to her plate. "Fine. I slept fine."

Her tone was too dismissive, too quick.

Lincoln wasn't the only one who noticed.

Bethany's brows furrowed slightly, her motherly instincts kicking in. She exchanged a look with Lincoln, both silently acknowledging that something was up with Waverly.

Lynx, standing off to the side, had caught it too—and instead of letting it go, he simply grinned knowingly.

Lincoln narrowed his eyes at his son.

Lynx's grin widened.

Lincoln pointed at him and silently mouthed, "Don't start with her."

Lynx's only response was to raise his hands in mock innocence, but the amusement dancing in his eyes said otherwise. He was thoroughly enjoying this.

Meanwhile, Waverly, sensing that she was under scrutiny, shot a quick glare at Lynx before shoving a bite of food into her mouth as if that would put an end to the conversation.

Celia, ever perceptive, observed the entire exchange with mild amusement, taking a slow sip of her tea. She knew her granddaughter well enough to recognize when something was swirling in that sharp mind of hers.

"Well," she finally said, breaking the tension. "Whatever is on your mind, Waverly, I hope you figure it out before you explode. Keeping things bottled up never did a Beaumont any good."

Waverly nearly choked on her food but quickly covered it with a cough. "I don't know what you're talking about, Gran," she muttered.

Celia gave her a pointed look. "Mmm-hmm."

Bethany laughed softly as she settled Maddox and Maya into their seats, they immediately started digging into their plates of food.

Ridge and Lorinda entered next with Monica who ran straight for Maya and Maddox, excited to start another day of adventure.

The tension eased as the morning meal continued, but Lincoln made a mental note to pull Waverly aside later. Whatever was on her mind, he wanted to make sure she was okay.

For now, though, he'd let it slide.

51

Just as Celia placed her empty cup on the table, a familiar voice rang through the open kitchen entrance of the pod.

"Good morning, Beaumont family!" Elara exclaimed cheerfully as she stepped inside, her presence filling the space with warmth.

All eyes turned to her as she smiled at the group. She was dressed in her usual flowing Arcmyrin robes, the iridescent fabric shimmering faintly as she moved.

"I hope this morning finds you refreshed and ready for a day of discovery," she continued, her golden eyes sweeping across the family. "I have gathered several villagers, and we would love to take you on a tour."

Excitement immediately spread through the room.

"Yay!" Maya, Maddox, and Monica jumped up and down, their enthusiasm infectious.

"I am certainly ready," Celia said, standing and smoothing out her dress.

"Me as well," Lorinda added, nodding eagerly.

The rest of the family quickly echoed their agreement, the anticipation for the day ahead growing.

Elara's gaze drifted down beside Lynx, where the porcufera was happily nibbling on a piece of Arcmyrin fruit. She crouched slightly to observe it.

"Lynx, is your friend still faring well and ready for the day?" she asked with a curious smile.

Lynx reached down and gently ran his hand over the porcufera's back, its quills shifting slightly under his touch.

"Absolutely," he replied confidently. "But I'm wearing the sling just in case Quillie needs a rest."

"Oh, it has a name now does it?" Elara asked.

"Yes," Lynx replied, "the children insisted."

Elara smiled and nodded approvingly. "Ok, well it's wise you are prepared to give Quillie a rest. The journey will take us through different terrains, so it may need a break."

Lincoln clapped his hands together. "Well then, what are we waiting for?"

Elara grinned. "Nothing at all. Let's gather outside and get started."

With that, the family quickly finished up, tidied their plates, and stepped outside, where a small group of Arcmyrin villagers and warriors awaited them. The shimmering sky overhead, with its twin suns beginning to rise higher, made the entire scene feel otherworldly yet welcoming.

"This is going to be incredible," Waverly murmured, taking in the beauty of the Arcmyrin morning.

Elara motioned for the group to follow her. "Then let's begin your journey of discovery."

And with that, the Beaumont family set off on an adventure through the breathtaking landscapes of Arcmyrin.

The journey through Arcmyrin's lush terrain had already been breathtaking, but nothing could have prepared the Beaumont family for the sight that awaited them as they turned a bend in the crystalline path.

Before them stood a massive, ethereal structure covered in what looked like soft green moss, yet unlike anything found on Earth. The entire surface twinkled and sparkled, as if infused with silver and blue glitter that pulsed gently, as though the structure itself was alive.

Ridge, unable to resist his curiosity, reached out and pressed his fingers into the strange surface. To his surprise, it yielded beneath his touch, creating a small indentation before bouncing right back, much like memory foam. The spot where he had touched glowed brightly for a moment before gradually dimming.

Immediately, a soothing warmth traveled up his arm and radiated through his entire body.

He stepped back, flexing his fingers. "What was that?" he asked, looking to Elara, both bewildered and amazed.

Elara chuckled at his reaction. "Welcome to our Consano Cella," she said, gesturing toward the structure with admiration. "Or, as you might call it on Earth, a healing center."

The family collectively gasped in awe.

"This is amazing," Lorinda whispered, stepping closer.

"Wait, so this whole building is a healing center?" Lincoln asked, his gaze traveling up the shimmering structure.

Elara nodded. "Yes. It is made of living, regenerative material that responds to touch, reading the energy of the body and sending restorative signals throughout it. That warmth you felt, Ridge, was the Consano Cella recognizing you and offering a small bit of renewal."

Ridge flexed his fingers again, still marveling at the sensation. "So... does it heal injuries?"

"Yes, in a way," Elara confirmed. "For minor ailments, just being inside the Cella is enough to stimulate the body's natural healing abilities. More severe injuries require guided treatments from our healers. The walls, the air, even the light inside—it all works together in harmony to bring balance to the body and mind."

Bethany's eyes widened. "That's incredible. So if someone were really sick, could they just live in here for a while?"

Elara smiled. "Not quite. Prolonged exposure would overstimulate the body, making it difficult to regulate its own healing over time. The Cella is meant for periodic treatments, a place to restore and rejuvenate when needed."

Maddox, who had been watching the glowing wall with fascination, suddenly turned to Lynx. "Do you think the porcufera would like it?"

Lynx looked down at his small companion, who was curiously sniffing at the air near the structure. "I think it might," he said, crouching beside the creature. "Maybe we should let it explore a little."

Elara nodded. "The Consano Cella welcomes all living beings. If your porcufera is in need of renewal, it will feel drawn to it naturally."

Lynx carefully set the porcufera down, and sure enough, it waddled toward the building, pressing its small body against the glowing surface. The moss-like material pulsed softly in response, and the porcufera let out a series of delighted chirps, its quills relaxing as though it was enjoying a soothing embrace.

"Look at that," Waverly murmured. "It's actually responding to the energy."

"This is beyond anything I could have imagined," Celia admitted, watching in wonder.

"Would you like to go inside?" Elara asked with a knowing smile.

The family exchanged excited glances before responding in unison.

"Absolutely."

With that, Elara led them toward the entrance, the shimmering doorway parting as if the building itself was inviting them in.

As they stepped through the shimmering entrance, the Beaumont family found themselves enveloped in a serene glow. The interior of the Consano Cella was unlike anything they had ever seen—spacious yet intimate, alive with soft light that seemed to pulse gently from the walls, almost like a heartbeat. The air smelled of earth and herbs, a fresh, cleansing aroma that immediately soothed the senses.

"This place is incredible," Lorinda murmured as she ran her fingers lightly over one of the walls, watching as the surface glowed faintly at her touch.

The building was divided into sections, each separated by tightly woven leaf curtains that swayed gently with the airflow.

Lynx immediately recognized the design. "These remind me of the leaf blankets at the Reficiat Haven on Tanzlora," he said, admiring the intricate weaving.

Elara nodded, pleased by his observation. "Yes, the Haven and the Cella share a lot in common. Both serve as places of healing, though their purposes vary slightly."

She gestured toward the softly illuminated hallways that branched off in different directions. "Here in the Cella, all herbal mixtures are prepared and distributed for the people of Arcmyrin, just like Sanodia does at the Haven on Tanzlora. However, there are no long-term stays here. The Haven provides extended care, whereas the Cella is meant for rejuvenation and recovery before returning home."

Bethany looked around in awe. "It feels like the walls themselves are alive."

"In a way, they are," Elara said. "Everything in this building is infused with the natural energies of Arcmyrin, working in harmony to enhance the healing process."

Lincoln glanced over at Ridge, who was still flexing his hand from his earlier experience with the exterior of the building. "That explains the warmth you felt, huh?"

Ridge smirked. "Yeah, I'm still wrapping my head around that. I've never felt anything like it before."

Maddox, still fascinated by the glowing walls, suddenly turned to Waverly. "Galen liked this place a lot!"

Waverly smiled at her little brother, crouching beside him. "What did he tell you about it?"

"He said that it is a perfect reflection of Arcmyrin's spirit—pure, balanced, and full of light."

Elara, overhearing their conversation, nodded solemnly, clearly pleased with that answer.

She motioned for them to follow her. "Let me take you toward the herbals area. While we're here, all of you can top up on your herbal mixtures to keep you refreshed for the remainder of our tour."

As they moved deeper into the Cella, the atmosphere became even more tranquil. The woven leaf curtains rustled softly as they passed, revealing glimpses of herbal preparation stations where Arcmyrian healers worked with luminescent plants and crystalline vials filled with shimmering liquids.

Celia, who had been quietly observing everything, finally spoke. "I have long wanted to see how the Arcmyrians prepare their herbals. I have witnessed Sanodia preparing them the Tanzloran way so I am eager to learn the differences between the methods."

A healer nearby, hearing this, smiled warmly and gestured for her to step closer. "Then you shall see, Mrs. Beaumont. I will be pleased to show you."

Celia's eyes sparkled with curiosity as she stepped forward, eager to absorb everything.

Meanwhile, Elara turned to the rest of the family and handed each of them a small iridescent vial. "Drink this," she instructed. "It will refresh you and help sustain your energy for the rest of the day."

Lincoln took his and gave it an experimental sniff before chuckling. "Smells like the herbal mixture we take before stepping through the Crystal Gate."

"It's similar," Elara confirmed. "But this one is infused with different elements to align with Arcmyrin's atmosphere rather than the portal's energy. It will help you adjust and keep your mind and body in balance."

Waverly raised a brow at her vial before glancing at Lynx, who had taken his without hesitation. She smirked. "You're way too used to this, huh?"

Lynx shrugged, a small smirk playing at his lips. "It's second nature now."

Celia held up her vial. "Well, here's to Arcmyrin and the journey ahead!"

With that, the entire family drank their herbal mixtures, the cool liquid spreading warmth through their bodies. As the effects settled in, Elara smiled.

"Now, let's continue our journey. There's still much to see."

52

Elara led the group along the perimeter of the community gardens, her voice light with amusement. "Now this should be very familiar to you, Waverly," she said, glancing toward her with a knowing smile.

Waverly nodded in agreement, the memory of her last visit to these gardens flashing through her mind.

Celia and Lorinda, however, were completely mesmerized by the sheer size and vibrancy of the gardens. Rows upon rows of plants, trees, and vines stretched out as far as the eye could see, their colors shimmering in ways that defied Earth's natural spectrum. Some plants glowed faintly, while others seemed to ripple as if responding to the soft breeze moving through the area.

"This is unbelievable," Lorinda murmured, taking in the wide variety of plants, fruits, and vegetables.

"It's much like the village gardens on Tanzlora," Bethany noted, nodding approvingly.

"Yes," Lincoln agreed, scanning the flourishing landscape. "Same concept—self-sustaining, community-driven, and tended by those who live here."

Waverly folded her arms and exhaled a small laugh. "Oh, it's very familiar." Then, with a more serious note, she added, "The last time I was here was when that unfortunate 'bump-up' happened with... you know who."

Celia immediately cut in, raising a hand in protest. "Oh no, let's not ruin today with that memory."

"Sorry, Gran," Waverly said with a sheepish grin.

As they walked deeper into the garden, Lorinda stopped abruptly, her attention caught by a particularly striking plant. Its long, elegant purple leaves were streaked with silver and it seemed to be... moving. The leaves would roll up and down, closing and then unfurling again, almost like breathing.

She pointed at it in fascination. "Elara, what kind of plant is this?"

Elara smiled knowingly. "Ah, you've discovered the *Virella*. It's one of our most adaptive plants. It responds to the presence of living beings, drawing in energy and releasing fresh oxygen in return."

"It reacts to us?" Lorinda asked, leaning in slightly.

"Yes," Elara confirmed. "It senses warmth and motion. It's part of what keeps Arcmyrin's atmosphere so pure."

"That's incredible," Bethany said, watching as one of the leaves quivered slightly when she extended her hand near it.

Maddox, ever the curious one, reached out excitedly. "Can I touch it?"

Elara nodded. "Gently."

Maddox brushed his fingers against the edge of a leaf, and instantly, the plant responded by rolling inward, encasing his hand in a soft, velvety texture.

His eyes widened in delight. "It tickles!" he giggled.

Everyone laughed, amused by his reaction.

"It means it likes you," Elara said, then looked toward Celia and Lorinda. "We have many plants like this—some medicinal, some for food, and some that serve to regulate the energy of the planet itself."

Celia shook her head in wonder. "I feel like I've stepped into a dream."

"It's not a dream, Miss Celia," Elara said warmly. "It's Arcmyrin. And this is just the beginning."

As the group continued their walk through the lush, radiant gardens, the path curved gently and opened up into a beautifully terraced space. The terraces were lined with stone benches and platforms, where several adults sat with the village children, guiding them through their learning lessons.

Elara lifted a hand in suggestion. "Let's pause here and just observe for a moment."

The Beaumont family quietly gathered along the edges of the terrace, their curiosity piqued. The setting was unlike any school they had ever seen—open-air, vibrant, and deeply connected to nature.

At the center of the space, a teacher stood before a group of young Arcmyrin children, who sat cross-legged in a semicircle. She gestured toward the sky, speaking in gentle, melodic tones, her hands moving with a fluidity that suggested she was weaving together more than just words—perhaps energy, perhaps knowledge itself.

The children were completely engaged, their expressive, golden-hued eyes wide with fascination.

Celia leaned in toward Elara. "This is their school?"

Elara nodded. "Yes. Education here is deeply immersive. Children are taught by experience, interaction, and connection—not just by words in books."

Bethany, ever the educator, was captivated. "They learn outside? All the time?"

"Mostly," Elara confirmed. "Each village has a designated learning space, much like this one. They study everything from planetary sciences to elemental energy and healing practices, and of course, languages. The structure of learning adapts to the needs of each child—some lessons happen in small groups, others through hands-on experiences with mentors."

Maddox tilted his head curiously. "Last night they said they built forts."

Elara chuckled. "They do, actually. Learning survival and construction skills is part of their development."

"Bronte created a little fort monster," Waverly whispered to Ridge.

"Of course," Ridge whispered back, "all little boys are fort monsters."

Maya piped up. "What about games? Do they have fun?"

Elara smiled. "Oh, absolutely. Games are a crucial part of childhood here. Many involve nature—chasing crystal blossoms, water-weaving competitions, even obstacle courses using the terrain. Some of our games might remind you of Earth's, while others are unique to Arcmyrin."

Just as she finished speaking, a small group of children ran past, giggling as they attempted to "catch" floating orbs of soft golden light.

Waverly's eyes lit up. "Is that a game?"

One of the teachers turned to them with a welcoming smile. "Yes, it is called *Lunaflare Chase*. The orbs respond to movement, and the children must use skill and timing to touch them before they vanish."

Maya gasped in excitement. "Can we play?"

The teacher chuckled. "Of course. Would you all like to join?"

Maddox, Maya, and Monica immediately dashed forward, eager to take part, while Lincoln and Bethany exchanged amused glances.

Elara looked to Celia. "Would you like to watch them play for a little while?"

Celia nodded warmly, watching the children blend seamlessly into the Arcmyrin learning experience. "Yes. I think we will all enjoy this."

As the family continued their walk through the village, Elara led them to a breathtaking structure—a small crystal cathedral that shimmered under the twin suns. The walls were made of Arcmyrin's unique crystalline stone, glistening with soft hues of blue, silver, and gold. Sunlight filtered through the intricate latticework of the exterior, creating a mesmerizing pattern of shifting light inside.

Waverly, still caught in her own thoughts, barely noticed as Lorinda let out a gasp.

"This is incredible," Lorinda whispered, spinning in a slow circle to take it all in.

"It's like a community center back on Earth," she told Bethany, "but a thousand times prettier and fancier."

Bethany chuckled. "Tanzlora has similar gathering spaces, though theirs are built more from natural elements. Arcmyrin, on the other hand, has this stunning crystal stone, and I can't blame them for using it. It makes everything feel like a royal hall."

Lorinda sighed dreamily. "I could get married in one of these."

Bethany laughed, shaking her head. "No, wait until you see the Crystal Cathedral on Tanzlora—the one Ridge talks about. Words don't do it justice."

Elara gestured them forward. "Come, let's get the little ones seated."

Inside, the space was warm and inviting, filled with large tables for communal meals, comfortable seating areas, and designated play spaces for the village children. The back of the building opened into an expansive kitchen, where villagers moved gracefully, preparing the meal with a sense of unity and joy.

They all sat at a long polished stone table, placing Maddox, Maya, and Monica near the center where they could easily be served. The children kicked their feet excitedly as platters of vibrant, fresh food were carried out—bowls of steamed root vegetables, grain-like breads, spiced greens, and fragrant fruit mixtures.

As they began serving themselves, Lincoln scooted his chair closer to Waverly, lowering his voice.

"We need to discuss this morning—whatever has you so preoccupied."

Waverly's fork paused midair, and she rolled her eyes. "Dad, not now."

"I think it may have something to do with Rykas," Lincoln pressed.

Waverly sighed deeply, setting her fork down. "Fine. Yes, it's Rykas. But there's nothing that needs to be done."

Lincoln studied her carefully. "If it's nothing, why does it seem to be weighing so heavily on you?"

Waverly bit her lip.

Bethany, seated across from them, subtly glanced at them but kept silent, letting Lincoln handle the conversation for now.

"Because," Waverly finally admitted, her voice quieter now, "it's something I can't change."

Her father nodded slowly, taking a bite of his food as he considered her words. "Then let's talk about it after lunch."

She sighed again but relented with a small nod.

"Alright."

Elara stood, a mischievous smile on her face as she clasped her hands together. "I have a big surprise for all of you," she announced, her eyes sparkling. "A huge elemental surprise."

At her words, the air around them shimmered, and suddenly, Mistara, Ignissa, Ambreela, and Terraveta appeared before them, their luminous forms glowing with radiant energy.

Ridge's brow furrowed. "What is going on?"

Terraveta turned to him, her voice smooth and knowing. "Patience, Ridge. It will serve you well."

The elemental spirits surrounded them, their presence sending a wave of warmth and calm through the air. Elara practically beamed with excitement. "Alright, follow me."

She turned and began walking, the elemental spirits gliding beside the family, their energies shifting and pulsing in sync with the natural surroundings. The Beaumonts exchanged intrigued glances but eagerly followed, anticipation building.

After a short walk, they emerged from the lush foliage to a breathtaking sight.

Before them stood a majestic waterfall, cascading down in streams of liquid silver and blue, its waters shimmering in the light of Arcmyrin's twin suns. The falls emptied into a large crystalline lake, its surface so clear they could see schools of magnificent, otherworldly creatures swimming beneath.

The children gasped in wonder, their eyes wide as they ran forward to the water's edge, peering in excitement.

Maddox was the first to spot them. "Look at all the creatures! They're glowing!"

Maya clapped her hands. "They're so pretty!"

The lake was teeming with vibrant fish with translucent fins, their bodies reflecting soft hues of violet and silver. Small, spiral-shelled creatures skimmed the surface, leaving behind trails of twinkling bioluminescent light.

Lynx felt a tug at his side as the porcufera started chirping melodically. He looked down to see it eagerly shuffling in its sling, clearly enthralled by the water.

"Alright, little guy," Lynx said with a chuckle, setting it down.

The porcufera waddled forward eagerly, reaching the water's edge, sniffing cautiously. Then, to everyone's delight, it took a few sips—before suddenly launching itself into the lake!

The porcufera rolled and tumbled in the water, emitting happy chirps as it floated effortlessly, its spiky quills softening and flattening in the cool lake. It wiggled its tiny limbs excitedly, diving under and resurfacing with pure, unrestrained joy.

"Oh my stars!" Bethany exclaimed, laughing. "It loves the water!"

"Looks like it's back in its element," Ridge observed with amusement.

The children squealed with excitement, kneeling at the water's edge, watching the porcufera's playful antics.

"Can we swim too?" Monica asked hopefully.

Elara smiled, nodding. "Yes, but first, let's share a little more about this place."

She gestured around them. "This is the Crystallum Falls, one of Arcmyrin's most sacred natural wonders. It is a place of harmony, where the balance of all elements—water, air, fire, and earth—can be felt most strongly. The waters here have restorative properties, not unlike the healing energies Bronte encountered on Pluboria."

Celia raised a brow, glancing at Ridge and Lincoln. "So you're saying this is a natural Arcmyrian version of that healing chamber Bronte talked about?"

Elara nodded. "Exactly. It is said that when one immerses themselves in these waters, any lingering exhaustion or tension melts away."

Lynx grinned, already rolling up his sleeves. "Well, I don't know about the rest of you, but I'm getting in."

He took a step toward the water—when suddenly, the porcufera splashed him playfully, sending a small wave of shimmering water right into his chest.

Everyone laughed.

"Guess that's an invitation!" Waverly teased.

"Fine, fine," Lynx grumbled, pulling off his boots.

The others began kicking off their shoes as well, eager to experience the magic of the Crystal Falls.

53

As the Beaumont family emerged from the shimmering lake, laughter still echoed through the air. The refreshing waters of the Crystal Falls had done exactly as Elara said—any exhaustion they carried from their journey melted away, leaving them invigorated and light-hearted.

They made their way back onto the soft, glowing grass, where they sat together to dry off, stretching out under the warm twin suns.

Lincoln sighed contentedly, running a hand through his damp hair. "That was exactly what I needed."

"Agreed," Celia added, squeezing water out of her sleeves. "I feel years younger!"

The children were still giggling, sitting cross-legged as they excitedly recounted their favorite moments from their playful splashing, competing over who had made the biggest waves.

As the group began pulling on their boots and shoes, the porcufera waddled up the gentle incline of the shore, shaking itself dry—

—right beside Ridge.

A spray of cool water exploded outward, soaking him from head to toe.

A stunned silence fell.

Then, the group burst into uncontrollable laughter.

"Oh, you've done it now," Ridge muttered, slowly turning his dripping face toward the porcufera, who simply chittered innocently, blinking its wide eyes.

"It chose you," Waverly teased, laughing so hard she clutched her sides. "You're its favorite now, Uncle Ridge!"

Even the Arcmyrian warriors accompanying them, normally so composed, let out rare chuckles.

Ridge dramatically shook his head. "Great. I travel to an alien planet, and out of everyone here, I'm the one who gets pranked by the fluffball."

The porcufera, clearly pleased with itself, chirped proudly before rolling over onto its back, exposing its belly like a playful pet.

"Looks like it wants a belly rub," Maya observed, grinning.

Ridge groaned, but still reached out, ruffling the little creature's fur. "Fine, you win."

The porcufera let out a series of melodic purrs, clearly delighted with itself.

Elara, still chuckling, shook her head. "It seems you've gained a new friend, Ridge."

"Lucky me," he muttered, wringing water from his sleeves.

Still grinning, the group stood, refreshed and rejuvenated.

"I'm glad we're rejuvenated," Lincoln said, rolling his shoulders. "Because we have got a long walk back to the living pods."

Elara, walking ahead of them, glanced over her shoulder with a knowing smile. "It will be an extremely short walk, Lincoln. Follow me, everyone."

She pivoted smoothly, leading the group down a shaded path—one that, oddly enough, veered in the opposite direction of where they'd originally come from.

"I'm confused," Ridge muttered under his breath.

"Me too," Lynx agreed, watching the trail wind through the towering crystalline trees.

Bethany, however, suddenly gasped in realization. "Oh! I see now."

Lincoln shot her a puzzled glance. "What do you see?"

"The portal system," she explained, pointing ahead.

And then—as they rounded the last bend—it came into full view.

A shimmering portal stood before them, pulsating with hues of deep blue and violet, edged with delicate silver symbols that danced along the outer frame.

The children's eyes went wide with excitement.

"Whoa," Maya whispered in awe.

"I forget about the portals," Bethany admitted, admiring the smooth, almost liquid-like glow at its center. "Where does this one lead?"

Elara gestured gracefully. "Step through and find out."

She stood to the side with one of her warriors while the other two moved ahead, leading the family toward the portal's threshold.

Ridge eyed it warily. "I know these are perfectly safe... but there's something unsettling about walking into it when I don't know my destination."

"You're being dramatic," Waverly teased, nudging him forward.

With a deep breath, Lincoln took Maddox's hand and was the first to step through, his form disappearing in a brief ripple of light.

Bethany followed suit, leading Maya through next.

Ridge sighed, looking down at Monica, who clutched his hand with eager excitement. "Alright, alright. Here we go."

As the rest of them passed through, Lynx turned to Elara, raising an eyebrow. "You're not coming with us?"

She shook her head. "I have a few things to tend to before I retire for the evening, but I will see you all in the morning. The warriors will escort you the rest of the way."

With a nod of gratitude, Lynx stepped through the portal last, the porcufera nestled safely in its sling.

As Lynx exited the shimmering portal, he found himself face-to-face with his family—gathered just beyond the threshold of their living pods.

The children were practically bouncing with excitement, their eyes wide with wonder as they turned to Lincoln and Ridge.

"That was incredible!" Maddox exclaimed.

"I still don't understand how it works," Monica added, her little brow furrowed in concentration.

Maya grinned at her. "I don't care how it works, I just want to do it again!"

Lincoln chuckled, shaking his head as he looked around. The portal had transported them directly to the edge of the interconnected pods, placing them just a few short steps from their temporary Arcmyrian home.

"This is impressive," Ridge admitted, rubbing his chin. "No matter how many times I see this technology, it still gets me."

Waverly nodded in agreement. "Imagine if Earth had portals instead of planes and cars—traveling anywhere in seconds?"

"I'd never be late for anything again!" Lynx quipped, grinning.

Just then, Rykas stepped forward, standing near the group with his usual composed expression.

"Welcome back," he greeted them, inclining his head slightly.

Celia stepped forward, smiling warmly. "Thank you, Rykas. That was a truly remarkable experience."

"I am glad you enjoyed it." He then turned his attention to the warriors who had escorted them, nodding in gratitude. "Thank you for your assistance today. You are dismissed for the evening."

The warriors bowed slightly before departing, leaving the family to settle into their space.

Once they were alone, Rykas addressed them again.

"The elders have requested that you spend the remainder of your afternoon and evening however you see fit. There are no obligations—just rest, explore, and enjoy. Our home is your home, so please feel free to wander as you wish."

He then gestured toward a small structure nestled near the perimeter of the community gardens. It was modest, yet intricately designed, its crystalline accents catching the Arcmyrian sunlight.

"If you need me for anything, I will be right over there."

Celia sighed happily, rolling her shoulders as if already feeling the weight of exhaustion settle in.

"Well," she said, "I, for one, am going to take a much-needed nap. This has been the most beautiful and eventful day, and I don't want to be a zombie for the rest of it!"

Bethany laughed. "I think you've earned that nap, Celia."

"You all have," Rykas agreed.

As Celia turned to head into her pod, the others began chatting among themselves about how they might spend their free time—some considering a walk, others simply wanting to lounge and take in the view.

Waverly, however, glanced toward Rykas' small structure, her expression thoughtful.

For the moment, though, she kept those thoughts to herself but as she watched him walk away, she knew that the time had come for a serious discussion with him.

Rykas felt the pull before he even turned around.

Somehow, he knew.

Still, when he glanced back over his shoulder and saw Waverly following him down the narrow path toward the hut, his brow furrowed in surprise.

He knew this was a bad idea. He should keep walking. He should ignore her and let her turn back.

But he didn't.

Instead, he stopped and turned fully to face her, waiting as she closed the distance between them.

She came to a halt in front of him, her expression serious, determined.

"We need to talk."

Rykas exhaled slowly, nodding once.

"Okay," he said. "I suppose I knew this moment was coming."

Without another word, he gestured for her to follow him into the hut.

The moment they stepped inside, Waverly took a moment to observe the small space. It was simple—a stone table at the center, shelves lined with weapons and tools.

It was practical. Uncluttered.

He leaned casually against the stone table, crossing his arms over his broad chest as he regarded her with a guarded expression.

"Go on," he said, his voice unreadable.

Waverly inhaled deeply.

"I never meant for this to happen," she said quietly, "but I have feelings for you."

His entire body tensed, though he didn't speak.

She pressed on, knowing she had to say it all—had to get it out before she lost her nerve.

"I know it's inappropriate. I know it's complicated. But I can't help it. I feel something when I'm around you. And judging by the way you look at me, I think you feel it too."

She saw his jaw tighten, his golden eyes darkening like a storm gathering in the sky.

For a long moment, he said nothing.

Then, finally, he pushed off the table and took a slow step toward her.

"Waverly," he said, his voice low, "this... cannot happen."

Her chest tightened, but she stood her ground.

"Why not?"

He hesitated—just for a moment. Long enough for her to see the truth flicker behind his eyes.

"Because," he said finally, "I cannot afford to want something I can never have."

And with that, he turned away, gripping the edge of the stone table as if steadying himself.

Waverly swallowed against the lump in her throat.

"Then we are both doomed, Rykas," she whispered. "Because I can't stop wanting it either."

Rykas gripped the edge of the stone table, his knuckles whitening. He stared down at the smooth surface for a long moment, his breath steady but heavy, as if holding something back.

Then, he turned to face her once more.

His expression was carefully composed, but his golden eyes burned with something unspoken—something dangerous, something undeniable.

"Waverly," he began, his voice low and measured, "the timing of this... after what has happened on Tanzlora, after Josephine, after Sylvaris' betrayal, after everything we are trying to build for the Triad—"

He exhaled sharply, shaking his head.

"It is unwise to pursue this."

Waverly nodded slowly, dropping her gaze.

"I agree," she murmured, "but I just needed to tell you. I wanted you to know how I felt. And I guess..." She let out a small breath, barely a laugh. "I guess I needed to know if you felt the same way."

Silence stretched between them, thick with things neither of them dared to say.

Rykas clenched his fists.

It would have been easier if she had just walked away, left it unsaid.

But she was Waverly Beaumont.

Brave. Honest. Willing to face the storm head-on.

And now he had no choice but to face it too.

Finally, he spoke.

"What I feel..." he started, but then stopped himself, as if choosing his next words with painstaking care.

He took a step closer, then another, until there was barely any space left between them.

"What I feel is something I do not have the luxury to act upon," he admitted, voice tight. "Not now. Maybe not ever."

Her breath caught.

She searched his face, looking for something—anything—that would tell her he wasn't just pushing her away because of duty or honor.

"So, you do feel it."

He didn't answer.

But he didn't have to.

The truth was there, in the way his gaze lingered on her lips before flicking away.

In the way his fingers twitched at his sides, as if fighting the urge to reach for her.

In the way his breath faltered, just slightly, when she took a step closer.

For a fleeting moment, the air between them crackled with something raw, something dangerous, something impossible.

Then, Rykas took a deliberate step back.

"I cannot."

Waverly swallowed past the lump in her throat.

"I know," she whispered.

And somehow, that made it worse.

For a moment, they just stood there, the weight of the unspoken stretching between them like a chasm neither could cross.

Then, finally, Waverly nodded.

"Thank you for telling me the truth," she said softly.

Rykas' jaw tightened.

"Thank you for trusting me with yours," he replied.

And with that, she turned and walked out of the hut, leaving Rykas standing in the silence—fists clenched, heart racing, and mind screaming at him to go after her.

But he didn't.

Because he knew if he did... he would never let her go.

54

Tears slipped down Waverly's face faster than she could wipe them away, her chest rising and falling with silent sobs as she clutched her arms around herself.

She had barely made it into the woods before her legs gave out beneath her, dropping her onto the first crystal rock she found.

The warmth of the stone surprised her, seeping through the fabric of her clothing like a gentle embrace—but it did nothing to ease the ache in her heart.

She buried her face in her hands and let the sobs take over.

How can her heart hurt like this?

She had known this was the right thing. She had told herself it would be fine. She had prepared for this moment.

But nothing could have prepared her for the way it felt to hear Rykas say "I cannot."

A hand touched her arm, warm and steady.

She looked up, startled, and through the blur of her tears, she saw her father.

Lincoln squatted down beside her, his expression full of quiet understanding.

Without a word, he pulled her into his arms.

That was all it took for the dam to break.

Waverly sobbed against his shoulder, her whole body trembling with the weight of emotions too big to carry alone.

"It's okay, sweetheart," Lincoln murmured, holding her tight. "Let it go."

For a long moment, she did just that.

She let the pain spill out, let herself mourn what could never be.

Lincoln held her through it all, never rushing her, never telling her to stop.

When the sobs finally faded into quiet sniffles, Waverly pulled back, rubbing at her red-rimmed eyes with the sleeve of her tunic.

She exhaled shakily.

"Dad," she whispered, voice still raw. "Doing the right thing really hurts, you know?"

Lincoln gave her a small, knowing smile. "Oh, I sure do, honey."

His gaze softened, distant for a moment, as if he were recalling a memory long tucked away.

"Your mom and I... we felt our hearts ripping out of our chests when we had to leave you and Lynx behind. It was the hardest thing we ever did in our lives."

He swallowed, eyes full of sorrow and love.

"Leaving those you love so much behind... it breaks you."

Waverly let those words sink in, feeling the weight of them settle deep in her chest.

For so long, she had wrestled with the pain of what she saw as abandonment.

For years, she had been angry.

She had told herself that she was fine, that she had grown past it.

But now...

Now, she understood.

Her heart ached not just for what she wanted and couldn't have... but for the sacrifices her parents had made.

"I think I'm beginning to understand that more now, Dad."

She let out a shaky breath, blinking at the stars starting to peek through the Arcmyrin sky as the twin suns set.

"I used to be resentful. Angry at you both."

She sniffled, shaking her head.

"And then I just quit thinking about it, because I was tired of feeling the hurt of abandonment."

Her voice broke slightly.

"But now? Now, I understand."

Lincoln tilted his head, searching her face.

Then, with a tenderness only a father could offer, he reached out, tucking a strand of hair behind her ear.

"You are wiser than you give yourself credit for, Waverly."

She smiled, a watery, fragile smile—but a real one.

Lincoln squeezed her shoulder. "And braver."

She let out a soft, breathy laugh. "I don't feel very brave right now."

"That's because you're still feeling the weight of it," he said simply. "But bravery isn't about not feeling pain—it's about doing the right thing anyway."

Waverly nodded, feeling the truth of his words settle into her bones.

The pain was still there. The ache hadn't vanished.

But somehow, sitting here with her father, she didn't feel so alone in it anymore.

She sighed and leaned her head against his shoulder.

"Thank you, Dad."

Lincoln pressed a kiss to the top of her head.

"Always, sweetheart. Always."

The golden hues of Arcmyrin's twin suns painted the sky in a soft, warm glow the next evening as the Beaumont family stood at the entrance to the portal. This one would transport them back to Sage Manor.

The atmosphere was filled with a quiet reverence, not of sorrow, but of deep respect and gratitude as the family took in their last moments on the planet.

Gathered around them were the Arcmyrin Elders, warriors, villagers, and familiar faces who had welcomed them so openly. It felt surreal to be leaving, even though they knew they would return.

Celia stood near the front of the family, her heart full as she gazed at the shimmering landscape one last time.

"I feel as though I'm leaving home," she murmured, half to herself and half to Releesia, who stood beside her.

Releesia's warm golden eyes crinkled with understanding. "That is how it should feel, Celia. That is the bond we share now. This place is part of you, and you are part of it."

Celia reached out and clasped the Elder's hands, overwhelmed with emotion. "Thank you. For welcoming us, for sharing your world with us. For making us family."

Releesia nodded solemnly. "You are family, Celia. And family is never far away, even across the stars."

Celia blinked back the sting of tears, giving Releesia's hands one last squeeze.

Rykas stood rigid near the warriors, his usual stoicism even more pronounced than normal. He had deliberately kept his distance from Waverly, but he could feel her presence, as surely as he felt the twin suns on his skin.

Elara, ever the perceptive one, stood beside him, watching him out of the corner of her eye.

"You will regret not saying goodbye," she said softly, but firmly.

Rykas didn't answer.

Elara sighed. "Do not let your pride rob you of closure, Rykas."

He clenched his jaw, torn between what he wanted and what was best.

Just then, Lynx approached him, carrying the porcufera in the sling over his chest.

"Thank you for everything," Lynx said, his usual playful grin replaced by a rare, serious expression. "You and your warriors kept my family safe. I won't forget that."

Rykas inclined his head. "It is what we do."

Lynx smirked. "Still, I owe you one."

Rykas grunted, but there was something close to amusement in his eyes.

Then, finally, he turned.

Waverly stood a few feet away, watching him quietly.

For a moment, neither spoke.

Then Waverly took a step forward.

"Goodbye, Rykas."

Her voice was steady, but her eyes held the weight of everything unsaid.

Rykas hesitated, then finally nodded.

"Goodbye, Waverly."

It was all he could allow himself to say.

She smiled softly, as if she understood.

Then, before the moment could linger, she turned and walked back toward her family.

Bethany approached Elara, warmth in her eyes.

"This has been an experience I will never forget," she said. "Thank you for welcoming us."

Elara smiled gently. "You are welcome here anytime, Bethany. Your heart is kind, and your spirit is strong. The Triad is better with you in it."

Bethany flushed slightly at the praise, but accepted it with grace.

"You must visit Sage Manor again soon," Bethany said.

"I would like that," Elara admitted.

Then, to Bethany's surprise, Elara reached forward and embraced her briefly.

"Safe journey, my friend."

Bethany beamed.

Celia stepped forward to address the gathered Arcmyrians.

"I have no doubt that this is only the beginning."

She glanced around the assembled faces, eyes filled with warmth.

"The connection we have built is unshakable. And though we leave today, we will return. Our planets, our people, and our futures are bound together now."

A murmur of agreement and reverence swept through the crowd.

She turned to Releesia. "Until next time, my friend."

Releesia nodded deeply. "Until next time."

Elara stepped beside the glowing portal, which had begun to pulse with light.

"It is time."

The Beaumont family gathered together, their hands reaching for the herbal mixtures.

Celia nodded to them all. "Drink up."

One by one, they took the herbal mixtures, the familiar taste settling into their systems.

Lincoln and Ridge took Maddox and Monica's hands, leading them forward.

Bethany scooped up Maya, holding her close.

Waverly, Lorinda and Lynx stepped up together, with Lynx adjusting the porcufera in the sling to keep it secure.

Celia took a deep breath, turning one last time to take in the breathtaking world of Arcmyrin.

Then, with one final nod to their Arcmyrian family, they stepped forward.

As they disappeared through the portal, the light swirled and pulsed once more—then dimmed.

The Arcmyrians stood in reverent silence for a moment, watching the space where their friends had just stood.

Then, finally, Rykas turned sharply on his heel and walked away, his jaw tight.

Elara watched him go, her expression unreadable.

Releesia sighed.

"The future of the Triad," she murmured, "is just beginning."

And with that, the Arcmyrians slowly dispersed, leaving the portal behind, but never the bonds that had been forged.

Thank You for Reading

Dear Reader,

Thank you for spending time with the Beaumont family and exploring the worlds of Pluboria, Arcmyrin, Tanzlora, and beyond. This story was written with love, hope, and a deep belief in healing, unity, and the extraordinary power of connection—both human and otherworldly.

If Bronte's journey or the adventures of the Beaumonts touched your heart, I hope you carry that light with you into your own life. And if you've ever felt broken or uncertain, may this story remind you that wholeness comes in many forms—and that love, faith, and community can help you find your way back to yourself.

With gratitude,
LG Rice

Visit my website: www.authorlgrice.com

Contact me: hello@authorlgrice.com

LG Rice is the author of the *Secrets of Sage Manor* alien fantasy adventure series and the creator of its spin-off, the *Galen Valley Chronicles*, a contemporary drama fiction series set in the same richly imagined fictional town of Galen Valley—home to Sage Manor. With a passion for layered storytelling, deep character arcs, and the secrets that bind both small communities and big personalities, LG Rice explores the intersection of fantasy and realism through powerful, emotional journeys that resonate long after the final page.